ARCTIC GAMBIT

LARRY BOND

ARCTIC GAMBIT

 FORGE®

A TOM DOHERTY ASSOCIATES BOOK

NEW YORK

ARCTIC GAMBIT

Copyright © 2018 by Larry Bond and Chris Carlson

A Forge Book
Published by Tom Doherty Associates
175 Fifth Avenue
New York, NY 10010

www.tor-forge.com

Forge® is a registered trademark of Macmillan Publishing Group, LLC.

The Library of Congress Cataloging-in-Publication Data is available upon request.

ISBN 978-0-7653-3492-3 (hardcover)
ISBN 978-1-4668-1895-8 (ebook)

Our books may be purchased in bulk for promotional, educational, or business use. Please contact your local bookseller or the Macmillan Corporate and Premium Sales Department at 1-800-221-7945, extension 5442, or by email at MacmillanSpecialMarkets@macmillan.com.

First Edition: May 2018

Printed in the United States of America

0 9 8 7 6 5 4 3 2 1

AUTHOR'S NOTE

It takes some time to total up the number of projects that Chris Carlson and I have worked on together. Even if you only count the ones that we actually finished, it's an impressive sum, spread out over thirty-plus years.

I will freely admit that the idea for this story came from Chris. I didn't even think the Status-6 torpedo was real until he showed me the information online—including the November 2015 photo "leaked" by the Russians. And it takes a creative (and dark) mind to make that nightmare weapon even more frightening.

One would think that after creating so many stories together, the process of writing would become routine, but each book has been different. Not only do we try to do better each time, but the structure of each plot can drive who takes on each role. Real-world circumstance can also impact who does what when, but our ability to jointly cope with such speed bumps is one reason we've been able to do this so long.

DRAMATIS PERSONAE

Americans

Hardy, Lowell, The President

Patterson, Dr. Joanna, The First Lady

Hyland, William, National Security Advisor

Peakes, Raymond, Director of National Intelligence

Richfield, Henry (Hank), Secretary of Defense

Lloyd, Andrew, Secretary of State

Gravani, Clifford, Secretary of the Navy

Schiller, Frank, GEN, Chairman, Joint Chiefs of Staff

Hughes, Bernard, ADM, Chief of Naval Operations

Sanders, Mike, RADM, Deputy CNO for Information Warfare

Chatham, Russ, CDR, CNO Intelligence Staff

Dorr, Robert, CAPT, CO SUBRON 12

Gabriel, Bradley, CDR, Assigned to Deputy CNO for Submarine Warfare

Forest, Mark, LCDR, Assigned to Deputy CNO for Submarine Warfare

Bartek, Representative Steve, D-WI, Member of House Armed Services Committee

Emmers, Senator Tom, R-KY, Member of Senate Armed Services Committee

Hendricks, George, National Security Council Analyst

Sellers, Dwight, White House Chief of Staff
McDowell, Evangeline, President's Personal Secretary
Brady, Melinda, Joanna Patterson's personal secretary
Perry, Dr. James, Tensor lead analyst, Central Intelligence Agency
Cavanaugh, Dr. Daniel, Army explosives expert
Berg, Jane, Lenny Berg's wife
Berg, Ethan, The Bergs' oldest son
Sheridan, Chad, USS *Shippingport* (ARDM 4) dry dock supervisor
Ulrich, Dr. Mark, Expert from Council on Nuclear Weapons

Submarine Development Squadron FIVE

Mitchell, Jerry, CAPT, Commanding Officer, DEVRON 5
Gustason, Dylan, CDR, Chief Staff Officer DEVRON 5
Matthews, Skip, LS2, DEVRON 5 staff, Logistics Specialist
Wheatly, Myron, LCDR, Maintenance Officer, DEVRON 5 staff
Mitchell, Dr. Emily, Mrs. DEVRON 5
Mitchell, Charlotte (Carly), Kid, DEVRON 5

USS *Jimmy Carter*

Weiss, Louis, CDR, Commanding Officer
Segerson, Joshua, LCDR, Executive Officer
Gibson, Paul, ITCM, Chief of the Boat (senior enlisted man aboard)
Malkoff, Kurt, LCDR, Navigator
Norris, Tom, LCDR, Chief Engineer
Hilario, Hector, LT, Main Propulsion Assistant (MPA)
Owens, Kathy (Kat), LT, Weapons Officer
Ford, Benjamin (Thing 1), LT, UUV Officer
Lawson, Steven (Thing 2), LTJG, Assistant Weapons Officer (AWEPs)
DiMauro, Philip (Mario), LTJG, Sonar Officer (Sonar)
Truitt, James, ENS, Chem/RADCON Assistant (CRA)

Alvarez, Miguel STS2, UUV Sensor Operator
Frederick, Lionel STS1, UUV Sensor Operator

Russians

Fedorin, Ivan Olegovich, President of the Russian Federation

Trusov, Aleksandr Aleksandrovich, GEN, Minister of Defense

Gorokhov, Nikolai Vasil'evich, VADM, Commander, Drakon Project

Apalkov, Sergei Ivanovich, CAPT 1st Rank, Construction leader

Kalinin, Boris Igorovich, CAPT 1st Rank, Chief of Staff to Admiral Gorokhov

Chekhov, Dmitry Mikhailovich, CAPT 3rd Rank, Meteorologist

Komeyev, Vladimir Olegovich, ADM, Commander-in-Chief, Russian Navy

Balakin, Viktor Yanovich, VADM, Deputy Commander-in-Chief, Russian Navy

Lavrov, Vasiliy Vasil'evich, CAPT 1st Rank, Senior intelligence officer

Drugov, Pavel Antonovich, CAPT 1st Rank, Chief of Staff to Admiral Komeyev

Zhabin, LT, Sever acoustic array detachment officer-in-charge

Mirsky, Stepan, CAPT-LT, Ka-27M helicopter commander

ARCTIC
GAMBIT

PROLOGUE

The darkness slowly diminished as the periscope head approached the surface. Fuzzy, indistinct blobs drifted lazily across a dim gray background. By the time they came into focus, the periscope had raced past, emerging from the water, pointed upward into the overcast skies above the Arctic Ocean. A large ice floe was briefly lifted by the periscope head before being pushed aside by the momentum of the unseen submarine below. The subtle shock from the collision was transmitted down the periscope's barrel, causing the eyepiece to shudder unpleasantly on the operator's face. A low growl escaped his lips as he announced, "Scope's clear."

"You okay, Skipper?" asked the executive officer. He'd seen the periscope shake and knew his captain had been thumped . . . again.

"Yes, XO," grumbled the commanding officer, "but I'm developing a severe dislike for ice." Rotating the periscope to the correct bearing, he paused to shift the optics to high power and focused the image. "Alright, XO, there's Master Two. Are you getting this?"

"Yes, sir, we're recording." The executive officer stared at the video display as the large icebreaker lowered a huge cylindrical object into the water. Whistling quietly he said, "That's one honkin' big sewer tube, Skipper. Could that be some sort of structural support member?"

The captain shook his head. "I haven't a clue, XO. But that's the second one we've seen being unloaded. Whatever *it* is, it's obviously a critical component to whatever the Russians are building on the seabed." Both men continued to watch in silence until the object disappeared below the water.

"Lowering number one scope," announced the captain as he slapped up the handles and rotated the overhead hydraulic control ring. Reaching over to the intercom, he toggled the mike switch. "Sonar, Conn. Any sign of our friend?"

The speaker crackled with the response. "Conn, Sonar. Negative. We haven't seen hide nor hair of Sierra eight. The ice noise to the east is particularly bad. Contact was last held on a bearing of one zero eight."

"Sonar, Conn, aye."

Pausing to consider his next move, the captain ordered the officer of the deck to get the boat back down to one hundred fifty feet and head northeast. Stepping down from the periscope stand, the CO motioned for his executive officer to join him at the navigation plot.

"Still concerned about that Akula?"

The captain nodded sharply. "Absolutely! The only thing worse than having a detected Akula wandering about is an undetected one hiding in the acoustic underbrush, waiting to pounce at the worst possible moment. Been there, done that, and I don't want to do it again!"

Taking a deep breath, he pointed to their current position on the chart, then traced a line with his finger. "Let's reposition to the northeast and see if we can't get a better vantage point to watch the next unloading evolution. Say . . . about here."

The XO leaned over to get a better look. His face became uneasy. Grabbing a set of dividers, he measured the distance to Bolshevik Island and ran an arc that nearly touched his captain's finger. "That's cutting it awfully close to the twelve-mile limit, sir."

"Agreed, but we're still a half mile outside and I don't intend to linger. We reach this spot, we'll take a few observations, and if nothing is happening we'll head north toward the pack ice. Is the SATCOM buoy ready?"

"Yes, sir," replied the XO. "Everything but the last video has been uploaded, and they're doing that right now. The video segment is a short one."

"Excellent! We'll launch it once we're clear of the damn ice chunks—" The captain didn't get a chance to finish the sentence; the loud beeping of the WLR-9 acoustic intercept receiver cut off his words.

"Conn, Sonar. High frequency active sonar, close aboard, bearing one six five. We hold nothing on that . . . Oh, God! TORPEDO IN THE WATER, BEARING ONE SIX FOUR! WEAPON IS RANGE GATING!"

The commanding officer leapt toward the periscope stand. "Captain has the conn! Helm, left full rudder! All ahead flank, cavitate! Launch countermeasures!"

The submarine's heading swung northward, its speed building at a painfully slow rate. Looking at the WLR-9 display, the captain realized the incoming weapon was on a steady bearing—right toward them. "Helm, steady on course zero two zero! XO, launch another set of countermeasures and get the SATCOM buoy away!"

"Sir, the ice . . ."

"To hell with the ice! Launch the damn buoy!"

For a brief moment the captain thought one of the countermeasures had broken the torpedo's lock on his boat. But the weapon's electronic confusion lasted but a moment and it swerved back toward the American submarine. Another pair of countermeasures was launched . . . no effect. The torpedo relentlessly closed the distance.

The explosion shook the boat violently. People were bounced out of their chairs, loose gear went airborne, and a loud roar could be heard aft. The submarine snapped over to port and pitched downward. The helmsman and stern planesman yanked on their yokes . . . the controls refused to respond.

"Emergency blow!" shouted the captain in desperation.

The lights flickered.

Suddenly, a monstrous jolt rocked the submarine, people and objects were thrown about like rag dolls, the screech of the hull yielding to the impact could be heard above the din. Then the lights went out . . . and darkness fell.

1

PHONE CALL

11 June 2021
0440 Pacific Daylight Time
Bangor, Washington

Emily felt Jerry's body tense, and she came fully awake. He was sitting up, rigid, listening to the phone.

Small-hours phone calls were hardly worth mentioning in the Mitchell home. Jerry had given his staff a fair-sized list of situations that required contacting the squadron commander immediately, regardless of the hour. She usually slept straight through them. Most were just a notification, or a simple question. Jerry would say a few words, hang up, and go back to sleep himself.

But this time, he listened and asked quick, short questions. If his body language hadn't alerted her, his tone would have—softly spoken, but intense, and Emily knew enough about submariners to become more concerned the longer he spoke.

"How long?" Then, "Who has been notified?"

After a long pause, he added, "Yes, go ahead, but I'm coming in anyway. Tell the driver I'll be ready in fifteen. Good work, Myron." Jerry set the phone down, then turned to Emily.

"It was Myron Wheatly," he explained softly, because four-year-old Charlotte was sprawled between them, thankfully still sound asleep.

LCDR Wheatly was the squadron maintenance officer, and the command duty officer that night. "We got a call from SUBRON Twelve in Groton. *Toledo* has missed her last three communications windows."

Alarm flashed through her, and she had to remember to whisper. "Lenny Berg's boat? It's overdue?"

"Not officially," he cautioned. "That won't be until it's due back at base, several weeks from now."

"But does Jane . . ."

Charlotte stirred, stopping Emily in midsentence. Jerry took the opportunity to smoothly disengage from the little girl's arm and ease himself out of bed. He'd heard the concern in his wife's voice, and came around to her side of the bed, kneeling down next to her head to whisper.

"There are a lot of reasons she could be out of comms, and SUBRON Twelve is already working the problem. They called me because Captain Dorr knows Lenny's a good friend of ours. I'm going in so I can get a classified briefing, and to make sure Myron didn't miss anything."

Emily nodded. Time to be the commodore's wife. "I can get Charlotte to daycare, no prob," she added. Sometimes she rode with daddy to the base's daycare, but not at 0440. "And this is still classified," she stated, although it was really a question.

"Tippy-top," Jerry confirmed as he got dressed. "But not officially. They're just keeping the information close-hold to avoid worrying the families. They won't even tell the other boats in Squadron Twelve until it's necessary. Hopefully, it won't be."

Long practice helped Jerry get downstairs and outside just as the duty driver arrived. As he got in, Logistics Specialist Second Class Matthews reached back and handed Jerry a printout. "Commodore, Mr. Wheatly said you'd want to see this, and there's a travel mug of coffee in the cup holder next to you."

"Bless you, Petty Officer Matthews," Jerry answered, taking the document and placing it in his lap. Reaching for the coffee with one hand while turning on a small reading light with the other, he saw that the document was a timeline of USS *Toledo*'s patrol, and now search. The last transmission from her was four days ago.

He frowned, feeling guilty about lying to Emily. Well, not exactly lying, but he hadn't told her that the navy's standard procedure after a sub missed two comm windows was to send out a priority message saying: "You OK? Please respond." The balloon officially went up when the deadline for an answer to that call had passed. That had been at 0700 this morning, eastern time, hence the predawn call to Jerry.

The part of Jerry still waking up groused that they could have waited another few hours to call, but the people on SUBRON Twelve's staff knew that Lenny and Jerry had been shipmates and close friends ever since they served together on *Memphis*. How many years ago? He and Emily were godparents to Lenny and Jane's oldest boy, Ethan. While Jerry's star had risen a little faster than his friend's, he was sure that after Lenny finished his command tour on *Toledo*, he would be moving up.

They were right to call, whatever the hour. Jerry's squadron, Submarine Development Squadron Five, controlled three boats, all fitted with advanced technology that might someday be fitted to the rest of the submarine fleet, or unique equipment that would allow a sub to perform a difficult, very specialized task, such as retrieving large heavy objects from the ocean floor, or carrying underwater robots for scouting. If any of that gear could help find *Toledo*, or save her if she was in trouble, he didn't want to waste a minute.

Jerry desperately hoped that some circumstance or combination of circumstances had prevented *Toledo* from communicating, although it was hard to imagine what that could be. Subs had more than one way of phoning home, and sub sailors were pretty creative.

Thinking about Lenny and their days serving together aboard USS *Memphis* made him think about *Memphis*'s captain, then Commander Lowell Hardy. Their skipper had also moved on and up since that cruise. Jerry had the urge to call Hardy. Not to tell him about Lenny. He'd already know. Just to talk and share their worries. But you can't just phone the president of the United States.

11 June 2021
0935 Eastern Daylight Time
The Pentagon
Arlington, Virginia

"He's agreed to let SUBFOR and SUBRON Twelve handle the search, at least for now." Commander Russ Chatham was on the CNO's intelligence staff. He leaned back in his chair, visibly relieved.

Rear Admiral Mike Sanders, Chatham's boss, smiled. "How was your first time briefing the president?"

Chatham just shook his head. "A typical nuke. He wanted to know everything. Thanks for warning me."

Sanders's smile widened. "Bitter experience, Rusty. You don't get a pass from Hardy because you're an aviator."

"He knows as much about *Toledo*'s status, and Tensor, as anyone in the Navy right now. I could tell he wanted to ask more questions, or tell us to do something else, but he knew there was nothing else to learn, and we were already doing everything we could."

"With any other politician, you would have lost an hour explaining why adding more searchers wouldn't help, or why we haven't already announced her as overdue."

Rusty countered, "But he still wants updates twice a day, and immediate word if something new pops up."

Admiral Sanders replied, "And hopefully it'll be good news. In which case this just becomes part of *Toledo*'s patrol report, and no fuss. If we do declare her overdue, with the search area right next to Russian waters, too many questions will be asked about why we were there. It's not a normal patrol zone. The last thing we want to do is draw anyone's attention to Tensor." Even in a very secure space, Sanders used the code word for the intelligence target, rather than its name.

"Since the location of our patrol zones are classified, we could just say it was a routine patrol zone, and only the Navy's head shed would know we were lying."

"The Russians have at least a general idea of where we normally operate. They would know," Sanders argued. "And nothing we say will prevent them from raising a very public fuss about operating so close to their waters."

"A lot of good it will do them." Rusty grinned. "Hardy doesn't put up with that crap."

Sanders nodded and returned the grin. "I voted for him, too."

15 May 2019
2330 Eastern Daylight Time
Georgetown, Washington, D.C.

"Let it go, dear."

Senator Lowell Hardy (D-CT) looked up from his newspaper. His wife, Joanna, lay next to him. They made a habit of reading together each night before they slept. For both of them, spending quiet time next to the most important person in their life was more than beneficial.

"I could hear your teeth grinding," she explained. "It's not worth the aggravation."

"I do not grind my teeth," Hardy protested firmly.

"No you don't. Well, at least not physically anyway," she said, smiling, "but you mutter and grumble any time you're reading something that upsets you, and we're supposed to be unwinding." She leaned over to look at the page. "I knew it! Another article on the primaries."

Hardy held the paper up in one hand, as if displaying evidence. "Walters is a moron. I learned more about economics at the academy than he did heading that committee. And that 'White Paper' on the military he's released is a piece of bovine excrement!"

"He's got to get his name out there, after all, dear. It's how the system works."

"Is this really the best the Democratic Party can do? And Walters is the favorite! The others are even worse! Would you divorce me if I voted Republican this time around?"

She shook head but smiled. "No, but you might want to buy a comfortable couch."

"I hear what passes for thoughtful policy in this town and I'm appalled. Reality doesn't stand a chance against ideology and political convenience. If I thought I had an ice cube's chance in a blast furnace . . ."

". . . I'd run myself," she completed. She leaned over and kissed him. "You've been saying that a lot lately. Be careful what you wish for." Turning around, she leaned over and opened the drawer on the nightstand by the bed. After some rustling, she pulled out a manila folder. "I've done a little research, and called a few friends." She opened the folder and withdrew a handwritten note. "Here, read this."

Hardy put the newspaper aside and fiddled with the reading light before focusing on the single half-sized sheet of paper. The letterhead leapt off the page. It read simply, "The White House," with the presidential seal embossed in gold over the letters.

> *Joanna,*
>
> *I think your idea is an excellent one, and if Lowell ever decides to run, tell him he will have my full support. Better yet, see if you can bring him around to that idea. I know he will do a great job sitting in my chair.*
>
> *Kenneth L. Myles*

It didn't take long to read, and Hardy read it at least twice more before noting the date. "This is over a year ago!" he exclaimed.

"Here's another one, it's a little more recent," she said smoothly, "from President Huber."

He started to speak, but she cut him off. "I waited until you'd made your feelings clear. I feel the same way—in fact, I think you'd make a great president, and I've thought so for some time."

"But these notes . . ." he protested.

"Only three people know about each of these notes, and two of them are in this room. I've also sounded out other friends in the party and outside, always privately: 'What if?' Their universal reaction was 'Yes!' and 'What's holding him back?'"

She pointed to the folder. "I've sketched out a rough campaign organization." Then grabbing his hand firmly said, "Lowell, you have more than just a chance. You could win. Seriously."

"I feel a little like I'm being railroaded," he mused.

She made a dismissive gesture. "You're too damn sensible, too practical to ever say, 'I want to be president.' It's my job as the objective observer in this household to point out the opportunity."

Hardy laughed. "You're not very objective, or unbiased in this case, my love."

"No, I'm not," she acknowledged, smiling, "but I've got thirty-plus years experience in this town, and I've worked directly for two presidents. You've made a lot of friends here, and more importantly, you're highly respected—even by those who disagree with you. And you're right. Walters is too focused on jobs, Mendoza's too inexperienced, and nobody can figure out why Pickering is running."

She laid a hand on his arm, reassuring him. "You can stop the train and get off any time you like. I can put this folder back in the drawer. It will still be good four or eight years from now, but you can run—and *win*—right now."

She watched his expression, or rather expressions, as he considered what might be the most important decision of his life. She knew what he would do, though. Lowell had never turned away from a job that needed to be done, regardless of how long it took or tough it might be.

He held out his hand. "Let me see what you've got in there."

22 June 2020
0940 Eastern Daylight Time
Columbus, Ohio
CNN Coverage of the Democratic Party Convention

"And that was really the last challenge to Senator Hardy's chances of winning the nomination. Waiting until this late date to choose a running mate was risky, but my sources tell me that the deal that allowed Mendoza to accept the VP slot was not finalized until very late last night."

"Literally at the eleventh hour," another commentator supplied. "But it really had come down to only Mendoza and Hardy, especially after Pickering's campaign imploded and Walters did so badly in the debates."

The woman anchor nodded her head and added, "The lack of any baggage didn't hurt Hardy, either. Both Walters and Pickering spent a lot of time on the defensive, attempting to justify their far left–leaning positions to a skeptical electorate. With Hardy's highly successful terms in both the House and Senate as a centrist, and Mendoza's one in the House, balance has become a virtue."

"But now with Mendoza's more progressive portfolio on jobs and immigration added to Hardy's strengths on national security, foreign policy, and the environment, he stands a good chance to win the presidency this November."

Jerry stared at the TV, half listening to the two commentators, and half struggling to come to grips with what was transpiring. It was all too surreal. His former skipper, friend, and mentor had just won the Democratic Party's presidential nomination . . . *What the hell just happened?* he asked himself, again.

Emily literally bounced with excitement beside him; she clearly was enthused by the prospect of their good friends taking up residence in the White House. "Jerry, isn't this marvelous! Lowell will be a fantastic president! It's a shame that Carly is too young to understand the honor of having the president and first lady as her godparents." She stroked the sleeping toddler's hair as she spoke, beaming with pride.

Emily's highlighting of the close relationship the two families shared caused Jerry to close his eyes and lean his head back on the couch. He didn't dare say what his inside voice was screaming, instead he merely pointed out the obvious. "It's a bit premature to schedule Christmas dinner at the White House, Emily. Lowell still has to win the general election."

An annoyed frown popped on her face. "Why are you so negative, Jerry? Lowell has far more experience than Crenshaw and is definitely more levelheaded. I don't understand why you're not thrilled for him and Joanna. Don't you want him to be president?"

There was no winning this presidential debate. Sighing quietly, he tried to keep his voice level. "Of course, I want to see Lowell become president, Emily, and yes, he most definitely has my vote. But, there will be professional complications with that outcome."

The frown melted away; she understood. "You're still having issues with your reputation, aren't you? People still believe you enjoy undeserved political favor, even after all you've done?"

Jerry nodded. "A month doesn't go by that I don't hear at least one offhanded comment from some general officer at the five-sided funny farm. My boss, and the other submariners, know better and are really supportive, but it still bothers me—maybe more than it should. I just can't see how things wouldn't get worse if Lowell is elected president, and I think it's very likely he will be. Being close to a sitting president has been difficult for my superiors and me. Can you imagine the strain Lowell's election will create? It's not like we've been hiding the close bonds we have with him and Joanna."

Standing, he reached for the sleeping child in Emily's lap. "In a way, I'm glad we'll be moving to Bangor before the election. I need to get away from all this bureaucracy and politics, and back to where I belong . . . back to the boats."

20 January 2021
1950 Eastern Standard Time
The Watergate Hotel
Washington, D.C.

A knock on the suite's door interrupted the aide. She opened the door and a dark-suited Secret Service agent reported, "Mr. President, we're ready to move."

Lowell Hardy, dressed in what was becoming an all-too-familiar tuxedo, called, "Joanna, it's time."

She swept into the room in a green-and-silver designer gown that almost reached the floor. They'd done things with her hair, still red but mixed with gray, piling up and holding it in place with small ornaments that matched her dress.

"Oh my. Wow!" Hardy clapped appreciatively. "Why did I even bother to put on a tuxedo? Nobody's going to be looking at me."

"Mr. President, Dr. Patterson, we really must proceed," the agent insisted. They were scheduled to personally attend a total of ten official inaugural balls that night, and there were over a hundred unofficial balls and other celebrations happening in Washington. Even the president had to allow for what would be crazy traffic.

Reflexively, Hardy checked for his car keys and cell phone, then stopped himself. He wouldn't need either of those for the next four years. At least he still had a handkerchief.

"We'll finish that message in the car, Jenny," he instructed. There were reports of troop movements near the Estonian border, and while there was no imminent threat, it was likely the Russians were getting ready to test the new administration. In between dances, he'd work.

14 June 2021
1800 Pacific Daylight Time
Bangor, Washington

It wasn't Jerry's preferred option, but in the end, he did talk to the president, although it was Hardy who called him. Jerry was still at the squadron offices when the call came from Dwight Sellers, Hardy's Chief of Staff. "The President would like to speak with you in about five minutes."

"I'll be standing by," Jerry answered. Sellers hadn't bothered to ask if he would be available. The chief of staff's tone implied that he was on a tight schedule, and so was the president.

Reflexively, Jerry sat up straighter and started neatening up his desk. He paused, laughing at his actions, then shrugged and continued. His desk was pretty messy. Besides, it gave him something to do.

The secure phone finally rang, and Jerry forced himself to wait for the second ring before picking it up. "Commodore Mitchell."

"Jerry, how's Emily? How's my goddaughter?"

"Charlotte just turned four, and Emily already wants her to take ballet lessons." He didn't sound happy.

"But she'll look so cute in that outfit. Every little girl wants to be a ballerina," Hardy argued.

"Have you been talking to Emily, again, Mr. President? I'm not hearing a lot of support on my end," Jerry said. Hardy laughed.

"A wise general chooses his battles carefully," Hardy quoted. "You're going to lose this one. Just like I always lost whenever you pushed an idea. And before you ask, yes, the SecDef and the rest of your chain of command knows we're speaking. I told the CNO I needed to hear your reasons straight from you, not third or fourth hand."

That was why Hardy had taken the time to call. Jerry got straight to the point. "*Jimmy Carter* is the best boat in the Navy for this kind of work. She's a full generation ahead of what *Seawolf* had on board when we went looking for *Severodvinsk* so many years ago."

Hardy said, "They briefed me on *Jimmy Carter*'s status, of course. She's been out running around the Arctic for over two months already. Do you have a plan to get her resupplied?"

"Absolutely, Skipper," Jerry replied using Hardy's old title. "But you're not sure if you should send her?" he prompted.

Hardy sighed. "Your logic is sound, Jerry, and I want to know what happened to Lenny as much as you do, but *Jimmy Carter* is a valuable, even unique, national intelligence asset. I know you read her last patrol report, so you're well aware of the kind of work she's doing for us. She earned another Presidential Unit Citation from that mission.

"What do we miss by having her do this job, instead?" Hardy continued. "And we can't afford to lose another boat, especially her."

Jerry understood immediately. The president was asking "Big Picture" questions, things possibly more important long term than solving the mystery of a lost submarine.

"Mr. President, *Jimmy Carter* is conducting weapons experiments right now and has all the equipment onboard to do a detailed search—she doesn't have to return to base. We'll have a Coast Guard icebreaker with a special navy detachment bring her the supplies she'll need, and she can head straight to *Toledo*'s last known location. *Carter* is used to getting in and out of sensitive areas. She can do it quickly, quietly, and by having her cross over the Arctic Circle, we deny the Russians any intel that she is even being sent to poke around their backyard. She can figure out what the hell happened without the Russians ever knowing she was there."

"That last part is more important than you know," Hardy remarked. "The borscht is bubbling quite enough as it is. We don't need to add any more heat to the fire."

The president paused briefly. "That's it, then. Get her there as fast as you can, Jerry. We'll transfer operational control to SUBRON Twelve for the duration of the mission. You'll get orders through the chain very soon. Tell Captain Weiss I said Godspeed."

"I will, Skipper. And good luck to you as well."

"Thanks, Jerry." Hardy broke the connection and Jerry glanced at the clock. He had some phone calls to make. It was 1815, but his staff's working day was not going to be over any time soon.

2

STORM CLOUDS

19 June 2021
1345 Eastern Daylight Time
Minsk, Belarus
CNN Headline News

The correspondent stood with the floodlit columns of the Palace of the Republic in the background. The foreground was filled with citizens milling about, some singing, others holding signs in Cyrillic. "This is Chad Gallagher for CNN. Kastryčnickaja Square is filled with peaceful demonstrators now, although that may be the wrong word to describe them."

The image shifted to a daylight scene, with the plaza much emptier. Wisps of vapor, either tear gas or smoke, partially obscured groups of men, mostly civilians but some police. The latter were in riot gear, and struggled with the civilians. "This was the scene early this afternoon as government forces fought to take control of the square from protestors.

"These images were taken as we arrived, before police told us to stop filming. Throughout the afternoon we interviewed citizens who said that earlier today, the square had been crowded with people protesting the government's decision to rejoin the Russian Federation.

"Throughout the afternoon, police cleared the square of all civilians, then pro-government 'demonstrators' began arriving by bus. A heavy police presence arrested any newly arriving antigovernment protesters. They also directed the bus traffic, and gave instructions to the new arrivals.

"A police official spotted us late in the afternoon. When we asked if we could use the camera, he said, 'Is okay.'

"Now Kastryčnickaja Square is filled with cheers and people singing Russian patriotic songs. It's been nearly forty years since Belarus declared its independence from the then-collapsing Soviet Union, but today, the government's message to the world appears to be, 'We're glad to be back.'"

The scene shifted to CNN studios. A map of Russia filled the background, with the different administrative divisions marking the various oblasts, republics, and krais. Belarus, highlighted, formed a bulge on Russia's western border, projecting farther west, in between Ukraine and the Baltic States.

"This is Christine Laird on CNN's International Affairs. We're following the incredible story of Belarus's joining, or more properly, *re*joining with the Russian Federation thirty years after the dissolution of the Soviet Union. As an autonomous republic, Belarus will retain its government and constitution, but she will now be represented by Moscow on international matters, and her economy and military will be integrated with the rest of the Russian Federation."

The camera zoomed out suddenly to show a man seated to Laird's right. "With me is Professor Samuel Kyvalyow, from Georgetown University's School of International Affairs." Kyvalyow was young for a professor, still in his thirties, with a narrow face and thick blond hair, hinting at Slavic ancestry. "I understand you have family in Belarus, Dr. Kyvalyow."

"Yes, not far from Minsk," he replied, his English completely unaccented. "We have been in communication, although I will not say how." He was nodding agreement, but his expression revealed how worried he was. "They are safe, although my uncle now regrets not leaving when my parents came here to America, shortly after the breakup of the Soviet Union."

"Please explain to us how this happened so quickly." Laird sounded puzzled. "Only a few months ago, Belarus was meeting with the European Union about regaining its membership."

"And that is likely the main reason why Russian President Fedorin decided to move," the professor answered. "Belarus has a strong economy, with a well-developed, modern industry. Closer ties with the West would move it even further away from Russia's orbit. As we've seen elsewhere, Russia used what has become their standard hybrid warfare approach of fomenting unrest in the ethnic Russian population while threatening military action if the Belarusian government takes action to suppress them. Meanwhile, the Russians invest heavily in Belarus's industry, often to where they hold a controlling interest, and give bribes to any government official who can be bought, which in this case included President Yatachenko."

"And Russia's economy becomes that much stronger."

"Along with many other benefits," Kyvalyow answered. "Belarus is now a captive customer for Russian products. Where before Minsk might have chosen to buy from the West, that avenue will now be more restricted. Russian industry will have a source for cheaper manufactured goods.

"And it's a huge triumph for Fedorin domestically, validating his long-stated plans for 'restoring Russia's greatness.' He was a young teen when the Soviet Union collapsed, and has publicly said that he has dedicated his life to restoring 'his father's Russia.' He accepts that military overspending caused the collapse, and that a proper understanding of economics is vital to rebuilding Russian power. That's why he studied economics, and he's written several books on the topic, which are now finally being translated and read in the West.

"Militarily, regaining Belarus restores part of the barrier that used to exist between Russia proper and NATO. During the Cold War, the Baltic republics of Lithuania, Estonia, and Latvia to the north, along with Belarus in the center and Ukraine to the south formed a geographic buffer against any NATO attack. Having been invaded so many times,

Russia wants satellite countries to keep an invader out of Russian territory."

"But that still doesn't explain how Fedorin was able to turn the tables on the West so quickly," challenged the CNN anchor.

"The advantage of hybrid warfare, Ms. Laird, is that it combines traditional military aspects with irregular warfare, criminal activity, and even terrorist attacks. All are applied against the target at the same time to achieve the desired political objectives. If the target is unprepared for this kind of coordinated political assault, the effects can be devastatingly rapid. Belarus was, frankly, unprepared for this onslaught, and by the time they tried to react, it was too late." Kyvalyow looked like he was going to continue, but decided he was coming dangerously close to ranting and fell silent.

Laird nodded her understanding, and then asked the obvious question. "What do you think will happen next?"

"In a general sense, especially given his success in Belarus, I am sure President Fedorin will continue to find ways to expand Russian influence, especially into what were Soviet or Warsaw Pact countries. Exactly how is harder to say, but he's shown a willingness to use any tactic that will exploit an opponent's weakness and strengthen his own hand—this is the essence of multimodal warfare. There isn't a fixed set of tactics. Each situation is approached individually. Where this will happen next, I can't predict.

"Russian foreign policy is often described as opportunistic. I agree, to a point, but Fedorin took advantage of the existing corruption within the Minsk government and skillfully exploited it, creating his own opportunity. The next step was to fan the flames, claiming Russian nationals were at risk, threatening military action on the one hand and economic benefits on the other. A classic case of 'the carrot' and 'the stick.' This 'overnight' takeover was actually months, or even years in the making. President Fedorin just had to wait until the time was ripe. There is this one thing: If we can watch Russian actions carefully, and see where they are active, we may be able to deduce their future intentions."

* * *

The cameras switched off, and Laird turned to shake Kyvalyow's hand. "That was well done, Professor. I'm sure your students enjoy your lectures."

He smiled, but there was a grim edge to it. "My classes have been very well attended lately."

"And good luck to your relatives still in Belarus."

Kyvalyow thanked her and left the studio. As he rode the elevator down, he checked his cell phone—still no word. He'd lied to the quite pretty reporter, but the last thing he wanted to do was tell her that early that morning, his uncle Artyom and his family had loaded everything in their car and headed northwest toward the border with Lithuania. It was about a two-hour trip, and he should have received word by now that they were in Vilnius, the capital. Kyvalyow and his parents were waiting to help arrange their passage to the United States.

He hoped his relatives were safe.

20 June 2021
0920 Eastern Daylight Time
Oval Office, The White House
Washington, D.C.

"They probably started moving at first light, Mr. President." The army colonel gestured toward a large flat-screen on one wall. "Two-thirds of the Western Military District is moving or will move within the next few weeks."

The flat-screen showed a map of Russia, with a big part of northwestern Russia highlighted in red. Colonel Collins knew they didn't need lots of detail. "There are three armies in the Western Military District. The First Guards Tank Army is in Moscow"—he tapped the map to the north—"the Sixth Army is in St. Petersburg, and the Twentieth Army is to the east of Moscow, in Nizhny Novgorod." Each army's headquarters was marked on the slide by a small numbered flag, with the garrisons of the different units marked by smaller flags, forming a cluster around each headquarters.

"Overhead imagery this morning showed units loading for what appears to be a permanent move." Collins pressed a control, and satellite photos appeared. Long columns of vehicles filled highways. Other pictures showed rail yards where tanks and artillery were loading. The map reappeared, linking the satellite photos to different flags. Then, on the same map, arrows appeared near two of the armies, both pointing west.

"The Sixth is staying put," Collins explained, "but the First is moving west, into Belarus, and the Twentieth is taking the place of the First in Moscow. Each of those armies has close to fifty thousand troops."

"It's like moving pieces in Risk," Secretary of Defense Richfield commented.

"But with a lot of hidden moves," Andrew Lloyd, Secretary of State, responded.

"Andy's right. They couldn't have decided to do this overnight," President Hardy stated. "How long?"

Collins answered, "The physical prep work for a move of this size takes weeks. The staff work would take months to organize, perhaps a year."

"So they were getting ready for this before they orchestrated the takeover in Minsk. And the cost?" Secretary Lloyd added.

Collins shrugged. "Hundreds of millions to rebuild or expand the old Soviet bases in Belarus. TRANSCOM and Army logistics people are working up estimates, which will be passed to the Joint Staff and the intelligence community. The move could cost even more than the money Fedorin spent in bribes to essentially buy Belarus."

"And Russian cash is in short supply right now," Lloyd added, "so Fedorin really wanted to do this . . . badly."

Richfield added, "He didn't need to move those troops. Our intel says that the Minsk government was on top of any dissent. Those Russian troops aren't there to back up Yatachenko's government."

Hardy asked, "Where will he do it next? What's his next move?"

Collins looked helplessly at the two cabinet secretaries. That question was well above his pay grade. Richfield broke in. "I'll answer that question, Mr. President. Fedorin's missed his chance in Ukraine. When Putin annexed the Crimea in 2014, he pissed off the Ukrainians so much that there's no way he can get it back now short of an overt invasion."

"That hasn't stopped him from backing the Russian militants in Ukraine," Hardy muttered.

Richfield continued, "And he'd love to bring the Baltic States back into the fold, but they're part of the EU and NATO now. Their economies and governments aren't as vulnerable as Belarus or Ukraine—and then there's that little issue of Article V." Lloyd and Colonel Collins both nodded agreement with the SecDef. Any military action against the Baltic States would invoke the collective defense clause that would bring the other NATO nations to their aid. No one thought Fedorin was crazy enough to try and push the NATO alliance that hard.

Hardy shook his head, frowning. "That doesn't answer my question. I understand that a Russian-style takeover needs a reasonable Russian national presence in the population and a weak government, one corrupt enough to be bribed." He paused for a moment, staring at the map. "You're all in agreement that he can't take over any more European states with the same tactics. Which means he'll have to change his tactics, try something else, somewhere else."

"Yes, Mr. President. And he'll be as sneaky as he can," Richfield added.

21 June 2021
1415 Local Time
Red Square
Moscow, Russia

Russian President Ivan Olegovich Fedorin was in his mid-forties; he looked young for his age, with only a few traces of light gray lacing his otherwise short brown hair. His eyes were gray, in a long narrow face that could switch from a smile to an angry scowl between two words.

He was as handsome as an actor, and just as adept at changing roles as the situation demanded. At the moment, he smiled broadly, waving to the cheering crowd, basking in their wild enthusiasm. A sea of Russian flags waved before him, celebrating the latest achievements as if he were a conquering hero of old.

A parade celebrating the return of Belarus to the Russian Federation had been announced the same day as the agreement was signed. Exactly one week later, Belarusian President Yatachenko and other Belarusian officials stood on the reviewing stand next to Fedorin, watching as tanks and troops marched by and jet aircraft flew almost dangerously low over the crowd, then spiraled up into spectacular aerobatics.

The moment the massed bands stopped playing, Fedorin almost sprang to the podium. He grabbed the microphone with one hand and leaned forward. "Comrades! Fellow Russians! Our country is larger, stronger, and richer today because our Belarusian brothers have rejoined us! And Belarus is stronger and richer as part of our Federation!"

Cheers would have drowned out whatever he said next, so Fedorin waited until the din had faded.

His exuberant tone mellowed, and he spoke more calmly. "There are many good reasons why Belarus should be part of the Russian Federation. Our common language, our cultures, our shared faiths, all make her return to us seem more than just a good idea." His voice rose to almost a shout. "But those do not matter as much as the pure joy I feel at part of our fathers' nation once again in its proper place!"

There was another cheer from the crowd, but Fedorin only waited for a moment before continuing. "Russia will be stronger still as our dismembered motherland rebuilds and heals. Soviet Russia was once the greatest, the richest, the most advanced country on Earth, but our leaders made mistakes, and our enemies seized on them, weakening our beloved nation and finally shattering it.

"Forty years later, we have returned to the world stage, and while I promise you that we will not make the same mistakes as our fathers did, our enemies are already sharpening their knives. They try to stifle us and strangle our country with sanctions and industrial espionage and boycotts and military treaties explicitly aimed at 'containing' us once more."

Fedorin paused and scanned the crowd. "They should be careful." He smiled wickedly. "We grow stronger while they grow weaker. Some day, perhaps not too long from now, the Russian Federation will be a union once again, with all of our lost peoples rejoined with us in a nation so powerful that the world will not only acknowledge our leadership, they will *beg* us to lead them.

"I will share my dream with you all, and I beg you all to make it your dream as well. Let us remake our fathers' Soviet Union, a nation unlike any before it, and still the greatest nation in history. But we will not be satisfied with recreating past glories, but will use them as a starting point to move forward, to do things we can only dream of now."

21 June 2021
2030 Eastern Daylight Time
CNN International Affairs
New York, New York

The background screen behind Christine Laird showed a constantly shifting montage with videos of President Fedorin and Russian military hardware, along with demonstrations both pro-and anti-Russia. The camera kept the background in view behind Laird as she began her broadcast.

"Fedorin's latest speech has already received over a million views, and the Russian Foreign Ministry has thoughtfully uploaded versions subtitled in English, French, German, and many other languages, even Malay. European leaders are becoming more open in expressing their concerns about Fedorin's revanchist policies.

"Senator Tom Emmers from Kentucky is a member of the Senate's Armed Services Committee. He is sponsoring a resolution calling for President Hardy to be more decisive in opposing Fedorin's actions. Welcome, Senator."

Emmers was a large man with thinning brown hair. His round face broke into a wide beaming smile as Laird introduced him.

"Thank you, Christine. You know, I had to look up 'revanchist' the first time I heard it. It turns out to be derived from a French word, and means wanting to regain territory that was lost, usually through a war or some such misfortune. There's also an element of revenge, implying that whoever made them lose the territory will suffer payback."

Laird prompted, "And you think this is an accurate description of Russian President Fedorin's policies?"

"They could put a picture of him in the dictionary next to the definition," Emmers asserted, "but while I had it open, I found another word: 'irredentism.' This one is from Italian and, boiled down, means people who want to claim territory where some folks with the same language or culture live. It doesn't have to even be a majority of the people living there. Does that sound like any Russian presidents we know?

"Fedorin believes in the 'good old days,' when the Soviet Union was a military superpower. He was barely out of school when everything fell apart over there. His dad and Putin were buddies, back in the day, so it's no surprise that the young Fedorin started his career in the KGB working for Putin, learning the dark arts from a master. Now he's in charge, trying to bring back something that's a mix of old propaganda and wishful thinking. In case the present administration hasn't figured it out, he wants to revive the good old USSR, and he doesn't care who suffers getting there."

Emmers sat up a little straighter, and his tone harshened. "I'm sending a dictionary to President Hardy with those two definitions highlighted. It tells him everything he needs to know about Fedorin, and will be much more than he knows now. The president did nothing to interfere with Fedorin's takeover of Belarus, and doesn't appear to be doing anything now that it's happened. If 'not doing anything' was going to be Hardy's foreign policy, he should have warned us before the election, so we could all start taking Russian lessons."

Laird referred to a paper on her desk. "Press Secretary Andrews read a statement today saying that they're continuing to quote, 'monitor the Russian actions for any violations of international law—'"

"'Monitor' is a word that means 'watching without acting,'" Emmers interrupted angrily. "And we already know what Fedorin thinks about international law. The only thing he cares about, or understands, is raw power, and until this administration grows a spine, the Russians will keep steadily reclaiming the old Soviet client states, and causing lots of damage along the way.

"Every state that used to be in the Soviet Union has suffered violent demonstrations and hacking attacks. There are even some 'accidental' deaths that this administration ought to be investigating. Even countries like Poland and the Czech Republic, which are both members of NATO, by the way, report incidents of cyber hacking, sabotage, and Russian economic sanctions."

The senator took a breath, and Laird quickly interjected, "You make some bold assertions, Senator, but isn't it true that everyone was caught by surprise by the sudden turnaround in Belarus? The universal response from the European Union countries certainly paints that picture, and if I may, neither your committee, nor any other in the House or Senate seems to have anticipated this development. Just what would you like the administration to do differently?"

Emmers grimaced briefly; he didn't like being challenged by this young upstart. Ignoring her jab, he went straight to answering the question. "We need to get some skin in the game. Get more troops over there, on a permanent basis. Help upgrade the military forces of our allies. How about some stronger economic sanctions? Don't wait for the Russians to do something. By then, it's too late. Hit Fedorin and his stooges in their wallets. And how about some decent intelligence briefings?" Emmers shrugged with an air of sarcasm. "Does the CIA know more and they're just not sharing? Or is this it? The Russians are busy all over Europe. What's their next move?"

21 June 2021
2250 Eastern Daylight Time
The Executive Residence
Washington, D.C.

They still read together in bed before sleeping, although it now some-times included watching recorded video. Hardy thumbed the control and the flat-screen went dark. "Why did Dwight think you needed to see that?" asked Joanna. There was irritation in her voice. She jealously guarded their "quiet time" together and the CNN clip was nothing but an ugly intrusion. "Emmers is going to criticize you no matter what you do or say."

Hardy scowled for a moment, then answered, "Emmers is a horse's patoot, but he's also right. We don't have enough intelligence to predict where Fedorin will move next. By the time we'd doped out what was going to happen in Belarus, it was too late."

"Maybe even Fedorin doesn't know," Joanna suggested. "He could just sit there and stir the pot until he sees an opening, and then act."

Hardy nodded agreement. "Being a dictator does let him move more quickly. But without taking the analogy too far, he has more than one bubbling pot on the stove, and there's lots of different things he can do: build up the fire or put in different ingredients, and we don't even know the recipes he's trying to make."

"But you do know," she insisted. "He's trying to make borscht, every time." Her husband's annoyed frown caused her to chuckle. She held up a hand, smiling. "Okay, I'm sorry. I broke your metaphor. I understand that you need more information, and that Fedorin has the initiative. He can choose the time and place, and all you can do is re-act. But you also know his goals."

"And Ray Peakes is working that angle, as he tries to improve our intelligence collection and analysis capabilities on Russia. We've been spread pretty thin with most of our attention being in the Middle East and Asia for the last couple of decades, as you well know, my dear. We need to essentially rebuild our Russian analytical cadre. You just can't or-der decent analysts online. They need to be recruited, trained, and grown. But this takes time, something that our allies, and my critics, don't get."

"Meanwhile, Emmers and his allies will snipe at you."

"I'm not worried about that; I'm already developing a thick hide. But Fedorin is not our friend, and wants to do us harm."

"He's trying to take over entire countries," Joanna persisted. "He can't do that entirely out of sight."

"Perhaps not. But, we're still depending far more on luck than I'd like."

23 June 2021
0700 Local Time
USS *Jimmy Carter*
Arctic Ocean

Commander Louis Weiss strolled slowly into the control room, carefully cradling his extra large mug. He wasn't completely awake yet and he didn't want to spill a drop of the precious hot black liquid. Although the mug was capable of holding twenty ounces, Weiss had only filled it to the "sea line," which meant a mere sixteen. A gift from his wife, it was a simple, sturdy design adorned with the ship's patch and motto, *Semper Optima*—"Always the Best."

Pausing to look around control, he found everything running smoothly, despite the fact that their deployment had taken a hard left turn. Two days earlier the boat had rendezvoused with the Coast Guard icebreaker *Polar Star* at Smith Bay, a remote ice-infested cove at the top of Alaska. *Polar Star* had hightailed it from Anchorage, on the other side of the state, after stopping just long enough to pick up a navy detachment and their cargo that had been flown into Elmendorf Air Force Base. It took nearly six days for the Coast Guard ship to reach the northern bay; thick broken ice slowed them down a little as they rounded Barrow.

By comparison, *Jimmy Carter* had it easy. Weiss was able to bring her in submerged until they were well within sight of land. Once tied up alongside *Polar Star*, navy and coast guard personnel quickly transferred the supplies, spare parts, mission data, and mail. Commodore Mitchell had promised the last item as compensation for what promised to be a long deployment. Five hours later, *Jimmy Carter* slipped back beneath the Arctic Ocean.

Acknowledging the officer of the deck's greeting, Weiss wandered over to the plotting tables. His executive officer, Lieutenant Commander Joshua Segerson was hunched over the port table, studying a chart of the Severnaya Zemlya area.

"Good morning, Skipper," hailed Segerson without looking up.

"Morning, XO. So how's the search plan coming along?"

"Nav finished it about half an hour ago, he was up all night tweaking the damn thing. I had him hit the rack."

Weiss nodded his understanding; the ship's navigator, Lieutenant Commander Kurt Malkoff, was a perfectionist. "Yeah, well, Kurt can get pretty focused when he thinks he needs to."

"Which is all the time," noted Segerson with confidence. "But still, after thirty-some hours staring at this chart I figured there was a distinct risk of us ending off of Australia, so I booted him out." The executive officer stood up straight, rolled the chart up and offered it to Weiss. "I've just finished looking it over, and it is one finely polished cannonball. It's ready for your review, sir."

"Thanks, I'll study it when I grab my second mug," said Weiss as he stuffed the chart under his arm. "But what's the bottom line, XO? How long does Kurt think it'll take to find *Toledo*?"

Segerson shook his head. "I asked him the same thing, Skipper, and I got a typical answer. If we're really lucky, about a week, if we're really unlucky, never, and then there is everything in between."

"I just hope we find her, Josh. There's a lot of attention on this mission. A lot of *presidential* attention."

"I'd say that's normal when a boat goes missing."

Weiss shook his head vehemently. "No, no, XO, it goes way beyond that. You see, the new president, our squadron commodore, and *Toledo*'s skipper all served together on *Memphis*. From what I heard, that wardroom got really tight during their last mission—a SPECOP in Russian waters."

Segerson whistled softly, then said, "No pressure." He hadn't been aware of that little fact.

"You got that right, Josh." Weiss paused to take a stiff drink of his coffee and then motioned toward the navigation chart. "We're still good, position-wise?"

"Yes, sir. We'll be in the search area in a little less than twenty-four hours. Then the real fun begins. I take it you still intend to make a quick pass of the area, get the lay of the land, in a manner of speaking?"

Weiss nodded. "Yes, XO, and we go in at battle stations. I don't know what happened to *Toledo*, but I'm not taking any chances."

3

DRAGON'S LAIR

24 June 2021
1100 Local Time
Prima Polar Station
Bolshevik Island, Russia

Vice Admiral Nikolai Vasil'evich Gorokhov steadied himself against the biting wind as he peered through his binoculars out into the Laptev Sea. He didn't like what he was seeing. Theoretically it was summer, theoretically. But at the far end of Cape Baranova he was nearly thirteen degrees north of the Arctic Circle, and while the current temperature of minus one degree Celsius was balmy by comparison to the frigid cold of a typical Arctic winter, it still wasn't all that cozy. The blustery northwest wind didn't help matters, coming in from over the polar ice pack with gusts of up to twenty-five knots. The wind-chill factor wasn't horrible; he'd experienced much worse while stationed in the Northern Fleet. No, his concern was the large ice floes the wind was pushing into his construction area.

From his perch on the small cliff, he could see the icebreaker *Arktika* and the floating workshop, PM-69, rocking at their moorings some thirteen kilometers away. The background was filled with large chunks of ice heaving in the swells, advancing slowly on the islands that made up Severnaya Zemlya. Sea spray and the ever-present overcast skies made it difficult to see any details; at times he could barely make out the vessels themselves. He felt bad for the men on the two ships as they struggled to get the last monstrous launch tube lowered over the icebreaker's side and down to the divers 180 meters below. But the weather would be the least of their worries if they didn't keep to the schedule.

A frustrated sigh escaped his lips; the warm air quickly formed a cloud that was instantly swept away by the wind. Turning, Gorokhov headed back to the command shack; there was nothing more he could do here. He had ventured out to see for himself if the bad news brought to him by the staff meteorologist was accurate—bad news confirmed. The walk back was short, only a few hundred meters, but it gave him time to organize his thoughts. He'd have to break the unpleasant news to the minister of defense carefully. Gorokhov knew from experience that General Trusov was a reasonable man; he would readily admit that weather-related delays were beyond human influence. Unfortunately, the man the defense minister worked for could be just as unreasonable.

The command shack was a large Quonset hut, just one of the two dozen structures that made up the Ice Base Cape Baranova Observatory, also known as the Prima Polar Station. Established in the late 1980s, the ice base was used for scientific investigation of the Arctic environment, glacier studies, and the research of Arctic fauna, especially birds. It also functioned as a base camp for floating ice stations, since it had a runway capable of handling medium-sized cargo aircraft. It was shut down in 1996 due to a lack of funding, yet another victim of Russia's severe financial difficulties. The ice base was reopened in the summer of 2013 and focused on studying the effects of pollution at high latitudes. It also became a tourist attraction for those adventurers interested in taking a cruise on a Russian icebreaker up to the North Pole. Business seemed to be rather brisk, but the ice base was closed again after the 2020 season. The official reason given was that the facilities were old and outdated, in dire need of upkeep and improvements that would take about two years to complete. The official reason was partially true, but the "improvements" had nothing to do with scientific research.

Gorokhov braced himself as the wind gusted again; was it his imagination, or was it getting stronger? He placed each step with care;

there was still plenty of snow and ice on the rocky surface and the wind-swept terrain hid the more slippery spots. He'd lost his footing on more than one occasion, and he had the bruises to prove it. As he approached the red-and-white hut, he noted the large number "14" painted near the entrance. During winter storms it was not unheard of for people to get lost walking from one building to another, sometimes with fatal results. Each structure had large numbers on its exterior to help guide those who had to go outside in poor visibility.

Once inside the entryway, the admiral removed his sheepskin mittens and *ushanka* and shook the snow off his heavy parka. Now that his "refreshing" stroll was over, he had to get back to real work. As soon as he opened the door to the inner workspaces he was met by his chief of staff, Captain First Rank Kalinin, with a steaming cup. Gorokhov handed his winter gear and binoculars to a waiting petty officer, then smiled as he reached for the hot liquid.

"Thank you, Boris. I definitely need this," remarked Gorokhov as he raised the cup. But before he took a sip, he paused, eyed his aide and said, "It is properly 'seasoned,' yes?"

"Absolutely, Comrade Admiral."

"Good," Gorokhov grumbled.

"I take it then that it's as bad as Captain Third Rank Chekhov reported?" Kalinin asked cautiously.

Gorokhov nodded, then added after a sip, "Perhaps worse. I don't know if Apalkov's men will be able to continue working under these conditions. The damn ice floes are coming right into the mouth of the strait from the Laptev Sea. That and the big swells will make it very dangerous for the men below."

"Ahh, I see," replied Kalinin. "Perhaps that is why Sergei called."

The admiral stopped drinking his tea, sighed, and asked, "When?"

"About fifteen minutes ago, sir. He said it was urgent."

"I'm sure it is." There was a note of resignation in Gorokhov's voice. "Very well, get him back on the secure radio. This isn't going to get any better by waiting."

"Yes, Comrade Admiral."

* * *

Gorokhov could hear the wind howling in the background as Captain First Rank Sergei Ivanovich Apalkov gave his report. The captain was the lead construction engineer for Project Drakon—Project Dragon, a long-range, nuclear-propelled, nuclear-armed land attack torpedo system. In Russian terminology, the Dragon was a deep-sea torpedo-rocket strike complex, a strategic weapon that combined an incredibly large torpedo with a hypersonic land attack cruise missile.

A follow-on development to the huge submarine-carried Status-6 land-attack torpedo, the Project Dragon weapon was even larger and heavier. With a diameter of nearly two meters, a length of twenty-seven meters, and a displacement of fifty-six tons, it was larger than any of the Russian Navy's current submarine-launched ballistic missiles. But unlike the Status-6, which had a multi-megaton nuclear warhead, Project Dragon had a very high-speed missile as its payload, able to reach targets well inland. The torpedo part of the new weapon had also undergone significant modifications and was a lot quieter than the Status-6.

Unfortunately, all these changes made the weapon so enormous that it couldn't possibly be carried by any Russian submarine currently at sea, or on the drawing board. This left a ground-based launcher as the only near-term deployment option, and that led the Russians to the far north. The Bolshevik Island ice base was an ideal location. Its high northern latitude made it difficult for imagery satellites and spy aircraft to get a good look at it. And that assumed the weather was conducive for visual reconnaissance, which it often was not. In addition, Cape Baranova ran right up to the edge of the Nansen Basin in the Arctic Ocean. This enabled the launchers to be placed in relatively shallow water, but still have easy access to water depths greater than one thousand fathoms. The trick was getting the launchers built in an environment that was anything but cooperative.

"Comrade Admiral," shouted Apalkov over the radio, "we need to temporarily cease the unloading evolution. The weather conditions have degraded and are causing the icebreaker to roll and pitch excessively. We cannot control the launch tube's position and it's getting very dangerous."

Gorokhov rubbed his forehead as he listened; he had expected as much. Apalkov was a very good engineer and knew his business. If he said the situation was too dangerous, he had already exceeded normal safety protocols. Still, the admiral had to hear for himself that everything that could be done had been done to continue the construction work.

"I understand, Sergei. Is there any way to stabilize the tube? Isolate it from the ship's motion?"

"I've used every trick I know, sir; the beast is wandering around like a drunken yak. It almost hit the launch complex; we only managed to just stop it."

Gorokhov winced at the very idea of one of the twenty-eight-meter-long steel tubes smashing into the reinforced concrete structure and steel frames that were to hold the six launchers. That would have ended any hope of having the Dragon system online by the fall.

Apalkov kept on going, "And it's not just the launch tube, it's a diver-safety concern as well. We were pushing it when the winds gusted to eighteen knots. By regulations I should have pulled the divers then, but we managed to keep going. Now that we're seeing sustained winds of twenty-plus knots, it's getting very difficult for the men to keep their footing, let alone trying to do their job.

"One diver has already been injured when his tether went momentarily slack and then snapped back as the floating workshop rolled. Thank God he was in an atmospheric diving suit and we were able to haul him to the surface immediately."

Gorokhov recalled how Apalkov had fought fervently during the planning meetings for the use of atmospheric diving suits, rather than the more traditional saturation diving approach. In the diving suits, the men didn't have to worry about the pressure effects normally associated with deep diving as the suits were kept at atmospheric pressure. In addition, the dry, comfortable environment meant that they could work longer without having to rest and recuperate. The disadvantages were that men in diving suits didn't have the same range of motion and control as a saturation diver, and the suits themselves were expensive. But in the end, Apalkov won the argument by showing how the project could be completed faster if the probability of diver injury, or death, were minimized.

"Very well, Captain," conceded Gorokhov. "Cease unloading operations and recover the divers. What do you intend to do about the launch tube?"

Apalkov chuckled over the airwaves. "I'll park it on the bottom, sir. The winds would have to reach hurricane force before they'll be able to move this twenty-ton son of a sewer tube."

24 June 2021
1130 Local Time
USS *Jimmy Carter*
Nansen Basin, Arctic Ocean

The submarine approached the Severnaya Zemlya archipelago from the northwest, passing by Komsomolets Island first, then October Revolution Island, and finally Bolshevik Island. Weiss kept *Jimmy Carter* in deep water and well away from the conventional twelve-mile limit on this first pass. Paralleling the major islands' coastlines from twenty nautical miles out enabled Weiss to get a good look at the Russian activity near the planned search areas. Using the edge of the pack ice as cover, *Carter* swept by at twelve knots, the sonar arrays scanning the area all around them. From the sound of things, it was really an ugly mess up on top. The background noise was deafening as massive chunks of polar ice violently smashed into each other. Weiss's senior sonar operator described the acoustic environment as akin to being inside a cement mixer. Fortunately, the two towed arrays were largely immune to the higher-frequency ruckus and had no trouble picking up the two ships to the south.

Weiss looked down at the plot that Malkoff had started as soon as the Russians were detected. All the bearing lines crossed the same spot—the ships were stationary. Using a pair of dividers, Malkoff measured the distance from Bolshevik Island.

"Looks like they're anchored about fifteen thousand yards northwest of Cape Baranova, Skipper. Right at the entrance to the Shokal'skogo Strait," remarked Malkoff, tapping on the chart.

"Easy for you to say!" Weiss shot back with a smile. "That's a bit of a tongue twister."

"Not to worry, sir. I'll have you pronouncing it perfectly by the time you give the mission brief."

Weiss shook his head in feigned exasperation then, pointing at the crossed bearings, asked, "Is this location consistent with what you used to anchor the search pattern?"

"Yes, sir. This estimate matches reasonably well with *Toledo*'s reporting before she disappeared. I just need a couple of hours to refine the anchor point, revise the search plan, and get it to Thing 2 for downloading into the UUVs." Malkoff pointed toward Lieutenant Junior Grade Steven Lawson sitting at the third fire control console. Lawson and Lieutenant Benjamin Ford were the two officers responsible for working with the "thingies," a shortened form of "thingamajigs" the executive officer liked to use when describing the unmanned underwater vehicles. Naturally, Segerson referred to Ford and Lawson as Thing 1 and Thing 2.

"Okay, Nav, two hours," Weiss insisted. "I want to get this search started ASAP."

"Aye, aye, sir."

Weiss walked back to the periscope stand, reached up, and depressed the intercom switch. "Sonar, Conn. Report all contacts."

"Conn, Sonar," squawked the speaker. "Hold two contacts. Sierra three, classified as a nuclear-powered icebreaker, bears one eight one degrees, and Sierra four, classified as an auxiliary, is at one eight three degrees."

"Sonar, Conn, aye." Satisfied, Weiss turned and motioned for Segerson to join him at the navigation plot. "Okay, XO, let's continue our run to the northeast, to Cape Sandy, and then turn north and clear datum."

"Understood, Skipper. Do you still intend to send in a status report?"

"I'd like to, provided we can find a semi-quiet spot to raise a mast without it getting scrunched."

Segerson looked skeptical, but said nothing. Weiss picked up on his executive officer's reservations. "Yeah, I know, Commodore Mitchell said to treat this mission like any other, but we both know that's not how it's being viewed back at the head shed," said Weiss quietly.

"Skipper, President Hardy was a submarine commanding officer.

He'd understand, no, he'd *expect* that we'd stay silent. Especially this close to the bad guys' backyard." Segerson's tone was respectful, but insistent.

"He's the least of our worries, Josh, for the very reasons you gave." Weiss paused as he considered his next move. "Look, if the situation isn't conducive to sending a quick message, then we don't and move on. But if we can do so safely, I think it would be a good idea."

"Yes, sir," answered Segerson. "I'll have the Commo get started as soon as we stand down from general quarters."

24 June 2021
1300 Local Time
Main Building of the Ministry of Defense
Moscow, Russia

General Aleksandr Trusov listened carefully as Vice Admiral Gorokhov gave his report. The minister of defense had been briefed on the deteriorating weather situation in the far north earlier, but Gorokhov's message put meaning behind the sterile maps with wind speed and barometric pressure. Unfortunately, the message's content was unwelcome news.

"Comrade General, we nearly lost control of the last twenty-ton launch tube due to the high swells. Captain Apalkov only just prevented it from hitting the launcher complex. I don't think I need to explain how disastrous that would have been."

Trusov sat back in his chair with a mixture of alarm and relief; he chased out the mental picture of him having to tell Fedorin that Project Dragon would be delayed for several months. The very idea sent shivers up his spine.

"No, Nikolai Vasil'evich, you don't have to explain it to me. I am well aware of how painful such an event would have been. And as unpleasant as it is for me to say this, you did the right thing by securing the launch tube unloading. I will have to find a way to break this unfortunate development to the president as gently as possible. He doesn't take disappointing news very well. Especially in regard to Project Drakon—he asked, again, if there was anything that could be done to speed the construction along. He raised the possibility of sending more workers to you so that you could pick up the pace."

Gorokhov took a deep breath, fighting the urge to howl in frustration; it would have been disrespectful and futile. The Russian Federation president hadn't met a law of nature that he didn't think could be cajoled into turning a blind eye to their activities. The admiral recalled an earlier meeting where Fedorin complained about the inconvenience of gravity.

"Comrade Defense Minister—" Gorokhov started to protest, but Trusov cut him off.

"Yes, Admiral, most of us are well aware that just adding bodies to a project doesn't mean the rate of construction will increase markedly . . . if at all. Particularly when the project involves a rather small structure almost two hundred meters underwater."

"My apologies, sir, I know you understand the situation. But I find it unnerving that the president doesn't seem to comprehend that for this plan of his to work, we must maintain absolute security. Sending more ships up here would only draw attention to this place. It would be like turning on a giant neon sign."

"Agreed, Nikolai. But rest assured, President Fedorin does understand the need for security, we've discussed it at length—he truly appreciates the necessity. The problem is that he has grown impatient; other aspects of his strategy have been incredibly successful. He wants to maintain the momentum, that's all. I'm sure you can sympathize with that desire." Trusov's calming wisdom had the desired effect on the aggravated senior naval officer, his faded breathing indicating he had calmed down.

"Now, back to the issue at hand. How long before you can get your people back to work?" asked Trusov.

"My staff meteorologist estimates it will be two days before the winds subside enough for the ships to stop bouncing about like toys. Once we can get men in the water, it should only take us a day to get the last tube in place. Then we get *Arktika* out of the way and shift to laying the computer network cabling."

Trusov nodded in agreement to himself. "I wish that I had better news for you, Nikolai, but my weather mystics have said the same thing. And I concur that we need to get the icebreaker out of the area soon; it looks like the cloud cover may desert us for a few days. I don't want to show the Americans any more than is necessary."

"We have been fortunate, Comrade Minister, but the sun does occasionally shine up here. It is summer, after all," chuckled Gorokhov.

"So I've been told," Trusov replied, amused. "Oh, before I forget, the Project 1274 cable laying ship, *Inguri*, will be leaving port by the end of the month. We've received word that the last of the seabed hydroacoustic modules you requested have left the factory and should be at Severodvinsk by the twenty-eighth. *Inguri* only needs a day to load, and then four days to sail to your location. With any luck your acoustic fence should be in place and operational by the end of the first week in July."

"That is very good news indeed, Comrade Minister," Gorokhov remarked, but there was a hint of irritation in his voice. "It certainly took Atoll long enough to produce the Sever modules. While the minefield provides a good deal of protection, I'd like to see the holes in the defensive perimeter filled."

"Don't be too hard on the people at Atoll, Nikolai Vasil'evich. Your last-minute requirement for MGK-608M Sever modules unexpectedly doubled their defense order for the year. The company has been scrambling to ramp up production as quickly as they could," scolded Trusov.

"I suppose you're right," grunted the admiral wearily.

"Of course I am! I'm a Russian general, don't you know!" Both men laughed, but Gorokhov suddenly ceased when a deep yawn forced itself upon him.

"Why don't you get some rest, Nikolai?" suggested Trusov. "You can't do any real work for a couple of days, so catch up on some sleep."

"That sounds like excellent advice, sir. I think I'll do just that. I'll inform you the moment the divers get back to work."

24 June 2021
0630 Eastern Daylight Time
Oval Office, The White House
Washington, D.C.

President Hardy was an early riser, much to the distress of his staff. It wasn't uncommon for him to swing by the Oval Office on his way to, or back from, his workout. Today, Hardy was on his way back. Garbed in his navy sweats and a towel around his neck, he only paused to see the pressing items on his desk; e-mail and other such electronic nagging would come later.

"Good morning, Mr. President," greeted Sellers as he entered the office with more paper in his arms. "How are you feeling today?"

"Old and rusty, Dwight, old and rusty," Hardy replied as he sorted through the growing pile. "Today's exercises were a little more annoying than usual." He rolled his right shoulder as he spoke. The slight grimace on his face betrayed the joint's tenderness.

"Perhaps you should see the physical therapist? He might be able to loosen that shoulder for you, that or WD-40."

Hardy laughed. "My shoulder doesn't want to speak to Chuck right now, thank you. His range of motion physical terrorism is why I ache so much. But I like the WD-40 idea. Too bad it doesn't work on humans." After pushing all the files around on the desk, he looked up at Sellers and asked, "So, what's on our docket for today?"

Sellers's eyes rolled slightly, a bad sign. "Where would you like to start, Mr. President?"

Hardy raised his hand, ending the discussion. "Belay my last! Let's resume after my shower."

"A wise decision, sir." Sellers walked by Hardy and started to rearrange the now unkempt stack. The president almost made it to the door when Sellers called out to him.

"Mr. President, I think you'll want to look at this now. It's a note from Admiral Hughes. *Jimmy Carter* is in area and will commence searching for *Toledo* shortly."

Hardy reached slowly for the single piece of paper. It took him only a moment to read the note; his somber expression hid the mixed emotions. He handed the paper back to Sellers. "Thank you, Dwight. I'll be back in half an hour."

Without another word, Hardy left his chief of staff to his duties.

24 June 2021
1300 Local Time
Golden Eagle Flight
Estonia

Major Ivar Talts gloried in flying his F-16AM fighter. It was one of twenty-seven aircraft purchased from the Netherlands by the three Baltic States. The price was quite favorable for the small NATO countries, and the United States provided funding and material support to overhaul the old aircraft. And for the first time in many decades, Estonia now had the ability to police its own airspace. A minor capability to be sure, but it was a huge step forward. A necessary step to counter Russia's increasingly belligerent behavior since Fedorin became the Russian Federation president in 2018. Major Talts didn't really care about the strategic implications right now; he was focusing on the moment as he and his wingman raced toward the Russian border at full military power.

"Golden Eagle flight, Ämari Air Base, the two bogeys bear one zero five degrees, range sixty-two kilometers, altitude five one double oh meters. Radar emissions identify the aircraft as Sierra uniform two seven Flankers."

Talts took a deep breath under his mask. *Here we go again*, he thought. "Understood, Ämari. I have radar contact on the bogeys. We're crossing over Lake Peipus now." The Russians had been getting more and more aggressive with aircraft skimming along the border over Lake Peipus. Sometimes they went a little too far and had to be herded back across. At least Talts didn't have to do this with the Aero L-39 anymore. An armed high performance F-16 made a far stronger impression than a lowly jet trainer.

Looking over his left shoulder at Captain Erik Lepp's aircraft, Talts toggled his mike. "Golden Eagle Two, follow my lead and keep it professional. No aggressive maneuvers. We just want to make sure our Russian neighbors stay on their side of the line. Understood?"

"Roger, Golden Eagle One."

It didn't take long to reach the middle of the big lake; a metallic flash to the southeast confirmed the Russian fighters' location. "Golden Eagle Two, visual contact to my right. Bearing one one zero." The two Estonian aircraft banked over and slowed down to cruise speed as the distance between them and the Russian Flankers evaporated.

"Golden Eagle flight, Ämari Air Base, the two bogeys have entered Estonian airspace. Repeat, they have crossed the border. A challenge is being made."

Talts swore then hit his mike again. "Golden Eagle Two, let's go. Keep close."

The Flankers were coming in fast. Talts watched his HUD as the tiny specs grew larger. He adjusted his course to close, but intentionally lagged behind their line of sight. Soon he could easily make out the twin rudders of the Su-27. Suddenly, the Flankers broke hard to the right and accelerated, hitting their afterburners. "Break left!" he shouted to Lepp as the Russian fighters screamed by a range well inside fifty meters.

"What kind of shit is that?" yelled Lepp. His voice was labored as the two F-16s pulled a hard five-G turn, coming around to follow the interlopers. Talts was angry. The Russian pilots were acting in an unsafe, unprofessional manner . . . on the Estonian side of the border. Just what the hell did these fools think they were doing?

Talts switched his radio to the emergency channel and issued a challenge. "Russian aircraft, you are in violation of Estonian airspace. You are ordered to withdraw immediately. Respond." There was nothing but silence. Either they didn't receive his warning, or they were blatantly ignoring it—more than likely the latter.

"Golden Eagle One, the bogeys have turned around. Closing at high speed," reported Lepp.

"Roger, Golden Eagle Two. Let's try this again."

The four aircraft hurled toward each other. Talts tried to keep his nose pointed behind the Flankers, but the Russians countered by angling toward him. When the range had closed to a few kilometers, the

Flankers broke hard left with the intent of making another dangerous close pass. "Erik, pull up and bank left!" ordered the major.

The sudden maneuver caught the Russians off guard and they pulled a hard turn to the right to get back in position. Lepp's fighter swung out of the tight formation, unintentionally moving closer to the incoming Russians. The lead Flanker reacted quickly and pitched down hard, but the trailing aircraft hesitated and then over-compensated—the Su-27's left wing smashed into Lepp's aircraft.

Talts continued his climb and then swung around. The other Flanker had pulled out of the dive and was screaming back toward the border on afterburner. Looking down, he could see both fighters were in flames, trailing dirty brown smoke as they plunged toward the lake. A sudden flash from the Flanker told him the pilot had ejected. A moment later a parachute blossomed, but there was nothing from Lepp's F-16.

Hitting his mike Talts shouted, "Erik! Eject! Eject!" There was no response and the plane continued to spin wildly downward.

"Eject, Erik!" he yelled again. Nothing happened. Talts could only watch in horror as the battered fighter crashed into the lake and exploded.

4

GRIM NEWS

8 July 2021
1130 Eastern Daylight Time
CNN International Affairs

"You just used the word 'datum,' Commander Chang. Is that where you—I mean the Navy, of course—think *Toledo* is?"

Commander David Chang was from Navy Public Affairs. His summer whites were almost blindingly bright, and he wore both a submariner's dolphins and a command pin. He'd most recently commanded *Annapolis*, an attack boat out of Groton, but was currently assigned to "hazardous" duty in the Pentagon.

"It's a Navy term that means her last known location. It's the starting point for our search," Chang explained.

Christine Laird asked, "And when did that search begin?"

"About fourteen days ago, when we became concerned that she wasn't responding to our messages."

"And yet the Navy only declared her overdue on July fifth," Laird pressed. "Why the delay?"

"Mostly, to avoid alarming anyone, hopefully unnecessarily," Chang answered quickly. "Submarines have been out of extended contact before and returned safely. But when *Toledo* didn't return by the scheduled time, the crew's families deserved to know."

"And yet, in that two weeks, knowing where to look, you didn't find a trace of the ship?"

"We call them 'boats,' Ms. Laird, and the initial search area involved millions of square miles. We've actually only scratched—"

Laird interrupted, "Could you show us on a map where you're searching, or where this 'datum' is?"

"I'm afraid not, ma'am. That location is classified."

"Why?"

"Because it's inside her patrol area, and the Navy doesn't want anyone to know where its subs are when they're on patrol."

"What about the families? Do they know?" She sounded hopeful.

Chang could see where Laird was headed. "Definitely not! They were told that *Toledo* would be operating in the Northern Atlantic Ocean. It was the same when my boat was at sea. Our families were only told the general geographic area where we would be operating. Information on a submarine's location and its operating area are strictly limited, even within the Navy."

"Well, can you tell us how much of the search area you've covered?"

"I'm afraid not. But even if I could, the search area will expand as we shift further and further away from the datum. Thus, any number would be meaningless."

"How is the Navy searching for *Toledo*?"

"All types of platforms are being used, including surface ships, submarines, and aircraft. Even satellites. The search is being coordinated between Submarine Squadron Twelve, in Groton, Connecticut, and Commander, Submarine Forces in Norfolk, Virginia."

"How are they searching?"

"Visually, for signs of anything on the surface, and with sonar, ma'am. We have side scan sonars accurate enough to give us an image of the seabed, but they only show a very small part of the bottom at one time."

"Could you search with radiation detectors?" she suggested.

"No, Ms. Laird. A submarine's nuclear reactor is so well-shielded that its gives off very little radiation, and actually, radiation detectors have a much shorter range than the imaging sonar."

"But if the—boat's—been damaged, could the shielding be cracked or breached, somehow? More radiation would be released then."

Chang disagreed. "The detection range underwater would still be very short; water is actually a very good shielding material. Besides, the pressure vessel that holds the reactor core is built to withstand tremendous force. The *Kursk* explosion in 2000 was so big that seismic detectors around the world picked it up, but her two reactor vessels remained intact. If something like that had happened to *Toledo*, we'd know where to look."

The commander sighed, hoping his impatience wasn't being televised around the globe. "Water is hard to see through. That's why submarines are so hard to find. The only sensor that works well in water is sound, and we are searching with that, guided by the best experts in the field."

"And when will the Navy finish its search? I did some research on the Internet, and the wrecks of lost World War II submarines are still being found. Isn't there a good chance that the Navy will never find *Toledo*?"

"As I mentioned earlier, the search area expands as we move outward from the datum. So, when we'll be finished, I really can't say. But we are nowhere close to stopping the search."

"Even though it's unlikely that any of the crew are still alive?"

He looked grim, but determined. "We won't stop looking while there is any hope of finding *Toledo*, whatever its current status," Chang declared firmly. "She experienced some sort of trouble, and we owe it not just to the families of the crew, but the entire submarine force, to find out what happened to her.

"After *Thresher* was lost in 1963, the Navy went to a lot of trouble to explore the wreck and figure out that the accident was caused by a combination of hardware problems and incorrect operating procedures. As a result, the Navy created a program called 'Subsafe' that made changes to submarine designs and training, so that failure would never happen again."

Laird picked up a sheet of paper. "I'd like to read part of a letter from Congressman Mark Rikell, head of the House Armed Services Committee, to the secretary of the Navy, that was sent two days after news of *Toledo*'s disappearance first broke." She asked, "Have you seen this?"

Chang seemed to be having trouble not frowning. "I've read it, along with the rest of the Public Affairs Office."

"The entire letter is available at our website under the heading '*Toledo*' but I'll just read the third paragraph.

"Congressman Rikell writes, 'I am unhappy with the information provided by the Navy to this committee. We find it impossible to exercise our proper oversight function when so much information regarding the search is being withheld from the members, even when meeting in classified session. Questions the Navy refused to answer included the duration of the search, the exact area where *Toledo* could possibly be located, and whether anything related to her mission could have caused her loss. We are very concerned that the Navy will not say how close the submarine was to Russian waters, or whether Russian assistance was requested.'"

Laird said. "Thanks to your explanations, I believe I can understand why the Navy hasn't disclosed the location information, but certainly the Russians know whether we've asked them for help. Is there any reason why the American people shouldn't know? So, I'll ask you here: Have you asked the Russian Federation for assistance in searching for *Toledo*?"

Chang smiled. "Congressman Rikell could have given the Navy a little more time to respond. Since the question involved a foreign country, the secretary of defense had to consult with secretary of state before answering, and the answer is 'No, we haven't,' and do not plan to."

"And can we deduce from your answer that you are not searching near Russian territorial waters?"

"You may draw any conclusion you like, Ms. Laird. I cannot tell you whether it is correct or not."

8 July 2021
0900 Pacific Daylight Time
Submarine Development Squadron Five Headquarters
Bangor, Washington

The quick-look report, the first information on what *Jimmy Carter* had found, transmitted within a day of the discovery, was just two pages. It was also classified at the Top Secret level, at least for the foreseeable future. *Jimmy Carter*'s UUVs had found *Toledo* rather quickly, which in one sense was great news. The crew's loved ones wouldn't have to wonder what had happened.

The second report was sent as *Carter* left the area. It wasn't much longer, but it confirmed everyone's worst fears. *Toledo* lay on the bottom, about 150 fathoms down, on her side with a hole in her hull that could not have come from any type of internal accident. The wreck was just a mile outside Russian territorial waters.

All sorts of emotions fought each other in Jerry. He felt pride for Weiss's work. It had taken considerable skill, as well as a little luck, for Lou's boat to locate *Toledo* so fast. Acoustic and bottom conditions were terrible in that part of the ocean, and having the Russians close enough to throw rocks at them had constrained his movements significantly. Jerry knew he'd be writing up another Meritorious Unit Commendation for this boat.

But conclusive word of *Toledo*'s fate also brought the dreaded sadness—delayed, deferred, and denied until hard proof tore away all his defenses. As much as Lenny's death saddened him, Jerry's thoughts went to Berg's family. They hadn't been informed yet, and wouldn't be until the higher-ups reviewed *Carter*'s full report and decided how much they could be told.

Weiss's boat wasn't due to return to Groton for another thirty-six hours, and that was with her making her best transit speed. It wasn't flank, but they weren't stopping at the gift shop on the way back, either. Until then, the "official" search would continue, while the Navy tried to absorb and understand what *Toledo*'s loss implied.

The few photos that were included with the transmitted report had been made by the UUV from a close distance. Thankfully the water was clear, but the UUV's lights still didn't reach very far. The image showed a ragged but roughly circular hole in a smooth surface. There was no hint of the hull's curve in the image, which confirmed the photos were taken from very close range. There was no sense of scale, and no details could be seen inside. The edges of the hole were pushed in, consistent with a weapon impact.

Weiss's report said that the hole was about two feet in diameter, located amidships, probably near the boundary between the forward and reactor compartments. Two feet was more than big enough to sink the boat. The Improved *Los Angeles*–class submarines only had three compartments, with the watertight bulkheads surrounding the reactor. On either side, there was nothing to stop the water from filling that part of the ship.

A hit in the forward compartment would quickly flood the front half of the sub, as well as knock out the control systems the crew would need to recover. If the weapon hit the engine room, aft of the reactor compartment, it would have been just as fatal. The boat would have lost all propulsion and electrical power. Even a hole this large in the reactor compartment would have overwhelmed the emergency blow system. U.S. submarine design emphasized stealth, not battle-damage resistance—at least not from a torpedo hit.

Naturally, the next question would be what made the hole, but *Carter*'s UUVs had actually answered that question before it had a chance to become a mystery. *Toledo*'s area of uncertainty had extended into Russian waters, but going across the border, at least during the initial search, had been ruled out. However, the two UUVs, dubbed "Walter" and "José," after the Jeff Dunham characters, had searched right up to the edge of Russian territorial waters. And they found something.

A long line of moored propelled warhead mines loosely followed the twelve-mile limit between October Revolution and Bolshevik Islands, blocking the approaches to Shokal'skogo Strait. A minefield? Jerry's surprise was understandable. Not only was it completely unexpected, but he could think of no reason to lay a minefield there—no reason that anyone knew of.

After *Jimmy Carter*'s UUVs had found the minefield, Weiss had shifted the search plan to check area near the Russian border first. That had been a good decision, although there was no joy in the outcome.

The mines were not relics from the Great Patriotic War. The UUVs' high-frequency sonars were good enough to get images from more than one angle, and Weiss's report identified the devices as very modern Russian PMK-2 mines. They were antisubmarine weapons, moored well below the surface. Each mine had its own sonar that would listen for an approaching submarine. The mine was smart enough to filter out noises that were not from subs. When it heard the right sounds, the mine would go active to determine the target's exact location and then release a torpedo that would home in and attack the sub.

But why was there a minefield around the northwestern edge of Bolshevik Island?

Jerry had never heard of it before, and had to look the place up. Off the central part of Russia's northern coast, it was one of the larger islands in the Severnaya Zemlya chain and marked Russia's northernmost territory, jutting well into the Arctic Ocean. An Internet search turned up information on a scientific base on the northwest corner, on Cape Baranova. The "ice base," as it was described, had no residents other than the people at the base, and no industry. The island's principal exports were ice, rocks, and birds.

Weiss's report said that the hole in *Toledo*'s hull was consistent with the size of a small torpedo warhead. The UUVs confirmed that the sub's location was consistent with the mine's detection range, and was within the range of the torpedo. In fact, while searching the ocean bottom around *Toledo*, Walter had mapped debris that could be part of a 324-millimeter torpedo propulsion section. The second report, brief as it was, conclusively answered the question of how *Toledo* had been lost.

There would be no accident investigation for *Toledo* and her crew. She had not been lost to mechanical failure or human error—the Russians had sunk her.

Even if the Russians hadn't wanted to sink anyone, they'd planted a very lethal minefield that had functioned exactly as designed. Whatever that minefield guarded on an island two hundred miles north of nowhere was important enough that they were willing to kill anyone who came too close.

SUBRON Twelve's cover letter to the two reports said that they would be continuing the official search, while waiting for guidance from above on what, and when, the families would be told. Jerry could well believe that Commodore Bob Dorr was seeking guidance from higher up in the chain.

Jerry's first impulse, and he imagined everyone's, was to tell *Toledo*'s loved ones immediately. But revealing the location, and especially the cause of *Toledo*'s loss would trigger an international crisis that would re-

veal the current "media firestorm" as the petty exercise in political the-
ater it was.

If the navy told the *Toledo*'s families what happened, it would have
to publicly accuse Russia of sinking her. Questions would be asked
about why the boat had been so close to the Russian border. Jerry
didn't know the exact purpose of her mission, but Fedorin wouldn't
miss the opportunity to raise a stink and accuse the U.S. Navy of
being up to no good. Especially now with Hardy as the president of the
United States; the man the Russian leader held responsible for the loss
of *Gepard*.

But the Russians were clearly up to no good. The longer they thought
the Americans were in the dark, the better.

Jerry's yeoman called into his office, "Commodore, your wife is on line
two." Emily usually called in the early afternoon, after Carly came back
from daycare. Emily claimed it was her desire to hear another adult
voice, but it was really just a chance to spend a few minutes together, at
least over the phone.

As soon as he answered, Emily asked, "Have you been watching
the news?" The squadron office usually had at least one TV set turned
to an all-news channel, but Jerry had ordered that the sound be muted
unless something important was happening.

"They just aired a short piece saying that the Navy was searching
close to Russian territory. That was news to me." She didn't sound entirely
happy.

"It's news to me as well," Jerry replied. It was only a small fib, since
while he did know where the search area was; it was indeed news that
the media had found out—and not good news. How much more did
they know? "Hang on one moment please, honey."

Jerry called to his yeoman, "I need to see Commander Gustason,
please," and Jerry's chief staff officer appeared at his door just a moment
later. "Emily's seen media coverage saying that the Navy's looking for
Toledo near Russia." Gustason's eyebrows went up in surprise, but he
could see Jerry's hand covering the phone, and remained silent. "Find
out what they're saying."

Gustason nodded and disappeared. The couple chatted about Charlotte's day and exchanged reminders about an upcoming house project. Jerry tried very hard to focus on his spouse's words, while the back of his mind processed the media's latest revelation. It kept intruding with a nagging question—*What else did they know?*

Gustason reappeared at his door after a few minutes, and Jerry excused himself. "Dylan's waiting to talk to me, honey." She finished her thought and hung up, yielding to the needs of the navy.

Jerry waved him in as he said goodbye and hung up. "I got more from the Internet than CNN," the commander reported as he sat down, "but it's very limited." Jerry relaxed a little, and his CSO continued. "A news article on CNN cites 'unnamed sources,' and just says that they're searching for *Toledo* in the Arctic Ocean, not the northern Atlantic, and that the searchers were concerned because of how close they had to go to the Russian border."

Gustason sighed. "Somebody talked to a reporter. Maybe someone who was worried they'd get shot at. There must be over a thousand people who know the search plan. It's not just SUBRON Twelve or SUBFOR. All the units taking part in the search, and all the people supporting those units, and all the people they're reporting to at the Pentagon. They all would know."

Jerry laughed softly, in spite of the news. "The reporters really should at least look at a map before saying we're searching close to Mother Russia. The search area is easily over a hundred miles from Franz Josef Land, and you can bet that the search plan included 'DO NOT CROSS THE RUSSIAN BORDER' in bold type."

"Written by some very wise staff officer," Gustason replied.

"At least the leak wasn't either of *Carter*'s reports," Jerry added, patting the document in question. "Any leak concerning *Toledo*'s loss is bad enough, but it could have been much worse."

"Your orders, Commodore?" Gustason asked.

Jerry scowled. "None, CSO. It's not our ball game. SUBRON Twelve and SUBFOR will have to carry on while the Russians go into a defensive crouch. Whoever leaked this to the press was not serving the national interest."

"Understood, sir. Oh, I've got your airline tickets and hotel reservation in Arlington all set. Your flight departs pretty early tomorrow morning, at 0645. Your driver will be by the house at 0430."

"Uggh." Jerry winced. "What an ungodly hour!"

"You're the guy who wanted to attend *Carter*'s formal debriefing at the Pentagon, so I don't want to hear any whining . . . sir."

Jerry saw the broad grin on Gustason's face. "You are a cold-hearted man, CSO."

Gustason nodded, accepting the compliment, and then left. Curious, Jerry turned on the television set in his office. How bad had the press coverage actually gotten? He flipped through different news channels, and all of them were now discussing the "stunning" revelations about possible Russian involvement in *Toledo*'s loss. A bevy of talking heads chewed on the new information, trying to make speculation sound like wise deduction.

Their conclusions were unanimous. There was some sort of navy cover-up, of that they were certain. Clearly, the navy was not doing its job properly, and of course was hiding the fact. They mentioned the "growing chorus calling for congressional investigations . . ."

8 July 2021
1900 Local Time
The Admiralty Building
St. Petersburg, Russia

The American news channel had a Cyrillic feed across the bottom of the screen, which obscured the different banners and messages the network ran, but Captain First Rank Vasiliy Vasil'evich Lavrov couldn't decode the scrolling characters quickly enough to make sense of them, anyway.

His spoken English comprehension was good enough to know that they were talking about the same things over and over again. The reports from the Main Intelligence Directorate (GRU) and the Foreign Intelligence Service (SVR) were far more interesting. Among their many surveillance activities, the two agencies tracked radio and cell phone emissions, listening in when the transmissions were in the clear. Any that related to the Russian Arctic, and now the loss of the American submarine *Toledo*, were routed to his office.

A navy captain first rank, a submarine officer, appeared in the open door and knocked on the doorframe. "Admiral Komeyev wants an update on the American search for their submarine." Lavrov started to rise, but the captain waved him down. "It doesn't have to be in person. He just wants . . ."

"Regular updates. Thank you, Captain Drugov. We've got some new intercepts from the GRU and SVR, as well as some data from other sources. All the search activity is well to the northwest of the island—about seven hundred fifty nautical miles away. The Prima station does not appear in any of the news reports or intercepts."

Drugov was the admiral's deputy and chief of staff. "So no news continues to be good news."

"The best news will be when the acoustic surveillance system is finally installed," Lavrov grumbled.

"The cable laying ship *Inguri* started installing the Sever modules the minute she arrived. Many sections are already operational," Drugov announced hopefully. "But the American news organizations are all crowing about this huge secret they've revealed."

Lavrov shrugged. "When the Western news media use the words 'near Russian territory,' they could possibly mean anywhere in the Arctic Ocean. They peddle drama, not information. I remember they used to describe our ballistic missiles subs in the Atlantic as patrolling 'just off the east coast of America' when the subs were many hundreds of miles out to sea."

After pausing a moment, he asked, "Did the admiral say anything about my recommendation that we place additional submarine patrols in the area, at least until the sensor net is finished?"

Drugov shook his head. "It was a reasonable request, but he turned it down. High submarine activity would risk drawing attention to the island. Coordinating the patrols requires more communications, both to and from the submarine. This could be perceived as unusual; it's well away from our normal training and patrol areas."

"And in the meantime, we are completely blind," Lavrov complained.

"Comrade Captain, we have insufficient assets to maintain a continuous presence, there will be gaps. The next submarine patrol is scheduled for later this month."

"Well, then," concluded Lavrov, "let us hope the Americans do us a favor and remain ignorant for a few weeks more. The longer the Americans stay in the dark, the better."

5

CONFIRMATION

9 July 2021
1600 Eastern Daylight Time
Ronald Reagan National Airport
Arlington, Virginia

A lieutenant was waiting for Jerry at baggage claim, holding a small sign that read "DEVRON." The shoulder boards on his whites showed that he was Judge Advocate General's Corps, but he also had a surface warfare pin on his chest.

As Jerry approached, the lieutenant came to attention, but didn't salute, since he was indoors. "Commodore Mitchell, I'm Lieutenant Abbott. We have a car outside." He grabbed Jerry's bag and headed for the exit. "If it's okay with you, sir, we'll have the driver check you in at the Crystal City Marriott while you're being briefed at the Pentagon."

A little confused, Jerry asked, "I thought the brief wasn't until tomorrow morning." It seemed a little late in the day to have a meeting.

The lieutenant nodded. "That's true sir, but this is a separate, though related matter." Outside, a navy car was waiting, and a petty officer took Jerry's bag from the lieutenant. Once they were inside and moving, with the windows rolled up tight against the Washington summer heat, Abbott explained, "We need to brief you into a special access compartment. It was the reason for *Toledo*'s mission. It will save a lot of time tomorrow if we get this administrative requirement done now."

"'We.'" Jerry repeated. "Are you part of the investigation, then?"

"Yessir, I'm Captain Gold's aide. He's the senior investigating officer."

"What about Commander Weiss?" Jerry asked.

"*Jimmy Carter*'s commanding officer? He's expected here late tonight. He's also booked into the Marriott. Do you need to speak with him before tomorrow morning?"

"No, tomorrow morning will be fine." Lou would be tired, and they had an early start tomorrow. And the things Jerry wanted to ask him couldn't be talked about in a hotel room anyway.

"I'm also supposed to pass on a message that a Mrs. Jennings will call your cell about nine tonight, and hopes you're available to take it. The brief this afternoon will only take about half an hour, Commodore."

"Will there be somewhere I can change into my whites first?" Jerry had traveled in civilian clothes.

"No, sir. It's not necessary, and in fact the briefer would prefer you come in civvies."

It was only a ten-minute drive in late-afternoon traffic from the airport to the Pentagon. Jerry held his questions as they were passed through security, then followed his guide down two levels. He'd been stationed at the Pentagon for two years, but it was big enough that they were soon in a part of the building he'd never seen, not that it looked any different from the rest of the place.

Abbott punched a keypad next to an anonymous gray metal door. "This is where we will have the debrief tomorrow." Inside, a light-green-painted hall ran past doors on either side. Abbot led him through one of these to a conference room. A civilian and a lieutenant commander sat at one end.

The civilian, a forty-something man in a short-sleeved white shirt, was fiddling with a laptop computer while the officer watched, but both stood as Jerry came in. Abbot introduced them as LCDR Travis and Dr. James Perry, "who works for the government."

As the civilian offered his hand, he protested, "Why don't you just tell him I'm CIA, Danny?" but Perry was smiling. He had a dark, tightly trimmed beard, probably to compensate for a receding hairline. "He'd find out soon enough anyway. This whole thing is a CIA show. That's why *Toledo* was up there."

Abbott left, promising to make sure Jerry's driver had checked him into the hotel.

Travis offered Jerry a clipboard with several forms on it. "You know the drill, sir. We need to read you into a sensitive HUMINT compartment."

Sighing, Jerry took the clipboard and began carefully reading. Sensitive compartmented information was used for the crown jewels of the intelligence system, very special kinds of secrets. Most classified information was labeled "Confidential," "Secret," or "Top Secret." If you had a confidential clearance, that meant you could read anything marked "Confidential," but not the higher Secret or Top Secret. Military service members had at least a confidential clearance.

Jerry had a Top Secret SCI clearance, but that did not entitle him to know everything in all compartments. Until the powers that be decided that he needed to know about something to do his job, the very existence of a particular "compartment" was hidden.

According to the paperwork, Jerry was going to be briefed into something called "Tensor." As with all sensitive compartmented information, he could not reveal the existence of Tensor to anyone else, or discuss Tensor-related information with anyone not also briefed into the compartment. The penalty for breaking these rules was severe.

Jerry did indeed know the drill, and was already briefed into several compartments that were required for his job as a submarine squadron commander. Nobody had ever explained to him how he was supposed to forget all that stuff after he left DEVRON Five. He was sure he had room in his brain for one more stack of super secret stuff, and handed the signed forms back to Travis, who checked them over before nodding to Perry.

Perry's tone was friendly, but businesslike. "This is a highly secure area, Commodore, more than your typical SCIF. Please do not discuss anything about Tensor with anyone unless you're in an accredited space like this one." He pressed a key on the laptop, and a large flat-screen display on the wall lit the darkened room.

It showed a drawing of what appeared to be a torpedo, but Jerry noticed the man-size figure placed next to it seemed much too small. The thing was huge. Then he noticed the title: "Status-6."

"Commodore, this is where it starts: the Status-6 nuclear torpedo. Excuse me, nuclear-propelled, nuclear torpedo. You're familiar with it?"

"Yes," Jerry answered, nodding. "We have weekly briefings for the squadron on Russian developments. What we got was scary enough. A nuclear-powered torpedo that travels thousands of miles at a hundred knots and armed with a very large warhead. The last data I saw said we didn't know the exact warhead size. Fifty megatons?"

"It's called the RDS-252, and has a yield of between twenty and twenty-five megatons, give or take a few kilotons." Perry smiled grimly. "Not that the difference will matter to whatever coastal city it hits. By the way, that information is in the Tensor compartment, for the moment."

Jerry shrugged. "Everything I've read said that this is a second-strike strategic nuclear weapon. The thing's as noisy as a cement mixer. We'd hear it coming hours before it reached its target, not that we could stop it. It's just adding more radioactive sunshine to whatever's left after the U.S. and Russia trade missile strikes. The material I saw reasoned that the Russians built it as a backup to their missile force. A ballistic missile defense shield won't help us against this thing. Wait a minute, does this mean . . ."

Perry stopped him. "Your understanding of the Status-6 is still what the intelligence community believes. And Russian actions are mostly confirming that evaluation. The Project 09851 *Khabarovsk* left on her first patrol last year, loaded with six of these monsters, and the second hull is close to being launched. We're still trying to confirm that the Project 09852 *Belgorod* mothership is also fitted with six launch tubes. So far, there isn't a smoking gun but it's starting to look that way.

"But Commodore, please remember that the Status-6 is just the starting point. Given that the Russians have designed the purpose-built *Khabarovsk*-class to carry this weapon, and are building at least one more of the class, what would you think of them building a coastal launch site in the Arctic?"

Jerry was confused by the question. "Do you mean a shore installation for launching the Status-6?" His mind quickly ran through the implications. It would be cheaper—much cheaper—than a submarine. And a *Khabarovsk*, and probably *Belgorod*, could only carry six weapons; after that, it would have to go home. Of course, since the weapons would be launched as the second wave of World War III, there would be no home to go back to. A shore installation could potentially launch more weapons, as many as the Russians . . .

Shaking his head, he stopped. "No, I don't see how that would work," Jerry decided. "It doesn't make sense. Status-6 is a second-strike weapon. Any static installation, especially one capable of launching nukes, goes right to the top of our target list. And it would be difficult, not to mention expensive, to harden it like an ICBM silo. Why build an unstoppable weapon and launch it from someplace that can be taken out as soon as the shooting starts?"

"Exactly!" Perry agreed enthusiastically. He tapped a key on the laptop with a flourish. "But look at this."

The screen shifted to a polar projection map of the Earth. From a point over the North Pole, the Arctic Ocean was almost entirely surrounded by land, with Canada's northern coastline and Greenland on one side, and Russia and Siberia on the other. A small star marked the center of the Russian northern coast, and Perry zoomed the map in until Jerry could see it marked an island. Then, as it continued to expand, he recognized the place: Bolshevik Island.

Jerry saw buildings clustered near the northwest corner of the island. "The Russians call it Prima Polar Station or Prima Ice Base. Considering how remote it is, it gets a fair amount of traffic, including tourist expeditions and scientists researching climate change and Arctic Ocean biology."

Perry explained, "A little over a year ago, we received information that people associated with the Status-6 program were being sent on trips to the Russian Arctic. Engineers on the program were also being consulted about ways to adapt the weapon to a 'different launch scheme.'"

They've got someone on the inside, Jerry realized. The deduction must have shown on his face, because Perry nodded. "That's why this is compartmented. We must not do anything that has the slightest risk of compromising this source."

Perry hit a key and markings appeared at several points on the image. "We wanted to confirm the report, and actually didn't have to look hard to find out that indeed something is going on at the Prima station. First, about the same time we received our information, those tourist cruises I mentioned before were canceled for this year's season. No explanation. Since the Russians get some much-needed foreign cash from those excursions, it must have been a good reason.

"At the same time, they closed the scientific station to foreign nationals. This time there was an explanation—the station was going to be heavily renovated and expanded. So we started watching the Prima base and the area around it, and sure enough, they did start upgrading the place. They refurbished the 1960s-era airfield, which has a two-kilometer runway, big enough to handle medium-sized transports, and started flying in people, machinery, and supplies. Until that time, everything had been brought in by icebreakers."

Perry pointed to several marked areas on the screen. The airfield was still basic, with a single runway and one hangar, but there were several radars, electronic vans, and a makeshift control tower. "Notice there are no air defenses, but the Russians have installed a full set of front-line radars and instrument landing aids." He pointed to several areas enclosed by white rectangles.

"They did expand the base itself, with several new buildings, and here"—he pointed to a spot a little distance away—"they are building something else, but we can't tell what. Whatever it is, it will be underground when they're finished."

Perry changed the screen again, and a close-up of the second site appeared. "This was taken last October. The weather was already pretty bad, but they worked until it was too cold for the machinery to function." The image flickered, and was replaced by a new one, but taken from a slightly different angle. The patches of snow had shifted, and the construction site looked further along.

"Look here, where there is a trench leading to the coast." Perry flashed back and forth between the two shots. "By March, when it's still colder than polar bear poop up there, they had not only restarted work, but had begun work on a cable landing station and installing cable anchors right up to the water's edge."

Perry turned off the flat-screen display. "That last image was the trigger for *Toledo*'s mission. The Russians must be building something underwater. Even if this activity wasn't connected to the Status-6, we'd be curious. Knowing that it's linked somehow to a monster unstoppable torpedo with a giant nuclear warhead makes it absolutely vital that we find out."

"Hence *Toledo*'s mission," Jerry concluded.

"Approved by the 'Big Skipper' himself." Perry used President Hardy's nickname within the Pentagon. "For what it's worth, I'm very sorry about what happened to her. I've read *Carter*'s reports, same as you." He sighed sadly. "In fact, it was my idea to use a sub, and I'll take responsibility for that. I believe our decision to send someone to take a look was sound, but that doesn't change the fact that we've lost over a hundred men. We've learned little, and have more questions than before. Anyway, that's Tensor. You have been briefed," Perry announced, and he closed the laptop. "Do you have any questions?"

Jerry did not, at least not right now, although he was sure there would be ones he could ask later. Perry and Travis assured Jerry they'd both be at Weiss's debrief tomorrow, and Abbott returned to escort the commodore to his ride.

At the hotel, in his room, Jerry ordered room service for dinner. He needed to sort out what he'd learned, and see where it fit in with Lou Weiss's two reports. He wanted peace, and for the moment, solitude.

His cell phone rang, and Jerry checked the time. It was 8:55; "Mrs. Jennings" was a little early, not that he minded. He answered, "Mitchell here."

"This is Melinda. Can you hold for Mrs. Jennings?"

Melinda Brady was Joanna Patterson's personal secretary. "Hello, Melinda. Of course."

There was only a short pause. "Jerry!" Joanna Patterson's voice was full of emotion. "I know why you're here in town. I'm so sorry." The phone line was completely unsecure, so she had to be careful what she said, but they both knew what she meant.

Jerry sighed without even meaning to. "At least we're moving forward," he said.

"Yes. I'm aware," she replied. "I'm hoping that both David and I will be able to come for the service. And we'll see you there, of course."

"David" was President Hardy's middle name, and much more common than "Lowell." It was a given that there would be a public memorial service for the crew, once the loss was announced, and Jerry thought it was not inappropriate for an ex-submariner president and first lady to attend. And Lenny Berg's ties to his old skipper were well known. In fact, questions would be raised if President Hardy weren't there.

"I'll bring Emily, and Carly, along." The public service would undoubtedly be held in Groton, *Toledo*'s homeport, but that couldn't be said right now.

"You'd better! Emily posted pictures of her in that ballerina outfit."

Jerry laughed in spite of his somber mood. "She wore it to bed that night, and most of the next day, but Emily finally got it off Charlotte for her bath."

They chatted about small matters for almost ten minutes, catching up and just enjoying being able to talk. Since becoming first lady, Joanna had been isolated by circumstance from her large circle of friends. He knew she had other things demanding her attention, but she seemed reluctant to end the conversation. Jerry was glad to talk to her, and waited patiently for Joanna to bring up whatever was her reason for calling.

"Jerry, I want to sit in on your meeting tomorrow."

He quickly suppressed his initial response—"What?"—and after a very short pause, substituted the more measured, "Is that a good idea?" He knew she was referring to the *Jimmy Carter*'s mission debrief. Jerry wasn't surprised that she knew about it. And come to think of it, classification wasn't really an issue, either. Joanna had been President Myles's national security advisor. When her husband Lowell had been elected, she'd had to resign, but she remained well connected. She'd hand-picked her successor, Bill Hyland, of course.

But she had difficulties with the transition. Emily and Jerry had spent more than one evening talking about what it must have been like to go from being one of the most powerful people in the U.S. government to someone who was supposed to host social events and encourage children's environmental programs. And to be completely on the outside of whatever was going on in the world.

"What does David think of the idea?" he asked carefully.

"He's against it, of course. And I can see his point," she admitted. "But this is very important to me, as well."

"Why?" Jerry asked, trying to stall, as well as understand. He didn't fly cross-country to get caught in a disagreement between the president and the first lady.

"I *need* to be there," she insisted.

"Mrs. Jennings, I'm trying to understand why," Jerry repeated.

"Because it was my responsibility," she replied sadly. "In my old job, I remember signing off on the . . . tasking. I didn't pick who did the work, but I was the one who endorsed the job."

Jerry made the connection. As national security advisor, Joanna had recommended approving a CIA request to send a sub north to investigate Bolshevik Island. No wonder she was so distressed.

Jerry could relate, but he wasn't moved. "This afternoon, I met the person who thought of the task. He feels pretty bad, too. And I'll bet the person who actually made the decision to execute probably feels really bad, as well. But I don't hold them, or you, responsible for what happened."

"That's what David said as well, but . . ."

Jerry understood how hard it was for her to let go of something she was so intimately involved with. "I don't think we'll arrive at any final answers tomorrow," Jerry offered. "We'll probably end up just asking new questions. And you are completely off the wiring diagram now. Even if they broke the rules and let you sit in, you couldn't ask any questions yourself."

She didn't answer right away. Jerry asked, "Won't you be there when they fill David in on what happened?"

"Of course," she admitted.

"Then you can ask the briefer all the questions you want," he pointed out.

"As long as David's sitting next to me!" Joanna fumed. "But I guess that's all I'm allowed."

"I think your new job is harder than your old one," sympathized Jerry.

"I should go," she said finally. "Give my love to Emily and Charlotte."

"And please tell David we're all behind you both."

She broke the connection, and Jerry relaxed.

10 July 2021
0930 Eastern Daylight Time
The Pentagon
Arlington, Virginia

Jerry took the Metro to the Pentagon, one more navy captain in a sea of uniforms passing through security and navigating the miles of painted concrete corridors. He found the office where he'd been briefed yesterday afternoon without a problem, but had wondered about the keypad. He assumed that there was an intercom, or at least a doorbell of some sort. But the gray metal door was propped open, with two armed sailors guarding the door and checking in all arrivals. Captain Mitchell's name was indeed on the list, and after carefully examining his ID, they let him pass.

The hall that was so empty yesterday was now filled with people in uniform, mostly navy, with a sprinkling of business suits. The conference room where he'd been read into the Tensor compartment seemed far too small for this many people, but the other doors appeared to lead to offices, so Jerry followed the crowd.

The conference room was nearly filled with people, and was clearly not the venue for the mission debrief, but in true navy tradition, had been furnished with two coffeemakers and numerous boxes of donuts, which showed signs of attrition.

A table at one end of the room had a large model of an Improved *Los Angeles*–class sub, while framed pictures in front of the model showed the crew of *Toledo* at different sporting events and group photos. It was a nice touch, Jerry thought, but it did make the briefing seem a little more like a wake.

He scanned the crowd. Dr. Perry was speaking with a two-star admiral while Abbott hovered nearby. Searching each knot of conversation in turn, he finally spotted Commander Louis Weiss, CO of *Jimmy Carter*, with SUBRON Twelve's commander, Captain Dorr. Weiss was almost as short as Jerry, thus hard to find in a crowd.

Fortunately, they were standing next to one of the coffeemakers, which saved time. Both saw Jerry's approach and by the time he'd reached them, Weiss was offering his commodore a just-filled cup.

Jerry shook hands with both, then gratefully sipped while he congratulated *Jimmy Carter*'s skipper. "Lou, you did a five-oh job up there. You're out here, so I'm guessing you're all prepped and ready to go."

Weiss nodded, but for someone who could maneuver a nuclear submarine close to the Russian border, he looked a little nervous. "Most of the submarine chain of command is going to be in there. Putting together the brief was easy, but I keep on worrying that my dolphins are on upside down."

Dorr reassured him. "I've checked twice, Lou. You're fine. And I don't blame you," the commodore observed. "The whole Navy wants to know what happened to *Toledo*."

"They aren't going to like the answer," Weiss replied grimly.

"I think it's more accurate to say they aren't going to like what the answer implies," Jerry added.

LCDR Travis appeared next to the three. "Gentlemen, the CNO's party is on their way down." That was the signal to find a chair, and Travis added, "Right and down the hall." He told Jerry, "You're in the second row."

A much larger conference room, almost an auditorium, looked tailor-made for debriefs. As Jerry entered, he could see that seats were being filled quickly. Neatly lettered index cards marked each chair, and Jerry found himself sitting between Commodore Dorr on one side and a civilian he didn't recognize, who turned out to be one of the deputy undersecretaries of the navy.

Weiss was at the podium, while Perry helped make last-minute equipment checks. The incoming stream thinned, but increased in rank. Jerry recognized two other east coast squadron commanders, who must have also flown in, then SUBFOR, a three-star who was responsible for every submarine in the U.S. Navy.

Travis called "Attention on deck!" as Secretary of Defense Richfield came in with the National Security Advisor, Bill Hyland, closely followed by the Secretary of the Navy, Clifford Gravani, and the Chief of Naval Operations, Admiral Bernard Hughes. The quartet was followed by a gaggle of aides and assistants. The instant all four were seated, the lights dimmed and Commander Weiss began speaking.

After introducing himself, Weiss quickly reviewed receiving his new orders and *Jimmy Carter*'s voyage to the designated search area. The trip had been routine, and without incident, but procedure demanded at least a summary. He then described the two unmanned underwater vehicles the submarine carried, their capabilities and limitations.

He spent more time on the search plan, especially since it had taken his UUVs within spitting distance of Russian territorial waters. There had been a contingency plan that actually extended the UUVs' sensors across the border, but this had required the remotes to maneuver right up to the edge of Russian waters, within what Weiss had described as the "control margin." Luckily, that was unnecessary.

The slide they'd all waited for appeared next.

It was impossible to get all of *Toledo* into a single photograph, but someone in the crew with very good graphics skills had created a mosaic of the UUVs' close-in shots. The viewpoint was almost directly overhead, but showed the boat on her starboard side, the sail half-buried in the mud. She lay on a slight slope, with the bow down and the screw, stern planes, and rudder well clear of the bottom.

A wave of sadness passed through Jerry, and he heard softly spoken comments from those around him. The most common was "Rest in peace." The image made it all too real. Then he took a mental breath and pushed his feelings to one side. He had to focus on the how and why, rather than who.

Carter's captain gave the audience a moment to take it in, then added a symbol marking the location of the torpedo hit. A *Los Angeles*–class submarine was 360 feet long and 33 feet in diameter, and the opening marked by the small red circle didn't look all that lethal. Of course, neither did a bullet hole in a corpse.

Weiss was explaining what they believed was the sequence of events. "We believe the hit flooded the forward compartment very quickly, but it appears the forward reactor compartment bulkhead was weakened by the blast and eventually gave way as well, so over half of the submarine's interior was flooded within minutes.

"She impacted the bottom very hard. Note the crushed sonar dome, and the impression along the seabed suggests the hull bounced two, possibly three times before coming to a stop. The propeller shaft was badly bent, which means the engine room probably also flooded, albeit the rate of flooding would have been slower. No one on board could have survived for any significant length of time, and she was too deep to attempt an escape. I had the UUVs listen carefully along the engine room, just in case; there were no indications of survivors."

Weiss's words were chilling and comforting at the same time. This was every submariner's nightmare, and the only mercy could be that it was over quickly. *Toledo* was far too deep to ever be raised, but they were no longer lost. The navy would be able to tell the crew's loved ones where they lay.

The next image zoomed out from the sub, including more of the surrounding seabed. A new circle appeared, some distance away from the hull. "We evaluate this debris as the rear section of an MPT-1 Kolibri torpedo, based on measurements of its diameter—324 millimeters." A close-up showed a crumpled cylinder with a tapered end and two propellers. "This torpedo is a copy of an early U.S. Mark 46 and is currently only used in the PMK-2 moored, propelled warhead mine and the 91R and 92R ASW missiles."

Another debris symbol appeared, closer to the hull. In the detail photo, it turned out to be a cylindrical object, even smaller than the torpedo remains. One end was damaged. Jerry recognized it instantly as a

SATCOM buoy. It was designed to be launched from a submarine's signal ejector, float to the surface, and transmit an encrypted message via satellite. It allowed submarines, who did their level best to stay hidden, to transmit messages without revealing their location. The satellite would relay the recorded message to nearby ships or planes, or back to shore, as needed. It even had a timer so the sub could be well away from the place before the buoy started sending. After transmitting, it would sink to the bottom.

From the damage, it appeared that *Toledo*'s buoy had never reached the surface, instead striking the underside of an ice floe. Even in June, the ice cap never disappeared completely at that latitude, instead turning into a mush of broken ice. Pieces ranged in size from a breadbox to a small town, and constantly crashed into each other, creating smaller pieces and enough noise to seriously interfere with sonar detection.

"Our UUV Walter successfully recovered the buoy, and our techs were able to download the information from the magnetic media."

Jackpot! Jerry felt excitement displace the sadness. That fact had not been in the earlier reports. In fact, Weiss's message hadn't even mentioned the buoy. It had probably taken *Carter*'s information techs several days of careful work to download the buoy's information.

A nautical chart of the Atlantic and Arctic Oceans appeared on the screen. "This shows *Toledo*'s track from Groton into the Arctic Ocean." The scene shifted to a close up of the northern part. "Here's her last twenty-four hours of movement." *Toledo*'s course arrowed directly toward Bolshevik Island and the Prima Polar Station. Initially, she closed to within twenty miles off the Russian border. *Toledo* then settled into a back-and-forth racetrack, paralleling the border. Each leg brought the sub slightly closer to the twelve-mile line that marked Russia's territorial waters.

The final leg almost merged with the Russian border. "It was shortly after turning onto a southbound leg, at one four zero degrees, that *Toledo* triggered the PMK-2 mine. At that time, the boat was inside a thousand yards of the border, and even at creep speed, and with the high background noise from the ice, was within the detection range of the mine's passive sonar."

Weiss answered one question before it was asked. "We saw nothing in *Toledo*'s logs about her using her own mine avoidance sonar." Mounted in the sail, the high-frequency active sonar was useless for general search, but could see small objects, like floating mines or underwater obstacles, at very short ranges. Nodding toward Admiral Gold, he said, "The investigating board will have to make the final determination, but Captain Berg had no reason to expect a mine or any type of barrier at the very edge of Russian territorial waters. Using active sonar, even the high-frequency set, would have increased the risk of detection, which he was trying very hard to avoid.

"Our analysis of *Toledo*'s sonar logs was limited by time, and the equipment aboard *Carter*, which while quite good, is not as extensive as that available ashore."

The commander pressed a key and a series of yellow lines appeared, all starting from some point on *Toledo*'s track and pointing toward to a single area, marked with a bright yellow circle. "After starting her back-and-forth approach, she would periodically go shallow enough to use her electronic surveillance mast. The logs note several aborted attempts because of the ice, but she detected several surface search, navigation radars that all seemed to be concentrated off the northwest coast of the island.

"As she got closer, her sonar started making passive detections at just under eighteen nautical miles from the coast. The noises were mostly transients, but definitely man-made. As she closed, they became steadier, more mechanical, but still showed no pattern. It wasn't until she'd approached within a few thousand yards of the CTML that they could be classified at all. To *Carter*'s very experienced and skilled sonarmen, they sound like metal clanging on metal, random but definite. They heard other more regular sounds. The frequencies they produced are consistent with electric motors and pumps. There were also occasional bursts of more common diesel propulsion, typical of diesel ships."

Weiss paused dramatically, and smiled. "In one case, we were able to correlate the engine noises to a specific vessel, a new Project 22220 *Arktika*-class icebreaker." He tapped the keyboard again and a photograph of the ship appeared, taken through a periscope.

Jerry could only smile, although it still hurt. Lenny had gotten close enough to use the periscope! He heard a murmur, and someone actually clapped. The vessel had a black hull with a high bow, typical of an icebreaker, and a bright red superstructure. A large crane mounted amidships was lowering an equally large cylinder into the water. Another barge tied alongside held similar cylinders.

"There were six images in the buoy's memory. This is the clearest of them. Two were taken at an earlier time, and then four in this sequence show this vessel supporting some sort of underwater construction."

And getting in close to take those photos is probably what triggered the mine. Jerry tried to guess at the cylinder's size and purpose. Fuel tanks? Pipes? Or launch tubes? They could confirm it with measurements from the photos, but he was willing to bet his dress uniform that a Status-6 torpedo could be fitted inside.

Weiss finished his brief with a burst of organizational and procedural information, and while the audience did not clap, Jerry could hear a murmur of approval as the chief of naval operations rose, shook CDR Weiss's hand, and took his place at the podium.

"Captain, well done! Thanks to your efforts, *Toledo*'s mission was not in vain. You brought home vital information that the crew of *Toledo* gave their lives to collect. Information that we now have to put to good use." Admiral Hughes had started out smiling broadly, but his expression became grimmer as he spoke. "However, as with most important tasks, processing the data is just the first step."

Nodding toward the national security advisor, Hughes ordered, "Our most urgent priority will be to make recommendations to NSA Hyland about Russia's responsibility for the loss of *Toledo*. We need to determine if this minefield is inside Russian territorial waters, or outside, in international waters. If it's the latter, then this is a violation of international law, of course. But is it a new policy? Are there other such minefields we should be concerned about near Russian military facilities?

"Our response to the Russians ties in with my responsibility to inform the families of *Toledo*'s crew. We are obligated to give them as much information as possible, consistent with security needs. Reconciling those two requirements will not be simple.

"And thirdly, we have to continue to investigate Russian activities at the Prima Ice Base. I won't be able to relax until we have a much clearer idea of what they're up to."

Jerry thought, *Which means we won't get to relax, either.*

6

GROWING CONCERNS

10 July 2021
2000 Local Time
The Admiralty Building
St. Petersburg, Russia

Captain Lavrov was not a happy man when his mobile phone buzzed. He had barely managed to slip away from his office when he received the urgent call to hurry back. Despite the inconvenience, the call was justified. It took him only a few minutes to review the latest satellite imagery, and with renewed energy he got back to work. An hour later, Lavrov phoned Captain First Rank Drugov.

"I certainly hope this is important, Captain Lavrov." Drugov's voice was sharp as he threw his cover on the couch, clearly displeased with being called in on a Saturday evening.

Lavrov's smile had a touch of irony to it. "I understand how you feel, Pavel Antonovich, I didn't even make it to Nevsky Prospect before my mobile phone rang." Then laying down a large photograph on the desk, he continued, "However, in this case the unfortunate inconvenience was entirely warranted."

Drugov picked up the photo and stared at it for a moment. "This is an American submarine base, Vasiliy, did the missing submarine magically reappear?"

"You're not entirely off, Pavel. A submarine did in fact recently appear, but it wasn't *Toledo*, rather it was the *Jimmy Carter*."

"And why should I be concerned with this particular submarine?" Drugov's face showed his irritation.

Lavrov sighed. *How typical*, he thought. "The *Carter* should concern you greatly, Pavel, for you see she is the U.S. Navy's premier spy submarine. Roughly akin to our Main Directorate of Deep-Sea Research submarines, only well armed, considerably faster, and far stealthier. Oh, and she is normally home ported in Washington State . . . on the Pacific coast."

The rapid change in Drugov's expression told Lavrov that he had the chief of staff's complete attention. "*Carter* showed up in Groton within the last twenty-four hours. According to GRU reporting, she's been at sea for the past three months; they estimated she was operating in the western Pacific Ocean, or possibly in the Barents Sea. But we really have no idea of where she has been; we would be hard-pressed to get a sniff of her, let alone track her. For this submarine to show up at an east coast base right now is very troubling, Pavel, very troubling."

"If the *Jimmy Carter* is a reconnaissance submarine, then it would make complete sense for the Americans to bring her to the other side of the continent to help search for their missing boat," Drugov concluded as he sat down. "Don't you think you're making up your own ghosts, Vasiliy?"

"Perhaps," considered Lavrov. "But it all feels so wrong. The Americans haven't lost a submarine due to a peacetime accident in over fifty years, why now? Right when we are at the most vulnerable stage of the Drakon's lair construction project. Discovery right now would be catastrophic. Then add to this the sudden appearance of a very capable spy submarine that has the equipment necessary to not only detect, but also identify the deep-water launch facility. Furthermore, if the *Carter* had been sent to help in the search, why did she pass by the very location on her way to the Groton submarine base?

"Is this all just a highly improbable set of coincidences? My intuition is screaming it can't be. So, no, Comrade Captain, I don't think I'm creating my own ghosts. I believe the *Jimmy Carter*'s arrival at Groton is an ill omen."

Drugov looked closely at his intelligence chief, there was no doubt the man was sincere in his beliefs. And he was correct; of course, Project Dragon was at an awkward phase in its development. Would it hurt to be just a little cautious? "What do you want from me, Vasiliy?" he asked.

"I request permission to brief Admiral Komeyev on these developments. Tonight if at all possible."

The chief of staff got up and started walking, thinking. The Russian Navy commander-in-chief had little patience for exaggerated threat assessments; he wanted accurate estimates of an adversary's capabilities and intents. Not some hyperbolic propaganda ploy for the masses, or a pitch to justify more funding. But Lavrov had a well-earned reputation as a levelheaded strategist. It didn't take long for Drugov to reach a decision.

"Very well, Vasiliy. I'll call the CINC *and* his deputy. You have thirty minutes to prepare your presentation."

An enlisted mess steward brought in a carafe of hot tea and some shortbread biscuits; he served the two admirals first and then the captains. Admiral Vladimir Komeyev took a seat on his couch; his deputy, Vice Admiral Viktor Balakin, sat next to his boss. Komeyev seemed to be in good spirits despite being dragged back into the office late on a weekend, Balakin not so much. His demeanor was one of annoyance.

"So, Vasiliy, what disaster threatens Mother Russia so badly that I had to drop everything and come running back to the office?" Lavrov heard both the light-hearted tone as well as the message behind it— "This had better be good."

"My apologies, Admiral, but I'm confident this won't be a waste of your time or Admiral Balakin's," began Lavrov. "It is my belief that there is a considerable risk the Project Drakon facility could be discovered by an American spy submarine."

Komeyev stopped drinking mid-slurp, his eyes focused on Lavrov. Balakin gasped and then coughed from the tea going down the wrong pipe. Putting his teacup down slowly, Komeyev said, "Please continue, Vasiliy."

Lavrov advanced the electronic presentation to the next slide; the satellite imagery shot that had started the whole thing jumped up onto the screen. "This photograph is of the U.S. submarine base in Groton, Connecticut. Please take note of this boat, here." The laser dot danced along the length of a large black hull alongside one of the many piers.

"It is the *Seawolf*-class submarine *Jimmy Carter*, America's premier intelligence gathering submarine. It appeared, unexpectedly, sometime late on July ninth at this facility—the imagery was taken during the mid-afternoon local time today. The last time we saw this submarine was on April eighth at Naval Base Kitsap-Bangor, in Washington State. We have no definitive information on her whereabouts between these two dates, although the GRU assesses she was operating in the western Pacific or perhaps the Barents Sea."

"Surely this submarine has been called in to help search for the *Toledo*," interrupted Balakin.

Lavrov smiled slightly; Vice Admiral Balakin could be quite predictable at times. "Yes, sir, that is the current working hypothesis, however, if one looks at the geography of the situation it makes little sense for the *Carter* to be at this base, at this time, given the officially announced search area."

"Go on," Komeyev insisted, his interest piqued.

The captain pulled up a large-scale chart that showed the location of the announced search area, as well as the Groton submarine base and the Prima Polar Station.

"We know that the *Jimmy Carter* was on the west coast of the United States in early April. Regardless of her mission and location, she would have taken the Arctic route to the other side of the country." Using the laser pointer, Lavrov highlighted the shortest possible route that *Carter* could have taken.

"If the *Carter* was sent to assist in the search for the *Toledo*, then why did she pass within a few hundred nautical miles of the announced search area and continue on sailing for an additional *three thousand five hundred* nautical miles to Groton? This is what makes little sense, and calls into question the validity of the hypothesis."

"Perhaps this spy submarine required additional specialized equipment to effectively conduct the search. Wouldn't that explain the long detour?" suggested Balakin.

"I'm afraid not, sir. The GRU's assessment of the *Carter*'s location allows ample opportunities for her to pull into an Alaskan port to pick up any necessary equipment and supplies. And even if she were actually already operating in the Arctic Ocean, the *Carter* could have easily pulled into Svalbard, Norwegian territory, which is far closer to the search area. The port of Longyearbyen has a three-kilometer airfield that could support any American transport aircraft, and there is nothing that the *Carter* could deploy that can't be moved by air."

"Are you implying the Americans have intentionally lied about the search area?" grumbled Balakin; he disliked being made to look like a fool.

"I'm saying that I'm very suspicious, Admiral Balakin," replied Lavrov tersely. Moving on to the next slide, he pointed to the announced search area. "The area where the Americans claim the *Toledo* was probably lost straddles one of the entrances to the Barents Sea. Their submarines have often used it in the past. Thus, this location wouldn't seem strange to us at all."

"A diversion?" suggested Komeyev.

"A distinct possibility, sir. The Americans are very capable of a coordinated disinformation campaign to try and pull our attention away from another location, another target."

"But the Prima Ice Station is . . ." began Komeyev.

"Some seven hundred fifty nautical miles to the southeast, yes, sir. But can you think of a more worthy target?"

"Captain Lavrov," Balakin snarled, "all I'm hearing is conjecture. Do you have any concrete evidence to support this theory of yours?"

Sighing, the captain replied, "I do not have what the Americans would call a 'smoking gun,' Admiral. However, let me put all the facts before you. First, the U.S. Navy last lost a submarine to a peacetime casualty fifty-three years ago. Their safety record is exemplary. Second, a well-equipped spy submarine that is normally part of the Pacific fleet mysteriously shows up at an Atlantic fleet base. Third, said submarine traveled thousands of miles farther to reach this base than would be required to reach the search area.

"Fourth, the area where the Americans claim *Toledo* was lost is a known approach to our waters, just on the edge of the Arctic Ocean. Fifth, if the *Jimmy Carter* is deployed to the search area, it is less than two days travel at moderate speeds to the Prima Polar Station. Furthermore, this route can take advantage of the unfriendly environment that will negate the use of surface and airborne antisubmarine forces. And finally, the absolute best reconnaissance asset to employ against the Prima station is a submarine because of the station's high latitude and typically overcast skies. If these factors are entered into our standard risk assessment algorithm, even with conservative values, then there is sixty-five percent probability that the Drakon launch facility will be discovered and identified for what it is."

Lavrov fell silent and awaited the judgment of his superiors. Balakin had an unconvinced smirk on his face, but Komeyev was more sober, clearly weighing the implications.

"You paint an ugly picture, Vasiliy," remarked the Russian Navy CINC. "And I appreciate your candor concerning what you know, and what you don't know. But I have some questions for you."

"Of course, sir."

"Do you believe that USS *Toledo* was indeed lost? Could all this noise be just part of the deception?"

"We have numerous and varied sources all telling us that a U.S. submarine by the name of *Toledo* is overdue and presumed lost."

Komeyev nodded, then pressed on. "And yet, you acknowledge the Americans have a stellar safety history during peacetime, how do you reconcile these two facts?"

"There is always a slight probability for a fatal accident, sir."

"How slight?"

"If one only looks at just historical occurrences over time, there is a five percent probability. However, this is likely on the high side. Without looking at the submarine's operational and maintenance history, it is impossible to give a precise answer, but I suspect the probability is less than three percent."

"And are you comfortable with that value, Captain?" Komeyev leaned forward, his voice harder.

Lavrov swallowed hard, before answering. "No, sir, I am not. I have difficulty accepting the sinking of USS *Toledo* as just an unfortunate circumstance independent of our activities in the Arctic Ocean. Simply put, I do not believe this is an amazing collection of highly improbable, independent events—the odds are enormously against it. They must be related!

"That is why I have been considering other scenarios that assume a relationship between the events. Scenarios that require a different explanation for the loss of the U.S. submarine."

"Such as?"

Lavrov paused, and then licked his lips. "This is pure conjecture, Admiral Komeyev, I have nothing to substantiate this theory."

"So noted, Captain, continue."

"Yes, sir," replied Lavrov. His uneasiness growing, he swallowed again before he spoke. "The theory I've been contemplating is the possibility that USS *Toledo* was engaged and sunk."

"Engaged? Sunk?" shouted Balakin. "By whom? We haven't had any contact reports on a foreign submarine sighting in weeks, let alone a report of an actual attack!"

"That is correct, Admiral Balakin. However, a minefield does not normally report back that it has conducted an attack."

Komeyev rose quickly from the couch, his face tense. "That's an alarming theory, Captain. Do you realize what you're saying?"

"As I said, Admiral, this theory is pure conjecture using what facts we have at the moment and the assumption of a worst-case outcome to our current military strategy."

"If we accept the 'worst case,' then it's entirely possible the Americans already *know* about Project Drakon!" replied Komeyev brusquely.

"Not necessarily, sir," Lavrov countered firmly. "We know the Americans are suspicious about something going on up north—it had to pique their interest when we closed the station to tourists and visiting scientists. The location is, at most, three days away from their routine Barents Sea deployment areas, so a submarine could have been sent up to the Prima base just to have a look around. If *Toledo* did investigate, and was engaged by our minefield and sunk, then whatever information they gathered likely died with them. In contrast to our practice, the U.S. Navy strongly discourages its submarines from communicating while on station . . . especially while off a hostile coast. Furthermore, the ice cover would be too dense, even if were broken, to use a communications buoy. The ice floes have been a major nuisance to our construction crews for the last couple of weeks."

Komeyev's expression eased as Lavrov explained. Still, the Russian Navy CINC wasn't thrilled. "The minefield was positioned inside our territorial waters. It was a purely defensive measure to protect the construction site. If the *Toledo* violated our borders, then she got only what she deserved."

"What about the *Carter*? Isn't it possible that she could have already been to the Prima area?" interrupted Balakin, his voice anxious.

"I seriously doubt it, Admiral. If the American spy submarine were where the GRU thought she was, it would take about a week just to get to the station at a high average cruising speed. Anything faster has too great a detection risk, they are well aware of the location of our Arctic hydroacoustic arrays. Even if the *Carter* were closer than estimated, she'd still need about four days. When you add in the ten to eleven days to make the journey to Groton, this leaves only two, perhaps three days at most to conduct a search. While the Americans are good, they are not that good."

"But that assumes you accept the Americans' timeline, when they claim they started searching, doesn't it?" Komeyev inquired.

"Yes, sir, it does. However, message traffic analysis and communications intercepts strongly suggest that the earliest the order went out was late on twenty-one June. This is consistent with the U.S. Navy's announcement, albeit a little misleading, as the first units didn't sortie until early on the twenty-second.

"But even if we take a more generous view and spot the Americans a couple of days more, it is still highly unlikely they would find the downed submarine in less than a week. I've been working with our own rescue service; they estimate at least two weeks would be necessary to find the sunken boat. The Americans simply don't have enough time to do all that has to be done and pull into the Groton submarine base yesterday."

Komeyev nodded his agreement. "When the *Gepard* was lost in May 2005, the wrecked hull was found twelve days after she was declared missing. But wasn't the search area also much larger in that case?"

"Quite so, Admiral. But also recall there were three oceanographic research ships with towed side-scan sonars involved in looking for *Gepard*. Their combined search rate would be two orders of magnitude higher than a single submarine attempting to remain covert."

The Russian Navy CINC began pacing, mulling over what he had heard. He shook his head as he walked. If Lavrov's analysis was correct, and the Americans were to learn of the deep-sea launch facility, it would unhinge President Fedorin's plan to recapture the former Soviet Union's lost territory. It could also move the Russian Federation and the United States closer to a full-blown nuclear exchange.

Lavrov watched as Komeyev paced. Seeing that the questioning had ceased, the captain wrapped up his presentation.

"The appearance of the *Jimmy Carter* is an alarming development, sir. She may, in fact, be sent out to search for *Toledo*, but it's unlikely *Carter* will be looking in the same place as the surface units we currently see running around off Franz Josef Land. If my theory is correct, *Carter* will go much further afield to search for their missing submarine.

"My greatest concern is that while they're looking for the *Toledo*, they will hear, and see, the Project Drakon construction effort, which is barely five nautical miles inside our territorial waters."

The room suddenly went quiet as Komeyev continued pacing; the three other officers looked on. Lavrov caught Drugov nodding his approval; the intelligence chief felt his stomach loosen up a bit. After half a minute of awkward silence, Komeyev stopped pacing, looked at Lavrov, and chuckled. "You think very darkly, Vasiliy Vasil'evich, but I find myself agreeing with your premise. What do you recommend?"

Relieved, Lavrov began running down his prepared list. "First, sir, we need to increase our intelligence collection on the *Jimmy Carter*. We have a limited inventory of imagery satellites, so we'll need to get an operative to the Groton submarine base to keep an eye on that boat. Second, we need to have the deep-sea research submarines *Belgorod* and *Losharik* search for *Toledo*. Those submarines are scheduled to assist with the loading of the Drakon launch tubes, but if we can get them up to the Prima Polar Station sooner, that would be ideal. Finally, we need to have a nuclear-powered attack submarine patrolling the area. Should the *Jimmy Carter* head north as I suspect, we need to keep her away from the launch facility."

"Reasonable," commented Komeyev. "What do you think, Admiral Balakin?"

"Captain Lavrov's recommendations are sound," replied the deputy. "The first is a matter of formality, one that the good captain can handle himself. However, the second will be much harder to implement. *Losharik* is currently in dry dock undergoing scheduled repairs. She's not due out for at least another ten days, and then she still has sea trials. I will see if the repairs can be accelerated, but I wouldn't count on it. Several key maintenance items involve her reactor and main propulsion motor. As for the third recommendation, we can have *Vepr* sortie immediately."

"With all due respect, Admiral Balakin," Lavrov interrupted. "Even though *Vepr* is an upgraded Project 971 submarine, she is still a third-generation boat. She is not the technical equal of a *Seawolf*-class."

Komeyev grunted his understanding. "Hmmm, so you're advising that we should send a fourth-generation submarine, a Project 885M boat?"

"Yes, sir, a modernized *Severodvinsk* submarine has the most advanced antisubmarine sensors in our fleet. It has the best chance of detecting an extremely quiet American submarine like the *Jimmy Carter*. Anything less increases the possibility of this spy submarine slipping past our outer defenses."

"What about *Belgorod*?" Balakin questioned.

"She is no match for a *Seawolf*, Admiral Balakin. Since in addition to being a mother ship for *Losharik*, she also carries her own load of Status-6 torpedoes, she is a priceless strategic asset. I do not believe she should be placed in a situation where there is the slightest risk of her loss. It would be best if *Belgorod* stayed inside the defensive perimeter as soon as we know the *Jimmy Carter* has departed the Groton submarine base. This will also reduce the possibility of a friendly fire situation."

"We could send two attack boats, split the area into two separate patrol zones," Drugov suggested, using his hands to illustrate the equally divided patrol areas.

Lavrov shook his head in disagreement. "The approaches to the

Drakon launch facility necks down considerably as you enter Shokal'skogo Strait. There is barely fifty kilometers between October Revolution and Bolshevik Islands, and the navigable waters are even narrower—that's far too small an area for two submarines to share. The potential for an unintended attack on a friendly unit is much too high.

"An alternative approach would be to use concentric rings for the search areas and put *Vepr* in the outer ring, but then again, if the *Carter* wanted to avoid her, the odds are in their favor they could do so."

Stillness filled the room again as the debate died off. Komeyev looked satisfied with the discussion and weighed his options in silence; it didn't take him long to decide.

"Admiral Balakin, please prepare the deployment orders for *Vepr* and *Kazan*. Have the staff generate two concentric patrol areas with *Vepr* in the outer ring. Schedule a formal review of their plan for 1000 tomorrow morning. And do what you can to get *Losharik* ready for sea as soon as possible.

"Captain Lavrov, I want your intelligence collection requirements on my desk by 0900. Thank you, Comrades, for your wise counsel; now we need to work quickly to implement your recommendations."

11 July 2021
1115 Local Time
Prima Polar Station
Bolshevik Island, Russia

Vice Admiral Gorokhov waited impatiently by the secure landline. He'd received word earlier that morning to stand by for an urgent call from Admiral Komeyev at 1100. Gorokhov mentally went over his recent progress reports to try and figure out just what the navy's senior admiral would want to discuss. Nothing leapt to the front of his mind, which only added to his agitation. He silently half prayed, half pleaded that it wasn't another friendly urging to speed up the construction of the launch facility. His musings were abruptly terminated by the electronic shriek of the secure phone.

"Vice Admiral Gorokhov here," he answered.

"Nikolai! How is life in paradise treating you?" Komeyev's voice was a bit warbled due to the encryption process, but his friendly tone was clear.

"Sir, I apologize a thousand times for whatever I did to deserve such a posting," replied Gorokhov jokingly.

"Ah, I'm afraid this is a different kind of self-inflicted wound, Nikolai. You have a well-earned reputation for getting difficult projects completed satisfactorily, and on time."

"Damn it! I knew I shouldn't be so efficient. Next time I promise to be as incompetent as my peers." Both men laughed, but it was short-lived.

"So, Admiral Komeyev, to what do I owe the honor of this call?"

"Bad news, I'm afraid. You see Nikolai, my intelligence staff believe the lost American submarine lies on the ocean floor just outside your doorstep, and that an American spy submarine will likely be coming to pay you a visit."

Gorokhov drew a sharp breath; he didn't believe what he had just heard. Stammering, he replied. "Yo . . . you're joking, right? Please tell me you're joking, sir?"

"I wish I were. There isn't a lot to go on, but the *Jimmy Carter* pulled into the Groton sub base a couple of days ago, and the only thing that makes any sense is that she came to look for their lost submarine. Unfortunately, the defensive minefield around your construction project is the most likely cause for the loss of USS *Toledo*."

"Dear God, that's incredible! How did the Americans find out so quickly? The minefield was to be a defense against a preemptive attack. It was intentionally placed just inside the twelve-mile limit for that reason."

"We don't think they have a clear idea as to what is going on, Nikolai, at least not yet, but we have to prepare for the worst. I'm sending two attack submarines, *Vepr* and *Kazan*, to patrol off your defensive zone. What is the status of your fixed hydroacoustic sensor field?"

"They just finished the calibration of the last Sever modules yesterday," grumbled Gorokhov. "We *finally* have a fully operational system monitoring the northern and southern approaches to the strait."

"That's good, Nikolai. Now, listen. Our two boats will be leaving within a day or two and should be in your area a few days later, so I think you'll be well covered. Drill your Sever system operators hard, Admiral. They have got to be on their toes if the *Carter* does come north. She's a *Seawolf*-class submarine, and I don't think I have to tell you what a bitch of a time we'll have in finding her."

Gorokhov found himself nodding; he was well aware of the capabilities of America's fourth-generation attack submarines. "I will begin additional training as soon as we're done with this phone call. Is there anything else, sir?"

"Yes, Nikolai," sighed Komeyev. "I'm briefing the president and the minister of defense in one hour; the president is going to ask what we are doing to speed up construction. I know what you've said before, what I need to know now is, are there any tricks up your sleeve that you or your project engineer haven't already used?"

"I'm sorry, Admiral Komeyev, but we are moving as fast as we can. The cabling has been laid to the launchers and we've just started installing the electronics modules. We are on schedule, but I'm working my divers as hard as I can right now. If nothing else goes wrong, and the weather holds, we can start receiving the Drakon torpedoes for loading later this month. That's a little ahead of schedule, but we can't afford to have any problems, at all, from here on out. And you know as well as I just how unlikely that is."

"I understand," Komeyev replied. "Just do the best you can, and I'll do what I can to keep President Fedorin off your backside. Good luck, Nikolai."

"Thank you, sir, now if you'll excuse me."

The click came without a formal farewell, but Komeyev knew his friend was probably screaming orders to his staff at this very moment. Well, he'd alerted the Project Drakon commander; now all Komeyev had to do was figure out how he was going to deal with the dragon in Moscow.

11 July 2021
1300 EASTERN DAYLIGHT TIME
CNN International Affairs

"Pentagon officials have confirmed that the First Guards Tank Army, which entered Belarus a little over a week ago, has not deployed into their new bases as previously announced, but continued moving, right up to the border of Latvia and Lithuania. In addition, the Sixth Army in St. Petersburg has begun moving units southwest toward the border with Estonia." Christine Laird paused to take a deep breath, as well as collect her thoughts. Within a matter of two weeks, the European border with Russia had been transformed into a powder keg, with both Russian and NATO officials now seriously talking about the possibility of armed conflict.

"Russian Federation President Ivan Fedorin has claimed the troop movements are precautionary and defensive in nature, to protect Russian citizens from unprovoked attack by NATO forces now building up in the Baltic States. Fedorin's rhetoric has been especially acerbic since the collision of a Russian fighter with an Estonian F-16 on June twenty-fourth. In his latest speech to the State Duma given yesterday, Fedorin accused the Estonians of attacking a Russian Federation aircraft, in Russian airspace, a hostile act on the verge of war.

"The North Atlantic Council, the principal decision-making body in NATO, has vehemently denied this accusation, pointing to the fact that the Russian pilot was safely recovered from waters of Lake Peipus nearly ten kilometers on the Estonian side of the border. These latest troop movements within the Western Military District, when combined with rumors of similar redeployments in both the Southern and Central Military Districts, all point to a Russian military that is mobilizing *en masse*.

"President Lowell Hardy has offered, on numerous occasions, to meet directly with President Fedorin to try and resolve the issues that concern the Russian Federation. Fedorin, however, has blatantly refused to meet with Hardy, stating that he can't work with a man that 'murdered' seventy-three Russian seamen on the submarine *Gepard* back in 2005 when Hardy was the commanding officer of the USS *Memphis*.

"Until President Hardy issues an apology for his actions, and pays compensation to the families, Fedorin will not even consider meeting with the American leader."

7

DISCOVERY

12 July 2021
1600 Eastern Daylight Time
Central Intelligence Agency, Office of Intelligence and Analysis
Langley, Virginia

The data *Jimmy Carter*'s crew brought back had been a revelation, critically important to many people, but taking them in several different directions.

Navy officialdom was occupied with deciding how much to tell *Toledo*'s families, without telling them too much. The civilian leadership was trying to figure out what *Toledo*'s loss told them about what was happening on Bolshevik Island. And James Perry's job was to answer the pressing question of why the Russians were going to such great lengths to build a shore installation for a weapon that needed to be launched at sea.

In strategic terms, the Status-6 was slow, even slower than a manned bomber, and about as non-covert as a weapon could be. Its only strength was its virtual invulnerability once it was launched. That made it an excellent retaliatory or second-wave weapon. Whatever the strength of America's ballistic missile defenses, now or in the future, they couldn't touch a torpedo that swam at a hundred knots a thousand meters deep.

But putting it in a fixed launch site offered few advantages, and took away its greatest strength. Because Perry didn't believe the Russians were blindingly stupid, he was determined to find out why they thought this basing concept was necessary.

The photos *Carter* had brought back provided a vital clue. One of the shots showed a section of pipe, more accurately a large cylinder, being handled by a crane. A junior analyst who worked for him, and who should have known better, had stated in a report that the tube's size was "consistent with a Status-6 torpedo." This was supported by a hatch on one end that could be used to load a weapon, and "different pipe fittings and connections that could be part of the launch mechanism."

Perry had summoned the analyst and chewed her out—politely but firmly. Exactly how big was the cylinder? Standard photogrammetric techniques could tell her that. What was it made of? Steel? Titanium? If steel, what kind of alloy could it be made of? Was a standard-sized industrial product used for this task, or a custom-built military component? That would help them track down the manufacturer. What could the fittings on the end be used for?

He understood she'd been under tremendous time pressure, but an intelligence analyst's job, especially right now, was to give the president every scrap of information possible. His job was to fit those scraps together into a coherent hypothesis, if he could, or generate more questions to help refine the analysis if he couldn't.

Her revised report, delivered the next afternoon, had estimated the cylinder's dimensions as two meters in diameter and twenty-eight meters long. Fuzzy close-ups of the fittings had identified possible air and hydraulic lines and probable electrical connections. According to the metallurgical experts she'd contacted, the tube was probably constructed from standard structural steel. No special alloys would be needed in this application. The fabrication methods required to construct such a cylinder were equally conventional.

A little disappointed, Perry had been hoping to get clues about the thing by locating the manufacturer, but without some unique feature, that was going to take a while. Still, it was a much better report than the earlier one, and every bit of information could be useful. Everyone said so, anyway.

The dimensions in her report matched his own back-of-the-envelope figures, but they bothered him a little. A Status-6 torpedo was 1.6 meters in diameter. The cylinder was close to two meters. The weapon was twenty-four meters long, while the cylinder was twenty-eight meters.

What was all that extra space for? Conventional twenty-one-inch torpedoes fit neatly in a twenty-one-inch torpedo tube with only a fraction of an inch clearance around it and a foot or two separation from the muzzle door. In fact, the weapon had to fill the space inside the torpedo tube, or it wouldn't launch properly.

So why did they need the extra half meter in diameter and four meters of additional length? The only thing he'd ever heard of going into a tube with the torpedo was the dispenser that carried some of the guidance wire. The Status-6 was definitely not wire-guided. Was their estimate of the Status-6's size incorrect? It was possible, but not very likely.

He spent several hours going through everything he had on the Russian wonder weapon, comparing its size to the subs that carried it and the engineering analysis that had been done. There was even a cutaway drawing, based on the now famous November 2015 "leak" of the Status-6, engineered by the Russians.

Perry grunted with satisfaction; earlier analysis still checked out. But that didn't help him explain what was going on now.

His next stop was the original HUMINT reports that had triggered the creation of the Tensor compartment. It was actually a cluster of three short messages. The first described an improved model of the Status-6 land-attack torpedo. The second mentioned Bolshevik Island and said that they were adapting the weapon for shore-based launch. The third reaffirmed the launch facility location and reiterated that the weapon would be much improved.

But what were the improvements? Perry wished the source had provided more details, but dismissed his feelings of frustration. He couldn't imagine what it was like for someone to do what the spy did; not just for a moment, or for a short time, but for weeks, months, perhaps even years. Perry knew he couldn't live with that kind of never-ending risk. That the U.S. knew about this project at all was a miracle.

The spy's three messages had been decoded, and then translated. The printout that Perry held displayed the original message in Russian, and then repeated it twice, first translated into English, and then a transliteration of the original Cyrillic.

"Improved." Perry's Russian was pretty bad, but he could follow along, comparing the English and Russian text. The word for "improved" in Russian was "*uluchshen*," and the spy had used that word in the first message. In the third message, though, they'd translated "*bolshaya*" as "improved." One of the meanings for *bolshaya* was "better," but others included "greater, major, larger, massive," and "big." Had the translator been thinking about the first two messages when he worked on the third? Was the improvement a "larger" torpedo?

His mind asked again, *But what improvements?* The thing didn't need to go any deeper or faster, and in both cases smaller was better. Its range was already ridiculously long. A bigger warhead, perhaps? Perry thought a twenty-plus megaton blast was quite big enough, thank you very much.

Perry rubbed his eyes; a larger size wasn't sufficient to justify being called an improvement all by itself. Something had changed, requiring the increased size. And that would, in turn, require a larger launch tube, which meant it wouldn't fit aboard the *Khabarovsk*-class subs or *Belgorod*. He'd just checked both subs' specifications for the third time. Hell, the torpedo wouldn't even fit in the missile tubes of the massive *Typhoon*!

It would take years to design a new submarine to carry the larger torpedoes, and many more years to build them. The new sub design might carry fewer weapons, but it would probably be much larger, and more costly. In that sense, a shore installation would be cheaper, and allow the weapon to be placed in service much more quickly.

Perry sighed. He had to write a daily report on his progress. Luckily, he was supposed to keep it short. DNI Peakes was a busy man.

"It is likely that the weapon to be deployed at the Prima site is larger than the Status-6 torpedo, with approximate dimensions of about 1.9 meters in diameter and 27 meters in length, compared with 1.6 meters and 24 meters for the first weapon. This increase in size may be required by a new payload, since an increase in speed or range is not necessary to accomplish its mission and are inconsistent with the change in dimensions."

It wasn't much, and after a moment's consideration, Perry added, "This does not answer the question of the weapon's vulnerability when fired from a shore installation. We will continue to search for this, as well as details of possible improvements being made to the Status-6 design."

13 July 2021
1730 Eastern Daylight Time
CNO's Intel Staff Office, The Pentagon
Arlington, VA

Commander Russ Chatham shook his head and laid the draft back on his boss's desk. "Why do we have to decide what the Navy will say? Isn't this Public Affairs's territory?" he complained.

"Public Affairs will say whatever CNO tells them to say," RADM Mike Sanders replied. "Our intel shop knows the most of anyone in the Navy about this issue. And we have to determine what's best to say in any case. It's simpler if we draft the release. I don't want to brief a bunch of PAO types into a compartment just so they can screw up the story."

Sanders continued, "Besides, my recommendation is 'Nothing.' As far as the rest of the world, and most of the Navy, is concerned, we're still looking for *Toledo*."

"But that keeps the families waiting."

"And that's on me," Sanders admitted sadly. "I'll take the karmic hit. Hopefully it won't be for very long, just until we figure out what the Russians are up to." He shook his head. "Nope. We can't say anything, because as soon as the Navy announces *Toledo*'s been found, we'll have to tell them how and where. No half measures."

Sanders held up one finger. "First, we'd have to announce that *Toledo*'s loss was caused by an external event, otherwise we would be required to investigate a material fault or personnel error that doesn't exist. That would be a major waste of time and effort, and disrespectful to the crew." Another finger went up. "Second, the only external cause that anyone will accept is a weapon of some type hitting her. There are no sea monsters or other navigational hazards in that area."

As he put up the third finger, he continued, "And we can't tell an obvious falsehood and say the weapon was somehow left over from World War II, because it will take about five minutes for someone to check the records and announce there were never any mines laid up there during the war.

"And that's just the 'how,'" Sanders explained. "The 'where' will really put the wind up the Russians' skirts. They'll flood the area with patrols, maybe even more minefields, and we'll never get a good look at that Russian whatchamacallit."

Chatham grimaced at Sanders's last point; he'd been worried about that particular issue. "Admiral, I'm not certain the Russians don't feel a breeze up their rears already. *Carter*'s arrival at Groton has to have been noticed."

"I know, Russ, I've been thinking about that too. We'll have to come up with a convincing story to explain her presence, but just saying she's here to help look for *Toledo* is pretty damn flimsy. We'll have to be more convincing."

13 July 2021
1830 Eastern Daylight Time
Oval Office, The White House
Washington, D.C.

"Is this the best the intelligence community can come up with?" President Hardy demanded. "'It's larger, and may have a different payload' is not good enough."

"He's still digging, Mr. President," Raymond Peakes replied. A thin man, with equally thin hair combed straight back, the director of national intelligence sounded defensive, and he added, "Dr. Perry is very good at this. He's methodical, but even more, he's good at filling in the gaps."

"But is he quick?" the president asked. "The Russians are building something and we don't know what it is, or when it will be finished. The public and the families are waiting for us to release more information about *Toledo*'s loss. Time is passing, Ray, and the problem is, I won't know when it's too late."

Joanna Patterson, sitting next to Hardy, asked, "Do we know any-thing about the Russians' timeline, Lowell?"

Peakes was still getting used to the first lady being present at Oval Office briefings. Anybody who knew Dr. Patterson knew she wasn't going to settle for just tea parties and civic causes, but the Tensor mate-rial was more than sensitive. Still, she was here, she had retained her clearances, and it was a good question.

Hardy nodded to Peakes, who answered, "They'll have to stop work by the end of September. After that, the weather gets a lot worse and the ice starts closing in again."

Evangeline McDowell, Hardy's secretary, knocked and opened the door. "Mr. President, everyone, Director Jacobson and Dr. Perry are on their way over right now. They say they have 'new information.' They should be here in about thirty minutes."

"Thank you, Evangeline," replied Hardy with a look of encourage-ment. "Maybe now we can get to the bottom of this mess."

Half an hour later, McDowell led Perry and Jacobson, the director of central intelligence, into the Oval Office. The two walked quickly over to the assembly, recently joined by National Security Advisor Hyland and White House Chief of Staff Sellers. Dressed sharply, Jacobson was calm and collected; his long slow gait rapidly chewed up the distance.

Perry, by contrast, was his complete opposite. Almost at a jog to keep up because of his short stature, he was clearly excited and looked more like a stereotypical hermit scholar. He entered clutching a locked briefcase and his sport coat with both hands. Customary dress at the White House was, at the very least, coat and tie. And while Perry re-membered to bring his sport coat, he hadn't remembered to put it on. It was obvious his mind was elsewhere.

"Good evening, George, Dr. Perry," Hardy welcomed. "What do you have for us?"

"And to you, Mr. President," replied Jacobson as he nodded to the other attendees. "My apologies for this brash entrance, but after Dr. Perry burst into my office an hour ago with his latest findings, I figured time was of greater concern than protocol. Dr. Perry, please explain."

The analyst faced the group, but looking directly at Hardy, Perry announced, "It is a different payload, Mr. President. *Very* different."

Peakes looked at him quietly for a moment before ordering him calmly, "All right, James. Please sit down and tell us what you've found."

Perry realized he was still holding his sport coat, and slipped it on before sitting down on a small couch next to Peakes. Hardy, Patterson, and Secretary Richfield sat on the opposite couch, with a small table between them. Hyland and Sellers stood behind them.

"I asked myself, 'How do you improve the Status-6?' It's virtually invulnerable once it's launched. It's got more range than it needs, and to make it faster, you'd be fighting the cube law. If anything, it should be smaller. I did some rough calculations, and the new version's larger size actually isn't big enough to hold a nuclear power plant with enough moxie to give an appreciable increase in speed. At the very best, we're talking about a three-knot increase."

Perry paused for just a moment, but nobody interrupted him. "That left the warhead, but an even bigger nuclear warhead doesn't give you much either. The cube law again."

He opened his briefcase and passed out sheets of paper to the president, SecDef, and the DNI. He'd only brought three, and Joanna looked on with Hardy. The others hovered over Peakes.

The single page showed a drawing of a needle-like missile, with a similar shape, much smaller, circled in a satellite photo. Provisional statistics were listed below.

"This is the Tsitrin missile. It means 'citrine' in Russian. They've been naming their missiles after minerals," he added. "We've seen tests at the Nyonoska Test Range on the Kola Peninsula for some time. It's a hypersonic weapon. We've watched it fly at Mach six, and it's big enough to carry a one-hundred-and-fifty-kiloton nuclear device with an estimated range of over four hundred miles."

Hardy nodded. "I remember being briefed on it. Scary. But what makes you think this is the new warhead—I mean, payload—for the torpedo?"

"The Tsitrin missile is very large—too large for either a submarine torpedo tube or the UKSK vertical launcher on Russian warships and submarines. The accepted wisdom was that the Russians were going to develop a new launch platform for it, probably a submarine, but the scramjet propulsion system is risky technology. We judged they wouldn't start the design until the missile's hypersonic engine had been thoroughly tested.

"Well, it's pretty late in the missile's test program, which it is passing, and we're not seeing anything being fitted out as a test bed. Typically, you take an existing platform, ship, plane, or sub, and modify it so you can proceed to launch trials. This time? Nothing."

"And this fits in the new torpedo?" Richfield asked.

"Yes, sir, rather neatly," Perry confirmed smugly. "We know how much of the Status-6 was taken up by the nuclear warhead. Add four meters to that and make the torpedo a little fatter and it matches the dimensions of the Tsitrin missile, nine meters, plus its launch canister. And the available space doesn't match the dimensions of any other missile in the Russian inventory, or under development."

Hardy sat back on the sofa with a *whoosh* as he exhaled. "So this improved torpedo will be able to approach the coast, and then launch a very, very fast missile that can reach over four hundred miles inland . . ."

Richfield, punching a calculator, reported, "At Mach six, it could reach maximum range in about six minutes. A more typical flight time might be four or five minutes." He shrugged helplessly. "Even if we knew exactly where it would be launched, we don't have anything that could stop it. We could build a radar able to track it, but we'd also need a new missile system that could hit it, and we'd have to line both coasts with radars and launchers."

"But it's still a second-strike weapon," Patterson insisted. She took the paper from Hardy and put it on the table in front of her, as if rejecting the idea. "It wouldn't be used until after a nuclear exchange between us and Russia. This makes a big expensive weapon even bigger and more expensive. Why go to so much trouble?"

Perry responded, "Exactly, ma'am. And it still doesn't explain how they expect to keep the Prima base from being destroyed immediately, in the first exchange. This weapon isn't like a missile; it takes some time to start up the nuclear reactor and bring it to max power before you launch it. Unless the launch facility was very well hardened, which would be another added expense, and a considerable one, it would never get a chance to leave its tube. And the more dangerous they make this thing, the more missiles we'll devote to giving it a quick and violent end."

Patterson shuddered. "So we know more, but we don't know enough to do anything."

Peakes turned to face the analyst. "This is good work, James. But we need you to be good again, and figure out why the Russians think the Prima station won't get nuked right away."

Hardy nodded agreement. "Yes, well done. There's a lot riding on this, Dr. Perry. And it would really help if you found the answer quickly."

14 July 2021
1030 Eastern Daylight Time
CIA, Office of Intelligence and Analysis
Langley, Virginia

With the "Big Skipper" interested in a fast answer, Dr. Perry's shop had been authorized to use any resource within the government, and their requests had top priority. While Perry couldn't call on an infinite number of monkeys, he hoped there were enough for at least one act from Shakespeare. In fact, he'd be grateful for a sonnet.

The U.S. wasn't the only military fascinated by shiny new stuff. The Russians seemed to also like dealing from the advanced-technology deck, so Perry spent the morning requesting a search of Russian scientific literature going back five years, which was about when he judged the idea of an improved Status-6 might have formed in the Russian leadership.

He also ordered a survey of all known weapon test sites, especially those connected with strategic or nuclear weapons, and finally, all possible submarine design houses for new programs or work to modify the *Khabarovsk*-class. One possible scenario that Perry had thought of was that the Russians were just in a tremendous hurry to deploy the new weapon. They might even make a demonstration launch to prove the credibility of the improved weapon as a deterrent. It actually was going to be sea-based, but the first submarine fitted with them was at least a decade away from sailing.

Perry was trying to think of more searches when someone said,

"Excuse me," from the open door to his office. An older gentleman with a lined face and snow-white hair stood at the door. "Dr. Perry, I'm George Ryskov, from the Office of Science and Technology. I don't think we've ever spoken."

Perry almost leapt out of his seat to shake Ryskov's hand and offer him a chair. Dr. George Ryskov wasn't just from the Office of Science and Technology. He was the office's chief scientist, and almost legendary throughout the agency. He had actually been considered for a Nobel Prize in physics some time back. He also had a gift for languages, and spoke several Slavic languages fluently. He knew more about Russian scientific research than anyone on this side of the Atlantic. Stunned, Perry could only wonder what the chief scientist wanted.

Ryskov sat down carefully and said amiably, "Several of my people are afflicted with flaming hair, evidently ignited by high-priority requests from you."

"I'm afraid so, Doctor," Perry admitted. "It's straight from the top, and . . ."

"I saw the requirement, and I'm willing to do whatever my office can to help. But the smoke is a distraction. I may have a more efficient search method."

Surprised, all Perry could do was agree. "By all means, sir. What do you suggest?"

The scientist smiled. "Let's talk for a little while about this new weapon. I've seen your analysis of the new payload, and it's quite insightful. Adding a missile is an impressive increase in the Status-6's capability. But apparently you believe that the Russians have made other changes to the weapon as well?"

Nodding, Perry replied, "We have to find out why the Russians would build a launch site on the ocean floor for a weapon that really needs to be fired from a submarine."

"A very secret launch site," Ryskov added darkly. "They could have chosen many places that are far less remote and where the weather is much more favorable for underwater construction. Construction that would have undoubtedly proceeded much more quickly, and the launch site could very well have been finished by now."

He paused for a moment, then continued, "That is what first struck me when I heard about this entire business. The remote location. The minefield. The Russians do not want anyone to know what they are doing. They had every reason to believe that they could complete the launch site and deploy this weapon before we were aware of its existence. They may still believe that. Without a certain 'special resource,' we would have been caught completely by surprise. This improved torpedo is a 'secret weapon,' in the classic sense," he concluded.

"Well, it won't be secret once it's launched," Perry countered. "Any scenario where these things are actually used becomes surreal very quickly, but the seabed sensors we have in the GIUK gap would easily hear these things the minute they started running. It might be hard to actually destroy the base before it could fire a lot of torpedoes, but the Status-6 or this new weapon would take literally days, even at a hundred knots, to reach a target here in the continental USA."

Ryskov nodded. "I cannot imagine a scenario where Russia telegraphs a strategic nuclear attack days in advance. This also highlights the question of their remote location, which with its increased distance actually increases our warning time. The Russians don't appear to be concerned with how long it takes to reach its destination, or how much warning we may get."

Perry's expression changed from puzzlement to realization. "Because the new weapon won't provide any warning. You don't think we're going to hear them," Perry stated flatly.

"One possibility—maybe the most likely one, given their choice of location, is that the improved torpedo is quieter than the original Status-6. We won't hear them coming because they have found a way to radically reduce their acoustic signature."

"New silencing technology?" Perry asked. "That makes sense. Silencing technology takes up space, hence the larger size. But wouldn't the Russians use it on their submarines first?"

"Actually, it would be easier to implement on a smaller vehicle than a larger one, and I would submit that a strategic nuclear system has an even higher priority than general-purpose submarines. If such technology exists, we might eventually see it on strategic-missile submarines now beginning construction, but it will likely be fielded first on these torpedoes by the end of the summer."

"That could narrow our search considerably," Perry observed.

"Yes, it does," Ryskov replied, smiling. "Assuming my hypothesis is correct. Since you haven't uncovered any flaws in my logic, I should tell you that after extinguishing several small fires on my staff, I've directed everyone in my section to concentrate their search on quieting technologies: acoustics, materials, hydrodynamics. For example, what if you could design a nuclear reactor of that size and power output that didn't need pumps or other supporting machinery? Or what if they've discovered a way to simply heat water with the reactor and expel it out the back? I know we've investigated those concepts ourselves in the past, but discarded them as unworkable."

Perry grabbed a notepad. "I'll restructure the searches I've already ordered. There's always the risk we will find nothing, but it's a good place to start."

"And hopefully whatever you find will corroborate whatever we find."

15 July 2021
2130 Eastern Daylight Time
National Security Council Meeting
The White House
Washington, D.C.

Knowing where to look had made all the difference. Perry was still working on his notes when Chief of Staff Sellers warned him softly, "The president is en route."

Dr. Perry had never been at a National Security Council meeting before, but he'd picked a good one to start with. Held to provide recommendations to the president on current national security issues, it was usually chaired by the vice president, and attended only by those agencies that were involved. That typically meant an undersecretary or a department head, and empty chairs were common.

There were no empty chairs at this short-notice session, with the secretary of defense, the chairman of the Joint Chiefs, the national security advisor, Bill Hyland, and numerous intelligence officials present and looking very interested.

He saw everyone start to stand up, and turned to see President Hardy, with Secretary of State Lloyd in close formation, come in. Lloyd's arrival caused a small delay as a seat was found for him, which then caused a ripple as the pecking order was adjusted.

The president's seat was arm's length from the podium where Perry stood. Some chief executives liked to be at the far end of the table, but Hardy preferred to be close to the briefer. Luckily, having spoken to him two days earlier had removed some of Perry's jitters. Besides, he was focused on his news.

Perry's brief was short, and he carefully avoided all mention of the original source of information—the Tensor compartment. The first slide was a diagram of the Status-6, which was familiar to most of the people in the room, but below it was the larger, modified version, with a missile in the front instead of a nuclear warhead.

The second slide showed the difference in capability, with a U.S. map marking likely coastal cities that would be targets for the first weapon, and then a colored band that ran 430 miles inland from each coast, showing how much of the continental U.S. it could reach. Perry heard a few quiet comments, but the bad news was still ahead.

"Here's the base they will be launched from," he said, and he put up a map showing Bolshevik Island, far to the north, and range/time circles showing how far the Status-6 could reach. It was almost certain that the new weapon would go just as far, which included the entire east coast of the United States.

"This all might seem a little academic for what our intelligence people tell us is a strategic second-strike weapon." Heads bobbed as many nodded their understanding.

"But it's only a second-strike weapon because the Status-6 is unbelievably noisy. It would take many hours to even reach the UK, much less our coast. We really don't have an effective way to stop them once they are launched, but the Status-6 will never be called 'stealthy.'"

He smiled at what seemed like a small joke, but it was a grim smile. "We have determined that the new weapon not only has a different warhead, but we believe a radically different internal structure surrounding the reactor and engine. This is the reason for the increased diameter. The reactor and propulsion turbine are, of course, the two main sources of radiated noise from the weapon. A new sheath, made of nanomaterial, completely encloses them in a structure that is very strong, but also absorbs and diffuses vibrations, which are what become noise when they reach the outer shell of the torpedo. Flow noise can be mitigated by an exterior coating and designing the propulsor properly."

Perry paused, and checked President Hardy's reaction. He knew Hardy's background, and that he would understand what this meant. "We conservatively estimate the reduction will make the new torpedo about as quiet as a Russian third-generation nuclear submarine, of course while still traveling at one hundred knots. It is possible that it may be even quieter."

Bill Hyland, the only person in the room who didn't look surprised, nodded confirmation. "I reviewed Dr. Perry's findings before I suggested this emergency meeting. There's not only scientific literature describing the early stages of this acoustic metamaterial technology, but we've been able to locate recent upgrades and activity at an acoustic range located at a lake in Russia. They'd never test this in the open ocean, where there's a chance they'd be observed."

Perry could see a mixture of reactions to the new information. Hardy, who was working it out, looked thoughtful. Others were simply puzzled, but a few faces held expressions of horror or disbelief. As he turned off the flat-screen display, he could see Hardy understood, and Perry connected the dots for those who still didn't understand.

"The Russians can launch these weapons and we will almost certainly not hear them approach. When the Tsitrin missile is launched, it will fly so fast that our air defenses won't have time to react, and its 150-kiloton warhead will burn the heart out of any American city it strikes. State-of-the-art satellite guidance systems will place the warhead within a few meters of its intended impact point; meaning even hardened installations are vulnerable.

"As terrible as a twenty-plus megaton warhead detonating off the coast of New York or Boston sounds, this weapon is an even greater threat. The most telling case, of course, is Washington, D.C. The Status-6 torpedo could never have negotiated the Chesapeake Bay and the Potomac River to strike here. The river meanders too much and the water's too shallow. The Dragon torpedo, with the Tsitrin missile, could put a weapon into the Oval Office or the south entrance of the Pentagon five minutes after it leaves the water off the coast.

"This new torpedo gives the Russians the ability to launch a decapitating nuclear first strike on the United States, with virtually no warning."

8

DETERMINATION

16 July 2021
1030 Eastern Daylight Time
CNN World News

"... don't know what the Russian name for the weapon is, but it has been assigned the NATO designation 'SS-NX-35 Shashka.' The 'SS-N' part means it is fired from a surface ship or submarine against a target on the surface. The 'X' means it is an experimental system, not in operational service yet, and 'Shashka' is the weapon's nickname assigned by NATO—a type of Russian sword. NATO names for Russian missiles always begin with an 'S.'" Defense Secretary Richfield looked up from the one-page press release at a Pentagon briefing room packed with reporters. "I can take a few questions."

President Hardy and Joanna watched the press briefing together from his private study, just off the Oval Office. They'd reviewed the final draft of Richfield's statement at breakfast. While a few trusted reporters had been "leaked" early copies of the draft statement last night, the missile's existence would be news to everyone else in the briefing room, in the country, and the rest of the world. In all probability, most Russians wouldn't know about the weapon their leaders had created.

Bill Hyland came into the study as Secretary Richfield was answering reporters' questions. Most were predictable. "When will it enter service? How can it be so fast?" Richfield had rehearsed answers ready.

Patterson silently gestured for Hyland to take a seat as the conference wound up. After Hardy muted the sound but left the screen on, the national security advisor said, "Well, it's not a secret weapon anymore." There was a note of resignation in his voice.

"And that's the entire point of this exercise, Bill," Hardy answered firmly. Hyland was still trying to come to grips with the president's decision to release highly classified information to the public. "After all, the Russians know all about it. They can still use it for a first strike, and that's a real problem, but we'll know who and how." He grinned. "Nobody likes having their secrets found out. And now they'll wonder what else we know. The Russians have been using information as a cudgel for years, I think it's time we do some thwacking of our own."

"The Russians use exaggeration, innuendo, and outright lies in their information operations, Mr. President," countered Hyland. "We are using information derived from highly classified sources, the use of which puts those sources at risk!"

Hardy frowned; they'd had this discussion earlier. "The DNI and DCI both agree that there is minimal risk to the HUMINT source. The Russians already know about other collection methods. Besides, facts are easier to keep track of and can have a greater impact on the intended target."

The television's image shifted from a briefing room to a news studio. Joanna grabbed the controller and turned up the sound. "It's Christine, Lowell." The CNN commentator had been one of the journalists to receive an early copy and a short briefing "on background." The story was within Laird's area of expertise, and the administration knew she'd be leading the coverage at CNN. Laird had evidently used the night and early morning to line up "talent" for her show.

". . . is from the Council on Nuclear Weapons, and is an expert on their design and construction. Dr. Ulrich, this not-quite-a-torpedo and not-quite-a-submarine swims incredibly fast and incredibly deep, then launches an equally fantastic missile that can reach hundreds of miles inland. I have to ask, is this really possible?"

Ulrich nodded, black beard framing his smile. "The Russians have built more than a few exotic weapons. The Shkval is a rocket-propelled torpedo that shocked everyone by how fast it traveled. It entered service in 1977. The Lun was a massive aircraft that skimmed the wave tops and carried six huge antiship missiles on its back. We've known about the Status-6 torpedo for some time. Putting a missile payload on it is both imaginative and potentially very effective."

Ulrich had brought a map of the U.S. with the missile's reach shaded in red. It ranged past Pittsburgh on the east coast, and well past Las Vegas if launched from the Pacific.

"The torpedo vehicle would arrive at the edge of the continental shelf, then rise quickly and eject the missile just below the surface of the water. Because they've reportedly made the torpedo quiet, the first detectable sign of an attack would be when missiles leave the water and fly inland. At six times the speed of sound, the missile would take just a few minutes, at most seven, to reach its target. Our military does not have an air defense weapon capable of shooting it down. Actually, it's questionable whether *any* nation has a weapon in service or in development that could hit something that fast."

"It certainly sounds scary, but Russia has had nuclear-armed missiles for decades. Why do you think are people so scared now?" Laird asked. It was a softball question, but that was deliberate on her part.

"We all grew up with the frightening knowledge that America and Russia could blow each other up, and the world along with them. The only thing preventing it was 'deterrence'—the idea that regardless of whoever launched an attack, the other side would see it coming and have twenty to thirty minutes to respond, firing its missiles in return. Both sides would be destroyed, so nobody wanted to start shooting. Mutually assured destruction was a stable defensive doctrine, and it worked for over sixty years."

"But now, with this new weapon, there's little or no warning," Laird prompted.

"Exactly. Many of our major cities are within its range, including Washington, D.C. and other military command centers. If they were all suddenly knocked out, that confusion would severely delay an organized response."

Ulrich explained, "It actually takes some time to order a nuclear attack, especially an all-out response. There is no red button, big or small. We should take comfort that weapons that can destroy the world are not on a hair trigger. This is why a 'decapitation' strike may actually work.

"It's likely the first thing anyone would do after hearing Washington had been bombed is ask for confirmation, then ask who's in charge. In the time it takes us to sort out who's next in the chain of command and then for that person to decide how to respond, a follow-on attack by Russian nuclear ICBMs could prevent or severely weaken our response. I personally believe it is still impossible to 'win' a nuclear war, but the Shashka might make it possible for the Russians to actually survive one. We would not."

The camera panned back to show two men, one on either side of Laird and Dr. Ulrich the center. The seating was a tactical move by her. Senator Emmers was on the Senate Armed Services Committee, and Congressman Steve Bartek was on the House Armed Services Committee. Both committees had received a classified brief that morning about the Shashka, and come to very different conclusions.

"He's given away the farm!" Emmers almost shouted. "Hardy's just admitted that the Russians can take us out anytime they want, and we can't stop them."

"President Hardy didn't create the weapon," Congressman Steve Bartek, a member of the House Armed Services Committee, argued. "Moscow built this weapon in secret. Hardy's administration deserves credit for discovering it and warning us that it exists."

"He doesn't seem to be doing much about it. This weapon is a gun not just pointed at our head, but with the hammer cocked." Emmers's tone was angry. "We have to match their move. Put our bombers back on round the clock airborne alert. Put nuclear warheads back on our Tomahawk missiles . . ."

"Just because the president hasn't said anything about a U.S. countermeasure doesn't mean there isn't one in the works, Senator. Besides, telling the bad guys what you're doing to stop him seems less than wise. Ramping up our nuclear forces to Cold War levels would only increase the volatility of the European crisis," Bartek reminded him.

"And this thing doesn't?"

"It would give Fedorin exactly what he likes—an outside threat to rail against."

"That's enough," Hardy ordered. "Turn it off."

Patterson protested, "Lowell, please, Steven's doing such a good job. After his committee was briefed, I warned him that he might get picked by Christine."

Hardy's shocked expression caused her to raise her hands in protest. "Through Bill, of course," she said, gesturing to the national security advisor. "It's just that Steven had been on Laird's show before, so we recommended that he study up, just in case."

The president surrendered gracefully. "It was a good idea, and Bill, thanks for passing her idea along." Hardy sighed. "It just sounds too much like our meeting last night."

"Nobody actually shouted, Mr. President," Hyland pointed out.

"I may have," Hardy admitted. "I know we're taking a domestic hit by not taking the overt steps to counter the . . ." he paused to check a note on his desk, "Shashka. But I won't give Fedorin a club to beat us over the head with, and we don't have the money or the planes to keep bombers aloft twenty-four seven. We can always crank up the DEFCON level later, if we really need to."

"Everybody agreed not to mention the base off Bolshevik Island, at least for now," Hyland offered.

Hardy nodded. "No point. And while I want the Russians looking over their shoulder, I don't want to tip them off we know what they're doing up there, at least until we know more and have a plan. Until then," the president ordered, "use every- and anything you can think of to track the activity at that place. If they order out for pizza, I want to know whether it's thick or thin crust."

16 July 2021
1800 Universal Time
ShippingNews.com

In a follow-up to our earlier report, Ukraine officials have confirmed that the Greek crude oil tanker *Xanthos*, which suffered an explosion and fire yesterday outside the port of Odessa, was mined. The tanker, fully loaded, was inbound to the port at low speed, in the channel, when an explosion under the hull sent a column of water over a hundred meters into the air. The vessel halted, dead in the water, with a fire in one of the amidships holds.

Ukrainian Coast Guard boats rescued most of the crew, but three are still missing, and may be trapped forward. The captain reported that the explosion knocked out the fire suppression system, but fireboats are trying to contain the blaze while other vessels rig a containment boom. The tanker's rated capacity is just over three hundred thousand barrels. The authorities are deeply concerned about a spill of this size so close to Ukraine's largest Black Sea port.

Even more troubling is the likelihood of more mines. All harbor traffic has been halted until the fire is put out, the spill contained, and the channel has been thoroughly swept. Some commercial operators are refusing to tow the crippled vessel away, and other shipping companies have already begun rerouting vessels or simply canceling sailings to the port.

Odessa is the only major port left to Ukraine following Russia's annexation of the Crimean peninsula. Sevastopol was its major port and the largest naval base. The economic effects of Odessa's harbor being indefinitely closed are still being calculated, but would certainly be severe. Among other things, Ukraine must import oil to supply much of its energy needs.

The Donbass People's Militia, a pro-Russian separatist group, claimed responsibility for the attack. An Internet announcement said their underwater commandos had laid "many" mines near the harbor. The Ukrainian Navy and other naval experts doubt this claim, though, because mines large enough to cause such damage cannot be carried or placed by divers. Such mines are typically laid by military aircraft, ships, or submarines, or covertly by merchant ships. While some pro-Russian groups do operate small boats, they do not have submarines or aircraft.

The Ukrainian Navy has one minesweeper, *Henischesk*. It was at Sevastopol when the Russians annexed the Crimea in 2014. While the vessel, along with many others, was eventually returned to Ukrainian control, much of its operational equipment had been sabotaged. Although still not fully repaired, the minesweeper will sortie sometime tomorrow to begin searching for other mines.

The Turkish Navy has offered to send several minehunters to Odessa to assist in clearing the channel. This gesture was widely praised by the Hardy administration officials and the European Union, while condemned by Moscow as another demonstration of the alliances' creeping invasion into Russia's Near Abroad.

17 July 2021
1600 Local Time
The Admiralty Building
St. Petersburg, Russia

Defense Minister General Aleksandr Trusov was President Fedorin's advisor and emissary. When he spoke, it was as the president's proxy. Anyone who spoke to him was, in essence, speaking to Fedorin. And when Trusov asked questions, it meant the president had already asked them and was expecting answers.

Admiral Komeyev, chief of the Russian Navy, offered a translated analysis of the American news conference. Trusov waved it off. He'd seen the video and read the analysis. "That's why I'm here," Trusov explained as he sat down. "We all know what they said publicly. What else do they know? What could they suspect, but they're not ready to say in public?" he demanded.

The matters they were discussing were extremely sensitive. Besides Trusov and Komeyev, the only other person in the room was Komeyev's deputy, Vice Admiral Balakin. He was younger than Komeyev by five years, and taller, thinner. "They've been aware of the Tsitrin missile trials at Nyonoska since they started, although the Americans haven't used that name."

"Or 'Drakon,' thank goodness, but they did link the missile to the new transoceanic torpedo," Komeyev added. "This announcement was made to upset and distract us. It changes nothing," he argued.

"It did upset and distract the president," Trusov remarked sternly. "Project Drakon—all aspects of it—was supposed to be secret, completely hidden, until the base was finished and we were ready to execute the plan. If the Tsitrin land-attack missile's relationship with the torpedo has been compromised, what else do they know? What can they know about the Drakon's Lair?"

Komeyev drew a breath; he was unsure of Trusov's reaction, but forged ahead. "As I reported earlier, sir, we know the Americans are curious about the construction on the island. We suspect their submarine *Toledo* may have been investigating the island when she was lost."

Trusov's expression became thoughtful as he recalled the video-conference several days earlier. Finally, he asked, "You still believe that the minefield was responsible?"

Both admirals nodded. Komeyev explained, "The mines were set up to protect the site from exactly that sort of threat: a creeping first-rank sub."

"That's not where the American navy is looking for the wreck," Trusov countered.

"Our intelligence people have analyzed the submarine *Jimmy Carter*'s movements, and they only make sense if the Americans were looking for their lost sub near Bolshevik Island."

"Yes, Admiral, I remember your conclusion. However, intelligence reports show the American spy submarine is still at Groton. What I haven't heard answered is why she's still there. Doesn't their slowness suggest another explanation?" Trusov challenged. "Besides, wouldn't we have heard a mine explode?" He sounded puzzled, but there was an edge to the question, as well.

Balakin replied, "It's a very noisy acoustic environment. The sound of the explosion could have been masked by the severe ice noise. Also, the ships and submersibles in the area are only fitted with very short-range high-frequency sonars. There is almost no chance they would have heard the blast, some five nautical miles or more distant."

"Our original plan was to set up the hydroacoustic sensor field first, and once that was operating, then lay the mines," Komeyev remarked.

"But that would have taken two seasons," Trusov continued. "I remember the discussion, and Fedorin's decision, which I supported. I still do, because the longer we take to build the launch facility, the more time the Americans have to find out its purpose."

The defense minister asked, "What could *Toledo* have learned? Worst case."

Komeyev answered easily. "If they put up a periscope, which is risky with all the ice, they could have seen the ships over the construction site. Their sonars are good enough to hear the sounds of work underwater. To gain any knowledge of its nature, they would have to use imaging sonars, which are very short-ranged, meaning they would have to cross the mine barrier, or a camera, which is even shorter-ranged. They have remote vehicles equipped with those sensors, but they would have to enter our waters and approach very close. If that was what *Toledo* attempted, then the minefield stopped her.

"Besides," Komeyev continued, "anything *Toledo* learned went down with her. Communicating requires a submarine to expose a mast or buoy, a precarious venture in the dense, broken ice field."

"In addition, we haven't detected any signals from that area," Balakin added hopefully.

"*If* the Americans are telling the truth," countered Trusov. "If they're lying about the search area, or perhaps the sub is not really lost. I assume you've sent vessels to search for the wreck. To confirm her loss."

"Not yet, unfortunately. *Losharik*, the only vessel currently in service for that type of work, is in dry dock for reactor and propulsion motor repairs. We're working to get her back in the water as quickly as possible, but it could take as long as another week."

Anticipating Trusov's next question, Komeyev quickly added, "Two attack submarines, *Vepr* and *Kazan*, have already sortied. They will arrive in their patrol zones by tomorrow and will remain there until the facility is operational."

Trusov nodded approval. "And I'm guessing there's no point in sending surface vessels or aircraft."

"They'd have to be icebreakers, Minister," answered Komeyev. "The ice is a problem year-round that far north. Our combatants aren't built for ice that thick, and their movements would only draw more attention to the area, as would aircraft. And the aircraft would be nearly useless anyway, as it is very difficult to use sonobuoys in those waters—they'd be crushed. I'm hoping the Americans don't get too suspicious about the two submarines we've sent out. We informed the crews they were going on combat maneuvers; it's likely this information will leak out in social media. However, if the U.S. doesn't accept this explanation, starts wondering where they've gone . . ."

Trusov gestured. The admiral didn't need to spell it out. "The risk of additional American interest is worth the security the submarines will provide. The instant the weapons are ready to fire, we win, but until then—for another four weeks, until the facility is finished, we are vulnerable. Secrecy was our greatest strength. With half the secret exposed, we must jealously guard what is left."

The defense minister sat back in his chair and announced, "I will inform the president that the Americans only have a vague notion that we are building something of a military nature on Bolshevik Island."

Both admirals nodded their understanding. Trusov continued, "We had hoped the facility would escape notice until it was operational, but as long as they don't know it is a launch facility for the Drakon torpedo, we are still safe. Even then," he smiled, "there are very few actions they can take."

Trusov sighed. "The sinking of the *Toledo*, if it was caused by the minefield, is unfortunate, but the alternative—the Americans getting close enough to discover its purpose—would have been a disaster. I see no reason to alter our plans on this matter. But now we need to discuss this upcoming countrywide exercise. What is the status of the Northern Fleet? How many units can you put to sea?"

Komeyev knew this was going to be brought up, and slid a sheet of paper across the table to the defense minister. "Here is the Navy's status, with details of all the ships currently in refit. We were adhering closely to the original schedule, but it is impossible that we'll be able to have our major units ready for this last-minute exercise. The best I can do in the Northern Fleet is to have the main surface task force led by *Admiral Nahkimov. Peter the Great* and *Kuznetsov* still need two more weeks in dry dock to complete their refits."

"I understand your frustration, Admiral," Trusov retorted. "But President Fedorin and the rest of the General Staff believe we need to ramp up our military readiness in preparation for the restoration offensive. The president also believes the exercise will rattle the NATO alliance, make them take a step backwards, force them to consider if they truly want to go to war over the Baltic States, Georgia, and Ukraine."

"I'm all for improved readiness, Defense Minister, but you know as well as I that a high tempo exercise has a price in materiel readiness. Ships, aircraft, and tanks often break down during these multi-theater wargames, and we'll have precious little time to make any necessary repairs." Komeyev's protest earned him a glare from Trusov. But the hard look melted away quickly, and the older general nodded his understanding.

"We've kept the Navy's portion of the exercise to a set of coastal defense vignettes to husband our assets. Your ships and submarines won't have to travel more than fifty kilometers from the coast." Trusov leaned forward to emphasize what he was going to say next.

"The vast majority of operational commands have no knowledge about Project Drakon, and President Fedorin believes that putting on a nationwide show of our military prowess will distract the Americans temporarily, force them to allocate resources to observe the massive exercise. We'll still get some useful training out of this, but what we really want to happen is to have NATO and the U.S. focus on our demonstrations of capability.

"This will pull some of their attention from our activities to the north, but, also, as you so wisely pointed out, Admiral, our adversaries will believe that we've worn ourselves out a bit with the size and speed of this exercise. They won't expect we'll transition into a two-front offensive within two weeks of this feint."

"I understand, sir. We'll give the Americans something worth watching. Perhaps I can find a dilapidated ship or two that we can sink during the live-fire portion of the exercise. As for Project Drakon, we should begin loading the launch tubes in two to three weeks. If all goes well, we'll be ready by the time the first ground units step off." Komeyev tried to look and sound confident. He'd glossed over a lot of things that could still go wrong. Things the defense minister wouldn't want to hear, nor would it have any impact on what Fedorin wanted the armed services to do.

"Good. Some in Moscow argued that the Americans already knew too much, and that the operations should be delayed, or even canceled." Trusov smiled broadly. "The president let them have their say, then argued we should continue as planned, that this was our best, and maybe last, chance to restore our nation. If only you could have heard him! By the time he was done, the doubters apologized for worrying. With President Fedorin leading us, we are unstoppable!"

Balakin's face showed he shared Trusov's unbridled optimism. Komeyev merely smiled politely; he hadn't been seduced by the confident prediction of victory. He knew there was a lot beyond their control, and whether the General Staff liked it or not, the Americans had a vote as well. Still, if the Americans could be tricked into looking elsewhere, it might be just enough time to get the launch facility finished. And given the key role Project Drakon played, it had to be operational.

17 July 2021
1800 Eastern Daylight Time
Naval Submarine Base New London
Groton, CT

Black puffs of smoke shot up from the stacks of two red tugs as they pushed and prodded *Jimmy Carter* into the dry dock. Ballasted down, USS *Shippingport* looked like two short gray walls projecting out of the water alongside Pier 15. The tugs held *Carter* steady as the submarine was slowly pulled into the flooded pontoon. The local newspapers had a small article in the business section announcing a contract had been awarded to General Dynamics to effect repairs on USS *Jimmy Carter's* propulsion shaft bearings. The submarine was expected to be in dry dock for about a week.

Across the Thames River, a man stood on a small boat pier watching the docking proceed with great interest. While he had an unobstructed view of Pier 15, he was still over seven hundred meters away and it was difficult to watch for long periods of time through binoculars without getting noticed. He would have preferred being closer, but it wasn't easy to get out on Mamacoke Hill without getting wet or seen. Silently, he hoped the American spy submarine would finally do something; it had been four days since he drove up from the Russian embassy in Washington, D.C., and those days had been filled with boredom. He'd wait until *Carter* was in the dry dock, then he'd head back to his hotel room and report before finding a place to eat that had decent vodka.

9

CONNECTING THE DOTS

18 July 2021
1800 Local Time
Barents Sea

The drone of the four turboprops had a hypnotic effect. The rhythmic beating of the engines, combined with staring at sonobuoy displays filled with background noise for hours, weighed heavily on the eyelids. The Tu-142MZ antisubmarine aircraft had been in the air for over eleven hours, and the crew was nearing its limit, and they still had another two hours of flying before they got back to base. Known as a Bear F Mod 4 by NATO, this large patrol aircraft was a variant on the Tu-95 Bear strategic bomber, and had incredible endurance. Patrolling just off the Russian coast didn't even come close to testing the aircraft's combat radius.

The Bear F had sortied from the Kipelovo naval air base deep inside Russia to conduct an antisubmarine patrol near the Norwegian border, and to loosely follow three Gazprom seismic survey vessels as they made their way to Murmansk. The survey ships had operated out of the former Olavsvern submarine base, near Tromsø, under lease to Gazprom. That was until early July, when the Russian government suddenly terminated the contract. President Fedorin announced the end of the lease personally, claiming that he didn't want the ships and their crews vulnerable to being held hostage by an aggressive NATO nation.

The aircraft had watched as the three ships chugged along, and once they were far enough away, dropped a standard twenty-four-sonobuoy search pattern. The fifty-by-fifty-nautical-mile search box ran parallel to the coast, from just inside the twelve-mile limit to well out into the Barents Sea. The two sonar operators struggled to stay alert as they monitored the RGB-16 sonobuoys drifting on the waves below them. Each man was responsible for twelve sonobuoys and rotated through his set at five-minute intervals. With the brief exception of two false alarms, there was little to break the monotony.

A drawn-out yawn distracted one of the operators, causing him to miss the weak line that had started to form. Two minutes later, the automatic detection function lit up on one of the buoys in the first line. Selecting the sonobuoy's output, he saw a distinct, stable, but very faint line in one of the lower frequency bands. The lack of a signal in any of the other bands suggested a submarine. Sighing, he activated his mike and reported.

"Sonobuoy Operator One to Combat Navigator, I have a possible submarine contact, buoy three, band five." A collective groan from the other crewmembers erupted on the internal communications net. The major at the command console rubbed his face in frustration. "Not again," he mumbled. Still, he had to acknowledge the contact report. "Sonobuoy Operator One, verify contact on buoy three. This had better not be another false alarm, Oleg." The major's tone was one of irritation.

"Combat Navigator, contact verified. Sonobuoy in position three has a weak narrowband signature in one band only, band five."

"Sonobuoy Operator Two, confirm contact on buoy three," demanded the major.

"Confirm contact, yes, sir. Stand by." The other sonar operator had already begun switching his display over to receive the sonobuoy's data, but he had to wait until the signal started showing up on his screen. It took but a minute for the waterfall display to reveal the thin line; there was definitely something there. "Sonobuoy Operator Two to Combat Navigator, confirm contact buoy three, band five."

The major lifted his face from his hands; his eyes were now wide open. He briefly paused to look at the radar display—nothing was even close to the sonobuoy field. With the two operators reporting a detection on the same sonobuoy, and given the lack of a corresponding radar contact, the object, whatever it was, had to be submerged. Any fatigue was forgotten. The hunt was on.

"Sonobuoy Operator One, prepare to drop a circular localization pattern; use four RGB-26 buoys." Before the man could answer, the major announced over the circuit, "Combat Navigator to Pilot, I have control of the aircraft."

"You have control," the pilot replied.

"Circular localization pattern set," called out the sonar operator.

"Executing maneuver!" the major called, while simultaneously pushing a button on the command console. The combat computer immediately began sending instructions to the autopilot and the large, clumsy-looking aircraft dipped down as it commenced a graceful turn to port. Lining up, it flew along the east-to-west axis, dropping two RGB-26 sonobuoys on either side of the alerting buoy. The aircraft then banked to starboard, circling around before running down from north to south, again dropping two more buoys. But before the last buoy could even deploy its hydrophone, two of the other buoys had already transmitted contact data.

"Sonobuoy Operator One to Combat Navigator, buoys twenty-five and twenty-seven have positive contact. Position uploaded for MAD run."

The major stared at the command display. The contact had to be a submarine, and it was operating eight miles outside of Russian territorial water. Ordinarily, they'd issue a contact report and track the boat for as long as they could. But these weren't ordinary times.

"Combat Navigator to crew, stand by for attack run with depth bombs."

The sonar operators turned toward one another; both were surprised and a little concerned by the announcement, but they had heard their orders as well as everyone else before they took off from Kipelovo. Any contact closer than twenty-five nautical miles was to be prosecuted and driven away. To that end, depth bombs were to be employed. No homing torpedoes.

The autopilot reduced the Bear F's altitude as it lined up for the initial MAD run. They had to get the position just right as the magnetic anomaly detector had a very short range, even against a larger nuclear submarine. The major doubted they were dealing with a U.S. or UK attack boat; far more likely the contact was a Norwegian diesel sub.

The aircraft roared over the submarine's estimated position and the detector registered the distortion in the Earth's magnetic field caused by the submarine's hull. Its precise location was recorded and fed back into the combat computer. Once again the big plane began another tight turn to get back over the area as quickly as possible.

As soon as the powerful Kuznetsov turboprops had hauled the aircraft around, the bomb bay doors slowly opened. Leveling out, the plane rapidly accelerated, racing to 450 knots. Just before it reached the sub's location, the first PLAB-250-120 depth bomb dropped away from the aircraft's belly, then another, and yet another. The Bear F then suddenly pulled up, climbing away from the ocean surface just as three large grayish-white geysers broke the surface and shot skyward.

18 July 2021
1715 Eastern Daylight Time
Office of the First Lady, The White House
Washington, D.C.

Dr. Joanna Patterson leaned back in her chair with a contented sigh; she'd just wrapped up the final details for her next event at a local science and technology magnet school. Thankfully her chief of staff had done all the legwork and Joanna just had to review and approve the agenda. She had found, much to her surprise, that she didn't mind many of the public responsibilities of being the first lady. She was particularly eager to promote education programs, especially those that focused on science, technology, engineering, and mathematics, but the more pure "social" aspects were drudgery.

The Office of the First Lady was on the second floor of the East Wing, about two hundred yards and one floor away from her old workspace in the West Wing. She'd rarely visited this part of the White

House before, and was surprised by the size of the office . . . and the staff. In addition to her chief of staff, Joanna had a dozen other assistants that helped her with everything from press releases, social events, state parties, floral design, and ad hoc special projects. Then there was the White House executive chef, Rob Wells. Chef Rob had an impressive culinary repertoire that spanned virtually all cultures and ranged from hearty rustic fare to extravagant, refined haute cuisine. Lowell had reluctantly commented after an exquisite meal that perhaps, possibly, *maybe* he was over-indulging a little in sampling Chef Rob's creations.

Still, Joanna's primary duties as first lady didn't prevent her from dipping her fingers in the national security matters bowl every now and then. And while the president didn't "formally" include her in the policy-making structure, he was no fool, and recognized that her talents and expertise were invaluable. They'd tackled more than a few complex problems together in the past, and both knew they made a good team. The real problem was with some of members of the Hardy administration and Congress.

She was unique; no first lady had served as the national security advisor in a previous administration, so there wasn't any precedence on how to handle such a complicated couple. President Hardy was sensitive to the awkwardness of the situation, and while he allowed Joanna to retain her clearances and access, he wanted to clearly separate her first lady responsibilities from those of unofficial NSA emeritus. This included her office in the East Wing. No classified information was allowed there, nor was there access to classified networks or a secure phone. If Joanna wanted to review classified documents, or discuss them with others, she had to physically move to a small office Lowell had set up for her near the Situation Room in the basement of the West Wing.

On the plus side, she was free to do her own analysis, provide opinions and recommendations, but she wasn't allowed to assign work or give orders. That last bit chafed. It had taken some getting used to, but by and large Joanna was satisfied with the compromise that was widely viewed as fair and reasonable. But that didn't mean everyone was thrilled with the arrangement.

Joanna still had a good hour before her husband would wrap up his day, and she wanted to catch up with the ongoing Russia crisis. She hurriedly cleaned off her desk and headed for the door, bidding her secretary "good evening" as she left. Aware that she too was suffering from Chef Rob's expansionist policies, she took the stairs down to the first floor at a brisk pace and crossed the East Colonnade into the residence villa. Strolling through the Center Hall with its arched vaulted ceiling, Joanna admired the beautiful architecture and the fine art on display. She then crossed the West Colonnade before entering the West Wing. After another set of stairs down to the ground level, she found herself back in her old haunts. Several people warmly greeted Joanna as she approached her "other" office. It was surreal; only seven months earlier these people had worked for her.

While Joanna logged into her top secret computer account, one of the duty officers stopped by with a fresh cup of coffee. They chatted for a brief moment as the classified network brought up her e-mail account. As the duty officer departed, he said a number of reports on Russia's latest impolite behavior were waiting in her inbox. He was sure she'd find them of considerable interest. He was right.

At the top of the electronic pile was a FLASH precedence message from NATO's Allied Maritime Command Headquarters in Northwood, Great Britain. The message briefly described an attack on the Royal Norwegian Navy submarine *Uredd* (S 305) by a Russian Bear F maritime patrol aircraft. The Bear F had made two passes on *Uredd*, dropping a total of six depth bombs before the Norwegian submarine could shake off the large ASW aircraft and escape.

The first five bombs were dropped at some distance from the submarine and caused no damage. The last depth bomb, however, detonated much closer, shaking the submarine violently. There was moderate damage to the periscopes and masts, minor damage to the combat system, and a hydraulic leak that was subsequently contained. The message also reported four personnel casualties, one serious. Joanna shuddered as she read the damage report; she knew exactly what *Uredd*'s crew had gone through. Even though it had been sixteen years, she could still vividly recall when a Bear F had bounced *Memphis*.

But it was the last paragraph that caused her the greatest apprehension. The Norwegian submarine had been well away from Russian territorial waters at the time of the attack. Given the deliberate, unprovoked nature of the incident, NATO was issuing a warning to all ships, submarines, and aircraft that Russian conduct was becoming increasingly erratic and belligerent.

Still shaking her head, she started looking at the other files her ex-staff had sent her; the majority was on the recently announced Resolve-2021 exercise. It didn't take long for her to realize that this exercise was going to be even larger than Center-2015. That exercise had mobilized over one hundred thousand members of the Russian Federation armed forces. In addition, Resolve-2021 was nationwide, involving all four military districts, not just two; the sheer number of messages on troop movements was mind-boggling. She grabbed the secure phone and punched a number.

"George, can you drop by if you have a minute? Good. Thanks."

Two minutes later there were two sharp knocks on the door. Joanna looked up and saw George Hendricks standing in the doorway. "Yes, ma'am, what can I do for you?"

"This exercise the Russians are spinning up, do you have a summary of the units involved? It looks like they are calling up four or five of their armies."

"Six, actually, Dr. Patterson."

"Six?"

"Yes, it looks like the Second Army got their marching orders the other day. We're starting to see train cars stack up at a marshaling yard near Samara."

"What does the JCS think of all this?"

Hendricks shook his head. "Ma'am, we've all been whipsawed by this guy lately. Just as soon as I think we're finally starting to figure out what the hell is going on, Fedorin pulls some more crazy ass sh . . . crap, and we're back to square one. It's . . . it's quite frustrating."

Joanna thought she detected something more in his voice, but let it go. These weren't her people anymore. "What do we know of the exercise's intent? Is there a clear theme?"

"Nothing has been formally announced, other than the exercise's name, but all the indications are that this is a multi-theater, general war exercise. However, given the number of units moving westward, I'd have to say there is a very strong anti-NATO flavor to this one."

"I noticed that the navy and the air force aren't involved anywhere near as much as the army. Any theories?" she asked.

"Both the navy and air force appear to have a lot equipment down for repair. There certainly was nothing to suggest this exercise was part of the annual training plan; on the contrary, we've heard of some belly-aching from unit commanders."

Joanna took a deep breath, this whole thing was a "soup sandwich," to quote her husband. She looked back up at Hendricks and smiled. "I'd better let you get back to work, George. Thank you for coming by."

"No problem, Dr. Patterson. It's always enjoyable hashing stuff out with you; just like old times. I'll send you the summary in a minute." As Joanna watched him depart, a concerned frown slowly appeared on her face. She'd heard the guarded words, the tight tone of Hendricks's voice. She made a mental note to ask Bill Hyland how things were going. Her musings were interrupted by a new e-mail with the list of Russian units and a map showing the rough deployment locations for the exercise.

She opened the list and map and started tracing the units' movements. The general shape of the exercise locations was a shallow crescent running all the way from the Kola Peninsula down to the Georgian border. But as she looked at the assessed starting positions, they looked more than a bit odd. Two of the armies had already started moving following the Belarusian reunification, and then after the incident in Estonia, the Sixth Army near St. Petersburg began moving westward.

Then she saw that the bulk of the Russian forces were moving south, toward Ukraine and Georgia, and north toward the Baltic States. The center was held almost entirely by Belarusian army units. Neither of these made a lot of sense; surely the Russian General Staff couldn't possibly believe that either Ukraine or Georgia would ever consider launching an attack against the motherland. Nor was it realistic to imagine that NATO would conduct a major thrust through the Baltics. The logistic lift required for such an offensive operation was well beyond

NATO's current abilities. Suddenly, a distant memory tugged on her consciousness.

In 2015 the Rand Corporation ran a series of war games that highlighted the vulnerability of the Baltic States from a Russian invasion and recommended that NATO shore up its conventional deterrence on the eastern flank against this unlikely, though plausible scenario. The debate over the published report's conclusions waged for many months. Several detractors thought that putting additional forces on Russia's northeastern border would only stir the pot, but improving the alliance's existing warfighting capabilities was worth considering. Others believed that the deterrent power intrinsic in the North Atlantic treaty's Article V was sufficient to keep a struggling Russia at bay. All sides of the debate believed that a war would be catastrophic, nor did they believe it would stay conventional.

Joanna pulled up the report's executive summary. Even though the judgments were in reference to Vladimir Putin, they were equally applicable to Ivan Fedorin, if not more so. The key assessment that hit home the hardest was the Rand study's conclusion that Putin viewed NATO's "presence on Russia's borders as something approaching a clear and present danger to his nation's security." The debate that followed hashed its way through Congress and the NATO hierarchy with an agreement, in principle, to send additional forces to the Baltic States. But before any troops could be deployed, the Sino-Littoral Alliance War erupted and the subsequent worldwide economic crash eliminated the funding. Years later, little had been done to bolster NATO's eastern flank. However, Russia had fared even worse when the two traditional sources of her national income, arms and oil, dropped to record lows.

She closed the file and slumped back in her chair; none of this was helping her explain Fedorin's aggressive conduct. If anything, Russia's economy was in a recession and open warfare is expensive—simply put, they couldn't afford a war. Even when she tried to look at the situation through Fedorin's "zero sum game" approach to diplomacy, it still didn't make any sense. Try as she might, Joanna couldn't justify her hypothesis that Russia was seriously considering, or actively implementing, a plan to attack the three smaller NATO nations simultaneously with an invasion of Ukraine and Georgia. "NATO would respond," she said to herself. "We would respond, and then nobody wins."

Staring at the map, her eyes followed the line of the Russian border from Estonia all the way down to Georgia. She was momentarily distracted by the slight dip around the tiny country of Moldova. Joanna sat upright; Moldova was split pretty much down the middle between pro-Europe and pro-Russia factions. The Russia-leaning group regained power in the 2016 election and civil unrest had been slowly brewing ever since. Then it dawned on her. If the Baltic States, Moldova, Ukraine, and Georgia could all be swept up in one swift stroke, Fedorin would re-establish the western boundary of the former Soviet Union. The Russian Federation would then have the buffer he claimed was desperately needed to keep NATO at bay.

But it always came back to NATO's commitment to the Baltic States, more accurately the United States' commitment, as most of the other NATO nations were suffering more from the global economic downturn. For his audacious plan to even have a chance, Fedorin would have to find a way to isolate NATO from the U.S. The Russian president had often used saber rattling to buttress his response to perceived alliance hostile intent, to include the threat of nuclear weapons. Fedorin's recurring reference to Russia's nuclear arms as the first line of defense disturbed many diplomats and national leaders, but this was just a cranky, unhappy Russian's babbling, right? Joanna then remembered an interview with Fedorin in the *Moskovsky Komsomolets* newspaper. In the article, Fedorin had quoted his predecessor as he outlined his "defensive" strategy to counter the increasing threat to Russia from NATO, both conventional and nuclear—"If a fight's inevitable, you must strike first."

"You must strike first," she mumbled. Suddenly, a cold shiver of awareness sped down her spine.

"My God!" she said gasping. "That's what it's for!"

She grabbed the phone and punched Lowell's number. The secretary answered after the second ring. "Evangeline, it's Joanna, is my husband still in the Oval Office? He is? Good. Please don't let him leave until I get there. Thanks."

With one hand she slammed the phone's handset while fumbling for a notepad with the other. She hastily scribbled a few notes and then logged out of her account. Before the screen had gone black she was already jogging for the stairs. After that it was a very short walk to the Oval Office.

Mrs. McDowell took one look at Joanna's face and motioned to the door. The secretary had seen that expression many times before and knew Joanna's urgency was authentic. So had the Secret Service agent who opened the door without a single word. Joanna gave him a stiff nod as she strode into the office.

As she walked into the Oval Office, she saw Lowell with Dwight Sellers and Bill Hyland huddled around the president's desk. All shared the same troubled expression. Hardy heard the door open, looked up and saw her as she walked in. He rose and greeted his wife with a thin smile.

"Good evening, Joanna. I must apologize for being waylaid, but there has been a troubling development with Russia." No sooner had he spoken than he saw her wince and understood she already knew. "Ahh, I see you've read the NATO message concerning the attack on the Norwegian boat. Brings back fond memories, eh my dear?"

Patterson ignored her husband's poor attempt at humor, and got straight to the point. "Lowell, I think I know what the Russians are trying to do."

Both Sellers's and Hyland's heads twisted instantly in her direction. Hardy leaned against his desk, folded his arms, and said, "I'm listening."

Marching over to the desk, she asked him to bring up the map she'd just been looking at. Joanna then pointed out where the Russian units were being positioned for the supposed exercise, highlighting the fact that it was largely Belarusian army units that were holding the center against NATO assets in Poland. Next, she summarized the Rand report and brought up the list of recent hybrid warfare-like events in Ukraine, Georgia, and Moldova.

"Now, if Russia were to use the six deployed armies, over half of her standing ground forces, in a sudden surprise attack, they would almost certainly overwhelm all six countries before NATO could even mobilize.

The hardest nut to crack would be Ukraine, but I think Russia is allocating at least two and a half armies against her. That's more than four to one odds, based on troop levels alone."

"But Dr. Patterson, there is very little air and naval participation in this exercise," countered Hyland. "Combined arms training is the hallmark of Russian command and control exercises. This suggests the exercise is more of Fedorin's 'strategic messaging' to us and the NATO Alliance."

"Normally I'd agree with you, Bill, but in past spur-of-the-moment exercises there were far more scenario events that called for air, air defense, and naval involvement—even if the number of participating units was on the low side. Resolve-2021 appears to be unusually ground-force heavy, uniquely so."

"Concur. And that's why I believe this is just a stern message, to us in particular."

As Sellers listened he nodded his head slightly, he knew where Joanna was going. "But Bill, moving well over a hundred thousand troops, and their equipment, is very costly. You said earlier today that the Russian economy is sliding deeper into recession, and the debt burden has skyrocketed in the past four years. From all that we've heard, this exercise wasn't part of the annual training cycle; the Russian MOD hadn't budgeted for it. Normally, supplies for this type of deployment are pre-stocked. This time they weren't, and some unit commanders have requested permission to dip into wartime reserve stocks to support it. That's a very expensive message, isn't it?"

"Not to mention that the navy and air force are doing everything backwards," added Joanna. "Many of the front-line units are down for maintenance, now, before the exercise. Normally the participating units go into a maintenance period after an exercise due to the higher wear and tear."

"So you're suggesting they're intentionally limiting the use of their ships and aircraft to keep them in prime operating condition? And that *this* was preplanned?" asked Hardy.

Joanna nodded. "Yes, and there appears to be a higher than normal number of ships, especially the major units, and Backfire bombers undergoing some type of maintenance. But what's just as important is that these assets aren't the limiting factor if you're planning an offensive, moving army units into position is."

"But what's the motivation? What does Fedorin hope to achieve by starting a war?" challenged Hyland.

"Take a close look at the map, Bill. If you fold the Baltics, Ukraine, Georgia, and Moldova back into the Russian Federation, along with Belarus, you get . . ."

"The Soviet Union!" Sellers almost shouted in surprise. "Well, at least the western end of it."

"That's a pretty ugly picture you're painting, my dear," concluded Hardy. "What I don't get is why you think Russia would even consider risking a war with NATO?"

Joanna smiled and motioned toward Hyland. "Dwight touched on this a moment ago. Bill's group has been banging the rocks together on the Russian economy; it's anemic and appears to be deteriorating more each year. What if the situation is worse than we think? Our information is limited; Fedorin's isn't. What if the Russian economy is in a nose-dive and the government either can't, or doesn't know how to stop it before it plows into the dirt?"

Lowell's eyes popped open. "It's the collapse of the Soviet Union, all over again!"

"Precisely, but only this time it would be the collapse of the Russian Federation. Fedorin's motivation is rooted in fear. If he seriously believes the existence of the Russian state is at risk, that NATO would be in a position to pick off fractured republics in a piecemeal fashion, then this would be sufficient justification for him to consider striking first. He said as much last year."

"I can see Ukraine, Georgia, and Moldova, but even Fedorin has to know NATO wouldn't allow him to invade the Baltics." Hyland's voice had a desperate edge to it, as if he was looking for something that would disprove her theory, but didn't expect to find it.

"Agreed. But without us, NATO doesn't have a chance."

"I'm sorry, ma'am, but that's absurd! Why would we not be involved?" protested Hyland.

"Oh, we would eventually get our act together and support our NATO allies, but by the time we did, it would be too late."

"I'm sorry, Joanna, but I don't understand why you think we wouldn't stand with our allies," replied Hardy. His demeanor reflected both confusion and annoyance.

"Because all of us here in this room would likely be dead, or struggling desperately to find some path out from under Russia's nuclear blackmail." The stunned look on their faces and complete silence told Joanna they hadn't made the linkage yet.

"Lowell, this is what the Dragon torpedo is all about. Fedorin knows that a war with NATO will very likely include the use of nuclear weapons, and therefore, he would want to find a way to strike first. The Dragon is a covert first-strike weapon. And, if the weapon itself could be kept completely secret, as was their plan, then the surviving national command authority would have to prove it was a Russian nuke. It would be extremely difficult to justify the damage a full-scale nuclear exchange would cause based solely on a hunch, even a good one.

"By then the Baltic States will have been overrun, and the rest of our NATO allies will be asking the question if Tallinn, Riga, or Vilnius is worth Paris, London, or Berlin. The ultimate goal of this new weapon being built at Bolshevik Island, Mr. President, is scaring us or knocking us out of NATO. Demonstrating that the Article V mutual security guarantee is meaningless dissolves the glue that holds NATO together. Without it, the alliance would fall apart."

Hardy's expression was a mix of astonishment and anger.

Sellers was tight-lipped and shaking his head. Hyland was dumbfounded; he just couldn't believe what he had heard. "That's insane, Dr. Patterson," he howled. "No nation, regardless of their economic situation, could ever view war as a preferred path. The damage from a nuclear exchange would be catastrophic!"

"Wrong, Bill!" snapped Hardy. "Japan, 1941. Many of that country's leaders believed it was preferable to go to war than lose face. As disturbing as my wife's conclusion is, she's put together a strong argument supporting it. And . . ." He paused as he looked toward Joanna and smiled. "She has an annoying habit of being right most of the time."

"Dwight, Bill, this is your top priority. Pitch the theory to the intel community, get them to give it a thorough scrub, take it apart if they can. But do not, I repeat, *do not*, say whose theory it is. I need some good, old-fashioned, impartial analysis of this assessment, not a bunch of 'yes sir, brilliant theory,' understood?"

18 July 2021
1830 Eastern Daylight Time
Naval Submarine Base New London
Groton, CT

USS *Jimmy Carter* rested high and dry on the keel blocks inside the floating dry dock. Out of the water, its true bulk was revealed—and *Carter* was a big boat. The Electric Boat dry dock supervisor made it a habit to inspect all submarines in *his* dry dock at least three times a day, but this was his fourth walkabout in as many hours. The U.S. Navy may own *Shippingport*, but it was Chad Sheridan's people that did the actual work. The problem was, he had no idea what work had to be done. There was nothing in the work breakdown section of the contract. Zip. Nil. Nada.

The submarine had been in the dry dock for twenty-four hours, and no one had a clue as to what had to be repaired, replaced, patched up, or painted. Sheridan had spent most of the day wandering from one senior executive to another at the Electric Boat shipyard main office only to get the same response, a shrug along with an aggravated "I don't know." It wasn't until Sheridan caught up with the vice president for Groton Operations that he got any useful information.

"Look, Chad, it's the Navy's dry dock. They can put anything they want in there. We just do the work."

"Which is backing up very nicely right now, sir. I don't have a problem with the Navy shifting priorities; I just need to know what *work* is required."

The executive was sympathetic to Sheridan's frustration, but this was outside his purview. Sighing, he said, "Why don't you find the boat's commanding officer? He has to know what repairs are needed."

* * *

It took a couple of hours to find *Carter*'s skipper and get on his schedule, but he was right on time. Walking toward the EB engineer along the wing wall, he was quick to introduce himself.

"Lou Weiss," he said while extending his hand. Sheridan accepted the handshake but got straight to business.

"Chad Sheridan, Captain, EB dry dock supervisor. I'm a little puzzled as to what your boat needs. The contract is woefully lacking in *any* specifics. I've checked your main propulsion shaft bearings and they're just fine, thank you. So what am I supposed to be doing?"

Weiss was visibly uncomfortable discussing his boat in the open. Looking around to see if anyone was watching, he asked, "Do you have a quiet place where we can discuss this, Mr. Sheridan?"

Bewildered, he replied, "Sure, my office is right over there." Sheridan turned and started walking over to the building when Weiss shouted, "Would you like to get some coffee first?"

"Coffee? Whose coffee?"

"My culinary specialists make a fine brew. I can have two mugs up here in a minute."

"Bilge water," declared Sheridan.

"Excuse me?"

"I said 'bilge water.' If you want a *real* cup of coffee, then come with me." Sheridan spun about and resumed his steady pace. Confused, Weiss followed the stocky engineer. Once inside the foreman's office, Weiss was offered a large mug.

"This is my personal stock, Captain. I purchase green coffee beans and roast them myself; these are from Sumatra."

While Sheridan filled the mug, Weiss scanned the office. It was small, but neat and well organized. The wall behind Sheridan's desk was covered with a large Oakland Raiders flag. On the desk was a parrot figurine with a similar eye patch. Once Weiss's mug was full, he thanked his host and raised it to take his first sip. The aroma was amazing, heady; the taste was rich, earthy, with just a hint of sweetness. It went down smooth, with no trace of bitterness or an acidic bite. He'd never had a cup of coffee like this before. "This is incredible!" praised Weiss.

"I thought you'd like it. Have a seat, Captain."

Once both men were comfortable, and after another sip or two, Sheridan got back to the issue at hand. "Captain, I don't know why the Navy had your boat put in the dry dock. Your shaft bearings are in perfect order, your hull is very clean, and I can't find any evidence of grease leakage from your torpedo tubes, control surfaces, or masts. So what the hell am I supposed to be looking for? I really don't mind a blank check, but a blank work order is very troubling. I have a lot of work to do on other submarines, and that's not a parking garage out there!"

Weiss took a deep breath; he had been equally surprised by the order to put *Carter* into the dry dock, but understood completely after he was told why. The problem was the EB engineer wasn't cleared to know why.

"I understand your frustration, Mr. Sheridan, but I'm not authorized to say why my boat was placed in the dock. But let's just say that this is more of a show than an honest-to-God maintenance period."

"I see. So you want it to appear that repairs are being done, when in reality we're to do nothing."

Weiss nodded, "Basically, yes."

"Well, Captain, the show would be more convincing if we had something real to work on. I just can't have welders cutting scrap metal in the basin; it would raise a lot of questions. And workers like to talk about strange occurrences at the bar after their shift."

Weiss sighed; the man had a point, a good one. "Okay, get with my chief engineer and see what small jobs we can have your people do. Oh, and you could give the ocean interface doors a thorough check. I have a hunch I'll be needing them."

"So besides making sure HAL can open the pod bay doors, you really don't have any exterior work?"

"That's correct. But whatever you can do to make it look like a lot of work is going on would be greatly appreciated."

Sheridan closed his eyes and took a deep breath; it wasn't much, but he could at least work with it. "All right, I'll get my folks busy. Maybe I can come up with a few odd jobs that we need to do on the dry dock itself."

Weiss thanked Sheridan for his understanding, and the coffee. As the *Carter*'s CO rose and headed for the door, Sheridan called out to him. Weiss turned just in time to catch a small bag that Sheridan had thrown at him. "A little of my special roast. No man should go into harm's way without a good cup of joe to sustain him."

10

READINESS

19 July 2021
1330 Eastern Daylight Time
Office of the Director of National Intelligence
McLean, Virginia

A commission formed after the 9/11 attacks found that the numerous U.S. intelligence agencies and organizations really didn't talk to each other in a useful way. Legal barriers, turf rivalries, and the demands of day-to-day operations all prevented effective sharing of information. Technically, the director of central intelligence, the "DCI," was supposed to collect information from everyone else and keep the president informed. In practice, it rarely happened.

The 9/11 commission recommended a new über agency, the Director of National Intelligence, whose sole purpose would be to collect intelligence information from other agencies and centers and present the president with an integrated intelligence picture. The "Office of the Director of National Intelligence" had no collection resources, and no ability to gather information itself.

More important than providing the chief executive with better information was the ability to produce "actionable" intelligence on a day-to-day basis. A huge intelligence center just inside the Washington, D.C. beltway not only gathered information, it then analyzed it and passed the finished products to those who needed it to protect U.S. citizens and territory.

"We don't know what they're calling it, but there's definitely something planned around the last week in August," Harry Mathias announced confidently from the podium.

"You make it sound like a state fair or a vacation." Ray Peakes was the director of national intelligence and Harry's immediate boss.

Mathias raised his eyebrows, a little surprised. "You could call it a road trip," he admitted, "and the late summer date is part of it. Still, there is a lot of—"

"Sorry for interrupting," Peakes apologized, "but this is still a discussion, not a formal brief." He tried to make eye contact with each of the dozen-plus people in the room. They were seated at a half circle of tables, all facing the obligatory flat-screen display on one wall. Smaller screens hung on the walls to either side. All three displayed the seal of the agency, an eagle with outstretched wings in a blue circle. One claw held an olive branch, the other a bundle of arrows. Not by accident, it was almost identical to the presidential seal. Brightly colored security warnings announced that the room was cleared for sensitive compartmented information.

"This is high-priority, but Harry is only going to summarize what we've learned so far. We need each of you to go back to your respective agencies with what you'll learn here"—he shrugged—"which is scary enough." Looking at his senior analyst, he said, "All right, Harry. What have you found so far?"

"I'll start with their overt moves. We all know about the Russian Army's movements in Belarus and on the borders of the Baltic States, but now we have units heading toward Ukraine and Georgia." Nodding toward the Defense Intelligence Agency team, he reported, "DIA has seen increased activity at all the European army garrisons. Traditionally, late summer is the end of their training cycle, but their judgment is the level of activity is higher than in previous years. The Russian units are staying in the field longer, and exercising in larger formations, battalion and brigade, not just company and battalion. Leo, just before this brief you said Ms. Miller has more to share."

Leo Odom, the DIA's chief rep, introduced, "Donna Miller, our senior naval analyst." She didn't stand but did fiddle with her tablet for a moment, and a graph appeared. It looked like something generated by an application, and had not been polished. The title was "Planned Northern Fleet Maintenance Schedule." Colored lines wandered across the chart's face, labeled "submarine, cruiser, destroyer," and so on; they represented the collective activity of Russian shipyards. A fair number of the lines took a sudden nosedive in late August.

She spoke quickly, as if she'd rushed to finish and hadn't slowed down yet. "This shows the ships being refitted. About three months ago, the Russian Navy began refitting and modernizing many of its first-line units. Also, instead of giving the shipyards a steady stream of contracts, they brought in a bunch of ships all at once, and we're not seeing any new contracts being let.

"Surprisingly, many Russian shipyard contracts can be found online, and normally they're awarded several months ahead of time. As of this morning, the amount of refit work scheduled for this coming fall drops by a factor of six." That got a reaction from the others, and she added, "And it's not for lack of work that needs to be done."

"It may be money," a CIA rep replied from three seats to her right. Young for his job, he sported a fashionable haircut, but still looked like an accountant. "Using National Security Advisor Hyland's hypothesis as a starting point, we looked for atypical spending patterns, and there is one. Russian defense spending is up almost everywhere, to support operations and maintenance, as well as procurement. It's at least twenty percent higher than last year. We've spent a lot of time trying to figure out where the money is coming from. We hadn't found it yet, but assumed we just weren't looking in the right places." The analyst turned from Miller to look at Peakes. "What if their income hasn't increased, but instead they're just spending what they have?"

The DNI answered, "I'll ask the obvious question: When would they run out?"

The accounting analyst shrugged. "Governments rarely just 'run out,' but at the estimated spending levels, they'll be hard-pressed to pay their people or buy fuel for their tanks in three, maybe four months."

Ray Peaks agreed. "And you figured that having suffered an economic collapse once from overspending on defense, the Russian government, not being stupid, wasn't planning to do it again."

Odom cut in, "Our logistics people have been making the same predictions. Their conclusions didn't seem to make much sense and they've been pushed to triple check their work to see if the math is right. So far, the analysis has been hanging together. The Russians can only run at this increased level for another four months. After that—pffft."

"Or less than four months if they increase their operational tempo," Peakes continued. "This is good, but I think Harry's still feeding grist into our mill."

"I am indeed, sir," Mathias answered. "Let me just roll it into one lump. Cyber attacks are up, nothing that's done serious damage, but there have been intrusions at financial institutions, infrastructure nodes like power stations and airports, Fortune 500 businesses, and in spite of their higher security, at military bases and command centers. The Russians deny it, of course."

Nodding toward the senior CIA rep, he reported, "I can confirm that the death of the Estonian defense minister last week *was not* a home robbery. Their interior minister had labeled it 'suspicious' from the start, and they've now told us that his office at home was searched very professionally. There were sensitive documents in a safe, which was opened.

"It's possible that other incidents, especially in the Baltics, Georgia, and Ukraine, may be due to increased Russian espionage activity. Even if they're not directly related to the military, they can be disruptive and distracting."

"Or they may be reconnaissance runs," the CIA rep interrupted. "I've got the counterintelligence section looking at things we don't usually track—industrial accidents and local crime rates."

Mathias put up a map of Europe and Russia. The border was dotted with red stars. "There are a large number of exercise-related scenarios planned for that same late-August timeframe. Again, that isn't unusual, but the folks with the experience in our shop say the level of activity is way up. This sudden exercise is considerably larger than the Center-2015 exercise, which was planned well in advance. They're also exercising right along the border with the Baltic States, Georgia, and Ukraine, which we've interpreted as Fedorin sending a message to his neighbors. And we've just discussed the Russians' cash situation. Running a lot of troops around in the field isn't cheap."

He summarized, "We're all familiar with the idea of using a military exercise to cover preparations for a real operation. It's been done before. But military operations across the border into NATO countries would trigger a general war, and if you think exercises are hard on a country's treasury, the cost and waste of a major conventional conflict in Europe would shatter the Russians' piggy bank. And Leo, why don't you tell them about the mobilization status?"

Odom nodded and explained, "I passed this to Harry last night. It's negative information really, but as far as we can tell, while the Russians are increasing the readiness of their first-line units, they have not mobilized any of their reserve units. The Russian army's pretty big, but if they were planning on taking on NATO, I believe they'd want at least some of their reserve units stood up, at least to provide garrison and rear security."

"Maybe they can't afford to," the CIA accountant suggested.

"That's possible, but whatever the reason, they don't have the forces to fight a general conflict with NATO," Odom replied.

"That ties in with the late summer date I mentioned earlier," Mathias added. "There's decent weather in August and early September, but it's not the ideal time to begin a military campaign. Putting it all together, they don't have enough troops, enough money, or enough time for a big theater-wide operation."

He turned to the last page. "Finally, there's the elephant in the room—Bolshevik Island." Heads nodded around the room. Everyone present had been briefed into the Tensor compartment, and was aware of the facility's weapons and completion deadline.

Peakes announced, "I think the Russian armed forces are moving to a timetable that is directly linked to the Dragon torpedo complex. Whenever the facility is completed, they will be ready to act. Does anyone disagree?"

The room went strangely quiet. When nobody spoke, Peakes added,

"Please, somebody disagree with me. We need to find alternate scenarios that don't involve NATO and the Russians shooting at each other, even though the evidence suggests that's where we're headed."

Mathias, still at the podium, raised his hands and shrugged. "Sorry, boss, but the data indicates there is a linkage."

"Then, how about indications and warnings?" Peakes demanded. "How can we know which way they're jumping?"

"Fedorin can walk away from this at any time," argued Odom. "We have to watch for signs that he is *not* walking away, that he's committed. It would be nice to know what he's committing to," he mused.

"If the Bolshevik Island base is driving their timeline, we need to know when it will be operational," offered the CIA representative.

"We'd have to get something or someone not just inside the program, but right up to the base and have a look," Peakes replied.

"A submarine with a robust UUV capability is the best option," Odom suggested. "But it means entering Russian territorial waters . . ."

"And looking over their shoulder while they're working," Peaks responded sharply. "I don't think that's an option. We've already lost one submarine up there. If there wasn't so much activity around the site, we could possibly argue to the president that the threat is worth the risk, but of course, once the activity stops, they'll be done."

"And ready to move," Odom agreed.

20 July 2021
0900 Local Time
National Cyberdefense Center
Berlin, Federal Republic of Germany

Dieter Hoffmann might have been born in the twentieth century, but he was a true child of the twenty-first. He'd been too young to remember the beginning of the millennium, and had grown up surrounded by personal electronics. To him, it was natural and essential that digital devices augmented his life.

His degrees were in mathematics and music, but he'd starved as a musician. He'd applied to the government because his family wanted him earning a steady income. Thankfully, the civil service exam didn't require the dreaded "prior experience." The Bundesnachrichtendienst, or BND, Germany's Federal Intelligence Service, was interested in his test scores, and the interviewer was intrigued by his extensive collection of pirated music. He'd admitted to the fact reluctantly, but the interviewer seemed genuinely interested, and promised that he was not in trouble.

Being broke, he'd found programs and learned techniques to get free music. Hoffmann had become quite skilled in searching out music he wanted while avoiding the many websites that used music as a lure to spread viruses and other malware. Hoffmann saw his interviewer taking notes, and thought that she was also a music enthusiast. Instead of offering him a job with maintenance or their records office, the BND asked him to go to war.

At the National Cyberdefense Center, he became not only one of their best analysts; he was promoted to supervisor with three other specialists working under his direction. He laughed whenever he thought of his grandfather, a solid German office worker, as ordinary as a signpost, and his grandson Dieter, piercings and tattoos, both working for the German civil service.

He loved the work. Nobody liked the criminals who stole credit card files and hacked hospital records, holding them for ransom. Finding them, identifying them, and then taking countermeasures to defeat or expose them gave Dieter great satisfaction. Often they were foreigners, Russian or Chinese, but occasionally they'd be German, or in a European country where the police could actually arrest them. It didn't happen often, but when it did, that was a very good day.

One of the reasons Dieter had been promoted to a supervisory position was his idea. Instead of simply reacting to news of an intrusion, the center should be actively searching for them. But with the entire Internet to hide in, where would you look?

Hoffmann remembered his collection of free music. Hunters don't search the forest for game. They set up blinds near places the animals frequent, or they put out lures.

Under Hoffmann's direction, the center created websites for fictitious companies or newly formed organizations. The websites were fully implemented, listing staff, with links to other pages that described operations and commercial activities. He liked to include touches like photographs of employees being promoted, or a ribbon cutting at a new facility.

His first attempt, flown solo, had been for an imaginary investment company. It boasted a long list of proven brokers and an equally long list of clients who had moved to that firm, bringing fat portfolios. It had taken almost a week to set up, then two more weeks to fix and polish after a real investment broker was asked to review it.

Within minutes of going live, applications monitoring the site registered the first intrusion. While their false front was equipped with the standard commercial-grade safeguards, a few ports had been left invitingly open, and cyber-criminals were quick to exploit them. While the crooks downloaded false data and installed their malware in code that led nowhere, the center's own programs traced their origins and isolated the viruses for further study.

Another benefit was that the intruders often sold the data they'd collected to brokers for all types of criminal activities, like fraud or identity theft. In this case, though, the data would hurt no one and, since it was known and unique, could be used to trace the hackers' connections, like marked banknotes.

It had been a heady eleven hours and thirteen minutes, with at least four and possibly six different intrusions recorded. The seventh wasn't interested in financial data, but simply trashed the website. Hoffmann mourned its loss, but his supervisor, Johann Klemmer, was satisfied. "If the website had withstood the attack, then the attackers might have become suspicious." Hoffmann could only think of all his work creating the website, now lost.

That had been almost a year ago. They'd become much better and quicker at creating websites. The team's latest effort was a midsized petroleum distribution firm. Not only was it modeled after a real company's website, but Dieter's team had concocted routines that would generate false reports showing equally false petroleum products being moved from ports to refineries to customers.

"Dieter." A call from one of his *"minionen,"* as they'd chosen to call themselves, pulled his attention away from the IP database he was updating. Greta, the youngest of the three, and notable for her lack of piercings and/or tattoos, reported, "It's the Russian Moskito virus again."

"Really." It wasn't a question so much as an expression of his amazement. "That didn't take long." Most viruses got by with a string of letters and numbers that described when it had been detected, its type, etc. Ones that appeared repeatedly were usually given code names. Dieter's team had chosen insects as their theme.

The Moskito virus was relatively new, discovered just over a week ago. It was subtle, and didn't appear to do anything, but slipped in disguised as a regular transaction. Once inside, it buried itself in the system and did nothing, as far as anyone could tell. The team had discovered it because the transaction information was all generated by Dieter's team, so the spurious input was flagged immediately.

Knowing what to look for, cyber center analysts had discovered the virus in six other real-world computer systems. Since it apparently did nothing, they had not removed it yet, but that's when it had been named.

The first intrusion had been on the team's previous false site, which mimicked a news operation. It was still running, with the virus inside, but since it was infected, it could not be considered safe, and a new fake website, a petroleum company named "Anders Oil," had been brought online. It had been live less than twenty-four hours before also being infected.

"Should I purge it?" she asked.

"Let me report first," he replied. Johann was still his boss, although he'd also been promoted, thanks to Hoffmann's success.

"That's very interesting," Klemmer answered when he heard the news. "I've ordered Hans's team to work on Moskito exclusively until we understand its purpose. We've found it on another eight websites."

"All of which were chosen to be attacked," stated Hoffmann confidently. "They have to create data that will mimic each site's actual traffic. Has anyone discerned a pattern yet?"

"No, but the information's moving up the chain quickly. The BND is sharing the data with counterintelligence, and we're contacting other countries to see if they've seen similar intrusions."

"And if they have?" Hoffmann asked.

"Then it is an even bigger problem—or potential problem," Klemmer corrected himself. "It has to be a state actor. Criminal organizations don't produce code this sophisticated, and with no purpose? It almost screams long-range planning."

"So, I should coordinate with Hans's team?" Hoffmann asked.

"Yes. They're the best at forensic work. You work at creating sites that might attract these *fieslingen*. We're not even sure we've located all of the viruses on the first system that was infiltrated. It turns out the thing breaks itself up into several pieces before deleting the original copy. We have made one breakthrough, though." Klemmer paused dramatically.

"What?" Hoffmann demanded. "Did they find out what it's supposed to do?"

"No, not yet," his boss explained. "But it turns out that it does interact with the host system in one place." He smiled. "It's connected to the real-time clock."

"A timer," Hoffmann realized.

"Most likely. We won't know the date until Hans's team has done more work, but until they do, I'm supposed to brief the interior minister twice a day."

20 July 2021
1300 Eastern Daylight Time
Situation Room, The White House
Washington, D.C.

It wasn't a full, formal meeting of the National Security Council, but it sure looked like it. The NSC's job was to give the president recommendations and options. In this case, the question put to them had been "How can we convince the Russians to abandon their plan, whatever it is?" which inevitably led to another question: "What do we do about the Dragon complex?"

After a long day and equally long night, Bill Hyland had presented the council's recommendations to the president early in the morning. Hardy had cleared his schedule, and following conversations with Lloyd and Richfield, had them clear theirs for an afternoon meeting.

Not every member of the National Security Council needed to be present. This meeting was about making a decision, and Hardy needed people who could help. Besides, since it was not a formal NSC meeting, Joanna could attend.

Andy Lloyd, one of the longest-serving secretaries of state in recent history, was the elder statesman. Richfield, as secretary of defense, had a good working relationship with Hardy and provided an overarching defense background beyond Hardy's submarine experience.

Bill Hyland reviewed the NSC's recommendations one more time. A few had been modified, based on viewing after a little rest. Some had been fleshed out with details, which led to one being removed from consideration. Hyland's list represented the best American counters to Russia's—Fedorin's—campaign of disruption and annexation.

Hardy tried to suppress his reflexive distrust of economic sanctions. "None of these—oil, insurance, travel—are decisive enough. And they take too long."

"They would have an effect, though," Hyland argued. "Some of these were used when they annexed the Crimea, and the Russians kept telling us how they weren't having an effect." He smiled.

"They didn't hurt enough to make them give the Crimea back," Richfield countered. "And you can't administer sanctions as a deterrent. Doing it after the fact won't correct the damage the Russians will have done by that time. And it will probably strengthen Fedorin's hand domestically. The old 'is that the best you can do?' taunt."

Hyland offered, "I told the economists at CIA to see if they can generate a synergistic effect . . ."

"It won't be quick enough, Bill. We're talking about weeks here, maybe days, not months or years," Hardy insisted. "We could freeze Russian assets here, and NATO could do it in every one of their member countries, and it still wouldn't be sufficiently painful to force them to pull back and rethink their plans. They're close to finishing whatever preparations they need to make. They've spent a lot of money and effort to build that facility, and they're not going to stop because we lock down someone's piggy bank."

"There still are no diplomatic options," Hyland reported sadly.

Lloyd agreed. "There never were. Fedorin's not interested in talking to us. We're the people who destroyed the Soviet Union in 1991, and he wants payback. Remember his bio. His father and grandfather were both old school KGB. His dad worked with Putin, and Putin was Fedorin's first boss, and mentor. His grandfather passed away before the collapse in 1991, but his father died in 1992. The official cause on the death certificate was cancer, but Fedorin always claims he died of a broken heart."

Joanna Patterson, who'd been listening quietly, said, "And you think this is about revenge."

The SecState nodded. "I've given this more than a little thought. Annexing the Baltic States, Georgia, Ukraine, and perhaps Moldova not only helps rebuild the old Soviet state, it weakens NATO, and humiliates the U.S. If we don't stop them, then countries like Poland and the Slovak Republic will know they're next on Fedorin's hit list, and will wonder if we can do anything at all to protect them."

"What worries me more than him taking over part of Europe is that he may be actually considering a preemptive attack using the Dragon torpedo. I've spoken to him twice," Hardy explained. "The first was a formal congratulatory phone call when I was elected. That was cold enough. He spoke through an interpreter, and he said exactly what was required and ended it, as quickly as possible. The second was that Economic Summit in Mumbai. Joanna came with me."

Patterson nodded agreement. "I remember that he didn't even want to meet with you."

"And when we met, it was completely formal, lots of people in the room, and he wouldn't even look me in the eye. The idea of those meetings was to establish some sort of personal relationship between two national leaders. He didn't want that."

"That leaves us with only military options, Mr. President." Hyland did not sound happy.

"I've reviewed them again, with General Schiller and some others," Richfield reported. "They all increase our readiness in some way, either by moving more conventional forces to Europe or trying to speed up our response in case of a nuclear attack. We can't put enough troops in Europe to stop the Russians if they want to come in. The greatest defense NATO had against a Russian invasion was the risk that it would quickly escalate into a general nuclear exchange. If that's gone—if Fedorin is willing to accept the risk—"

"Maybe even wants that risk," Hardy added.

"—then we'd need a larger standing military," Richfield said. "This would require legislative action, if we want to radically change the number of people in uniform. And even then, it will take time to build and prepare the new brigades, ships, and squadrons."

"And this doesn't change the fact that we cannot block a Russian sneak attack should Fedorin give the order," Hardy concluded.

"Mr. President," pleaded Bill Hyland, "if none of these options are effective, what should we do?"

"Actually, I like the economic sanctions a lot," Hardy announced brightly. He turned to Lloyd. "Have your people put together a plan for implementing these as soon as possible. We may have some NATO members join us, and some may balk, but tie them to things the Russians have already done, not what we're worried about them doing."

"Yes, Mr. President." Lloyd acknowledged the order, but sounded a little puzzled.

"Bill, you did a good job leading the council's deliberations. Those are all good recommendations, but you and the council filtered the list. You missed one."

Hyland looked shocked. Hardy's tone was friendly, but the president had just accused the national security advisor of not doing his job properly. "Mr. President, we spent hours searching . . ."

Hardy raised his hand. "This is no reflection on you or your staff. I doubt if anyone even considered it, but I can see that if we're playing on Fedorin's turf, we're going to have to use different rules. The key to the Russian offensive, and the thorn in all our strategic plans, is the Dragon and its launch facility on Bolshevik Island. That's the new factor compared with earlier confrontations. That's what has upset the balance."

Hardy paused for moment, thoughtful, then finally said, "We have to destroy the launch facility before it becomes operational; in other words, as soon as possible."

Patterson looked shocked. He hadn't discussed this with her, still a little unsure if it was the only viable course. This second review had convinced him.

Lloyd looked thoughtful. Richfield and General Schiller looked as shocked as the first lady. Hardy had been speaking to Hyland, who sputtered, clearly searching for a reply other than "Are you nuts?"

Pausing to take a breath, Hyland finally stated firmly, "You're right, sir. That option did not come up in the discussion. I can personally state that it did not even occur to me to suggest it, since an attack on Russian soil would be an act of war. We were trying to avoid that." There was a subtle edge to his answer, as if Hardy should not even be talking about this.

"Fedorin's shaken things up, Bill, and we need to do the same. Hybrid warfare is about living near the edge, then figuring out how far to hang over the side. Andy, you're the only one who's not shocked."

"I was thinking about parallels between this and the Cuban Missile Crisis, Mr. President," Lloyd replied calmly. "When the Russians put the ballistic missiles in Cuba, it dramatically shortened the warning time we would have, although there were other reasons for putting missiles there. President Kennedy considered it a grave threat to U.S. national security."

"Yes, Andy, I was thinking the same thing. I believe the Russians will put a bargaining chip labeled 'nuclear blackmail' on the table, asking us if Europe is worth a nuclear war that would destroy the United States."

"President Kennedy only ordered a quarantine," Hyland argued, "and still, we almost had a nuclear war in 1962."

"I remember reading the declassified invasion plan," Richfield remarked. "I wrote a paper on the crisis when I was at National Defense University. The Russians didn't think we'd react, that we'd accept the missiles' presence there."

"And instead he forced the Russians to put that piece back in the box," Hardy replied. "Secretary Richfield, I don't even have to ask you about the best method to take out the facility. Tell the CNO to give me a plan for using a submarine to covertly approach the facility and destroy it. I don't mean to disable or damage it, either. I don't want the Russians to be able to repair it, or make it partially operational. It needs to be obliterated."

Richfield, a little walleyed, acknowledged the order, but Hyland protested. "This entire discussion has been about avoiding a war with Russia! Mr. President, this gives Fedorin the excuse he needs to start one! He still has all his other nuclear forces."

Hardy frowned, but paused for a moment before replying, "No, Bill, I don't think it will. Fedorin believes we're weak, that we'll just give in and let him take those former Soviet republics. This will give him something new and unexpected to consider. And the Bolshevik Island complex is his trump card. If we take it away, then the Russians lose the strategic cover they were depending on for this whole operation."

He looked over at Richfield and General Schiller. "The DNI is telling me that the Russians are running short of money, that they're not bringing everyone to the party, just their first-line forces. I think they aren't expecting any real opposition; they believe that they can occupy those countries while forcing us to accept the new status quo. If the U.S. backs away, and we don't honor Article V, the NATO Alliance will collapse. Do you agree with that assessment of their military forces?"

Richfield confirmed, "Yes, I do, Mr. President."

"So does the Joint Chiefs of Staff, Mr. President," echoed Schiller.

Turning back to Hyland, Hardy asked, "And why is attacking a remote, covert military base, whose sole purpose is a decapitation strike, more escalatory than allowing the Russians to complete it? Once it's operational, we will be at a much higher risk of nuclear war every time the Russians cause a crisis, and this will only be the first of many."

"Mr. President. I cannot recommend . . ." he started again, protesting. "The chance of war with the Russians . . ." He shook his head. "Sir, we have to give this more thought."

Hardy sighed. "Bill, it's time to make a decision here. Do you know who Arleigh Burke was?"

Hyland shook his head.

"Former chief of naval operations. He was so good, he served three tours as CNO. Destroyer skipper in World War II, but nobody's perfect. He dealt with more than his share of crises. He said, 'The major deterrent to war is a man's mind.' This launch facility is Fedorin's baby, his vehicle for personal revenge against the U.S. It needs to go away."

Hyland seemed muddled. He definitely had not understood what Hardy had meant. "Mr. President, you can't . . ."

"Bill, we're done talking about this. It's time to act." Hardy glanced over toward Joanna, recalling their discussion the night before. She'd been deferential and diplomatic, but she felt she had to voice her concerns about Hyland. Some of the points she'd made had just been painfully demonstrated. Hyland couldn't handle dissention; he preferred to avoid conflict, and this had had a negative effect on the NSC staff.

Hyland opened his mouth to reply, then closed it quickly. Deflated, he simply answered, "Yes, Mr. President." He silently sat down in his chair.

Hardy felt a little regret at having to run his NSA over, but he had a job to do and the younger man was getting in the way. The president turned to Richfield. "Hank, use whoever can get up there quickest and do a proper job of it. I'll want to see the rough plan on my desk tomorrow morning. We don't know what the Russians' timetable is, so we'll have to go flat out until we find out otherwise, or until it's done."

11

DEEP THOUGHT

21 July 2021
0730 Eastern Daylight Time
CNO Intelligence Office, The Pentagon
Arlington, Virginia

"And they can't put a cover over *Shippingport*," RADM Sanders confirmed, hanging up the phone. "Their best estimate was a week to make the modifications—once they figured out how."

Chatham shrugged as he typed. "We had to ask, sir." He reviewed his work, then hit the print button. "Here you go, Admiral, the draft press release for your review." He offered the hard copy to his boss. "I put this together in a hurry, and that's when people make mistakes."

Sanders carefully read the hard copy statement.

PRESS RELEASE-THE U.S. NAVY ANNOUNCES A NEW CONTRACT
WITH THE ELECTRIC BOAT CORPORATION FOR REPAIRS TO
USS *JIMMY CARTER*'S PROPULSION SYSTEM. THIS CONTRACT
DOES NOT INCLUDE WORK ON THE SUBMARINE'S NUCLEAR
REACTOR OR ITS SUBSYSTEMS. THE CONTRACT IS OF UNSPEC-
IFIED DURATION, WITH WORK TO START IMMEDIATELY. A
NAVY SPOKESMAN SAID THAT THEY WOULD TAKE ADVANTAGE

OF THE UNEXPECTED DRY DOCKING TO MAKE A NUMBER OF
MINOR REPAIRS AND MODIFICATIONS.

The admiral handed it back. "That looks fine, Russ. Given that the earlier release put her in dry dock for 'propulsion repairs,' this one definitely says 'there's more wrong than we thought, and EB's going to be working on her for a while.'"

"And one of EB's graving docks can be covered," Chatham remarked as he hit send. "Public Affairs will have this out shortly, but word's already gone out to everyone from EB to the harbormaster. They've ordered the tugs to stand by to move *Carter* out of *Shippingport* as soon as the EB dock is ready."

An aviator, Chatham had only a passing knowledge of things like dry docks. "How long will it take them to cover the dock, sir? It's not routinely covered, is it?"

"No, but it's pre-assembled arches. It takes about half a day to rig the frames and spread them over the entire length of the dock. They can put the frames up while they prep the keel blocks *Carter* will rest on. They'll bring her in, pump the water out, and let everyone see her sitting there. Then they'll spread the canvas over the riverside opening. To get her out, we wait for a window at night when there won't be any satellites overhead. It takes two or three hours to flood the dock, and about another six to get her propulsion plant up and running. We get *Carter* headed down the Thames River, then de-ballast the dock and run the canvas out so it covers the end. Nobody will be inside, but the Russians won't know that."

The admiral smiled. "I'm going to see if we can get a few 'yard workers' spreading tales in Groton's bars about how 'totally messed up' *Carter's* propulsion system is. We'll build a legend—figure out exactly what's supposed to be wrong, maybe even put in urgent orders for parts . . ."

"But all this is actually costing the Navy real money, Admiral," Chatham protested. "Electric Boat will charge us by the minute for using one of their graving docks . . ."

"It's money well spent if we can convince the Rooskies they 'know' where *Carter* is, when she isn't."

23 July 2021
0800 Eastern Daylight Time
The Pentagon
Arlington, Virginia

It wasn't the first time he'd gotten an evening phone call from the Pentagon. Daniel Cavanaugh was an explosives expert, a civilian working out of the U.S. Army Explosives Laboratory in Adelphi, Maryland. He was good enough at his job that the army let him pick his own research projects, and would lend him out when his skills were needed.

As per the phone call, the car picked him up at his home in the morning. It was early enough to be cooler, but it was high summer in the south and it was going to be hot and muggy again. He left a little earlier than he normally did for work, but it was worth it to get ahead of the Washington traffic. The driver had orders to drop him at the south entrance, where he would be met.

"Dr. Cavanaugh?" The young civilian who met him and ushered him through security never identified himself, but led him through the passageways and down to a gray metal door labeled "PLAN 1." After buzzing the intercom and announcing their arrival, at 0800 hours sharp, he disappeared down the hall.

Probably not cleared into whatever was going on, Cavanaugh thought. This wasn't his first visit to some high-security project. He was glad to be of use, and flattered to be in demand, but expected just another routine technical question-and-answer meeting.

He was wrong, of course.

A crew-cut officer whose name tag read "Forest" brought Cavanaugh inside, both literally and figuratively, getting the civilian's signature on several security forms before letting him past the entryway. Inside, he found a suite of offices, complete with its own restrooms and small kitchenette. Forest, a lieutenant commander, introduced him to Commander Gabriel, the team leader, and Petty Officer Brady, their assistant and computer specialist. The two officers both wore gold dolphins, and Gabriel a command pin. Brady's dolphins were silver.

"This is the entire team, Doctor," Gabriel said, shaking Cavanaugh's hand. It hurt, just a little. Although the two were about the same age, Gabriel had obviously worked at staying in shape. Cavanaugh's exercise program consisted of twenty minutes on a treadmill, when he couldn't think of an excuse.

"Please, just Dan is fine."

"Fine, Dr. Dan. Everything you see and hear is Top Secret, including the existence of this planning cell," Gabriel continued.

"Although that will probably change," LCDR Forest added smugly.

Gabriel nodded and grinned. "It's likely." The pair led him to a small conference room. There were signs of long use, including plastic trays with the remains of breakfast. Papers lay in organized piles on one side of the table, while a detailed chart of the Arctic Ocean and the Kara Sea covered one wall.

A carefully drawn course line came up from the south toward an island on Russia's northern coast. The neatly lettered annotations were too far away for Dan to read, but "Top Secret" had been written in large red marker on each corner.

Gabriel saw Cavanaugh studying the chart. "That's our third draft of the voyage plan for USS *Jimmy Carter*. As soon as we can put a plan together, she will leave Groton."

He walked over to the chart, and tracing the track with his finger, explained, "She will sail north, pass Iceland to the west, then make as straight a course as she can for here." He tapped the island. "It's called Bolshevik Island. They send people from there to Siberia to warm up. And that's why we need you."

LCDR Forest handed the civilian two hard copy printouts of a color photo. The first showed the original image. Taken through a periscope, it showed a large tube or cylinder suspended from a crane on some sort of ship. The second sheet had the part with the cylinder blown up to almost illegibility, and was enhanced with lines and dimensions.

"The Russians are building an underwater launch facility at that island for the very large Dragon transoceanic torpedo that has a SS-NX-35 Shashka missile inside. That beast there is a launch tube."

Cavanaugh had followed the news coverage on the Shashka with interest, both professionally and personally, since he lived within four hundred miles of the Atlantic. "It's a scary system," he replied. "But all the reports said it's a strategic weapon, with a nuclear warhead. If you give me the dimensional data, I can calculate what size a conventional . . ."

CDR Gabriel shook his head. "That's not it, Dr. Dan. We want to blow up the launch cylinders."

"Where are they located?"

"Underwater, just off Bolshevik Island." He offered Cavanaugh a marked-up satellite photo of the island. "This shows our best guess at the exact location."

Confused, the civilian didn't take it immediately. "But this map says Bolshevik Island is Russian territory."

"Chart," Gabriel corrected, then added, "And it is." The civilian saw Forest nodding agreement.

Astonished, Cavanaugh didn't know what to say. He wasn't sure what his expression was, but Gabriel must have thought the newcomer was reluctant to participate if it meant attacking Russian territory. Truthfully, Cavanaugh's thought processes hadn't taken him that far.

The commander pulled a chair up next to where Cavanaugh was, facing him. "Here's the drill," Gabriel explained. "The Russians are building a launch facility in secret. Its purpose is to launch weapons capable of a covert nuclear first strike on the U.S. east coast. The president has ordered that it has to be destroyed before it becomes operational.

"Only a few hundred people in the U.S. know what the Russians are doing up there. You're the thirteenth or fourteenth person to know about this operation, and that includes the Big Skipper, who gave the order. This is all flash priority. The operation doesn't even have a code name yet. We've spent two days working on how to get *Jimmy Carter* up there, and we've got some ideas about how she could do the job, but we need a reality check.

"You're not only an explosives expert, which we are not, but you specialize in blast effects on complex structures—including underwater targets. We're only going to get one shot at doing this, and the destruction has to be complete."

Cavanaugh absorbed the commander's explanation easily enough, but did he agree with the conclusion? In reality, it really didn't matter what he thought; Gabriel was merely repeating the president's conclusion. President Hardy thought the danger was so great that he was willing to risk starting a war with Russia.

It wasn't his place to agree or disagree, but Cavanaugh found he did agree with the president's call. He read the papers and watched the daily news, and the Russians were up to several kinds of no good.

Time to do his job, and the questions were simple enough. "All right. How many of these cylinders are there? What's the water depth? What can you tell me about how they're constructed?"

"The water depth where that cylinder was photographed was ninety-eight fathoms," Forest reported.

Trust the Navy . . . Cavanaugh thought. He did the mental math and came up with 588 feet deep. Call it a 180 meters.

"We're not sure how many cylinders there are. Our best guess is more than four, but less than twelve. We don't think there's anything fancy about their construction. Standard structural steel, most likely."

"And is there a diagram of the installation?" Cavanaugh asked hopefully.

"I'm afraid not." Forest shrugged. Gabriel looked apologetic. "All we really have is the photo. Everything else is deduced from that."

"Then how can I tell you where to place the charges?"

"We can't use demolition charges. *Jimmy Carter*'s unmanned underwater vehicles can't carry anything heavier than thirty pounds. But the submarine carries as many as fifty Mark 48 torpedoes. Their warhead is six hundred fifty pounds of PBXN-103."

That was something he could hang his hat on. "All right," Cavanaugh announced. "Given that warhead, I can tell you what it can do to that cylinder at different distances. But how will the torpedoes find the cylinders? Aren't they acoustic homing? And what type of fuzing are you looking at?"

"We're working on those," Gabriel said hopefully.

24 July 2021
1820 Eastern Daylight Time
Situation Room, The White House
Washington, D.C.

They clustered at one end of the long table near the podium. They certainly didn't need all the space. There were only a dozen people involved in planning or approving the mission, and for the time being, it was going to stay that way. Besides CDR Gabriel, LCDR Forest, and the somewhat surprised Dr. Cavanaugh, it included Admiral Hughes, the chief of naval operations; General Schiller, chairman of the Joint Chiefs of Staff; and the secretaries of the navy and defense.

Gabriel sat at a laptop, working the mouse and keyboard as the others stood behind him, studying the notes on the laptop's screen.

It had been a long day and a half for Cavanaugh, with meals inside the small planning cell as they worked out ways to get the torpedoes to home on target, the warheads to detonate, and what their effects would be—thank Heaven at least the depth was known. Then they spent almost as much time trying to imagine what could possibly go wrong, and how they could adjust to still get the job done. He'd been outside exactly once, with LCDR Forest as an escort, so that he could call a neighbor to ask them to feed his cats. He'd spent the ride from the Pentagon to Pennsylvania Avenue rubbing his chin and wondering how scruffy he looked.

President Hardy entered unannounced, with a navy commander close behind, and everyone quickly stood. Hardy introduced the commander as Lou Weiss, skipper of *Jimmy Carter*, a submarine. He'd arrived only a short time ago from Groton. While everyone exchanged introductions and greetings, Cavanaugh noted the contrast between the officers' crisp summer uniforms, *de rigueur* for the White House, and his own bedraggled sport coat and tie. Even Hardy managed to make slacks and a polo shirt look military. The shirt was navy blue with a submarine and the name "Memphis" embroidered in gold.

Hardy sat as Gabriel moved to the podium and called up the first slide. "Mr. President, Captain Weiss, this is *Jimmy Carter's* route north. It's nine days, five hours, transiting at an average speed of about twenty-two knots. We optimized speed while maintaining a high level of covertness—especially for the last twelve hundred miles where interactions with Russian navy assets have a greater chance of occurring. We've prepared a draft of a complete voyage plan for your review."

Hardy nodded and looked to Weiss, who observed, "Having just been up there, the final approach leg has to be at a much slower speed, of course."

Gabriel shrugged. "We weren't sure how you'd want to use your UUVs during the final leg, nor do we have any insight into changes in the area's defenses, so that last part's pretty much a placeholder." He gestured to the rest of the planning cell. "We're a little thin on experience with unmanned underwater vehicles, and again, you were just there."

"And I can't decide how I'll make my approach until I see how we're going to make the attack."

Gabriel grinned. "We've made a lot of progress with that." He pressed a key, and the slide shifted to show an acoustic target transponder beacon. The two submariners had explained the device to Cavanaugh that afternoon. The navy used them in torpedo tests and in live fire exercises when they wanted a torpedo to home in on a particular target.

The commander explained, "We've arranged to fly in every beacon in the Navy's inventory from Norfolk, Bangor, and San Diego. They should arrive in Groton late tomorrow. Counting the beacons already in storage in Groton, that will give us eighteen. Captain Weiss, these weigh about ten pounds each. They're cylindrical in shape with a length of fourteen and a half inches and a diameter of three and a half inches. How many do you think each UUV could carry?"

Weiss looked thoughtful. "The vehicles have a small cargo module that can carry a total weight of one hundred and fifty pounds. So weight won't be an issue. The trick will be packing the beacons into the existing deployment tubes we currently use for the deep-water positioning beacons. The two beacons are similar in size, more or less. I'd say four, maybe as many as six if we get creative."

Cavanaugh saw LCDR Forest making notes. Gabriel continued,

"The beacons are built with a transponder mode that transmits a frequency-shifted chirp. We can set it up so each beacon will respond to a particular torpedo, and that torpedo will only home in on that beacon."

Carter's skipper nodded understanding, and looked a little relieved. "I like the transponder idea. It won't make any noise until the torpedo goes active, which will be at short range. The Russians would almost certainly detect the beacons if they just started pinging as soon as they were planted. The less warning time the Russians have, the better."

Gabriel nodded agreement, but he wasn't smiling. "That's true, Captain, but we can't depend on the Russians being complacent. We'll have to use the UUVs to first scan the perimeter, then we need to get a good look at the facility so we can see how the launcher is laid out."

"We have no idea what it looks like?" Weiss was asking Gabriel, but he looked at the others as well, almost begging someone to say he was mistaken.

"Captain, the only way we even know where the facility is located is because we know the locations of the ships supporting the construction. We're reasonably sure that the launch facility will be within a hundred yards of the location *Toledo* provided."

"So we will preload the UUVs with beacons, send them out to do a reconnaissance, and then . . ." Weiss trailed off.

Gabriel explained, "Once we know what the facility looks like, you figure out the best spots for the beacons, and then drive the UUVs to each location. After the last beacon is in place, the vehicles can head back to the sub, and you commence launching torpedoes."

"It's better if the UUVs stand off and watch," Weiss replied. "That way we can get a real-time battle-damage assessment. If we need to set more beacons, the UUVs will already be in the neighborhood."

"Good point," Gabriel responded. Forest took some more notes.

The lieutenant commander asked, "Captain, how far away can you control the UUVs?"

"Six thousand yards, maybe eight, in good conditions. It was pretty noisy up there, and my controllers had problems with anything over five thousand yards."

"Which means you'll have to get through the minefield," Gabriel concluded. "We were pretty sure of that, and neither of us could figure a way to program the UUVs without bringing them all the way back to *Carter* after they scout the target."

Carter's skipper and the president both shook their heads at the idea. "They don't have to come all the way back," Weiss replied. "They just have to get close enough for us to communicate reliably with them.

"We can also use the vehicles to place small neutralization charges on some of the mines." Weiss sounded confident. "My crew has actually practiced that in the simulators, and we know exactly what type of mine the Russians laid."

"We budgeted time for that in the plan," Gabriel added. "Still, the torpedoes have a range of ten miles at high speed. If we could operate the UUVs at a greater distance, *Carter* herself would never have to enter Russian territorial waters."

Hardy cut in. "I think the subtle difference would be lost on Moscow."

"I'm comfortable with making a gap in the minefield and taking *Carter* inside if we need to, but I can see if my crew can boost the communication range while keeping us covert," Weiss decided. "The biggest unknown is how long it will take to reconnoiter the place and how many beacons to use, as well as where we're supposed put them. Have you put together any guidance for us on how to do that?"

Gabriel nodded. "That's what we have Dr. Cavanaugh for. Go ahead, Doctor," he urged the civilian.

Cavanaugh had not expected to be briefing the president that afternoon. Especially after working nearly thirty-six hours with little time for rest or basic cleanliness. He suppressed his nervousness by focusing on the numbers. "I've calculated the optimum and maximum distance at which a Mark 48 warhead will completely wreck the steel launch tubes. We investigated using two torpedoes homing on the same beacon, or two beacons next to each other, but that wasn't reliable. There are many possible layouts the Russians could use, and I'm halfway through writing guidance . . ."

Hardy interrupted. "How confident are you of these possible layouts?"

Cavanaugh shrugged. "They're all likely, Mr. President, and I can't say it's exhaustive. There are many different possible configurations, depending on what assumptions—"

"That's what I thought," the president intruded. Turning to *Carter's* captain, Hardy asked, "Captain Weiss, do you have any issues with letting Dr. Cavanaugh ride with you?"

"None at all, Mr. President. We've plenty of space. He'd be our honored guest."

Everyone was looking at Hardy; some with amusement, others were perplexed. Cavanaugh swallowed hard. The only submarine he'd ever been aboard was at the *Nautilus* museum in New London. In his line of work, he'd done his best to avoid being in the water at the same time as something that was going to explode.

It wasn't being aboard a submarine that gave him pause. It was being aboard a submarine that was going to attack Russia—after navigating a minefield. But they would only get one shot at this, and Cavanaugh wanted it to work as much as anyone.

"I can do it, Mr. President," he answered, feeling awkward and pretentious, and trying to sound confident. "I'll have to get Mrs. Gray to look after my cats," he added, thinking out loud.

Hardy nodded. "Problem solved. Don't worry, Doctor. The food is great, and you'll love the Bluenose ceremony." The president smiled broadly.

Cavanaugh nodded silently, not wanting to confess he'd never heard of it. He saw LCDR Forest making more notes, and then started a list of his own.

Gabriel stepped away from the podium. "That's all I have."

Weiss said, "Then I should go over the voyage plan Commander Gabriel has put together. I'd like to get back to Groton as soon as possible. Tonight, if it can be arranged."

"Definitely," Hardy answered. "If those beacons are arriving late tomorrow, how quickly can you be ready to sail after that?"

"Six hours or so, sir, if the yard does everything properly and we warm up the reactor while we're still in the dock." Looking both at the president and ADM Hughes, he asked, "When will Captain Mitchell be informed, sir? Technically, I'm still part of DEVRON Five, but I'm betting he hasn't heard about any of this."

"No, of course not," Hardy answered almost automatically. He appeared distracted, and after a moment said, "I wish you and Captain Mitchell could spend some time together working out tactics for using the UUVs."

"Is there any way to bring him in, sir?" Weiss asked. "We could organize a video conference."

Both the CNO and Hardy immediately disagreed. Hughes said, "I wouldn't trust a conversation about this operation being transmitted, secure channel or not."

Hardy added, "And that's not what I meant, Captain. I mean a couple of skull sessions where you can brainstorm ideas, then beat them to death and see which ones refuse to die." He paused for a moment, then another, and finally said, "All right, Lou. I'm putting Captain Mitchell onboard as mission commander."

Cavanaugh watched the others' reactions. He understood what the president's order implied about his confidence in Weiss, but the other officers' protests, in spite of Hardy's position, surprised him.

Weiss looked almost like he'd been slapped. "Mr. President, if you don't think . . ."

The CNO was ready to intercede, and put an arm out to stop Weiss before he said something that couldn't be unsaid. Even Gabriel and Forest looked like they wanted to say something, although he couldn't image what.

Hardy held up a hand, motioning them all to calm down, which they did. "Lou, I'm going to be a hard-ass here. There's a damn fine chance that you'll pull this off brilliantly, but it's not one hundred percent. It never will be, but I need it to be as high as we can possibly get it—the consequences of a failure are astronomical.

"I've been where you are. I understand this will reflect on you no matter what I say, but this mission is more than vital. I get better vibes with both Mitchell and you aboard than with just you. I'd put your entire chain of command on *Carter* if I thought it would help.

"This mission *has* to succeed, and I want you to put the success of the mission above everything else, including your personal feelings."

Cavanaugh watched as numerous emotions passed across Weiss's face. He remembered that Hardy was a former naval officer, and a submariner, too. He was giving *Carter*'s skipper plenty of time to absorb the news and deal with his feelings.

Weiss finally nodded. "I understand, Mr. President. Two heads are better than one. We'll get it done." Cavanaugh relaxed a little. *Carter*'s captain had used the pronoun "we" instead of "I."

Hardy looked over to the CNO, who said, "I'll get Commodore Mitchell moving right away. I'm sure we can have him in Groton by sailing."

"Then I'll leave you to work out the details, and wish you Godspeed and good hunting." The president offered his hand to Weiss, who didn't hesitate to take it, and even managed a small smile.

The president left, and Forest hurried over to Cavanaugh. "While Commander Weiss is working with us, I'll have a driver take you home. Pack, and don't bother with any cold weather gear. *Carter* probably won't even surface until you're back in Groton. I'll send the driver instructions on where to take you after that, but you'll be flying up with *Carter*'s captain to Groton, probably very late tonight. I hope you can sleep on airplanes."

Cavanaugh grabbed the unclassified to-do list he'd started. It was the only thing he could take out of the room.

Forest warned him again, "Don't speak to anyone about any of this. If you have to tell someone why you're gone, just say it's DoD business, and you'll be 'on the road.' And that 'Godspeed and good hunting' applies to you too, now." Forest shook his hand solemnly. "And don't forget about Mrs. Gray."

24 July 2021
1930 Pacific Daylight Time
Bangor, Washington

Emily was just beginning the bedtime festivities when the squadron duty officer called. She could tell it was from the squadron because the phone had a different ring. It was impossible to hear what Jerry was saying over splashing water and Charlotte's singing. It didn't last long, and after that, she was fully occupied with bathing a four-year-old who insisted, "I can do it!" As a mom, she'd learned long ago to set aside any expectation of efficiency and just accept the sheer randomness of it all.

The normal routine was for Jerry to clean up the bathroom while Emily carried a towel-wrapped Carly into her room for pajamas and stuffed animal selection. This time, though, he wasn't standing by at the bathroom door, and by the time their daughter was in bed, he still hadn't appeared.

Poking her head out in the hall, she could see the bathroom, untouched and unoccupied. She could hear him in their bedroom, though, and sternly warning their little one to "Stay in the bed!" she promised to be right back.

Then she saw his sea bag, laid out on the bed, already half-full, and her heart sank. Jerry sometimes rode his subs on short trips, but those were always planned well in advance. And Jerry was in a hurry, with that expression he wore when he was focused.

Emily didn't bother with any of the obvious questions; besides, she didn't want to distract him. "How long?" and then, "Where?"

He looked up at her questioning face, but didn't stop moving. As he headed for the master bath with his empty shaving bag, he answered, "Three weeks. They want me in Groton as soon as possible. There's a plane waiting for me."

The overalls he wore underway were already in the bag, so she knew he wasn't spending all that time in Groton. "You're going out on a boat," she stated flatly.

"Yes." His reply was just as flat. She'd always been very open and vocal about the joys of a squadron commander's wife, who got to see more of her husband than the spouses of the submarine crews. This would be the first time he'd be gone for so long since he'd taken over the squadron.

She'd put up with it while he was a submarine captain, sometimes for many months, mostly because she didn't have any choice in the matter. Now, she found herself resenting even a three-week separation. *Must be out of practice*, she thought.

Jerry had a checklist on his smartphone that he used when he packed. He glanced at it one last time, paused, and looked around their bedroom. He grabbed a paperback from the nightstand and stuffed it into the bag before zipping it shut.

Emily had stood silently for the few moments it had taken him to finish. Jerry came over to where she stood and put his arms around her waist. "I'm sorry about this. If it's any consolation, I'm not thrilled either."

"Like you have a choice," she responded glumly. She leaned against her husband's chest, already missing him.

"Actually, this time they didn't even ask. But I'm still sorry for the extra work it means for you, and being away from you and Carly. I'll miss her first day of preschool."

Emily did the math and knew he was right. She hadn't even thought that far ahead. She tried to be supportive. "I'll take lots of pictures."

"Thank you for being a Navy wife." He kissed her, and added, "And for marrying a sailor like me."

"And you can't tell me anything about where or what." It was a statement of fact, but she hoped she was wrong, or that Jerry could give her a hint.

"I really can't say anything because they didn't tell me squat. Dylan read the whole message to me, Flash priority by the way, verbatim. 'Get to Groton ASAP, transport being arranged. Be ready for a three-week underway.'" After a short pause, he added, "You know you can call Dylan if things get crazy here. The whole squadron will come running if you ask."

"Hopefully I won't have to," she answered, but felt a small tug on her leg.

Charlotte, plush owl in tow, looked up at her. "You didn't come back. I almost fell asleep," she complained.

Jerry laughed and scooped her up. He announced, "Group hug!"

After a collective squeeze, Emily stepped back. "Well, it's definitely your turn to read to Carly tonight. I'll let you explain where you are going and how long it will be."

"To a four-year-old? I'll do my best," he said bravely. "The driver is due any time. Please tell him to stand by. I'll read *Goodnight Moon* to her at least twice."

12

WORKING AGREEMENT

25 July 2021
0420 Eastern Daylight Time
Graving Dock, Electric Boat Company
Groton, CT

Lieutenant Commander Joshua Segerson came awake to violent shaking. He couldn't imagine the source, since they were in dry dock, but the possibilities brought him wide awake instantly. Then the light suddenly came on in the stateroom. Blinking, he saw Petty Officer Bailey stepping back. "Sorry, XO," she apologized. "You weren't answering your phone, and the quarterdeck just got a call from the skipper. He's inbound, ETA about fifteen minutes."

Rubbing his face as he sat up, the XO answered, "All right, Tiff. Thank you."

Segerson glanced at the clock, squinted, and took a moment to put his glasses on. It still read 4:20 in the morning. It was going to be a very long day, but the captain had been summoned to Washington in one hell of a hurry. Evidently, he was coming back the same way. That meant there might be news, which would be welcome.

Segerson dressed and washed up quickly. It wasn't mandatory that he meet the skipper as he came aboard, but it was his policy. He was out of his stateroom in ten minutes, and threaded his way aft toward the forward escape trunk.

It was cool but clammy as he came topside and crossed the brow to the side of the graving dock. *Jimmy Carter*'s massive hull was lit by hundreds of work lights on the sides of the dock. More lights clustered around the quarterdeck shack. Ensign Truitt, the duty officer, saluted as the XO approached. "Skipper should be here any time, sir."

After the XO returned the salute, Truitt asked, "Sir, do you think he'll finally have some word on what the f— I mean, what we're supposed to be doing?"

"I'm hopeful, Jim. If we do get word, is your division ready?"

"Twelve hours' notice, sir. We've gotten a lot of stuff done. I've scheduled training today for . . ." He stopped as a pair of headlights appeared. They turned off as the car got closer, and Segerson saw CDR Weiss get out, accompanied by a fortyish man in civilian clothes.

The watch took care of their luggage while Weiss introduced Dr. Daniel Cavanaugh to the XO. The skipper's explanation that the civilian was a "subject matter expert" did nothing to satisfy Segerson's curiosity, but he understood the skipper would tell him what he could, when he could.

The three went aboard and down the escape trunk, then forward. Weiss led the way, then Cavanaugh, following clumsily, and Segerson in trail to keep the newcomer from making a wrong turn. Reluctant to slow down the two submariners, Cavanaugh tried to move too quickly at first, and paid for it by connecting solidly with a valve at shin level, then collected what had to be a bruised shoulder from a junction box. The second hit was enough to make him slow down and look carefully before taking each step.

When they reached officer's country, Weiss disappeared into his stateroom, while Segerson helped the civilian get settled in the XO's cabin next door. This involved moving stacks of papers off the extra upper bunk while Cavanaugh unpacked. Segerson mixed instructions about life on the sub with general questions. The civilian seemed pleasant enough. The last thing Segerson needed was a finicky or abrasive roommate.

Weiss rapped on the open door, and simply said, "When you can, XO," then went back in his stateroom. After making sure that Cavanaugh knew where everything was, including the head between their stateroom and the CO's, Segerson closed his door, took three steps, and knocked lightly on the captain's stateroom door.

He heard "Enter," and then as he came in, "Close the door." Weiss motioned to an empty chair. As the XO sat, the captain announced, "We're getting underway tonight. There's a six-hour window when there are no Russian or Chinese imagery satellites overhead. They'll begin flooding the dock at 2115 tonight, and not a moment before. The shipyard will recover the dock, and pump it back down after we leave. If we do it smoothly, we'll be gone with no one the wiser."

Segerson grasped the plan's intent instantly. "How long does the deception have to last?"

"As long as possible," Weiss answered. "A week would be nice, two would be ideal."

The XO nodded his understanding and Weiss continued, "The crew will find out about the destination after we're underway. It's close enough to reveille now that we'll give all hands the word about the sailing at officer's call and quarters. Make sure everyone hears two things: when everyone is to be onboard, and that nobody outside this graving dock should know we've left. Nobody talks to anyone outside EB, no social media, no phone calls home, no e-mails, no nothing. The rest of the world needs to believe we are still high and dry in this dock."

Weiss handed his XO an envelope. "This is where we're going and what we'll do when we get there. For the moment, just concentrate on getting us headed in the right direction."

He gestured toward the XO stateroom. "Dr. Cavanaugh is completely briefed about our mission, so we can speak freely around him. I'll give you the details about his role later."

Segerson nodded. "Aye, aye, sir." He didn't know where they were going, but knowing they were going somewhere lifted his spirits. He was impatient to look at the material the captain had given him, and one part of his mind was already trying to remember where the tide would be late tonight.

"There's one more thing, XO." Weiss's tone remained serious, almost grim. "Commodore Mitchell has been assigned as mission commander. He's en route, and will arrive sometime this morning."

The XO stifled his first reaction, an incredulous "What?" but really couldn't think of what to say. There was a small chance he'd misunderstood the skipper, and he asked, "COMDEVRON Five is going with us?"

"Yes," Weiss replied, then explained. "This mission is huge, Josh. I was briefed with President Hardy sitting next to me. He's the one who decided Mitchell should be in charge."

Segerson's mind followed several tracks at once. The first thought to leave the station was *Where the hell are we going?* Pulling out shortly after that was *He couldn't say "No" to the Big Skipper.* Finally, *This sucks* brought up the rear.

Lieutenant Commander Joshua Segerson had been aboard longer than Weiss, and comparing his current skipper with CDR Prindell, the last captain, he'd already decided that Weiss was the better officer, and the better leader. Prindell had been competent, methodical, and easy to work for. Just do whatever the book said. But he'd been cautious, and a little withdrawn. Weiss was outgoing, wanting to know everything, and had nerves of steel. He wasn't reckless, but on the last two patrols he'd shown a keen ability to know when to take risks, and then ride out the results, good or bad.

But both of them paled in comparison with their squadron commander, Captain Jerry Mitchell, a legend in the flesh. The stories about what he'd done to earn several Navy Crosses would fill a book, and there were reliable eyewitness reports that he had some very ugly bullet scars. That he'd been in the thick of it was clear. He hadn't been squadron commander all that long, but he'd done a good job. And by the way, he was best buds with POTUS.

The skipper must be feeling completely crushed. Segerson knew Weiss looked up to Mitchell, but *Jimmy* was Weiss's boat. Nobody did this job entirely for glory, or pluses on fitness reports, but whatever the mission was, when they did it, it would not be Weiss's mission. And understanding that didn't help Segerson know what to do or say.

He finally shoved all his feelings into a corner labeled "pending." His job was to take care of the boat and its captain. "Skipper, I'll run this any way you want."

Weiss smiled, and the XO realized how sad his expression had been. "Thanks, Josh. I'm still sorting out how I want to run it, but then

I realize it's not really my call. It's how *he* wants to run it." There was anger and frustration in his tone. "It all makes perfect sense when you think about it, but damn it! This was my mission until President Hardy got that bright idea to stick the commodore aboard! This is one of the few times I wish the Navy Way was something other than a smart salute and a cheery 'aye, aye, sir.'"

The XO couldn't think of a reply, but just listened.

"But the president said the mission has to come first, and I completely agree with that. So I'm going to set my personal feelings aside, and focus on making sure *Jimmy*'s as good as she can get." After a short pause, he affirmed, "And we'll let the commodore call the shots." Then Weiss added, "This will make a little more sense after you read what's in that envelope."

Weiss let out a frustrated sigh, and then shrugged. "I think we should go do our own stuff for a while. Why don't you look at that"—he pointed at the envelope—"and let's get together just before breakfast, at 0615."

Segerson nodded and stood. "Aye, aye, Captain." He was reluctant to leave Weiss alone. He didn't think the skipper was a suicide risk, but wanted to help his captain. He was just unsure of what to do. Finally, he left, closing the door to the CO's stateroom behind him, thinking about "the loneliness of command."

Dan Cavanaugh watched the executive officer leave, and focused on organizing his possessions into a very limited space. He was reluctant to explore the room too thoroughly, since it was Segerson's personal stateroom, but the XO had made sure that the civilian knew what parts of the room were his to use.

Still, he was curious about his new roommate, the second in command of a nuclear submarine. The bulletin board behind his fold-up desk had a few clues: family man with three young kids, a purple-and-gold "Geaux Tigers" miniature banner, and a handwritten list of restaurants in Groton. He hoped Segerson didn't mind snoring.

He didn't sleep well on airplanes, and it had been an awkward flight with CDR Weiss, who obviously had a lot on his mind. Luckily, the military version of the civilian bizjet was designed to carry ten passengers, so he was able to give the disappointed officer some physical space.

The upper bunk called to him, but by the time he had everything properly "stowed," it was after five, and they said "reveille" was at 6:00 A.M. He wanted to explore, but didn't think that was wise. He'd probably trigger some sort of security alarm. Finally, he pulled out some notes he'd made during the flight, intending to organize them, opened the second desk, and sat down.

Cavanaugh awoke with a start to find a young officer standing next to him. The ensign offered his hand, and as the civilian groggily shook it, explained, "I'm Jim Truitt, the chemistry and radiation control assistant. The XO asked me to check whether you wanted any breakfast."

Even half-asleep, that was an easy answer, and Cavanaugh let Truitt lead him a short distance down a passageway aft to the wardroom. It was full, almost to capacity, but Truitt led him to a side table with juice, fruit, and fresh-baked cinnamon rolls. Their aroma completed the revival process, and while the two collected plates, Truitt ordered eggs and ham from the galley. Cavanaugh followed his example.

Truitt led him to two empty seats, explaining, "Underway, we'll eat in shifts, so it won't be quite this crowded." They were surrounded by animated conversation, and to Cavanaugh's ears, it had an excited tone. Word of getting underway had already spread, and he was sure that at least one conversation was about whether they'd be going home. He remembered that *Carter* was based in Washington State, and had been away for some time.

He spotted the executive officer approaching, and after making sure the civilian was being properly cared for, Segerson broke into the buzz of conversation to introduce their guest. "He will be with us for the patrol, and is new to submarines, so be gentle." There were several laughs, and Cavanaugh felt a non-specific uneasiness.

Ensign Truitt spent their meal explaining some basic submarining rules and nomenclature. The first imperative was "if you don't know what it's for, don't touch it." *Jimmy Carter* was a "boat," not a ship, in spite of her size and commissioned status. Hatches were in the deck, doors allowed passage through bulkheads. There were no stairs between decks, just ladders. He was cautioned to follow all the posted directions, in the order listed, when using the head. Failing to do so would have adverse and unpleasant consequences.

They would check in with the yeoman after the sub's office opened, and he would get a dosimeter, which was Truitt's department. The ensign explained mealtimes, General Quarters, and other "evolutions." Cavanaugh did his best to take it aboard, but accepted that even if he remembered everything perfectly, he was still the "New Guy."

Breakfast ended at 0700, with quarters on the dock's wing wall at 0715. Per Truitt's instruction, Cavanaugh retreated back to the XO's—his—stateroom, where Segerson collected him and led him back outside. He'd only been aboard the sub for a few hours, but coming back out into the open air had a novelty he'd never felt before. He was not claustrophobic, but open space had a new value.

Drawn up in neat rows, grouped by division, the crew cheered and clapped at the XO's announcement they were getting underway. They listened as Segerson warned them about concealing their departure. Any hopes of a homeward-bound course were scuttled when he introduced Cavanaugh, who would be accompanying them on their "mission."

After quarters, Cavanaugh stood back, waiting while a long line of sailors filed back aboard. Truitt found him. "The XO wants to get you checked in ASAP. I'll take you to the office, and then maybe on a short tour." Cavanaugh nodded his agreement.

Then Truitt asked, "You came aboard with the captain this morning. Do you know why the commodore will be going with us?"

That surprised Cavanaugh. The XO hadn't mentioned Commodore Mitchell's name, or that anyone else would be going with them. Evidently, submarines had a well-developed grapevine. "It has to do with the mission," he answered as carefully as possible. That should have been a good way to politely end the conversation, but Truitt pressed his point.

"But don't they think our skipper can cut it?" Truitt sounded almost personally offended. "This is my first boat, so I can't say anything, but I've been thanking my lucky stars I got Captain Weiss as my first commanding officer. I know they're not all this good. Mitchell is the commodore, and way more experienced, but it's the skipper's boat. Why put the commodore in charge?"

Cavanaugh couldn't say anything.

25 July 2021
0750 Eastern Daylight Time
Subbase New London Navy Lodge
New London, CT

The car was early, which was fine, because so was Jerry. The civilian driver was already taking care of the paperwork when Jerry arrived in the lobby at ten minutes to eight. He was a little jet-lagged, but he was functional. A small, pale woman with jet-black hair approached and offered her hand.

"Commodore, good morning. I'm Valerie Adams, one of Mr. Sellers's assistants. Are you ready to go?"

"Yes." As instructed, he'd brought everything with him, and as the driver smoothly took his carry-on and sea bag, Ms. Adams guided him outside. A black, imposing-looking limousine with dark-tinted windows waited at the curb.

Once inside, she pulled out a hard-sided briefcase, unlocked it, and handed Jerry a manila envelope. It wasn't sealed shut, but it was vividly marked with several security warnings. "Chief of Staff Sellers asked that you read this material on the way, to save time. We have about twenty-five minutes until we're at Pendleton. The car is screened, so we're secure."

He opened the envelope and pulled out a dozen-or-so-page document. The first one repeated the security warnings, and was titled "Overcharge." The second page was a map of the Kara Sea and Arctic Ocean. He started reading.

The Secret Service had instantly turned down President-Elect Hardy's first choice for a presidential residence, a five-acre estate right on the Thames River. Not only were they concerned about water access to the site, but the security perimeter would have to extend well offshore, and would interfere with traffic on the river. Besides, while the house was grand enough to entertain distinguished guests, five acres was simply not enough room. For example, there was no good place for the helipad.

Eventually, they'd settled on Pendleton Hill in Stonington, forty-two acres purchased in the 1890s by a robber baron that fancied himself a gentleman farmer. Hardy and Patterson got it at a good price, since the previous owners had not been able to keep it properly maintained. The place would have to be renovated anyway, before the new occupants could move in. There was a small stream on one edge of the property, which would have to satisfy the president-elect's desire for water.

Jerry had been there once before, with Emily, at the official housewarming for the "Connecticut White House." He remembered the first guard shack, just after turning off the main road. They didn't even stop, but Jerry knew they'd been reported.

The real security came five minutes later, at a converted gatehouse that now served as the Secret Service's local headquarters. Everyone showed their IDs, while dogs checked the car. Jerry, in the middle of his second, more thorough reading of the document, replaced it in the envelope and offered it to Adams, but she waved it away. "Please keep it for your meeting. The Secret Service will keep your luggage until you're done."

Once past the gatehouse, they drove by an ornamental garden dotted with small statues, as old as the house. Any further security was well concealed, and aside from a few people working on the grounds, there was nobody in sight.

The car pulled around to a side entrance, where Dwight Sellers was waiting for him inside. Hardy's chief of staff greeted him warmly. "You're early. That's good." He pointed to the envelope. "Did you get a chance to go over it?"

Jerry barely nodded yes before Sellers had them moving down a long central hall. He apologized, "Lately, the weather's been good in the morning, and the president and first lady have been taking break-fast in the garden, but today they're in their private dining room." Jerry, his mind filled with what he'd just read, completely understood. He didn't want even a sparrow to overhear their conversation.

"I've cleared his morning, so you shouldn't feel rushed. We weren't sure how long he would need—how long this meeting would take," Sellers explained. "But there's a lot going on . . ."

"I understand," Jerry replied as Sellers knocked lightly and opened the door.

The first couple were seated, but they both rose and Joanna Patterson almost ran from behind the breakfast table to where Jerry stood, sweeping him in an enthusiastic and familiar embrace. "Jerry, it's wonderful to see you."

Jerry responded with a small squeeze and a peck on her cheek, but turned as quickly as he could to face Hardy. "Good to see you, Skipper." Hardy's handshake was firm without being competitive.

Jerry served himself from a trolley loaded with fruit, bacon, pastries, and almost anything he could imagine asking for. He noticed the other two were both eating light, and resisted the impulse to load up. As he sat, Joanna asked about Emily and Charlotte, and then Hardy asked about how the squadron was reacting to *Toledo*'s loss.

More questions followed. It seemed like they were hungry for news, or more properly, unfiltered, personal news. Jerry and Emily occasionally sent photos and short messages to a special e-mail address they'd been given, but they'd been reluctant to clutter the first couple's inbox. As the conversation progressed, he made a mental note to send more personal e-mails to Hardy and Patterson. They might as well be living in a foreign country for all the contact they had with their old friends.

Jerry waited patiently for Hardy to get around to business. The three finally cleared the dishes away, by themselves, onto the bottom shelf of the trolley. It was clear to Jerry that this was to be a very private conversation. Hardy poured a second cup of coffee for all three of them, and then asked, "What's your opinion of Lou Weiss, Jerry?"

That was an easy one to answer. "He's very good. He took over *Carter* about a month after I arrived, so we're both the 'new guys' in DEVRON Five. It's his first command, but he's done well, witness his last two outings. He's energetic and methodical, almost to a fault, and is always thinking about what comes next." Jerry gestured to the manila envelope, now resting on one corner of the table. "He's got as good a chance as anyone in the fleet of getting this done."

"What do you think of Overcharge? Any qualms about attacking a Russian base in Russian waters?" Hardy asked.

Jerry almost laughed. "After all we've been through? It's almost old home week." Then his tone became more serious. "I haven't heard anything about this base since I was at the *Toledo* debrief. When I got the phone call, I wondered if Bolshevik Island was involved."

Then he shuddered, not entirely theatrically. "Overcharge scares the hell out of me, because there is a small, hard-to-measure chance of triggering World War III . . ."

Hardy nodded reluctant agreement.

"But it seems like Fedorin's getting ready to start one anyway. If not now, then whenever he feels like it, and we wouldn't be able to stop him. I completely agree with what someone wrote in the plan about it 'being the best way to remove a key element of the Russians' strategy.'"

"Do you see any problems with the mission plan?"

Jerry sighed. "The only dicey spot I can see is having to snoop around and figure out the layout of the place before they can place the beacons. The Russians are still working there, so it'll be a lot like a boat slipping into an enemy harbor during World War II, dodging the escorts until he can get close enough for a shot. If the UUVs are spotted before they start putting the beacons in place, or even before they're done placing them . . ." Jerry shrugged. "And we've no idea of their timeline?"

"None," Hardy answered, "except that the weather's going to get progressively worse, and they won't be able to work at all starting in October. It's reasonable to assume they're close to being done."

The president added, "I'm also working with the Joint Chiefs on a massive no-notice deployment 'exercise' to Europe. The planners don't know anything about Overcharge and don't need to, but if this"—Hardy tapped the envelope—"fails, then the troops won't be taking part in an exercise. They'll be the first wave of reinforcements in what will be a very bad war."

"It will work, Skipper. Lou is new, but he's had time to learn his boat and his crew."

Hardy made a face, not quite a frown. "But he's never fought. He's done well with the UUVs, and you just pointed out how tricky this will be . . ."

"Skipper, do you have some concern about Lou Weiss? Please, tell me."

"Jerry, I'm putting you aboard *Carter* as mission commander."

"Then you are concerned about Lou's ability," Jerry accused.

"No," Hardy replied sharply. "Not a bit, and I understand what this will mean for both you and him, but as I told Commander Weiss yesterday, there's a better chance of the mission succeeding with both of you aboard than just him. And this *has* to work, Jerry."

Jerry didn't reply immediately, sorting through the implications, then asked, "So Lou knows, then? How did he react?"

"I told him myself yesterday evening. And as you'd expect, he wasn't happy," Hardy admitted, "but he took it aboard. 'Two heads are better than one.' His own words."

Jerry was still frowning, and Hardy pressed his point. "You have more time with UUVs than almost anyone else in the Navy, and you've used them in combat situations. You've fired torpedoes in anger; he hasn't. I need that experience on board *Carter*.

"The arrangement will be awkward, but I think the two of you will figure out how to deal with it. After all, if a pair of hyperactive Type A's like Joanna and I can do it . . ." Hardy looked toward his wife and smiled. Patterson stuck out her tongue. "Then you two can."

"And if the president of the United States gives me an order, it's up to me to do my best to follow it." Jerry nodded solemnly. "We will make it work somehow, sir."

"Which gives me a better feeling about this mission," Hardy replied. "Dwight will get you down to Groton. *Carter* sails tonight." He offered his hand. "Godspeed and good hunting."

The car dropped Jerry off at the EB graving dock just before ten o'clock. Civilian workers were busy preparing for *Carter*'s departure. He'd been involved with enough undockings to see that everything was proceeding properly. There were few sailors visible in the basin. There was plenty for them to do inside.

The quarterdeck watch was waiting for his arrival, and a messenger ran up to collect his bags. He would have liked a moment or two to gather his thoughts, but realized he'd just be stalling. As he saluted and crossed the brow, he heard a bell ring four times, and "DEVRON Five, arriving."

Jerry started to follow the messenger down the forward escape trunk, then paused. Instead, he told the quarterdeck, "Ask Captain Weiss if he can come topside for a few minutes." The OOD relayed the message, and Weiss appeared only moments later. He approached Jerry, standing on the aft casing, and snapped a salute sharp enough to cut a mooring line.

"Welcome aboard, Commodore." After Jerry returned the salute, as crisply as he could, they shook hands.

Jerry asked, "Can you step off the boat for a few minutes, Lou? Can they spare you?" He tried to sound as sincere as possible. The last thing he wanted was to slow down preparations while he and Lou Weiss hashed things out.

"Certainly, sir. It's going pretty smoothly, and you know as well as I that the XO is doing most of the work," Weiss reported, gesturing toward the brow. As he followed the commodore, he added, "Everyone's been waiting for the 'go' signal."

Jerry saw the quarterdeck watch preparing to render honors again as they stepped ashore, but he waved them off. "We'll be close by," he explained.

Electric Boat's graving dock was surrounded by a concrete apron as wide as an eight-lane highway. While there was plenty of activity near *Carter*, they quickly found a quiet spot in sight of the boat. They sat on a low, wide packing crate long enough to hold a school bus. A cool breeze off the water offset the sun's heat, reflecting off the surrounding concrete.

Jerry knew Weiss would wait for him to speak first, and lacking anything better to say, he tried to sound positive. "I just came from a meeting with the president; that's when he told me I was going along. This is still your mission, Lou."

"Thank you for saying that, sir, but it can't be, not with you aboard." Jerry opened his mouth to respond, but Weiss held up a hand and kept talking, the words pouring out. "I've seen how you operate, and I've done my best to follow your example. I'd be nuts not to. But I have to be honest. Every time I give an order, my guys will be looking to you for confirmation. You are senior, and you are much more experienced."

Jerry couldn't disagree, but there was more to it. "I don't want the crew looking to me. That moment of indecision could be disastrous. The president told me to back you up, not take over. I won't tell you how to run your boat, Lou. My job is to advise you and help you complete the mission."

Weiss nodded. "And it makes sense for you to come along. You've got more command time and combat experience, not to mention working with UUVs."

"You did good work with them on your last patrol," Mitchell offered.

After a short pause that threatened to get longer, Jerry explained, "If it's any consolation, the president knows exactly what he's asking us to do. I was with Lowell Hardy when he was the CO of *Memphis* and Joanna Patterson was the mission commander—also assigned by a president. That was my first boat, and my first patrol. I watched them *not* work together. It took time, but they hammered out an arrangement that got the job done."

"So that story is true?" Weiss asked.

Jerry shrugged. "I don't know which version you heard, but there was a 'process' both of them had to go through." He smiled. "But they managed to work it out. We can do that, too."

"She wasn't Navy," Weiss observed.

"And she had a lot of learning do to, which we can skip," Jerry countered. "Saves time. Think of it this way—let me be your *consigliore*. You have seen *The Godfather*?" he asked.

Weiss nodded. "Yep, and you'd be a wartime *consigliore* at that."

Jerry relaxed a little, and expanded his idea. "On the trip up, we are going to work out tactics for *Carter* and the UUVs, and drill until they're second nature. If we have any differences, that's when we resolve them. Later on, if things get sticky, or you're looking for a second opinion, I'll be there."

Weiss was considering what Jerry said, but he still looked like a kid who'd just gotten underwear for his birthday. He might really need it, but he didn't have to like it.

Jerry said, "I really don't expect, and don't want to ever give an order when I'm in control. If I do have to give one, I'll expect you to follow it, but that's not how I see things sorting out. Think of me as a coach, prepping you for the big game, and standing by on the sidelines while you run the plays."

"I like the *consigliore* analogy better," Weiss observed. "Thanks for taking the time to talk about this, sir."

"I owe you at least this much, Lou." They shook hands again, then turned back toward *Carter*.

25 July 2021
1900 Local Time
The Admiralty Building
St. Petersburg, Russia

Vasiliy Lavrov was a frustrated man. It had been over two weeks since the *Jimmy Carter* had first arrived in Groton . . . sixteen days, and half that time was spent in a dry dock. He threw the latest report from the embassy's observer back on the desk. The man was nearly useless. He had no way of knowing what was going on, even though he spent many hours each day peering across the Thames River. Once the Americans put *Carter* in a covered graving dock, he no longer had an unobstructed line of sight, and yet he still reported there was evidence work was ongoing.

Rubbing his face to ward off the effects of fatigue, Lavrov struggled to figure out where his analysis may have been flawed. Could it be that he was still right, but mechanical difficulties prevented the spy submarine from heading toward Bolshevik Island? There were plenty of news reports of a problem with the submarine's main propulsion train, and the Americans did move *Carter* into two different dry docks. The observer had taken plenty of photos of the submarine as it was moved first into the dock at the submarine base, and then to an Electric Boat graving dock.

Stretching, he tried to understand the Americans' activities. Was the boat truly suffering from a significant mechanical failure? Or was this just part of a well-run disinformation campaign? Drugov and Komeyev were both convinced the submarine was broken and no longer a concern. Lavrov's instincts couldn't accept that; he had to know what was actually happening. Grumbling, he sent an e-mail to the embassy demanding their observer expand his efforts beyond staring at a covered dry dock from across the river. The captain suggested that the man frequent some of the local bars and listen to the workers' conversation. Perhaps he might learn something that would shed some light on this vexing situation.

13

NEW AND OLD

25 July 2021
1015 Eastern Daylight Time
Graving Dock, Electric Boat Company
Groton, CT

Cavanaugh tried his best to keep out of the way as they prepared for leaving the dry dock. The excited tone he'd heard in the wardroom now infected the crew's conversations, although he still heard a lot of speculation about where they were headed. Ensign Truitt brought him to the sub's office, then disappeared, reappearing while the civilian was just finishing his paperwork. "Here's your TLD . . . a portable dosimeter," he explained, placing it in Cavanaugh's hand. "Wear it at all times when you're up and about the boat. Just loop it through your belt." Truitt pointed to his own on his waist. "But I'd recommend having the case under your belt. You're less likely to snag it on something. And trust me, there are a lot of somethings to snag on a submarine."

"Yes, I've discovered that," Cavanaugh replied, reminded by the aches in his shin and shoulder.

Truitt smiled. "So, ready for a quick tour? This won't be very detailed; it's just to show you how *Jimmy*'s laid out."

"Do you have the time right now?" Cavanaugh wondered. Everyone seemed to be in a hurry.

"My guys are ready. Actually, it was going to be my turn to take her out, and normally I'd need some time to prepare for that, but the skipper decided that my boss, Lieutenant Commander Norris, will take her out of the dry dock." Truitt scrunched up his face a little and intoned, " 'There will be ample training opportunities later.' "

Cavanaugh had to laugh at the ensign's impersonation. It was very bad, but still clearly recognizable as CDR Weiss. "Has the Captain ever seen your impression?"

Truitt grinned. "Why do you think I'm still an ensign?" He gestured toward the office. "This is a good place to start. We're about as far forward as you can get. The only things in front of us are the three main sonar arrays, basically one big ball that is passive, listens only, with a smaller active array under it. The third is a low frequency bow array, a series of hydrophones that wraps around the entire front end of the boat." He pointed down. "The torpedo room is below us. Follow me."

It was only a few steps to the control room. Cavanaugh had seen enough submarine movies to recognize it immediately, although it was not as spacious as he'd imagined. It wasn't manned, of course, but crewmen—and women, he noted—were busy at different terminals. "We're right under the sail," Truitt explained, then pointed a single cylindrical pole in the middle of the room. "We only have one traditional periscope now. The other is a photonics mast that doesn't penetrate the pressure hull. Both feed that console over there, but we can route the output to one of many video displays." Cavanaugh wanted to ask questions, but Truitt kept moving.

The civilian did his best to listen as he followed the young officer, who moved easily through the passage, barely wide enough for two people to pass each other if they turned sideways. The "bulkheads" and "overhead" were cluttered with boxes and cabling, with faux wood paneling and green-painted metal underneath. Truitt smoothly dodged people and obstructions, while Cavanaugh seemed to mutter "Excuse me" to everyone he met. For their part, the crewmen often answered with, "Welcome aboard!"

Past the control room was the "hab" area, with berthing, the galley, and the wardroom, then the "Ocean Interface Hull Module," the special one-hundred-foot section that was added during *Carter*'s construction.

It could launch and recover remote vehicles or underwater swimmers, although Truitt said there were no SEALs embarked right now. "I wonder if any will show up before we leave tonight," he mused aloud, with a sidelong look at *Carter*'s guest. Cavanaugh remained silent.

Next was a short section of passageway with comparatively empty sides, but strangely enough, a heavily framed glass port in the deck. Truitt invited him to look through it. "This is the tunnel. It connects the ocean interface module with the engine room. That's the reactor under us. This space is heavily shielded, of course, but don't lounge around in here if you can help it." Cavanaugh looked through the yellow-tinted window and saw several large shapes surrounded by pipes. It wasn't obvious which blob was the reactor. Truitt quickly pointed out the various components. The army engineer still wasn't certain what he was looking at, but appreciated Truitt's attempt to identify the bits and pieces. He led Cavanaugh toward the other end of the passage, which opened out into a space three stories high and just as wide. They stood on a grating on the upper level, looking down.

Truitt gestured, pointing aft toward the tangle of piping and machinery. "Everything from here back to the pumpjet belongs to engineering, and has something to do with making us move or keeping the lights on." He pointed out different parts of the "steam cycle," starting with two huge valves that sent steam from the reactor compartment, or RC, to the massive turbines, the condensers that converted the steam back into water, and dozens of pumps that tied it all together.

Cavanaugh asked, "Can I come back here when we're at sea?" He found himself fascinated with seeing an actual nuclear reactor and the machinery that drove this steel monster.

"No problem, Doctor. I'm sure the Engineer will give you permission. And now that we're back here, let's visit the aft DC locker and get you acquainted with an EAB." Responding to the civilian's blank look, Truitt said, "It means 'damage control,' and EAB stands for the emergency air breathing system, a respirator mask that you put on if the atmosphere inside the boat becomes toxic."

He now looked worried as well as confused, and as they went down the stairs—*ladder*, Cavanaugh corrected himself—Truitt explained,

"Even a small fire puts out lots of smoke, and in a closed environment there's nowhere for the smoke to go."

They reached a locker labeled "EAB Storage" and Truitt reached inside, returning immediately with a bag that had what looked like a gas mask in it, except for the rubber hose trailing from it. Truitt explained about the emergency air supply piping that ran through the sub, with quick-connect fittings. He showed the civilian how to get the mask on, test to make sure it was tight, and then find and hook up to one of the fittings. "I'm still memorizing where all these fittings are. It's one of the things I have to know before I can get my dolphins." He tapped the empty spot over his right shirt pocket.

"How many are there?" Cavanaugh asked.

"There are 204 manifolds with four or five connections each," Truitt replied instantly. "I also have to be able to draw the piping network from memory, know where the air comes from, and what to do if we need to isolate a manifold." He handed Cavanaugh the bag and helped him stow the mask properly—another thing for the newcomer to practice. "Each space has EABs in it, including your stateroom. It's really a good idea to know where the masks and manifolds are in each space—even if you're not getting qualified in submarines. And don't be surprised if the XO makes you grab a mask and show him you know how to use it," Truitt warned.

It was now almost eleven o'clock, and Truitt got Cavanaugh headed back toward officer's country before taking his leave. He jokingly warned the civilian, "If you see daylight, you've made a wrong turn."

But the main passageway was fairly straight, and once he spotted the wardroom, Cavanaugh's uncertainty vanished. Navigating his way back to "his" stateroom, he opened the door and walked in to find someone else in the middle of changing from a white uniform into the dark blue coveralls Truitt said were called "poopie suits."

Confused, Cavanaugh started to back out, saying, "Excuse me," but then he saw his own belongings, confirming that he was in the right stateroom. Even more confused, he noticed a puckered, circular scar on the other's shoulder.

"No, you're good," the stranger barked as he straightened up, pulling on the coveralls and zipping them closed, and turned to offer his hand. "I'm Jerry Mitchell."

Cavanaugh saw silver eagles on the collar tabs of Mitchell's coveralls. *Mitchell. This is the guy that President Hardy put aboard to run the mission.* "Captain—I mean Commodore . . ."

"Either will suffice, but just Jerry is fine when we're in a private setting. And you're Dr. Daniel Cavanaugh. *Carter*'s captain has already briefed me on your role. I have some questions for you, but there's time for that later."

"Of course—Jerry, anything I can do . . ."

As Mitchell was pocketing different items, Cavanaugh looked for the third bunk.

Jerry saw his confusion, and explained. "I've taken over the XO's stateroom, but you're staying here. I think the XO will be bunking with the engineer on this trip. Rank does have some perks. The only stateroom with more space is the captain's."

"But then shouldn't I move?"

"No. Not only are you a guest on board *Carter*, but your civil service pay grade makes you roughly equivalent to a captain. Not that you'd give him any orders, but technically, you outrank Captain Weiss." He grinned. "So you and I get to split the extra two square feet of floor space in the XO's stateroom."

Mitchell grabbed a clipboard from what was now his desk and said, "I've got to run now, but I would like to get together. Can we meet after dinner?"

"Of course," Cavanaugh answered, and Jerry was out the door.

Cavanaugh nodded as Jerry left, then grabbing the chair by his desk, he sat down, his brain overloaded with all the new information that had just been crammed into it. He tried to organize what he'd learned, where everything was, and sort out who he'd met. It was very different from what he'd expected. His impressions were all of people and technology packed into tight quarters. It was at odds with his first sight of *Carter*'s massive black hull in the dry dock.

As he sat, the excitement faded, and a wave of fatigue washed over him. The morning would have worn him out even if he'd been well rested.

Climbing into the upper bunk was another challenge, but he made it. Truitt said that they started serving lunch in the wardroom at twelve o'clock, which gave him just under an hour for a quick nap.

He missed lunch.

Jerry headed aft to the mission spaces, specifically the UUV bay, passing through the berthing area as unobtrusively as possible. He greeted those he knew by name. There were even a few of *Jimmy Carter*'s crew who had served with him on other boats, including *Carter*'s chief of the boat, or COB. Jerry would chat for a moment with his former shipmates, but always excused himself as soon as possible. Everybody had more than enough work to do, getting ready for the undocking, but more importantly, he didn't want to answer any questions about why he was aboard. The best way to do that was to not give the crew any chances to ask them. Jerry knew he'd have to sit down with Master Chief Paul Gibson eventually and explain what was going on, but that would have to wait. Although, Jerry was confident Gibson already knew he was coming along on the mission.

Carter was doubly familiar to him. Not only had he been aboard as the squadron commander, but he'd also served as navigator aboard *Seawolf*, the first boat of the class. *Jimmy Carter* was the third and last boat of the same class, and differed from her sisters only in having an extra hundred feet hull section added amidships.

The multi-mission bay held, among other things, the UUV hangar and control center. Climbing down the ladder into the hangar, Jerry saw the two UUVs in their cradles. Looking at the blunt, rounded nose, Jerry was sometimes reminded of a loaf of bread; it was eighteen feet long, four feet wide, and painted blue-black. It had an almost square cross-section, which allowed more internal space for batteries and other equipment. The back end was sharply tapered, with a stubby x-tail and a simple five-bladed propeller. In many respects, they were similar to the UUVs he had on *North Dakota*.

The two vehicles sat in large cradles that allowed the crew to service them and then move them to what the U.S. Navy had designated the "Ocean Interface Module." *Carter*'s crew called it the "Hatch."

Besides being used to launch a UUV while submerged, it could also be used as a lockout chamber for combat swimmers.

As Jerry entered the space, officers and enlisted men were clustered around the UUV named José. A stack of metal cylinders, the acoustic beacons, lay to one side. LT Kathy Owens, *Carter*'s weapons officer, stopped what she was doing and came to attention as he came in. She didn't salute, of course, since they were indoors. The others kept working. A chief petty officer held a tablet that was connected by a cable to José. As he typed commands with the tablet, a petty officer lying underneath the vehicle's payload bay reported the results.

"We're making good progress with the beacons, Commodore," Owens reported brightly. She was short, even for submariners, with curly hair that threatened to explode out from under a blue ball cap. "I've still got my techs working on them. The beacons all work, of course, but my guys are making doubly sure they're watertight, programming in the unique ID codes, and disabling the 'pinger' mode. Transponder only."

"Good. How about the fit?" Jerry asked, looking at the group working on the UUV.

"No problem, sir. The target transponders are the same diameter as the positioning beacons the UUV is designed to use, but they're just a bit longer. Each vehicle will carry six. We're testing the entire sequence soon, from loading to deployment; if there's any problems, we'll know by this afternoon," she announced confidently.

Jerry nodded approvingly. "That's good. If we need anything else to make this work, it would be nice to know before we're underway. I came looking for a manual, if you've got a spare."

"Of course, sir," she answered and walked past the two vehicles to a cabinet. She pulled out a loose-leaf binder and handed it to Jerry. "This one is up to date, Commodore."

"Thanks. I can have it back to you this evening."

"We have several, sir. Please keep it for as long as you need."

Jerry nodded and headed back the way he came. He settled down in the wardroom to work, after grabbing a fresh cup of coffee. There were few places on a sub for quiet study, and with the civilian in his cabin, the wardroom between meals was an acceptable alternative. The mess stewards were setting up for lunch, so he sat at the side table.

It felt familiar to him, even comfortable. Not only was the wardroom's layout almost identical to the one aboard his earlier boat *Seawolf*, it had the same sounds and even smells as all the other subs he'd ever been aboard. It was an environment he knew so well, and thrived in.

Jerry could never tell Emily how much he loved serving aboard subs. To do so would imply that he didn't miss his family. He did miss them, especially at meals, and in the evening, before going to bed—the times when he wasn't practicing his chosen craft. Even this, poring through a UUV manual for obscure facts, was rewarding, even enjoyable.

After lunch, Captain Weiss had scheduled a meeting to review preparations for the undocking that evening. Jerry debated not even showing up. He wasn't technically part of the evolution, and didn't want to be a distraction. But he wanted to watch Lou at work, and it wouldn't be proper for him to pretend he didn't care.

Counting the sixteen officers and eight chief petty officers crammed into the wardroom, Jerry didn't so much watch *Carter*'s captain at work as listen to him, as well as the reports from the sub's leadership. Weiss marched everyone through the timeline, with everything starting at exactly 2115, when the last Russian satellite disappeared below the horizon.

In dry dock, out of the water, the sub's reactor was of course completely shut down. Weiss spent some time with LCDR Norris, the chief engineer, and LT Hilario, the main propulsion assistant, going over what could be done before they were floated out to shorten the startup process, but there wasn't much they could do. "We've already begun warming up the primary system, but the fact is, we don't have enough time to get us to the normal startup temperature. So, we'll use the emergency diesel and the EPM to get us moving down the river while we finish heating up, and then bring the reactor critical."

Jerry heard a few soft groans. The emergency propulsion motor wasn't very powerful, and that meant slow slogging, but Weiss continued. "Yes, I'm aware this will be a slow egress. Three knots, max. We can't go much faster than five knots down the river anyway, at first, and our top priority is to be well away from this dock by 0220, when the next Russian satellite makes its appearance. If we're out of the dock by

2345 as planned, and the boat can answer a flank bell two hours later, that will put us over thirty miles away, counting the current. This gets us through the Block Island Sound and out into the Atlantic before the next imaging satellite gets a chance to take a peek."

Jerry agreed with Weiss's plan of action. It wasn't the most auspicious way to start a patrol, but it would work.

In the end, Jerry didn't say a word until the very end of the meeting, when Weiss asked him, "Commodore, would you like to join me on the bridge during the undocking?"

"That would be fine, Captain."

Jerry stayed busy in his stateroom until just before it was time. He wanted to avoid joggling Lou Weiss's elbow, and was sure that was the right thing to do, but he did feel a little out of touch.

A few minutes after 2100, Jerry left officer's country and headed forward to control. It was fully manned now, although most of the workstations were dark. They would stay dark for a while, too, even after they were in the water and underway.

While in the dry dock, *Carter*'s electricity came from "shore power." That cable would have to be disconnected once they started flooding the dock. Her reactor normally drove two steam-powered generators that provided all the electricity the sub needed, but until it was online, the emergency generator, a large diesel engine, would have to serve. It not only had to power the electric propulsion motor that would move the boat, but the control systems that steered her, cooling water for the diesel and the reactor plant monitoring circuits, as well as continuing to heat up the primary plant. Nonessential systems would stay secured until the reactor could take over.

Jerry went up a deck to the bridge access trunk and climbed up the ladder inside the sail. He was just near the hatch when Maneuvering passed the word over the intercom, "Bridge, Maneuvering. The electric plant is in a half-power lineup on the diesel." Weiss acknowledged the report, and although he didn't sound relieved, Jerry knew that a problem with the diesel generator right now would have shut down the entire evolution.

"Permission to come up?" Jerry asked.

Weiss answered "Granted" almost automatically, as the bridge inter-com reported shore power had been secured and the cables were being removed. They would continue to receive cooling water from shore until the water level in the dock was deep enough to cover the auxiliary sea-water suction ports. *Carter*'s captain was following a checklist even more detailed than Jerry would have used. A phone talker passed other re-ports, and a walkie-talkie buzzed and chirped with reports from the graving dock workers. Lou was fielding the information smoothly, and everything was going according to plan.

Maybe he really didn't need to be here, Jerry thought, but that would be the best of all possible outcomes. He always tried to be ready for the worst.

A hundred feet below the bridge, the dry dock floor was already hid-den by swirling white-frothed water. Floodlights illuminated the streams pouring into the basin from six-foot square sluice valves opened in the dock's floating caisson gate. The level still hadn't reached the keel. *Car-ter* sat on sturdy wooden blocks about six feet off the bottom of the dock, and it would take almost two hours for the sub to float off the blocks.

Normally after coming out of dry dock, a sub, still not much more than an inert mass of metal, would be towed to a nearby dock to finish lighting off its reactor. After that, it would prepare for sea, and leave a day or so later. This time, all the preparations for sea were being done at the same time as the undocking.

"Commodore, thank you again for these nifty PRC-148 secure radio hand sets," exclaimed Weiss in between the stream of reports. "They're much appreciated. Any way we can hang on to these for future use?"

"You're welcome, Captain. But I'm afraid the radios are on loan from a SEAL team. I'm probably just overreacting, but if we're striving to keep this departure as covert as possible, then we need to eliminate the possibility of someone listening in as you give orders to the tug. However, I *will* have to return them."

"Pity," replied Weiss with a disappointed tone. Jerry chuckled.

"Request permission to come up?" The voice sounded a little uncer-tain, but Weiss replied "Granted" and Daniel Cavanaugh clambered up. The bridge watch hadn't been set yet, so there was space for Weiss, Jerry, and Cavanaugh, along with the enlisted phone talker.

"Not a lot of room up here," Cavanaugh commented. He tried to find a corner that would give the others as much space as possible.

Weiss was responding to another report, so Jerry answered, "At sea, it's just the OOD and a lookout in here, what we call the cockpit. The extras, like you and me, ride up on the flying bridge." He gestured to a small platform with railings up behind the bridge. "But subs really don't spend much time on the surface, usually just while leaving port and coming back in."

"I wanted to watch us get underway, but that won't be for a while, will it?"

"It will take about two hours to flood the dock and lift *Jimmy* off the blocks. That tug"—he pointed to a cluster of running lights in the river—"will actually tow us clear. That's when it will be safe for the pumpjet to turn and she can move under her own power."

Jerry was content to answer Cavanaugh's questions, all very basic, about submarines while *Carter*'s captain oversaw the undocking. The civilian had questions about the UUVs, about submarine training, the inevitable question about how deep the sub could go, and how long they could stay submerged.

Lou Weiss chimed in occasionally, and the conversation even included a few sea stories, designed to edify and warn the civilian about the importance of staying on the crew's good side. Submariners had tools, access to really sticky duct tape, and a wicked sense of humor. It passed the time, and Jerry felt the ice was beginning to thaw between him and Lou Weiss. He also learned a little more about their civilian guest—completely ignorant of submarine operations, but curious and intelligent.

They'd all been marking the water's progress as it rose, slower than the minute hand of a clock, but steadily creeping up the sub's flanks. "Right now our ballast tank vents are open, so it's filling them as well as the dock," Jerry explained. "When the water gets high enough, we'll close the vents, and soon after that we'll be afloat."

Cavanaugh watched the tug approach and hook up a towline as Weiss communicated with it over the secure walkie-talkie. The water had risen high enough in the dock to cover the openings in the gate, eliminating the waterfall noise and leaving the tug's diesels the loudest sound. Commodore Mitchell stood silently in his corner, watching the action, evaluating the performance of *Carter*'s CO and crew. Cavanaugh could understand some of the reports Captain Weiss received, but most were a complete mystery to him.

Weiss received yet another report and immediately ordered, "Close all main ballast tank vents." Jerry leaned over and told Cavanaugh, "That's our cue. We should go below now, to make room for the bridge crew."

So the sub was close to actually moving. Things were just going to get more interesting. Hesitantly, the army engineer asked, "Can't I stay topside?" like a kid wanting to watch the late, late movie.

Mitchell shrugged, and looked to Weiss, who nodded. "Just stay where you are for right now," *Carter*'s captain ordered. Cavanaugh nodded happily.

Jerry disappeared down the hatch, to be replaced almost instantly by a lieutenant commander and two petty officers. One petty officer, wearing a harness, climbed up to the flying bridge and clipped a safety strap to a fitting behind him. It hadn't occurred to Cavanaugh until that moment that once the sub began moving, the platform might not be all that steady.

The officer introduced himself. "I'm Tom Norris, the chief engineer. We met below. I'll be the OOD—officer of the deck—once we're underway."

Cavanaugh felt the deck shift a little underneath them. It was so small it could have been dismissed as a vibration, but a second shift, and then a sliding movement followed it.

"And we're off the blocks," Norris announced. Pushing the intercom switch, he reported, "This is Mr. Norris. I have the deck and the conn."

While the EB workers disconnected the auxiliary cooling water connection, two lines on the submarine's bow came taut. The slack also disappeared from the mooring lines that held *Carter* in the center of the dock. Cavanaugh noticed that line handlers had appeared on the hull in front of and behind the sail.

There was still no sensation of movement, but rather one of not being part of the earth anymore. Eddies and currents pushed the hull in different directions, and while the lines kept the sub in one place, she was definitely ready to move.

The radio crackled again, and Weiss confirmed, "Understood, removing the gate." That was clear enough, and Cavanaugh saw a crack at the end of the dock grow wider as the dock's interior connected with the Thames River. He could see no sudden rush of water in either direction. The two levels were exactly the same. Just outside the dock was a tug's stern, loitering smartly in place. Another line was expertly transferred from the submarine's bow to the tug.

The radio crackled again. Weiss smiled broadly and clapped Norris on the shoulder. "And that's it!" he announced happily. "Take us out, Eng."

Norris accepted the secure radio from Weiss and told the phone talker, "On deck, take in all lines." *Carter*'s captain disappeared below, followed by the phone talker, making more room, but Norris took it all in as he moved from side to side, watching the line handlers and the distance between *Carter*'s hull and the dock, now that she was free to move.

"*Tug Paul*, dead slow ahead," Norris ordered, and the tug's rumbling increased. Cavanaugh felt the gentlest of jerks as the towline went taut, and they were moving.

He had half a dozen question he wanted to ask, but knew better than to distract Norris. Even a gentle scrape on the sides of the dock could mean a delay of hours, but more likely days or possibly even weeks. *Carter* wasn't going fast enough for her rudder to work, not yet, and was at the mercy of whatever currents the river sent them.

Norris's head was on a swivel as he tried to judge not only *Carter*'s current position, but where she'd need to be in the next few minutes. The only good direction was straight ahead; anything else was trouble.

Cavanaugh marked their progress by watching the dock slide past. They were moving slightly faster than a walk. He spotted the floodlit opening ahead, and was encouraged, but Norris checked aft, and the civilian was reminded that three-quarters of the sub's length was behind them.

Norris turned and spoke to him, the first time since he'd taken over. "The tricky part is coming up. The river's current will hit us from the side, and the tug will have to compensate."

Cavanaugh nodded his understanding, thinking to himself, *now comes the tricky part?*

Norris ordered, "*Tug Paul*, slow ahead," and waited only a moment for the acknowledgement before resuming his bouncing back and forth motion in the cockpit.

Marking their progress along the dockside, it suddenly changed up from a fast walk to a jog, and the end of the dock seemed to fly past them. He turned to look aft, and knew Norris was doing the same thing on the other side of the sail. Cavanaugh heard Norris give a few orders to the tug, but they were always in a calm voice.

And they were out, as if they'd been launched. In the island of illumination behind them, he could already see the dock gate being closed. If he understood the plan properly, they'd de-ballast the dock, and extend the canvas cover over the end again, so that it would be impossible to tell that USS *Jimmy Carter* was not there anymore.

Norris was now telling the tug what course to take up as they headed south down the river. Then he received word that the sub's pumpjet had been unlocked and the EPM was ready to answer bells. Soon the tug was detached and fell in line astern as *Carter* proceeded down the Thames River's southbound channel at a stately three knots. "The tug will stand by until the reactor's on line, just in case the diesel craps out," Norris explained.

The action seemed to be over, and Cavanaugh asked, "When will we reach the ocean?"

"At three knots, we'll reach the mouth of the Thames River in about forty-five minutes. It will be another hour before we reach Block Island Sound. By that time we should be able to commence a normal reactor startup. An hour later the main propulsion plant will be ready to answer all bells and we'll get to go a lot faster."

Cavanaugh looked around them. Out from under the canvas, there was a quarter moon and clear sky. There was no wind to speak of, just a cool breeze from the sub's movement. The water on either side of the submarine was black as ink, rippled by the sub's passage. He could see lights on shore to either side, but it was hard to tell exactly where the water ended and the shore began.

He looked at his watch, realized it was too dark to read it, then he saw the time readout on the navigational display: 0000—midnight. He should be exhausted. Truitt had said reveille at sea was at 0600, but there was too much to see and Cavanaugh, filled with excitement, was wide-awake. Besides, he'd had that nap.

"Is it all right if I stay up here for a while longer?"

14

APPROACH

Jerry kept his eyes glued to the large flat-screen display. The three icons representing *Carter* and the two UUVs moved slowly along the digital chart as they crept in from the north. They were cautious, watchful.

A day earlier, they'd picked up the sounds of an Akula-class attack submarine. The acoustic traces were faint, but discernable. The low bearing rate suggested she was some distance away. Nonetheless, Weiss adjusted *Carter*'s course to give the Russian boat a wide berth.

The presence of a front line SSN that far west suggested, at best, that the Russians were extending the defensive barrier around the Dragon launcher facility. At worst, they believed an attempt would be made to prevent the covert launcher from becoming operational. Paranoid, these Russians, but with good reason; their entire plan hinged on this facility.

The UUV control center on *Carter* was spacious by submarine standards, with plenty of room for the two control consoles, a command workstation linked to control, and two vertical large-screen displays similar to the ones Jerry had on *North Dakota*. Each control console had two positions, one for the pilot and the other for the sensor operator. In keeping with the UUVs' nicknames, the first console had a photo of the Jeff Dunham character, Walter, and the words "Holy Crap!" taped on the support frame. The other console had a picture of José Jalapeño along with the predictable phrase, ". . . on a Stick," embellishing its framework.

The trio was in a loose inverted V formation, with the UUVs four thousand yards ahead of *Carter*—Walter to the left, José to the right. Jerry glanced at the secure Fathometer readout; the ocean floor was a scant twenty feet beneath the keel. This was a little closer to Mother Earth than he was accustomed to in a submarine, but Weiss and his crew didn't seem too concerned. The plan they'd hashed through on the way up emphasized a low and slow approach.

Five days after departing New London, Jerry held the last of his preliminary planning sessions with Weiss, Dr. Cavanaugh, and *Carter*'s senior leadership. The boat had just passed Iceland to the west, through the Denmark Strait, cutting across the Arctic Circle. So far, there hadn't been any sign of Russian naval or air activity . . . so far. And while this suggested the navy's ruse was still working, neither Jerry nor Weiss were willing to push their luck. *Carter* would randomly slow to fifteen knots every now and then to allow the sonar shack to conduct a thorough sweep before the boat cranked back up to their twenty-five-knot transit speed.

Jerry was in the wardroom enjoying a cup of coffee before the meeting when Cavanaugh walked through the door—his nose still a stark shade of Prussian blue. Jerry quickly looked down at his notes, struggling to suppress his laughter. Poor Dr. Dan was the only "warm body" on board during this trip and the crew had fallen upon him like hungry sharks during a feeding frenzy. Jerry recalled his own Bluenose ceremony on *Memphis*, and shuddered to think how much worse it would have been if he were the sole victim. Unexpected, a memory of Lenny Berg, his shipmate on that patrol, flashed to the front of Jerry's thoughts, and his smile vanished. It was with a feeling of vengeance that he focused his thoughts back on the attack plan. There was a score he intended to settle with the Russians.

Others began to arrive for the session, and soon the wardroom was filled to capacity. Jerry started going over the issues one by one. The biggest problem was, of course, the minefield. *Carter*'s initial survey was incomplete, but what they had collected showed the mines were rather close to each other. Spacing was at most one thousand three hundred yards, usually a little less. The intelligence estimated the mine's passive sonar had a detection range of five to six hundred yards, leaving them almost no room to maneuver between the mines. That is, until Jerry looked closely at the weapon's physical characteristics.

"The PMK-2 is an interesting mine," Jerry began explaining. "Like our old Mark 60 CAPTOR, it's a propelled warhead mine that uses a lightweight torpedo as the payload. In fact, the Russian MPT-1UM Kolibri torpedo is a copy of our old Mark 46. But while these two mines are very similar, there are some differences. First, the Russian mine can be laid in much deeper water, but more importantly for us is that it's over twice as long as a CAPTOR. This is key, as the acoustic sensor is located on top of the mine."

He pulled up a brochure photo of the PMK-2, and with a laser pointer emphasized the mine's size. "The length of the mine is 7.9 meters, nearly twenty-six feet." Jerry then shifted to the next slide with a diagram of a deployed mine.

"Your earlier survey, Captain Weiss, showed the mines are tethered about thirty-three feet off the bottom. When you add in the length of the mine, the passive sensor, way up here, is fifty-nine feet above the ocean floor. Furthermore, the passive sensor only looks upward. Therefore, I believe we can creep in under the mine's acquisition cone if we hug the bottom—a nap of the earth approach, if you will. We'll also come in slow and at ultra quiet, to keep our radiated noise to a minimum. Just in case."

Weiss looked intrigued and gestured toward the screen. "That cone looks like it covers about sixty degrees off the vertical, one hundred twenty degrees overall. If that diagram is even close to accurate, Commodore, then we won't have to take out any of the mines. That would be preferable, as we would remain covert." Then looking over at LT Owens, said, "Sorry, Weps, but I don't think we'll be blowing up a mine on this trip."

Owens visibly pouted while the crowd laughed. Jerry chuckled at the junior officer's feigned disappointment, but he quickly moved on. "Agreed, Captain. But I'd like your sonar techs to go over a number of detection simulations with historic sound velocity profiles and varying acquisition cone size just to make sure we're not missing something obvious. Once we get closer to the minefield, we can do a final check with the actual acoustic conditions."

"You've got that one for action, Mario," chimed in Segerson, pointing to Lieutenant Junior Grade Phil DiMauro, *Carter*'s sonar division officer.

"Yes, sir, we'll get started ASAP. Commodore, I'd like to borrow this material when I brief my division. I'm afraid my artistic skills leave something to be desired," DiMauro replied.

"Not a problem, Lieutenant. Your XO already printed out a copy for you and your people. Get with him after we're done."

"Aye, aye, sir."

Jerry nodded and moved on to his next slide. "Now, getting past the defenses is just the first phase of this operation. Next we need to look at how we're going to destroy the launchers. Dr. Dan, that's your cue."

Cavanaugh stood up and squirmed his way around the tightly packed bodies to move up next to the flat-screen. A number of stifled chortles could be heard bubbling up from around the room.

"Have you finally managed to warm up, Dr. Dan?" teased Segerson.

"Despite your best efforts, Your Majesty, yes," Cavanaugh shot back at his main tormentor. Still, his tone was amiable and there was a wide grin on his face.

"I have no idea of what you're talking about, Doctor," protested the XO. "I thought King Boreas was quite lenient in the trials he demanded of you."

"I'm sure you do. But all of this has convinced me that the rumors I've heard about submariners are absolutely true. You people are certifiably crazy and should be locked up in a padded cell!"

"Nah, that's why they send us to sea," Segerson scoffed. The wardroom erupted again in laughter.

"All right, people, let's move along," chided Weiss. "Please begin, Dr. Cavanaugh."

"Yes, Captain, um, could you bring up the next slide, please." Cavanaugh picked up the laser pointer and drew the crowd's attention to a series of crude diagrams. "Since we left New London, I've analyzed about two dozen possible launcher configurations. The seven shown here are the most likely possibilities. The number of launch tubes considered ranged from four to eight, and each scenario assumes an open, rigid steel frame with columns embedded in concrete slabs. Next slide please.

"Commodore Mitchell and I have studied the estimated timeline provided by the intelligence community, and this construction technique not only provides the necessary load-bearing structure for these very large torpedoes, but it also has the advantage of being easier and faster, since the major components can be manufactured on land and then trucked to the construction site and lowered into place.

"The disadvantages of this are that the Russians have to use human divers to do much of the final construction work. This will be a critical factor in how fast they can build this beast. For us, it means that placing the beacons on the structure will be somewhat problematic. My hope is that the large warhead of the Mark 48 torpedo will compensate for a less than optimum placement."

"Is there anything we can do to alleviate this problem?" asked Owens.

Cavanaugh took a deep breath. "The best way to maximize our chances, Lieutenant, would be to conduct a full survey of the target facility, then pull back and analyze the data before we try to place the beacons. Unfortunately, the tactical situation isn't conducive for this approach, and we'll just have to wing it. That's why we've been doing the detailed number crunching on these scenarios. Once we get an idea of what the launcher actually looks like, we'll match its configuration as best we can to one of the preplanned structures."

"Dr. Dan and I have looked at this at some length," interrupted Jerry, "and I don't believe we can count on having unobstructed access to the area near the launcher. There is the minefield, of course, but it's almost a certainty that we'll have to deal with at least one, and possibly more Russian submarines. ONI has reported that the *Severodvinsk*-class submarine *Kazan* and the Akula II–class sub *Vepr* have been out for some time. They haven't been seen or heard in their traditional gate-keeper patrol areas, so it's a good bet we may run into one of them. Then there is the special purpose submarine, *Belgorod*, that disappeared from Olenya Guba around the same time we left New London.

"Skirting the minefield will restrict our ability to maneuver. That's not an advantageous position to be in should a Russian SSN suddenly rear its ugly head. We can probably sneak inside the perimeter once, but we'd be pushing our luck to try it twice."

Weiss nodded his agreement. "There isn't a lot of sea room around the Dragon torpedo launch facility. If we get caught up in a short-range melee with one or two Russian boats it would be like a knife fight in a closet. I want to minimize the amount of time we have to spend in such tight quarters. We get in, find the launcher, drop the beacons, fire our weapons, and then get the hell out of Dodge. Once the first Mark 48 goes off, all hell is going to break loose."

"Concur, Captain, that is why I think we should change the UUVs's beacon loadout," Jerry declared.

Weiss was momentarily confused; the current plan was to carry as many beacons as possible. "In what way, sir?" he asked.

"The UUVs are currently configured to carry six transponder beacons each. Dr. Dan's analysis indicates that the maximum number of torpedoes that we would need to take out the launcher complex is six; with four being the most likely. Since you've already stated your intention to have two tubes reserved for self-defense, we should only employ six beacons. A one hundred percent redundancy is unnecessary, and I believe we should replace two transponder beacons with NAE Mark 3 acoustic countermeasures.

"This way we can also use the UUVs to get our butt out of the sling, should we run into any trouble. During my engagements in the Sino-Littoral Alliance War, I found a decoy-carrying UUV to be a very handy tactical asset."

Heads nodded all around. "Wise guidance, *consigliore*," responded Weiss.

"UCC, Control. We are five thousand yards away from the minefield," reported the voice through Jerry's headset.

"Control, UCC, aye," he replied. A cold shiver abruptly washed over him, but passed quickly. Jerry had never had to deal with mines during the Pacific war, or during his pursuit of the Indian Akula, so this threat was new to him. And while he was confident that they could slip under the mine's acquisition cone, Lenny Berg's dead boat lying nearby testified to the weapon's effectiveness.

Behind Jerry, hovering near the plotting table, Dr. Cavanaugh kept watch in silence. Being more of an army guy, the paper plot was more useful in helping him to figure out where they were, and where the mines should be.

"José report all contacts?" demanded LT Ben Ford, Walter's pilot. Normally he would be in the chair Jerry was occupying, overseeing the two UUV control consoles, but with the commodore on board, Ford was more than happy to relinquish his spot and fly one of the UUVs.

"No contacts," replied Sonar Technician Second Class Miguel Alvarez.

"No contacts, aye. Walter?"

"No contacts," said Walter's sensor operator, Sonar Technician First Class Lionel Frederick.

"Stay sharp, guys. We should be making contact in about five minutes. Make sure the imaging sonar is in single-frequency mode," ordered Ford. Both sonar techs acknowledged the command and confirmed the setting.

Jerry had pulled up the sonar display for both UUVs on his command console and watched as small rocks, soft coral, and the occasional fish passed through the sonar's beams. Each UUV was equipped with a bow-mounted, high definition 3-D imaging array that operated at a very high frequency. This would be the primary means of identifying underwater objects as the camera and lights had been replaced by the transponder beacons and NAEs in each UUV's cargo module. In the single-frequency mode the sonar had a detection range of just over a hundred and twenty yards, and produced a reasonable picture of anything within its field of view. With the exception of the odd color scheme of the display, the objects appeared as slightly blurry, but easily recognizable images. In dual-frequency mode the range dropped to seventy-five yards, but the resolution improved considerably. And even though the UUVs were actively transmitting, the frequencies they were using were so high that it was unlikely any Russian sensor would be able to hear them.

As the distance to the minefield slowly shrank, Jerry listened to the four operators as they exchanged information with one another. He was impressed with their professional decorum and the finely tuned working relationship. During the workups for this mission, the crew spent a lot of time preparing both the UUVs and the control consoles. Every subsystem was checked and triple-checked to ensure all was in order. And while they understood the seriousness of what they had to do, they still swapped jokes and teased one another while working.

Since he had more day-to-day contact with the two lieutenants, Ford and Lawson, Jerry hung out as often as he could in the hangar and UCC to spend more time with the two sonar techs. Frederick was a particularly interesting fellow. A short and slender African American—no, Jerry had to admit the guy was just plain scrawny, so much so that he made Jerry look big. Frederick was also several years older than his commodore. Given the sonar tech's age and rank, Jerry initially assumed the man had some disciplinary issues. He couldn't have been more wrong.

During one of the numerous casualty drills Segerson ran, Frederick had confided that he had joined the navy at the eleventh hour, fifty-ninth minute mark. He beat the navy recruiting age limit by just a few months, after aimlessly wandering about for most of his early life. Jerry silently wondered how a thirty-four-year-old man would've handled boot camp, "A" school, and then submarine school with snarky adolescents nearly half his age. It didn't take him long to figure it out. In spite of Frederick's small stature, he projected an aura of authority. That he knew his trade cold was obvious, and he expected the more junior personnel in his division to do likewise. Armed with an infectious smile, bright eyes, and a firm but fair leadership style, it was no surprise that the younger sonar techs called him "Pops."

"Conn, Sonar, hold two new contacts. Sierra one four bears one six five, and Sierra one five bears one seven zero. Both contacts appear to be submerged."

The report jerked Jerry back to the here and now. He wasn't surprised that they'd picked up two submarine contacts; they were almost certain Russian boats would be in the area, but detecting them reminded him of the dangerous nature of their mission. Switching to the TB-33 towed array input, Jerry saw the faint narrowband signature build on the waterfall display. After only two minutes, he was pretty sure that Sierra one five was a Type 6 nuclear boat—an Akula-, Sierra-, or Oscar-class sub. That likely meant the special purpose mothership, *Belgorod*. His suspicions were confirmed with the sonar supervisor's next report.

"Conn, Sonar, classify Sierra one five as an Oscar-class nuclear submarine with position-keeping thrusters. Sierra one four is classified as a nuclear-powered submarine with turbo-electric drive and thrusters. Both appear to be stationary and are in close proximity to Sierra one three that bears one six zero."

Jerry heard Weiss acknowledge the report. "Sonar, Conn, aye." So far, so good, no big surprises yet. Suddenly, Frederick's light blue North Carolina Tar Heels ball cap lunged forward toward the console.

"Contact!" he barked. "I hold a mine anchor and cable bearing one six eight, range four thousand one hundred yards from own ship."

"Control, UCC, Walter has detected a mine. Bearing one six eight, range four thousand one hundred yards from own ship. Recommend coming left to one seven zero," advised Jerry.

"Come left to one seven zero, UCC, Control, aye."

Jerry looked past his console to see Ford glancing over his shoulder. "All right, people, here we go. Execute the breakthrough plan, Ben."

"Aye, aye, sir. Slowing Walter down to one knot while maintaining contact on the mine. José come left to one one zero and find the next mine in the line." Lawson acknowledged the order and soon the display showed José starting to cut across *Carter*'s bow. Six minutes later Alvarez sang out. "Contact! Mine anchor and cable bearing one eight zero, range three thousand seven hundred yards from own ship."

"What's the distance between the mines?" Jerry shouted to the fire control technician at the plotting table behind him.

There was only a brief delay as the enlisted man plotted the mines' positions and measured the distance. "Mines are one thousand one hundred yards apart, Commodore."

Jerry nodded and toggled his mike. "Control, UCC. José has detected another mine, bearing one eight zero, range three thousand seven hundred yards from own ship. Distance between the mines is one thousand one hundred yards. Own ship's course looks good."

Carter began inching even closer to the bottom; the secure Fathometer now read just twelve feet. Jerry took a deep breath and whispered softly, "Now we make like Robert Mitchum and crawl our way through the enemy's defenses on our belly," referring to the movie the crew had watched the night before, *The Longest Day*. And at a speed of three knots, *Carter* would cover just three hundred yards every three minutes—this would be a long approach.

For the next half hour, *Carter* crept closer and closer to the minefield. The mine that Walter had discovered was barely one thousand yards away, just off their port bow. There was no idle chatter now, and when a report was made, everyone spoke in hushed tones. Soon, very soon, Jerry would find out if all the analysis they'd done was correct— *Hell of a theory to practice exercise*, he thought. The commodore fidgeted in his seat as he stared at the UUV sonar displays. Walter was holding position, keeping the first mine in view as the larger boat advanced. José had altered course to the south and was now three thousand yards directly in front of *Carter*, scouting the path ahead.

"Contact!" called Alvarez. "Contact bears one six eight, range three thousand three hundred yards from own ship. It looks like some sort of cable."

Looking at José's bow sonar input, Jerry could just make out the line on the silty bottom. "UUV range to target?" he asked.

"Ninety-five yards, sir," was the response; still too far for the dual-frequency mode.

"It looks like the line is running parallel to the minefield. Is the PMK-2 a controllable mine?" asked Lawson.

"Not according to the intel reports," Ford answered.

Jerry was confused as well, and he didn't like it one bit. They needed to identify this object, and fast. "Alter José's course to the east. I want to know what this thing is ASAP!" he ordered.

"Yes, sir, coming to one one zero. Switching to dual-frequency mode."

The moment the sonar mode changed, the line transformed into an obvious cable. To the west, Jerry saw that it kept on going . . . beyond the imaging sonar's range. After watching for a few seconds, he made out what looked like bumps on the cable. There appeared to be four of them, evenly spaced. Then he saw the cable connect with a long cylindrical object. Immediately, Jerry froze with recognition. He knew exactly what he was looking at. Slowly shaking his head, he growled, "Oh shit!"

4 August 2021
1145 Local Time
Prima Polar Station
Bolshevik Island, Russia

The petty officer adjusted the portable heater and then cradled his cup of hot tea. After taking a couple sips of the steaming liquid he glanced at his watch; it would still be another hour and fifteen minutes before he would be relieved. Sighing, he started running through the Sever modules monitoring the defensive perimeter. Even though the system had an automatic detection function, the base commander had instructed the operators to look at the outputs of each module as well. It was dull and boring work, as they hadn't heard anything but ice noise and the loud banging from the construction site for several weeks. The first three modules were clear, but the fourth showed something odd. There was an unusual signal on the audio channel, but it didn't sound like anything he'd ever heard before. The narrowband display had strange diffuse bands of acoustic energy and the bearing to the "contact" was vacillating wildly. He then noticed that the auto-detect feature would momentarily blink and then reset.

Thinking that the module had a malfunction, the operator ran the diagnostic program. When it reported all subcomponents were functioning normally, he ran it again with the same results. Confused, the petty officer flagged the watch center supervisor. "Lieutenant, I have a very weird situation with Sever module four."

"And what would that be, Petty Officer Yolkov?" yawned the officer as he got up from his chair and stretched. It had been a long and uneventful morning and all he wanted right now was a hot meal, then his rack.

"I have a signal on module four, but it looks like nothing I've ever seen. The narrowband display is very fuzzy and the contact's bearing is all over the place." The lieutenant walked up behind the operator and looked at the display. After studying the screen for a moment, he frowned and muttered. He too was puzzled.

"That looks very strange, how long has the module registered this signal?"

"About six minutes, sir."

"And there was nothing before then?"

"No, sir. There was nothing."

"Have you run a diagnostic test on the equipment?"

"Yes, Lieutenant, twice. The module passed both times."

An annoyed grumble escaped his lips as the lieutenant went over to the surface search radar and checked the display. There were no contacts on the scope except the icebreaker and the barge—and they hadn't moved in days. There was absolutely nothing along the bearing to the alerting Sever module. Baffled, the young officer weighed reporting such a bizarre contact. But it was Captain Kalinin's stern warning that anything unusual was to be reported that finally convinced him to pick up the secure phone.

The phone rang only twice. "Captain Kalinin, Lieutenant Zhabin, we have an anomalous acoustic contact on Sever module four."

"Define 'anomalous,' Lieutenant," snapped the chief of staff.

"There is a signal being received by the module, but the frequency and bearing data is unlike anything we've ever seen. There is also no corresponding contact on the radar."

"Is the module malfunctioning?"

"The operator has run the diagnostics program twice and the module passed both times, sir."

"Very well, Lieutenant. Begin recording the signal if you haven't already done so, and pass what data you have to the helicopter operations detachment. I'll order them to go out and investigate."

4 August 2021
0800 Local Time
The Admiralty Building
St. Petersburg, Russia

Lavrov tapped his fingers impatiently on his desk as he waited for the next satellite imagery pass of Groton to be processed. He was old enough to remember when it took nearly a day to get the latest images. Now the raw digital photos were usually available within a few hours. And yet, today that seemed like an eon. The latest report from the embassy stated the situation remained unchanged at the Electric Boat Shipyard. The graving dock was still covered, and the operative reported the bars hummed with rumors of significant engineering problems on the *Jimmy Carter*. The embassy also asked that the "unproductive" and "expensive" collection operation be terminated. It had been two weeks since the American spy submarine went into the graving dock, and there was little point in maintaining the surveillance when all the data said she wasn't going anywhere, anytime soon.

The "ding" from his computer terminal caused his head to snap. He opened the long awaited e-mail and then held his breath as the image was downloaded. As soon as the file opened up he moved the cursor over the Electric Boat shipyard and zoomed in. A quick study of the infrared photo confirmed that nothing had changed since yesterday afternoon's image. Frustrated, Lavrov scrolled over to the New London submarine base just to take a look. Nothing readily appeared out of the ordinary, except that the base seemed to have fewer boats in port than what he thought was normal.

Pulling up yesterday afternoon's naval intelligence summary, he paged through until he reached the deployed U.S. forces section, and that's when it struck him. The number of attack submarines at Groton in the newest imagery was three fewer than the latest intelligence report. Curious, he ran down the list of Atlantic and Pacific submarine bases to see if they showed a similar trend—what he saw sent chills down his spine. He grabbed the encrypted phone and called Drugov.

"Pavel, Vasiliy, I think we have a problem. It looks like the Americans may be on to our plans."

An exacerbated sigh was the first response Lavrov heard. "Vasiliy, we've been over this many times in the last two weeks. The *Jimmy Carter*, by all indications, hasn't left the shipyard and we don't need to waste—"

"Pavel, I'm not talking about the *Carter*!" growled the intelligence officer. "The Americans have put five attack submarines, one cruise missile submarine, and two ballistic submarines to sea in the last twelve hours. Now, unless you know of a nationwide exercise that I'm not aware of, this sudden surge brings their deployed assets to over fifty percent of their strength—and that is on both the Atlantic and Pacific coasts!"

"Are you sure of this, Vasiliy?" asked Drugov hesitantly.

"I just looked at the recent imagery for both the east and west coast bases and compared them with the latest summary report, Pavel, I do know how to count!" Lavrov insisted firmly.

"All right. Bring the imagery and your notes up immediately. I'll fit you into Admiral Komeyev's schedule somehow before he leaves for Moscow." The click on the receiver told Lavrov that Drugov hadn't even waited for his acknowledgement.

Lavrov started printing out the latest imagery, then grabbed the intelligence summary and his notes. If he was correct, and the Americans were sortieing their submarine forces, then they had to have a very good reason for doing so. He feared he knew exactly what that reason was.

15

ROUGH NEIGHBORHOOD

4 August 2021
1200 Local Time
Prima Polar Station
Bolshevik Island, Russia

The helicopter detachment used the airfield office as their headquarters. It was the only properly built structure near the airstrip, and it had the all-important telephone. They tacked status boards and charts to the walls, and worked from laptops. They all slept in prefab huts that had been brought in along with the detachment's equipment.

The four pilots, eight flight crew, the weather officer, and ten mechanics had all arrived a little over a week ago. A hurry-up order from the Northern Fleet headquarters had snatched personnel and machines from wherever they were handy and sent them to the Prima Polar Station on Bolshevik Island to defend . . . something. They weren't quite sure what it was, but orders were orders.

The pilots passed the time in the office. They played cards or chess, received a weather briefing every six hours, and wondered who they'd angered to end up in such a desolate place. Talk alternated between guessing what they were supposed to be protecting and when they would get to go home.

Captain-Lieutenant Stepan Mirsky, the detachment commander, took the call, while the others waited, deducing what they could. After scribbling a few numbers, still holding the phone with one hand and listening, he gave a thumbs-up with the other. The two duty crews started zipping up their flight gear, while the enlisted men left at a run to prepare their aircraft.

Theoretically, the standard was to launch within five minutes, but drills since their arrival had shown six to eight was more feasible, especially since they didn't have as much ground-handling equipment as they would at a regular base. The command pilots, Senior Lieutenants Sharov and Novikov, each grabbed a fresh printout from the weather officer. The two co-pilots and sensor operators didn't wait, but immediately headed out, right after the mechanics, to warm up the helicopters' mission systems.

After a short while, Mirsky, listening and writing, finally responded, "Understood. Logged at 1203," and hung up. Senior Lieutenant Sharov was still scanning the weather report, while Senior Lieutenant Novikov tried to read what Mirsky had written upside down. The detachment leader announced, "Mission orders."

Both pilots came to attention, and Mirsky said, "A Sever acoustic module has alerted, bearing three four two degrees, fifteen kilometers from Center. They confirm it's not a drill. Standard rules of engagement apply. Sharov is the flight commander." The captain-lieutenant handed them each a slip of paper with the information, and added, "If there's something there, find it and kill it."

Sharov could hear turbines spooling up outside, and left the office at just a little less than a run, Novikov sprinted to his own aircraft. Still carrying his helmet, Sharov pulled it on as he reached the left-hand cockpit door. Climbing in, he connected his comm leads in the same motion. Petty Officer First Class Lukin, sitting at the sensor operator's station behind the cockpit, was already reaching for the mission data, and Sharov handed him the paper.

"Red 81 is ready to fly, Senior Lieutenant." Copilot Lieutenant Migulov's voice over the intercom was calm and businesslike. Sharov hadn't flown with his copilot before being assigned here, but standard procedures and a few practice flights had gotten them used to each other. The younger officer was eager to prove himself, and Sharov was happy to have such an energetic second.

The helicopter's engines sounded smooth, and Sharov scanned the instruments carefully before telling Migulov, "Go ahead and taxi; course after takeoff is north-northwest, max cruise." That would get them headed in the right direction while Lukin worked out an exact vector. On the radio circuit, Sharov sent, "Red 81 taxiing," and received two microphone clicks in acknowledgement.

There was a stiff wind, forty-two kilometers an hour, which would make for a very short takeoff run and an equally bumpy ride. Up on the concrete, away from the row of parked helicopters, Migulov turned the machine northwest, facing into the wind, and revved the engine. The helicopter almost jumped into the air.

Sharov barely noticed. The lieutenant would get them where they needed to go. As the mission commander, he was working with the tactical display. A red pip showed where Lukin had already entered the last reported contact, marked "Datum 1."

"Center" was marked as a yellow box on the navigation display. It was a spot about thirteen kilometers offshore. As far as anyone could tell, it was empty water, although they'd seen ships anchored nearby. The helicopter detachment used it as a navigational reference point, although they were instructed to stay at least two kilometers away from the place. It would be nice to know what was there, but for Sharov and the others, it didn't really matter.

A yellow moving symbol showed the position of the helicopter, and as Sharov watched, a second yellow symbol appeared and the course indicators swung right to the course he'd ordered. A symbol on the upper edge of the machine appeared, showing that his aircraft, Red 81, was now data linked to Novikov's Red 50.

They were flying relatively new Kamov Ka-27M helicopters. The design first flew in the eighties, but these machines had been refitted with the Lira antisubmarine system. Normally the Kamovs operated from helicopter pads on the stern of Russian warships, but flying from a land base was also fine. In fact, taking off and landing from a land base was far simpler than the pitching and rolling stern of a ship that was also moving through the water.

"Recommend course three four zero degrees. Passing over Cape Baranova. Recommend first dip point at twenty-seven kilometers, seven minutes at this speed."

"Go to full military," Sharov ordered over both the radio and the intercom. That would increase their speed from 240 kilometers per hour to 270. They were very close; the increased fuel consumption was far less important than getting on top of the contact and beginning the search.

"At full speed, time to dip point is now six minutes." Sharov watched the other aircraft match his speed, a kilometer behind.

The first real bump hit them, and Sharov tightened his harness and returned a few items to their proper places. The airframe rattled, but bulled through the turbulence. Flying this low would be a rough ride, but you can't dip from thousands of meters up. And you had to be low to use MAD as well. They hadn't even bothered to load sonobuoys. They were useful tools for finding subs, but the buoys needed open water. The loose ice around the island, combined with the waves' action, would crush any sonobuoy within moments.

Even dipping would require a little open water. Drills after they arrived had allowed them to figure out just how big the gap in the ice had to be, although it had cost them one sonar finding out. Luckily, openings in the ice five meters square weren't too rare. After all, it was high summer.

"Two minutes to the dip," Lukin reported.

"Red 50, assume a contact will break off to the north."

This time, Novikov answered with a short, "Concur, taking station."

"Prepare for auto-attack."

Novikov answered, "Ready," and Sharov ordered, "Go to auto-attack" on both the intercom and radio circuits.

Lukin was faster, but his acknowledgement was only seconds ahead of Novikov's.

Another symbol appeared at the top of Sharov's mission screen. The helicopters' autopilots were now flying both machines, and would automatically head to the proper dip point, transition to hover, and lower the sonar without any human intervention. Based on which search pattern Sharov chose, it would then calculate the next dip location for each machine and fly there.

The roar of the turbines decreased as the helicopter's symbol slowed, merging with the symbol on Sharov's screen marked "Dip 1." They revved again as the helicopter went into a hover, using full power to hold it aloft and stationary. He watched as Migulov tapped a few keys, and the Kamov crept ahead and slid left a dozen meters to center itself over a patch of open water.

Sharov heard the winch start up at the same time he got Lukin's report. The sonar winch was a big thing, filling half the helicopter's cabin behind the pilots with one hundred fifty meters of stout cable and the one-hundred-and-eighty-kilogram sonar array on the end. An opening in the cabin floor allowed the array body to be lowered into the water, while the operator, Lukin, monitored the procedure.

The winch started and stopped automatically, the Lira system stepping through a standard procedure: Lower the sonar projector to a water depth of twenty-five meters, listen for thirty seconds, then lower it to fifty, listen again, then one hundred, and finally one hundred and fifty meters. The entire sequence took several minutes.

Sharov read the status indicators on the mission display while splitting his attention between the ice-covered horizon, the engine instruments, and Red 50's position, loitering a little to the northeast. It was waiting for Red 81 to finish her search. The results would determine where she had to dip. It was very unlikely that the first dip would be right over a contact, but if Red 81's sonar picked up anything, then Red 50 would do its best to dip closer to the contact. Working as a team, the helicopters would use leapfrog tactics to first detect, then localize, and finally attack any submarine in the area. Assuming there was anything to find.

"Passive search completed, no contacts," Lukin reported. "Request permission to go active." If their sonar didn't hear anything, then they could send out active pulses to look for a very quiet contact.

"Yes, go to active search."

1215 Local Time
USS *Jimmy Carter*

The intercom report was expected, but it still startled everyone in UCC. "Conn, Sonar. Active sonar, bears one seven one degrees." While Cavanaugh was still trying to figure out where that was in relation to everything else, LT Ben Ford immediately ordered, "Walter, José, all stop, and hug the bottom." Behind Ford, the commodore gave a small nod of approval.

As Petty Officer Alvarez typed on José's console, Petty Officer Frederick sang out, "Walter holds the active sonar at one eight six degrees." Alvarez gave the bearing from José seconds later. Jerry pointed to the fire control technician at the geoplot, instructing him to plot the bearings and get a position on the helicopter that was pinging away.

Sonar came back on to announce, "Conn, Sonar. Active sonar is classified as a Lamb Tail. It's unlikely that they detected José. No chance of seeing Walter, and own ship is well out of range."

A moment after that Jerry reported over the intercom, "Control, UCC, we've got a three-point fix on the Lamb Tail. It's two thousand one hundred yards to the south of José. Recommend sending José northwest before bringing him back. Own ship should also head west."

Weiss's voice came up on the circuit and responded "Concur, changing course to the west."

Cavanaugh felt the deck shift slightly. *Carter* had started turning.

"Commodore, what kind of sonar is a Lamb Tail?" he asked, breaking his long silence.

"It's a NATO code name for a dipping sonar. It's a high-frequency set, and relatively short-ranged, but putting it on a helicopter makes it very mobile, and of course we usually can't hear the helicopter until it puts the sonar in the water and starts pinging."

"And it didn't detect the UUV," Cavanaugh stated hopefully.

"No, or his partner would already be dipping on top of José, and we would be in a very different situation," Mitchell explained.

"His partner?"

"ASW helicopters operate in pairs, usually from ships, but these were probably flying from the island."

"Why didn't the active sonar detect the UUV?"

"Like *Carter*, the UUVs have anechoic coating that absorbs active sonar pings, reducing the amount of energy that is reflected. That can cut the detection range by roughly half. And since the UUV is very small, was moving slowly, and was close to the bottom, the acoustic processor would have a hard time telling José from a rock. Just to be sure, LT Ford had them put José on the bottom and stationary until the sonar stopped transmitting. Right now, the two helicopters are positioning for another dip. They'll listen first, and then if they don't hear anything, they'll ping."

"Then shouldn't the UUV shut down its own sonar?"

"No, it doesn't need to. José and Walter use really short-range, very high frequency sonars. They operate at several hundred kilohertz, but the Lamb Tail is transmitting and listening at twelve to fourteen kilohertz. It simply can't hear the UUVs' sonar, the same way we can't hear a dog whistle.

"Same thing goes for the acoustic modems that allow us to communicate with the UUVs. They don't operate anywhere near as high as the imaging sonar, but the modem frequency is still up there and is outside the frequency range of the dipping sonar. That and the transmissions use pseudo-random noise sequencing to hide the signal."

"And the sensor can't change the frequency it listens to?"

"Nope," Jerry announced confidently. "They'd have to have a separate receiver. And it's hard to passively search for sounds at such high frequency. Remember, Doctor, the higher the frequency, the greater the attenuation loss. The UUVs use it for close-range navigation and imaging, so range doesn't matter as much. Its best range is just over a hundred yards. The Lamb Tail is a dedicated search sonar. It can see and listen to contacts several thousand yards away . . ."

"And *Carter*'s sonar is even lower-frequency, for greater range," Cavanaugh concluded. The physics made sense, once he remembered to apply it properly.

"Lower frequency means larger size, too. The UUV's sonar transducer is the size of a microwave oven. The Lamb Tail's sonar is the size of a mini refrigerator. And *Carter*'s active bow array is like a big hot tub by comparison."

During their discussion, José had been motoring west at a brisk four knots, but still just off the bottom.

The intercom chirped "UCC, Control. Report status of comms with Walter?"

Jerry relayed the request to team Walter, and Petty Officer Frederick checked the display. "We're good, sir. Signal strength is still strong, but I'd recommend limiting any transmissions. At least for now."

"Very well, have Walter head west at slow speed and secure communications." Clicking his mike, Jerry replied, "Control, UCC. Comms are good, however, we are securing them for the time being. Walter has been ordered to head west."

1225 Local Time
Red 81
Northwest of Bolshevik Island

Sharov put in a search axis of three five zero, based on nothing more than a guess. Standard tactics was to dip on each side of the axis, with an interval just slightly less than twice the sonar's detection range.

The sonar contact had been northwest of Center. While there was more open water straight north, the intruder might zig west instead of zagging north. The Lira combat system calculated the two next dip points, based on the sonar conditions and the contact's estimated speed, which Sharov believed was slow. Both helicopters would go active simultaneously this time, but Sharov had biased the dip points so that the sonars' detection ranges just barely overlapped.

The air was still rough, and he kept one eye on the engine instruments. He'd heard stories of turbulence shaking things loose, and considering how low they were to the water, there would be little time to correct, or even autorotate down if the engines failed. They wore immersion suits, which would give them a little time in the water before they died of hypothermia, but hopefully long enough for Red 50 to fish them out.

Sharov shook off those thoughts. That was one problem with the new Lira system. There was time to think now, while the computer ran the search. *Focus on the hunt*, he thought to himself.

Looking out his left cabin window, he saw Red 50 in the distance mimicking his own helicopter's motions, smoothly slowing and settling into a hover, then the transducer array appeared under the fuselage. It took about ten seconds for it to disappear below the water's surface.

1230 Local Time
USS *Jimmy Carter*

"Two separate Lamb Tail signals this time," Sonar announced over the intercom. Petty officers Alvarez and Frederick fed the bearings from their UUVs in turn to the geoplot.

"Control, UCC. We've got two three-point fixes. The eastern helo doesn't have a chance of picking up José, so you can angle him toward us as soon as they stop pinging. Walter's course is good."

Jerry paused to study the tactical display, and jumped out of his seat to inspect the paper plot. Then keying the switch, he said, "Control, UCC, the other helo to the northwest is not close to either UUV, but it's closer to own ship. I recommend increasing speed on both UUVs to eight knots so we can get some sea room."

Weiss's voice responded only a moment later. "Concur. Increase UUV speed to eight knots."

Cavanaugh actually understood what they were doing and why. Because of the modem's limited range, they could only get so far away from the UUVs, so moving the remotes faster allowed them to close the distance between them and *Carter*. But what if the Russians heard the UUVs? He started whispering to Mitchell, then stopped himself in mid-word and began again in a normal voice. "Aren't you worried about the helicopter sonars hearing the UUVs' propeller noise?"

Jerry made a face, but shook his head. "No. We ran the numbers several times. Unless they've done something to dramatically increase the sonar's sensitivity—and I mean a lot—we should be fine. Not only is the Lamb Tail not that sensitive, but between the shallow water and the ice chunks, this is a noisy environment. Also, the UUVs use a permanent magnet electric motor. Not as many moving parts to make noise."

Cavanaugh could understand that. "And a three-point fix is accurate, right?"

"Yes, it does mean an accurate fix, but it should really be called a 'three-bearing fix,'" Jerry apologized. "It means we have three sonar bearings to the source of the sound, one from *Carter* and one from each UUV, and that they all cross at the same point. Of course, you only need two bearings to get a fix, but the third one is nice to have. Three bearings won't automatically give you a perfect fix, though. If the bearings are fuzzy, you can end up with a triangle, and all you know is that the source is somewhere inside."

1240 Local Time
Red 81
Northwest of Bolshevik Island

Novikov announced "No contacts" over the radio, which was really unnecessary. Obviously, he would have reported a sonar hit immediately. Sharov interpreted the transmission as "What next?"

This was why it was important to pay attention to the search. Assuming there was something to find, and Sharov always assumed there was something to be found, it was within a circle of uncertainty that was constantly expanding at the contact's speed. It was likely the contact wasn't moving all that fast or their passive sonar search would have heard it, but time wasted planning their next move meant a larger area to look in. Sharov posited a low speed for the intruder, no more than ten knots, but plugging that value into the formula for the area of a circle still meant that time was against him.

He had already decided what to do if they didn't find anything with their current dip. Responding to Novikov's transmission, he entered a new search axis into the Lira computer, and announced, "New axis is due north, double interval."

Red 50 acknowledged with his customary two clicks on the microphone switch, and his helicopter peeled away. Perplexed, Migulov asked,

"I can see the contact trying to go north. If he tries to evade west he'll just get trapped against October Revolution Island. It's too close. But why the double interval?"

Sharov smiled. "What if our underwater friend knew it would take five or ten minutes for us to respond? What if he sprinted for several minutes and then slowed to creep speed?"

His copilot responded, "And you're hoping to catch up."

"Or get ahead of him."

Migulov shrugged. "At this point, one patch of water is as good as another."

Sharov shook his head, disagreeing. "No, Lieutenant. I am looking for one very special patch."

They reached the new dip points almost at the same time, and Sharov thought that the Lira system delayed Red 50's dip until his Red 81 was also in position.

"Listening," Lukin reported.

1250 Local Time
USS Jimmy Carter

Lieutenant Ford was marking the time. "He's probably dipping again," he estimated.

"Concur," Mitchell answered.

Cavanaugh reasoned, "That means he—I mean, they are listening for us now, before they start pinging again."

Jerry nodded. "It's likely, given the time between the first two active searches. That's about how long it takes the helo to lower and listen first."

"But we don't know where they are."

The commodore nodded again. "They only reveal their position when they ping. But we're at creep speed, and remember the captain ordered 'Ultra Quiet.'" Mitchell turned to Lieutenant Ford. "How close does a Lamb Tail have to be to hear *Carter* passively?"

Ford picked up and read from a clipboard. "In these conditions, with us creeping and at ultra quiet, four hundred yards for a fifty percent chance of detection. It's theoretically possible out to about nine hundred, but beyond that, we're lost in the ambient noise."

"And if they go active?" Cavanaugh asked.

"Effective range? About 3,500 yards, but they could still get a sniff out to about 4,200," Ford replied, reading from the clipboard.

Cavanaugh was surprised at the difference between the passive and active ranges. "That's an impressive difference."

"It's really their best tool in this environment," Ford remarked casually. "It isn't affected as much by the ice noise, but the shallow water depth is to our advantage."

The intercom announced, "Conn, Sonar, one . . . no, two active sonars bearing two eight six and zero eight four."

Cavanaugh now knew to wait for the sonar cross bearings to figure out the dippers' new location. It only took a moment for the computers and the human to plot the different bearings.

Jerry reacted while the civilian was still trying to understand the display. "Control, recommend immediate course change to two nine zero! Dead slow, and as deep as you dare go!"

Two nine zero was staring straight at the nearest dipping helicopter to *Jimmy Carter*. Then Cavanaugh saw the range: thirty-nine hundred yards. A biting shiver did laps up and down his spine.

The intercom answered with a simple "Concur," and the deck tilted again, this time in more than one axis.

Jerry saw the civilian's panicked expression, and spoke matter-of-factly, "The other one's safely out of range, but that near one, he's a problem." He shrugged. "The turn will put us bow-on to the active sonar, so we will send back a smaller echo, but it also means we get closer to him. Sort of a game of chicken."

Cavanaugh had suppressed his original reaction, but he couldn't hide his worry. "When will we know if they've spotted us?"

"If the one in front of us keeps pinging and the other one stops. That'll be a good clue that we've been picked up," Jerry answered.

According to the clock, the two Russian helicopters pinged for about thirty seconds. To avoid thinking about what being found would mean,

Cavanaugh did math. At a dead slow speed of two knots, in thirty seconds *Jimmy Carter* would cover just thirty-three yards. It was glacially slow, but they were still moving toward the searching helo, reducing the range. They didn't dare turn. That would present a broad aspect to the sonar array, and they'd send back a bigger echo. He decided it was like slow-motion chess, with explosives.

Moments later, both sonars stopped pinging, and next to him, Cavanaugh saw Mitchell exhale. The commodore explained, "Standard tactics for the dippers would be for the helicopter with a good contact to guide the other one to a spot right on top of us, or as close as possible. That's the 'leapfrog' tactic. If they get a solid contact, it's very hard to escape, because they can move at better than a hundred knots. They're impossible to outrun."

Cavanaugh felt the deck tilt under him again, and Jerry, surprised, turned back to study the displays. *Carter* was turning south.

Even as he reached for the intercom switch, Weiss's voice ordered, "UCC, Control. I'm turning to close on José and Walter. Compute an intercept course for the UUVs to us based on a course of two four zero degrees at five knots. We'll collect them ASAP and get out of here."

Cavanaugh saw Mitchell pull up short, then look hard at the tactical display. He frowned, which turned into a scowl. Finally his expression became less severe, but remained unhappy. He pressed the intercom switch. "Control, UCC, strongly recommend immediate new course to the northwest at a fast creep. Meanwhile, we program the UUVs to go to the bottom and remain stationary. We can pick them up later, after the helicopters leave."

The reply was immediate. "UCC, Control, the UUVs are mission critical. We can recover them safely." Weiss's voice was neutral, but everyone realized he was disagreeing with the mission commander.

"We don't know when, or where, the helicopters will dip next," Jerry argued.

"Likely to the north, Commodore, while we zig southwest. Computed intercept to José is five minutes, Walter is nine."

"They're just as likely to start dipping randomly within their uncertainty circle. They've got nothing but the initial contact to go on, so from this point on, we can't predict where they'll search," Jerry protested.

"With the uncertainty area expanding, the odds are in our favor." Weiss sounded confident.

Jerry sighed. Cavanaugh could see that he was worried. Was it about being detected, or his reluctance to issue a direct order? The commodore could simply tell Weiss what to do, but he knew that was the last thing Mitchell wanted. And of course, the crewmen in control and UCC were hearing this as well. What would they think if their skipper was overruled?

Finally, Jerry pressed the switch again. "Concur the odds are low, but they're not low enough. With your plan, we will have three moving contacts for the helicopters to find, instead of just one. Also, we'll have to stop to recover each UUV. If they find us while that's going on, we are done for. The Helixes only have—what? Another hour and a half of fuel until they go home, hopefully without finding anything."

Jerry paused, but kept the intercom switch pressed. He added, "We can't risk a second detection. It's not enough to just evade contact. We have to convince them it was a false alarm—that there was nothing to find in the first place."

Jerry released the switch, and waited for Weiss's response. From the commodore's expression, Cavanaugh saw that Mitchell was willing to overrule *Carter*'s captain if he had to, but he wouldn't be happy about it. Was Weiss weighing his superior's arguments, or the effect on his authority if he was countermanded?

It seemed to take forever, but it was only a few seconds, according to the clock. "UCC, Control. Concur. Ordering new course three three five at five knots. UCC, program the UUVs to go to ground for later recall."

4 August 2021
0900 Moscow Time
The Senate Building, Kremlin
Moscow, Russia

Defense Minister Aleksandr Trusov was the second most powerful man in the Russian Federation. He spoke to others with Fedorin's voice, and he told Fedorin whatever he heard. It wasn't simply a matter of being loyal, or a toady to the president. Trusov was a good listener, and was careful about when to wield the president's authority. Yes, Fedorin demanded complete loyalty, but he also demanded competence.

And good teams need to complement each other. Trusov would never have Fedorin's ambitions, or his ability to see a path from their present to a greater future. His skill was in finding ways to anchor the president's dreams in reality. They were great dreams, and Trusov believed in them wholeheartedly.

Fedorin knew he needed Trusov, and respected his ability, but he sometimes chafed at the restrictions the real world, incarnated as Trusov, placed on him.

He was chafing now, more properly worried, as a hundred different actions began to converge on a single goal. If their plan didn't work, Russia would sink even further into ruin. Fedorin was taking the risk because he believed his homeland was headed there anyway, unless he acted.

Fedorin's office was on the third and highest floor of the Kremlin's historic Senate Building, first built in the late 1700s. While the exterior remained as it had been built, numerous renovations had destroyed most of the original internal structure. Trusov saw hints of the building's past in glass exhibit cases, mixed in with the portraits and banners that decorated the corridors.

The entire building was considered a secure site, of course, and even Trusov had to submit to a scan and show his identification before being allowed enter the dedicated elevator for the president's third-floor office complex.

The outer offices were bustling, and the presidential security detail checked him one last time before admitting him to the inner office.

Even, then, the president's personal secretary asked him to wait while she announced his arrival.

Fedorin's working office was large, of course, lined with wooden, glass-fronted bookcases and illuminated by a grand chandelier that highlighted a vaulted ceiling.

A large table with a settee on each side sat in front of a massive desk. The president sat at the table, surrounded by stacks of documents. He was wearing his glasses, which he rarely did in public, and studying a heavily annotated map of Europe. A side table held the remains of his breakfast.

It was the president's custom to work late into the night, and then rise early. Trusov's regular daily briefings, usually three, were like the chimes of a grandfather clock. The 0900 briefing marked the beginning of the president's workday.

"Results from the latest round of snap drills, Comrade President." They used the euphemisms "snap drills" or "exercises" to refer to the armed forces' preparations for the invasions of the Baltic States, Georgia, and Ukraine. In truth, if for some reason the attack was canceled, then this was indeed just a massive exercise.

He offered Fedorin a multipage document, but the Russian president waved it off. "Good news or bad, Defense Minister?"

"More good than bad, sir. The Twentieth Army has made up some of its lost progress. Another seven field-grade or higher officers have been relieved for dereliction. They all failed in their duties."

"From the Twentieth?" asked Fedorin, alarmed.

"No, sir, please excuse me. That is the total from all the branches of the armed forces over the last week. Three from the Army, two from the Navy, and one each from the Air Force and the Strategic Rocket Forces."

"Make sure word of their fate is well-known, Minister Trusov." Fedorin paused, then added, "We are too weak to leave any of that rot in place. How many were for drunkenness?"

Trusov sighed. "Three, Comrade President."

Fedorin glanced over at the side table. A tray held a crystal service with a decanter full of vodka in the center. The president drank little, but many of his visitors showed less restraint. "'Vodka spoils everything except the glasses,'" he quoted.

Trusov tried to sound positive. "It's much better than when we started, Comrade President. Discipline is improving. And so far, the only country to react decisively is Estonia. They've ordered a full mobilization."

Fedorin smiled, then actually laughed. "The mighty Estonian army. That's it?"

Trusov nodded. "Partial mobilizations in the rest of the NATO countries, and they're still arguing over whether or not units should be deployed to the Baltic States. Everyone's assuming the United States will step forward and commit the bulk of the forces. There are signs that the United States may be preparing a large 'no notice' exercise of its own."

"This is based on?"

"Signals intercepts and spies, mostly relating to long-term logistics, slightly higher than usual naval deployments. It's apparently still in the early stages"—Trusov smiled—"and of course, it's pointless."

"All the more embarrassing when we force them to cancel it," Fedorin predicted. Then his smile disappeared. "What of the progress at Bolshevik Island?"

"It's going well, Comrade President. The Project 09852 submarine *Belgorod* and *Losharik* have been assisting with the installation of the Drakon weapons being brought in separately by icebreaker. They are on schedule for completing the loading and testing process by eighteen August. The antisubmarine forces are in place, and aside from a few false alarms, no contacts have been reported."

"False alarms?" Fedorin asked.

"From the Sever sensor net," Trusov explained. "One of the acoustic modules will on occasion report a detection." He saw Fedorin's face, and the president started to rise from the settee. Trusov held out a hand. "Each detection is thoroughly investigated by helicopters, and so far all have proved to be false."

"I don't know if I like a warning system that is prone to false alarms," Fedorin muttered angrily.

Trusov was unconcerned. He'd studied the matter in depth. "It's a question of sensitivity, sir. A passive acoustic sensor capable of hearing a modern submarine will sporadically pick up enough random noise to signal a detection. Within reason, the greater the sensitivity of the sensor, the more false alerts, but also the better the chance of detecting a real enemy."

Fedorin frowned. "That sensor net and the minefield are the only things guarding our greatest asset, and what I hope is still our greatest secret." Trusov knew Fedorin had been greatly upset by American President Hardy's public exposure of the Drakon system. It had shaken his faith in their security, and was the only thing that had seriously threatened the upcoming operation.

Hardy's announcement had caused Fedorin to momentarily question relying on the new torpedo-missile complex and pushing up the timetable for the army. Trusov had spent a long night with the president, reviewing their campaign, trying to imagine what else could go wrong, and what the Americans could do with their knowledge of the weapon. It didn't take long for Fedorin to regain his confidence in the operation.

"I don't like it, Defense Minister. We need to do more to make sure those false alarms are just that, and not a Western submarine poking around where it shouldn't. Our whole plan hinges on that facility, and it is at its most vulnerable point!"

"I understand, Comrade President. A second group of ASW helicopters and support equipment is being organized right now. It should arrive the day after tomorrow."

"Why is it so hard to get helicopters to Bolshevik Island? The Navy has dozens in the Northern Fleet alone!" Fedorin was clearly irritated.

"Most have been assigned to Northern Fleet warships in preparation for the operation. The ones sent to Bolshevik Island were spare aircraft, or those just coming out of a modernization overhaul . . ."

"I don't care if we lose half the fleet to submarine attacks!" Fedorin shouted angrily. "That facility is the key to everything, and its defense must have the highest possible priority."

"A larger helicopter detachment could draw attention, and will need more flights to supply them. Those may be hard to conceal," argued Trusov.

"Do it!" Fedorin ordered peremptorily. "What about submarines?"

"Both the attack submarines *Vepr* and *Kazan* are on station, watching the western and northern approaches to the island."

"Move them in closer to the island, as soon as possible. Position one within striking distance of monitoring arrays. Maybe it can catch the next 'false alarm' that appears."

"Yes, Comrade President."

"And while you're at it, have naval intelligence do a complete check of all Western submarines. Positively confirm the location of any that are capable of reaching the Arctic."

16

MAKE A HOLE

4 August 2021
1400 Local Time
USS *Jimmy Carter*

They moved well away from the island to the north and west. The water wasn't that deep, just a little over one hundred fathoms, and Weiss hugged the bottom. *Jimmy Carter* couldn't actually sit on the bottom like World War II submarines could. Back then, subs did it to save battery power, as well as hide from active sonar, but nuclear submarines used cold sea water—a lot of it—to condense the steam after it had spun the ship's turbines. The intakes for the main seawater pumps were near the bottom of the hull, and if *Carter* got too close to the bottom, she could start vacuuming up silt, clogging the whole system and possibly losing propulsion.

At Weiss's orders, the sub remained at ultra quiet, creeping at bare steerageway as close as he could to the sea floor. LT Kathy Owens was the officer of the deck, and she ordered random zigzags, on the outside chance anyone had detected the sub and was trying to track it. Unlikely as that was, *Carter*'s crew was taking absolutely no chances. They might be in international waters, but they were certain the Russians would shoot first and explain later.

Setting ultra quiet was a mixed blessing. It reduced the submarine's noise signature, but it also adversely affected normal operations. Those not on duty were confined to their bunks, reading or catching up on their sleep. No maintenance or repair work was allowed, and the galley was limited to simple meals that didn't require cooking. Maintaining the submarine's trim became difficult, since the pump used to shift water from one variable ballast tank to another had to be used sparingly.

Jerry had come to control to consult with Weiss; a face-to-face discussion was preferable to debating over an IC circuit. Dr. Cavanaugh had followed the commodore and, with the OOD's permission, remained in control, silent and still. He listened to the sonar reports as they tracked the Russian helicopters' search. While the Russian Lamb Tail sonar could detect a sub only a few miles away, the pinging could be heard much farther. The control room watch plotted the bearing of each dip, and compared their results with the plot in UCC, watching for changes that showed them getting closer to *Carter*'s position.

Meanwhile, LT Owens had to solve a word problem: "If two helicopters with endurance X were detected at time Y, when will it be safe to return and recover José and Walter? Show your work. You will be tested on the material."

Their intelligence pubs told them how much fuel the helicopters could carry, and they knew where the airstrip on the island was located. Commodore Mitchell, the only one on the boat with actual aviation experience, told her about how much fuel the helicopters would likely keep in reserve, which shortened their time aloft somewhat. Then factor in the travel time back, as well as the detection range of the sonar, if they were listening.

She reported to Weiss, "I compute turnaround at 1445, and ETA for rendezvous with Walter at 1530, assuming we tell the UUVs to wake up and close on our position at four knots." Although speaking to Weiss, she did glance over to the commodore, who stood well off in a corner of the control room, pretending to study a tactical display.

Still watching Owens's report, Cavanaugh quietly slid over next to Mitchell and asked, "What if they send another pair of helicopters to continue the search?"

"Then we'll hear more pinging after the first two should have gone home," Jerry responded. "But it's unlikely. From the Russians' point of view, all they had was the initial contact from that fixed acoustic sensor. They sent out a pair of aircraft to check it out, and found nothing. False alarms are a fact of life for any sonar system."

"But what if the next pair are just listening?" Cavanaugh persisted.

"Remember the difference between active and passive ranges," Jerry countered. "They'd have to be listening in exactly the right spot. There is a small risk in going back at all," he admitted, "but we're fighting the clock. I'm confident we'll be able to recover the UUVs safely. The larger question is what we're going to do about those *ublyudok* sensors."

"Can you speak Russian?" Cavanaugh asked. As capable as Commodore Mitchell seemed to be, it wouldn't surprise him.

"No, but I know how to start a fight," Jerry answered.

1430 Local Time
USS *Jimmy Carter*
UUV Control Center

Jerry studied the navigation display with Cavanaugh, Weiss, Segerson, Malkoff, and Ford. Joining them was Master Chief Paul Gibson, *Carter's* chief of the boat or COB. The large flat-screen showed a composite chart of the waters off Bolshevik Island. The launch facility lay seven miles north-northwest of Cape Baranova, in five hundred and ninety feet of water. A circle showed its position, determined by the location of the ships Weiss had seen through the periscope on *Carter's* first mission and from observations taken an hour earlier—a quick check to make sure the helicopters had left the area. The recorded video showed a cylinder being lowered into the water by the icebreaker.

"I'm pretty sure those are smaller than the ones we saw earlier, Skipper," commented Segerson.

"Concur, XO." Weiss nodded as he spoke. "Which means—"

"That they're probably loading the launchers," interrupted Jerry. "I'm willing to bet those are transport launch canisters for the Dragon torpedo."

"And that means we're running out of time," Segerson concluded.

"Pretty much," said Jerry.

"So, how do we get to the launcher complex?" asked Cavanaugh. "I'm not much good to you this far away."

It was a good question. The UUVs' surveys had counted at least twenty PMK-2 mines. If spaced at an optimal distance, it would take fifty to form a complete barrier twenty-seven miles wide. There was probably another line to the south, but that was irrelevant. They'd figured out how to deal with the mines, but they were just the first layer of the facility's defenses. The second layer, comprised of MGK-608M fixed acoustic modules backed up with helos, was more of a challenge.

"I guarantee these were not here the last time we scouted the area," Weiss stated.

"It makes sense that the Russians were still installing their defenses," Jerry remarked philosophically. "I've encountered these acoustic sensors before, and just like last time, we found them by literally tripping over one. José's image looks identical to the one I saw earlier. The system is called 'Sever,' and it can obviously detect a *Seawolf*-class boat."

"What did you do about them the first time?" Ford asked.

"We ran like thieves, with most of the Northern Fleet after us," Jerry answered, smiling.

Ford wasn't deterred. "The UUVs were originally designed to find and destroy mines. This acoustic sensor is just like a bottom mine, except it listens instead of exploding. I recommend we put a mine-clearing charge on top of the cylindrical body and knock it out."

Weiss and Jerry considered the suggestions, but only for a moment. Jerry waited for *Carter*'s skipper to speak first.

"No good, Ben, for two reasons. First, the modules on either side will transmit the sound of the explosion, but even worse, the network is almost certainly designed to show when a module has stopped working. Either way, we draw attention to ourselves."

"And cutting the cable with a mine-clearing charge does the same thing," Ford muttered. "That was going to be my second suggestion."

Weiss observed, "What we have to do is get through the sensor net without alerting it in any way. But we couldn't even get a UUV close to the sensor without being detected. How are we going to get anything close enough to do any good?" He didn't sound optimistic.

Jerry smiled broadly. "No, there is something we can do." He turned to Ford. "Has anyone ever measured the glide slope on the UUVs?"

"Like a plane?" Ford asked. When Jerry confirmed the meaning, the UUV officer answered, "Definitely not. I can tell you how far it will coast, given its speed when we stop the motors, but the UUVs are neutrally buoyant. And they're shaped like a brick. There's nothing to generate any lift like an airplane."

"Okay," Jerry replied, "so it's not so much a glide as a controlled fall. If we put a UUV at the right depth off the bottom, and make it negatively buoyant, it will start to sink. We then point the nose down . . ."

"And you will get some forward speed," Ford concluded.

Weiss nodded approvingly. "After we recover José and Walter, we'll move some distance away from the island and test the idea. We will start a UUV moving, then shut down the motors and angle the nose down. We can measure the rate of depth change, then play with it until we find the best combination of angle and buoyancy." *Carter*'s captain smiled. "So we launch the UUVs and they glide silently over the sensor's position and then . . ." He stopped, unable to finish the sentence and scowled.

"If we can't knock the sensors out," LT Ford mused, "could we blind them by launching countermeasures? Use the UUVs to place several at different spots along the barrier and then drop one ourselves as we go through. We could even launch a mobile decoy while this is going on and point it north so they're chasing the simulator while we head toward the island."

"So instead of sneaking in, we just kick down the door?" Jerry asked.

"Doors and windows, all at once," argued Ford. "Give them three, five, or even more major noise sources that blind portions of the net. Even if they assume we've crossed the barrier, they won't know exactly where."

Weiss wasn't convinced. "But instead of letting them sleep, they'll go to battle stations for sure. Going through the fence safely and undetected is just step one. We still have to get the UUVs to the facility, survey the target, place the beacons, fire the torpedoes, and then get out of there."

Jerry calculated, "Given the distance from the airstrip to the facility, the Russians can have helicopters overhead in about fifteen minutes or so. Instead of alerting them at the very end, we would be waking them up as we come in. Kind of like kicking the bee's nest before you get the honey."

"I'd much prefer being on the way out by the time any ASW helos arrive," declared Weiss.

"And I'd like to withdraw my suggestion," Ford replied sheepishly.

"Not entirely, Lieutenant," Jerry countered. "I like the idea of blinding—or more properly muffling the sensor. Don't knock it out, just keep it from hearing anything."

"Cover the cables with something," Weiss suggested.

Jerry explained, "Technically, we only need to cover up the hydrophones that stick out on either side. The center body holds the electronics. You can't break or damage the cables, though. The system would interpret that as a fault."

Weiss concluded, "So we bury it. The bottom is mostly silt and sand. If we could scoop up some of the mud . . ."

"Even if we could jury-rig some way of getting the mud and loading it into UUV canisters, it would take too long," remarked Jerry.

Lieutenant Ford had followed the two senior officers' reasoning carefully. He knew the UUVs' design better than anyone else aboard. He tried to imagine some way of gathering material from the bottom . . .

"Captain, would lead shot work?"

"The ballast!" Weiss exclaimed.

Ford nodded and expounded on his theory. "We'd have to make the UUVs negatively buoyant for their 'gliding' approach. To restore neutral buoyancy, I'd have to dump ballast anyway." He smiled. "We could come in and drop the lead shot on the hydrophones . . . sort of like a dive-bombing run."

"More like glide bombing, but the idea is similar. This could work." Jerry thought for a moment, then added, "The UUVs' 3-D imaging sonar is more than accurate enough to locate the individual hydrophones and guide the vehicle over them. Well done, Lieutenant." He clapped Ford on the shoulder.

"Two UUVs, left and right hydrophone sets," Weiss observed. "We follow the UUVs through the gap and we are in. But where? Until we cover the hydrophones, we're still vulnerable. I'm betting if we have to get low enough to avoid the mines detecting *Jimmy*, one of the Sever modules would still be able to hear us as we approached."

Ford scratched his head. "Theoretically, the UUVs could create a gap in the field by placing a mine-clearing charge. But the sensor net would hear the explosion . . ."

Jerry's expression became solemn. He tapped a spot on the navigation chart display. "Walter's closest to this location?"

Ford nodded.

"Then instead of recovering Walter first, we should pick up José while Walter surveys this section of the minefield." The others noted the small cross that someone had added to mark the place where *Toledo* lay.

"You believe the mine that sank *Toledo* left a gap in the mine barrier," Weiss realized. "But wouldn't they refresh the field?"

Jerry shrugged. "I don't think so. The Russians have been pretty busy. They may not have gotten around to it. And it's entirely possible that they don't even know there is a missing mine. Remember, the sensor net wasn't set up until after *Toledo* was lost. The Russians couldn't possibly have heard the mine explosion that far away, not with the sonars they have on the ships near the construction site. We just have to confirm this theory with Walter."

"Thank you, USS *Toledo* and Captain Lenny Berg," Weiss observed. "By the way, when we found her, we hovered overhead and held a memorial for her crew. Tom Norris is an ordained minister, and he led the service."

Jerry smiled, although it was a sad one. "I hadn't heard about that. Thanks, Lou. After this is all over, hopefully we can tell Jane Berg everything. And I'll say a prayer, when we're nearest. That's about all we'll have time for right now."

"A missing mine should give us a thousand-yard gap," Weiss reasoned.

"Which we can hit precisely, with the UUVs navigating for us," Jerry argued.

Weiss nodded. "Agreed, but we'll have to line up well out in front of the opening, and once we commit to entering the gap, we'll be unable to maneuver freely for ten, perhaps fifteen minutes. In fact, we'll probably have to manually guide the UUVs to begin their 'bomb run.'"

"I suspected as much," said Jerry. "And we'll need to be close to the hydrophones so the lead shot doesn't scatter too much; say a foot or two off the bottom. Tricky."

Ford looked at Mitchell with apprehension. "Commodore, the minimum range for the imaging sonar is one meter, three point three feet. For the last foot or two the pilot will be essentially blind. We won't be able to accurately place the lead shot on the target."

"We'll work on that, Mr. Ford. If I can train a pilot to drive a UUV into a torpedo tube, I think I'll be able to help you and Mr. Lawson on this."

Incredulous, Ford stammered, "Dr . . . drive a UUV . . . manually . . . into a torpedo tube? That's . . . that's impossible!"

"Mr. Ford," Gibson chimed in, "they did it. Twice. I was there."

Ford swallowed hard and looked at Jerry with amazement. The lieutenant then started writing down his to-do list. "I have to calculate the amount of ballast that the UUVs will be able to drop and still stay neutrally buoyant."

"And the battery levels," Jerry added. "You'll save some power during the 'bomb run,' but once they're past the sensor net, you'll want them to use their best speed to reach the facility so they can begin the sonar survey."

Ford continued to make notes.

"After we figure out how to glide the UUVs properly, we'll practice a little 'formation flying.' Once you and Lawson get comfortable with manually flying the UUVs, we'll do a few dry runs to familiarize you with how it feels." Turning toward Weiss, Jerry asked, "How long before we're ready to make the attempt, Captain?"

"We'll need to recharge the UUVs' batteries once they're recovered.

That will take about five, maybe six hours. Then the practice runs. Top off the batteries again and load the lead shot, at least twelve hours, Commodore."

"Very well. Let's get started, people."

With the planning meeting over, Weiss and the others headed forward, that is, with the exception of the chief of the boat. Gibson caught Jerry's eye and motioned for the commodore to join him over at the DC locker at the back of UCC.

Walking over to Gibson, Jerry spoke quietly, "What can I do for, COB?"

"Sir, we've been shipmates before, so let me get straight to it. Some of the crew is a little uneasy about the 'incident' you and the skipper had earlier. A lot of people heard it, and there is some concern that it has raised doubts as to the skipper's abilities; doubts that might have unfortunate consequences later. It was felt that I should quietly bring this to your attention."

"I see," replied Jerry, a slight grin on his face. "Well, you can assure the XO that this is still Captain Weiss's boat, and that I have no desire to take over."

Gibson smiled. "I didn't figure it would take you long to see through that smokescreen."

"Nope, it's pretty obvious. But that just means he's a good executive officer. You can also tell him I appreciate his tact. You're the perfect messenger, Master Chief."

"Mr. Segerson thought as much," chuckled the COB. "But, shipmate to shipmate, sir, what are your intentions?"

Jerry grew serious, determined. The question was a little unsettling, but proper. And he owed this man a truthful answer. "My sole concern is that we complete this mission successfully, and I'll do whatever I believe is necessary to make that happen. And it's not just because the president of the United States personally put me onboard this boat." He paused as he pointed in the direction of *Toledo*'s lifeless hulk. "A good friend and his crew lie over there, Master Chief. I will not let their sacrifice be in vain. And if that means I sometimes have to be a little rough on Captain Weiss's ego, then so be it."

FLASH

040900Z AUG 21

FROM: USS JIMMY CARTER (SSN 23)

TO: CNO WASHINGTON DC

INFO: COMSUBFOR, SUBRON TWELVE

TOP SECRET//SCI

SUBJ: MISSION STATUS REPORT

1) SURVEY OF DRAGON LAUNCH BASE DEFENSES BY UUVS COM-PLETED. BASED ON PERISCOPE AND PASSIVE SONAR OBSERVATION, WEAPON LOADING HAS LIKELY BEGUN.

2) SURFACE UNITS AT SITE INCLUDES ICEBREAKER, TRANSPORT BARGE, SMALL DIVING SUPPORT CRAFT. SUBMARINES BELGOROD AND LOSHARIK ARE PRESENT, IDENTIFIED THROUGH PASSIVE SONAR ANALYSIS. ASSUMED TO BE SUPPORTING DIVING AND LOADING EVO-LUTION.

3) DEFENSES INCLUDE PREVIOUSLY OBSERVED PMK-2 MINE BARRIER, RECENTLY ADDED NETWORK OF SEVER BOTTOM-MOUNTED ACOUS-TIC SENSORS, SUPPORTED BY KA-27M HELICOPTERS.

4) PROCEEDING AS PLANNED. INTEND TO PENETRATE MINE AND ACOUSTIC BARRIERS USING UUVS. EXPECT TO COMMENCE OPERA-TION WITHIN THE NEXT TWELVE HOURS.

BT

4 August 2021
0500 Eastern Daylight Time
National Military Command Center, The Pentagon
Arlington, Virginia

Captain Tony Monyihan, USN, had the 2000–0800 watch in the National Command Authority's monitoring center. His job was to over-see a small group of civilian and military personnel as they kept track of not only the positions and status of all U.S. military forces, but of allied and adversary militaries as well.

A movie screen–sized display showed a map of the world, divided into operating areas and dotted with symbols for not only navy, but army, air force, and marine units. Foreign units were similarly marked, but with the three-letter country designation below the unit's name.

The captain had a big-picture view of the United States' armed forces, but that didn't mean he always knew what was going on. He could see where all the units were, and had a pretty good idea of where they were going. But he didn't necessarily know exactly why.

Monyihan hadn't seen a general sortie order in the message traffic, but he knew that subs were leaving port individually, always at night, and when weather or satellite windows hid their movements. The U.S. Navy had fourteen active submarine squadrons, SUBRONS, organized into five Submarine Groups, with a total of seventy-four boats.

Under normal circumstances, Monyihan would see twenty to twenty-five subs, one-third of the force, at sea, on patrol at any given time. Another third would be in port, training and performing routine maintenance on their complex systems. The last third would be in refit, in dry dock, or with vital machinery dismantled for upgrades or repair.

His latest count showed over forty submarines at sea. Not only attack boats and cruise missile submarines, but also ballistic missile submarines were sortieing out of the regular schedule. He couldn't tell where the "boomers" were going. Their patrol areas were not displayed on the map. That information was too sensitive even for this space.

At this rate, soon the only submarines left in port would be those in dry dock or extended maintenance. Seeing that many attack boats at sea piqued his curiosity, but extra SSBNs going to sea made him consider buying canned goods and bottled water. When he saw that carrier strike groups were beginning to deploy out of sequence, he knew the Russian crisis was getting really serious.

Were those "snap exercises" that Russia had announced really just practice drills? Apparently, the Joint Chiefs of Staff didn't think so. War with Russia, a nuclear war, had been the boogeyman of U.S. national security for sixty-five years. He hoped he wasn't watching its opening moves.

17

UNWELCOME COMPANY

4 August 2021
0700 Eastern Daylight Time
CNN International Affairs

"The Russian military exercises in Europe have been harshly criticized by the Hardy administration as 'designed to intimidate Europe' and as 'a rehearsal for a full-scale invasion.' President Fedorin personally responded to the administration's comments in a speech before a pro-Russian rally in Moscow today, saying that the 'West can draw whatever conclusion it likes. Russia's armed forces are ready to carry out the will of its people.'

"Historically, America's response to an adversary's military exercises is limited to rhetoric, plus careful observation to learn what they can of a potential opponent's capabilities. This time, though, there are indications that President Hardy and the Joint Chiefs of Staff may be considering more direct action.

"There have been rumors that the Pentagon is planning its own 'snap drills,' mobilizing and moving several rapid-reaction forces to Europe. In addition to increased activity at several military bases, most notably naval installations, the president and many national security officials have suddenly canceled, or rescheduled, long-standing appointments over the last few days.

"The famous 'Pizza Index,' using the amount of take-out pizza ordered by Pentagon offices as a sign of long hours, and thus of impending action, has become less reliable in recent years. A survey today of Arlington pizzerias showed only a small increase of ten to twenty percent over usual, compared to the doubling of orders before both Gulf wars and the Sino-Littoral Alliance War. A Pentagon source said that standing orders now forbid ordering take-out from nearby pizza places, and that to accurately measure late-night hours in Washington, one would have to poll every type of take-out cuisine . . ."

4 August 2021
0715 Eastern Daylight Time
Oval Office, The White House
Washington, D.C.

The message came while President Hardy was already receiving a briefing by Director of National Intelligence Peakes about non-military Russian activities. The large-scale military exercises were worrisome enough, but covert actions worldwide were on the rise. Peakes had started with news of another assassination, this time of a German counterterrorism official. Several different extremist organizations were claiming credit, but it didn't really fit any of their normal operating patterns.

Cyber attacks had increased as well, often demanding ransom for padlocked data, but they included an alarming number of infrastructure organizations: electric and transport utilities especially. A smaller number of sabotage incidents added to the overall pattern.

"Ray, will these really disrupt a country's infrastructure or economy that much?" asked Hardy.

"No, Mr. President," Peakes answered, "not at their current level, but look at how they're spread all over Europe. The cyber warfare people at both NSA and CIA believe that the Russians are demonstrating their capability, or European vulnerability, to these attacks. These incidents could easily be used as a coercive bargaining chip if the Russians make demands."

"You mean a threat," Hardy replied, "which is what we believe the Russians will do, once the balloon goes up."

"They may not have to even go that far," General Schiller remarked. The Chairman of the Joint Chiefs had already briefed the president on the status of the American exercise, Operation Fortify. "I'm very concerned about the Polish defense minster's remarks this morning. If they aren't prepared to—"

Secretary of State Lloyd cut in. "He only said that full mobilization depended on NATO showing a united front. And he's right. Germany and France are the big players. The smaller countries have said quite clearly that they're waiting to see how Berlin and Paris respond. And those two countries are looking to us. The U.S. has always been the *de facto* leader of NATO. The sooner we announce Fortify, the better."

"I agree it will encourage our allies, but I'm concerned that it will also increase international tensions." Bill Hyland looked genuinely worried. "I've looked at our post–World War II history, and this situation is every bit as unstable as the Berlin Blockade or the Cuban Missile Crisis."

"You're afraid we'll end up unintentionally in a shooting war," Hardy concluded.

"Of course," Hyland responded. "Fedorin doesn't want war any more than we do. But he's seeing how close to the edge he can go. In fact, he'll hang out over the edge and wave at us. He's willing to take risks because he believes that's where the big payoffs are. We can't know how far he's willing to go, and he obviously doesn't know everything we're doing."

Hardy was listening, but frowning. "Come to the point," he demanded.

"The world had come through East-West confrontations before, but later scholarship has shown us that we were always closer to disaster than was known by either side at the time. The danger is not from our or Fedorin's intentions, but rather unforeseen interactions or mishaps. And the more pieces both sides have in play, the greater the chance of an accident or incident. At best, it will cost lives. At worst, it literally means the end of the world." The national security advisor sat back, looking a little drained.

Hardy looked over at Joanna, sitting a little to one side. Bill

Hyland had been on Joanna's staff while she was national security advisor under President Myles. His specialty was nuclear strategy. He'd written several books on international relations and military force that were brilliant, and when she'd recommended the relatively junior staffer as her replacement, Hardy and his people had thought him an excellent choice. Youth was not necessarily a down check on the list of qualifications. It was an extremely demanding job and younger bodies usually could handle the stress and lack of sleep better. Hyland had been working twenty-hour days.

The president sighed. "Bill, that risk is going to be there, no matter what we do. We all know that we're using live ammunition, but so are they, and at the moment, Fedorin seems almost eager to shoot." He paused, then added, "I think the job of every president is to understand the risks each crisis presents as best he can, and do whatever he can to reduce those risks."

"Mr. President, I believe that sending those troops to Europe will escalate the current crisis. It may be enough to demonstrate that we're able to send them, or even just announce the conditions . . ."

"That's enough, Bill." Hardy's tone was firm. "Our allies need to see concrete actions even more than the Russians do."

Secretary Lloyd agreed. "The situation in Europe right now is extremely unbalanced. Our presence will give the Russians pause. Their chance of success goes down when a determined U.S. presence is factored into their planning."

White House Chief of Staff Sellers opened the door without knocking. "Mr. President, gentlemen and lady, Admiral Hughes has new information . . ."

"Please, send him in," Hardy urged.

Hughes entered, looking rushed. As he sat, he announced quietly, "We've received word from *Jimmy Carter.*"

Everyone sat up and leaned forward, and Hughes passed a copy of the message to each person. It had been sent two hours earlier.

Hardy took the time to read it twice, then announced, "There's our timeline for announcing Fortify. At the same time that I report the success of Overcharge, we'll announce the plan for reinforcing Europe."

"That should settle Senator Emmers's hash," muttered Lloyd.

Hardy nodded. "What I want it to do is set President Fedorin back a few steps. Give him pause for second, maybe even third thoughts."

Hyland looked alarmed, almost panicked. "Mr. President, Overcharge is exactly the kind of incident that could trigger a nuclear catastrophe. That launch site has to be his personal cause. A deliberate attack by us gives him precisely the excuse he needs. But to be honest, I can't predict how he will react, because a successful attack will come as a shock to the Russian leadership. Even if it fails, it will enrage him."

"God forbid," General Schiller added, scowling.

Hyland was insistent. "The more unusual the circumstance, the harder it is to predict how your adversary will respond. Fedorin could easily see it as a personal challenge, and feel compelled to respond or suffer a monumental loss of face."

"The Russian population doesn't even know about the facility," Schiller retorted.

"They will after President Hardy announces it!" Hyland's voice wasn't shouting, but it was a level of intensity rarely heard in the Oval Office, and it was clear from his tone that he thought the announcement was a mistake. "And regardless of whether the attack succeeds or not, we will have committed an act of war."

The chief of naval operations countered, "Placing those mines so they could attack and sink one of our subs in international waters is also an act of war."

"Fool! You can't see the difference between *Toledo*'s loss, which was completely hidden from view, and the public humiliation of the Russian president." At this point, Hyland was shouting, hands balled into fists.

"Bill, that's enough," Hardy ordered sharply in a raised voice. Hyland turned to look at him, and seemed to be composing a response, but the president cut him off. "Mister, you are relieved."

Chief of Staff Sellers had opened the door to the Oval Office a crack at the sound of raised voices, and Hardy motioned him into the room. "Dwight, Mr. Hyland is no longer the national security advisor. Please have the Secret Service collect all his badges and personal electronics, then escort him to someplace where he can rest under observation. He is to remain incommunicado until I say otherwise."

Hardy had been speaking to Sellers, but had kept his gaze fixed on the now former national security advisor. Hyland stood up a little straighter, but in the process also seemed to shrink. He nodded his understanding and turned to leave, then dithered for a moment about whether to take his notepad and tablet. He finally left them behind and walked slowly toward the door.

He stopped halfway and turned to face Hardy. "I will pray that I am wrong, Mr. President, and that your plan succeeds. Thank you for allowing me to serve in your administration, if only for a short time." A moment later, he was gone, and Sellers closed the door.

"Incommunicado?" Lloyd asked.

"He knows about Overcharge," Hardy answered. "Bill said it himself. We can't predict someone's actions when under severe stress. What if he went to the press?"

Lloyd's eyebrow rose, and he nodded his understanding. Hardy continued, "It won't be for long. The Secret Service will park him in a safe house where he can catch up on his sleep. If *Carter*'s message is accurate, Overcharge will be very public very soon."

Hardy also looked over to the first lady. Her expression was completely neutral, a mask. The others in the room all knew that she had recommended Hyland for the NSA post. But if they assumed it was a silent apology to his wife, they were wrong.

"Joanna, I need your help. Will you please take over as national security advisor?"

"What!?" Lloyd half rose out of his chair. The others, not as senior, stifled their own outbursts, but wore expressions varying from surprised to stunned.

Hardy waved him down. "Interim only, Mr. Secretary. This is not a good time to lose a key member of our national security team. She certainly is qualified for the job."

Lloyd sat back down, deep in thought. General Schiller and Admiral Hughes conversed in whispers, while DNI Peakes spoke the obvious. "It's unprecedented, and the potential for conflict of interest . . ."

"Will no doubt be investigated at great lengths by numerous congressional committees," Hardy completed. "However, I plead urgent necessity."

Lloyd nodded, but observed, "You're already receiving her advice, which has been very good, by the way," with a nod toward Patterson, "but there's no need to make it formal."

DNI Peakes responded. "That's not true, Mr. Secretary. Unless she's officially the NSA, she can't have access to all the intelligence sources that the position of national security advisor allows. The President has been walking a fine line on this, but without a formal NSA, that line becomes blurred. Unless there is someone officially occupying the NSA box in the wiring diagram, information can't flow, by law."

"What about Bill's deputy?" Lloyd asked.

"He's busy enough already," Joanna answered, joining the discussion. "My husband is right . . ."

"I love those words," Hardy interjected.

Patterson shot Hardy a look. "Sandy Hall's an excellent deputy, but he will cease to be so if he's suddenly promoted to the top spot. And we'll have to find someone to take Sandy's job. That means we'll have two critical positions operating at less than full efficiency. If I take the NSA post, he provides continuity."

Hardy turned to the two military officers. "Do you have any reservations on the appointment, Chairman?"

General Schiller, senior of the two officers, spoke for both of them. "The national security advisor is not in the chain of command. As far as we're concerned, nothing has changed."

"True, but is the military willing to work, on an *interim basis*," Hardy emphasized, "with an NSA who is also the first lady?"

Schiller nodded sagely. "Absolutely. And woe betide anyone who says otherwise," he promised.

Hardy smiled. "And by the time we announce Bill's resignation 'for health reasons,' in all likelihood, Overcharge will be public. By the way, when you all write about this in your memoirs, please be kind to Bill. He's right that this could spiral out of control."

In response to their surprised looks, Hardy explained. "The Russians are still getting ready. If they'd already started moving, if Fedorin and his generals had committed themselves, I believe the risks of escalation would be much greater. But we have a narrow window that *Carter* is doing her best to sneak through. Bill couldn't see the difference between now and what's to come."

The president tapped *Carter*'s report on his desk. "The good news in this message is that the Russians have not finished construction. Sun Tzu said that if you aren't trying to wipe out an enemy, leave him a line of retreat, and he won't fight as desperately. Unless they are going to try something in Europe in the next twelve hours, *without* their nuclear trump card, they'll be able to pretend it really was an exercise, back out and save face."

4 August 2021
1530 Local Time
USS *Jimmy Carter*
Off Cape Baranova, Russia

The UCC crew had just started recovering José when Walter reached the part of the mine belt nearest *Toledo*'s grave. It had taken some careful figuring to find the best combination of depth and distance from the minefield to avoid triggering either the acoustic sensors or the mines. Luckily, the mines were easy to see on Walter's imaging sonar.

While *Jimmy Carter*'s crew had mapped much of the minefield during her first visit to the area, they had not plotted the position of every mine. They'd established the extent of the field, its shape, confirmed that it was composed of a single mine type, and then kept as far from the area as circumstance allowed.

Walter actually began its search over a mile short of where they believed there would be a gap. The UUV crept parallel to the barrier at two knots, twenty feet off the seabed, using the long-range mode on its navigation sonar.

José was docked and recharging by the time Walter saw the first mine, but after that it became easier. They had been placed about eleven hundred yards apart. Once the precise location of the first mine was known, Walter's operators brought him a little farther out, increased the speed, and motored over to where the next one should be. It was exactly where they expected. The next mine was also in its proper place, and the next one. They were now a little over a mile and a half from their starting point, and all they could do was keep looking and hope they didn't find one.

Carter remained close enough to maintain good communications with Walter, but as far away from the minefield as that allowed. Cavanaugh knew that eventually they'd be getting much closer to the minefield, and hoped he could hide his nervousness.

The fifth mine was in place, but the sixth one was not. After Walter had gone several hundred yards past where the next mine should have been, Ford ordered the operator to circle the remote back and switch to high-res mode.

They were so close that as soon as Walter had finished his turn, they saw it. A long tube lay on the seabed. One end was connected by a cable to a large round disc close by—the anchor. "Tallyho," Jerry cried. "Finally!"

The empty canister that had held the torpedo had flooded with seawater and was no longer buoyant. In high-res mode, the sonar image was so clear they could see the open end of the cylinder. Jerry knew that everyone in the control room could see the image on their own displays, but he hit the intercom switch and reported, "Control, UCC, we just found the center of our path through the minefield. We will begin looking for the acoustic sensors."

That took longer. Under Ford's direction, Petty Officer Frederick had Walter look straight toward the mine barrier at dead slow, with the imaging sonar reset to its longest range. Cavanaugh stared at the screen along with the rest, watching for something that would look like a squat oil drum. Each time Walter approached one hundred yards from the line without seeing anything, Ford backed the UUV out and then moved it along the barrier to a new spot.

It was boring to watch, but nobody complained. Control could see what was being done, and did not hurry them. Cavanaugh knew that *Jimmy Carter*'s sonar watch was keeping an ear tuned for the sound of a Lamb Tail sonar, or any other kind, for that matter. He tried to calculate if they could avoid being found again, and wondered what Mitchell and Weiss would do if that happened.

It took over an hour of careful probing to find one of the Sever nodes on the seabed. Its location was not helpful. "I should have guessed," said Ford, frustrated.

"I made the same assumption," Jerry admitted. "At least we know where the one on this side of gap is located. We'll just have to look a little longer."

Forty-five minutes later, they'd found the second acoustic sensor and entered everything on the geoplot. While the UCC team prepared to recover Walter, Jerry, Ford, and Cavanaugh joined Weiss in control and tried to decide what could be done.

It was clearer on the paper plot, and Cavanaugh immediately understood their dilemma. The gap in the minefield was covered not by one acoustic sensor, but two, one to either side.

"It makes sense that the mines and sensors wouldn't line up," Weiss remarked. "They have different detection ranges, after all."

Now we have to muffle two sensors," Ford muttered. "The Russians are not playing fair."

"They don't even know we're playing," Jerry reminded him.

They'd added in circles that represented the detection range of the acoustic sensor on the geoplot, along with the diamonds that marked their actual positions on the sea bottom, and the two mines on either side of what everyone now called the "The *Toledo* gap." Cavanaugh was visualizing them as goal posts.

The two acoustic detection circles overlapped in the gap, a little to the left of center. Weiss asked, "What if we use the UUVs to mask this one on the right?"

Ford tapped a few keys, and measured the distance. "Four hundred yards," he reported. "Maybe four twenty-five."

"Compared to a thousand before," Jerry observed. "I'm sure we could get through that, carefully, on the way in. It's the way out I'm worried about. We can't expect to have the UUVs navigating for us."

"And we might be in a hurry," Weiss added, smiling.

Jerry asked, "How long to 'bomb' one sensor, come back to the sub, reload ballast, and then do it again?"

"Assuming we can do it at all?" Weiss asked. "Too long. I feel like the clock is ticking."

Other heads nodded, and Jerry suggested, "Then let's see first how well the UUVs can imitate a glider."

1900 Local Time
USS *Jimmy Carter*
Near October Revolution Island, Russia

With both UUVs back aboard, *Carter* proceeded five miles northwest for "flight tests." To Cavanaugh, it seemed they should have moved farther away from Russian territory, but Captain Weiss reassured him. "We can't hear the Russians this far away, and I guarantee we have a much better sonar suite than they do."

While Jerry and the UUV team tested Walter, Captain Weiss had the sonar crew keep a close watch. Although she wasn't particularly vulnerable with a UUV deployed, it would be highly inconvenient if a Russian stumbled across *Carter* while they were occupied experimenting with the remotes.

They launched José with as much ballast as the UUV could hold, almost a hundred pounds of lead shot. The UUVs normally carried some ballast to maintain neutral buoyancy, but the UCC crew had filled the ballast compartment, so the UUV was "max heavy" when it left the sub.

Lieutenant Ford, worried about the extra weight, watched the battery charge and speed carefully as LTJG Lawson moved the UUV a few hundred yards off *Carter*'s port beam. While *Carter* hovered above the bottom, José rose, or more accurately, "clawed for altitude" like a heavily loaded airplane. The UUV needed full power and a nose-up angle to slowly rise. It took longer than normal for the vehicle to reach a depth of twenty-five feet below the ocean surface, but once leveled out, it proved to be only two knots slower than its normal eight-knot maximum speed. It still needed a little up angle, and of course maximum power.

After taking copious notes during the UUV's ascent, LT Ford reported, "I've got the numbers I need, Commodore. Ready for the first test."

Cavanaugh watched Mitchell glance at the recorded values, and at the display, before reporting on the intercom to control. "Ready for glide test."

Weiss immediately replied, "Proceed." The displays in control would let them see everything that they saw in UCC.

Jerry nodded, and told Lawson, "All stop, five degrees down angle."

The bottom lay some three hundred feet below José. They'd calculated the sink rate using the standard formulas in the UUV manual. That much was easy. What they couldn't calculate was how far forward José would move as it descended. The UUV had no wings, just small control fins at the back.

Everyone's attention was focused on the readouts: battery charge, depth, and especially speed. Even though everyone could see the displays, Lawson still read them out loud. "Showing six knots." Normally, at that speed, the vehicle would coast to a stop within a minute of the motors stopping. It had a smooth exterior, but nobody who saw one would describe it as "streamlined."

"Still showing six knots," Lawson reported hopefully. Up in control, they were plotting the UUV's position, as well as its depth. They needed to know exactly how long the "bomb run" would have to be.

Cavanaugh watched the display along with everyone else. It actually showed the UUV's speed to a tenth of a knot. When Lawson had nosed over, it read 6.2 knots. Then it went up, to 6.4.

After another moment, the lieutenant announced, "Speed is up to seven knots," a little surprised.

"Sink rate matches what we expected, more or less," Ford commented.

Cavanaugh watched the speed go up again, to 7.5 knots. Well, most things go downhill faster than they do over level ground.

"Eight knots!" Ford announced proudly, as if José were in a race. "Sink rate is increasing as well."

"End the test," Jerry ordered suddenly. "Engage the propulsion motor and bring it level. Be ready to bring the nose up. Steve, watch the sink rate and depth carefully."

Puzzled, Ford gazed at the commodore, who looked genuinely

concerned. The vehicle had only gone down about a hundred feet, and Cavanaugh knew the plan had been to let the UUV drop until it was much closer to the bottom, and maybe even find a feature on the seabed to practice their aim.

Jerry repeated, "Watch the depth carefully. Be ready to angle up if I say so," he ordered. Lawson acknowledged the order, but both he and Ford looked confused. Jerry explained to the two lieutenants, while keeping his eyes on the display, "We've determined that the UUV will gain sufficient speed as it sinks, in fact, a little better than expected. But it's translating some of that speed into downward motion. We know it will dive like an airplane. The question is, can it pull out of a dive like one?"

Cavanaugh imagined one of their priceless UUVs plowing into the bottom at ten-plus knots.

"Speed's not dropping a whole lot. Sink rate is slowing . . ."

"Raise the nose ten degrees," Jerry ordered.

Ford, making notes, announced, "That's the trick! Look at the speed drop. And the descent rate is decreasing." After a long pause, he reported, "Sink rate is zero."

"That's called a 'flare,'" Mitchell explained. "Pull the nose up just a little, and the bottom of the plane—the vehicle—turns into one giant speed brake. The trick is going to be flaring close enough to the bottom to kill the sink rate, but leaving the UUVs at the right depth to drop the lead shot on the sensor."

"A steeper up angle—a flare—would do that quicker," Ford suggested hopefully.

"But we don't want the UUV to rise," Mitchell cautioned. "We want to slow the vehicle down just a bit as we're approaching the sensor node. In aviation, they call that 'dumping speed.' But the borderline between losing a little speed and losing a lot is very fine."

"We need to do some more tests," Ford realized. "Maybe a lot more."

Jerry reached for the intercom. "I'll inform Control. You figure out exactly how much longer this is going to take, and then how to do it faster."

"Some more time will be required." Jerry passed on to control what had happened. He could hear the frustration in Weiss's voice over the intercom. "But I concur. It has to be done. Besides, my sonar gang just came up with a way to solve the problem of the buoys not lining up with the *Toledo* gap."

"Oh! Do tell, please," Jerry asked.

"We mask the left hydrophone set on one module and the right hydrophone set on the other. If we cover the sides facing the gap, we should have about an eight-hundred-yard passage through both the minefield and the sensors."

2030 Local Time
USS *Jimmy Carter*

In the wardroom, dinner had turned into an extended planning session as they discussed the results of the "glide bombing" trials and worked out a detailed timeline for the complex attack. To Jerry, tracking and engaging a submarine in open water was simple, compared to the precise interlocking steps that would lead to the destruction of the Russian launch facility. Any one of them failing could throw the entire operation off the rails.

Where did *Carter* have to be when the UUVs started their run? How close should she actually get to the facility? The closer they were, the shorter the time lag between the UCC crew giving a command and the vehicle executing it. What should they do if *Belgorod* detected them during the approach and reacted aggressively? She had a decent sonar suite, and torpedoes.

One interesting fact came from the sonar officer, LTJG DiMauro. "I've had my operators listening to the noise coming from the construction site, to see if they can determine exactly what's going on. There's a lot of clanking as metal bangs up against metal, and they are sure they've heard pounding, as if a stubborn piece is being shifted into place. That won't help us, but we've found a pattern," he announced proudly.

By now, most of the sub's chief petty officers were also present, and the remains of dinner cleared away. He paused dramatically, enjoying the moment, but didn't push his luck.

"It appears that every eight hours, the transients stop and the broad-band noise levels go way down for about fifteen to twenty minutes. It's been very regular."

"A shift change for the divers," Weiss concluded.

Jerry nodded agreement, along with many others.

"It makes sense. They will have as many divers down there as possible to speed the work. At that depth, they have to be in atmospheric diving suits with long air hoses, so they can't send the next batch down until the other set comes up."

Weiss smiled. "It's pitch black down there except for any lights they've set up, which will be concentrated wherever they're working. I'd been wondering about the chance of a diver spotting Walter or José, even if the UUVs are dark-colored. When is the next shift change?"

"There should be one at midnight, 0000 hours, give or take a few minutes," the sonar officer answered.

"Then that's where we'll anchor our timeline. We want the UUVs in position to start surveying a little before then, and as soon as the transients stop, we send them in, followed by torpedoes soon after."

It had already been a long day. The UUV operators had been constantly busy, and the rest of the crew had been operating at modified general quarters for over twelve hours. Cavanaugh had done nothing more than listen and watch, and he felt worn out.

But he could feel the energy in the room as Weiss gave orders for the final preparations. They'd have to move quickly to take advantage of the window, but there was enough time. And time was against them. Not only did they not know when the Russians would finish their work, but as long as they stayed in Russian waters and close to the island, there was the constant risk of being detected. Better to be done and gone.

2130 Local Time
USS *Jimmy Carter*

USS *Jimmy Carter* was at general quarters, two nautical miles away from the *Toledo* gap, pointed south. Six of her tubes were loaded with the modified torpedoes, the other two held standard warshots . . . just in case. The UCC crew had launched the now fully charged and heavily loaded José and Walter, one right after the other. Both UUVs were now climbing to carefully calculated locations, defined not just in range and bearing, but depth as well. Once they were in position, *Carter* would slowly accelerate to creep speed, just three knots, and head straight for the center of the passage.

As before, Jerry was in UCC, along with Cavanaugh. If the engineer needed to change the preplanned survey, the commodore wanted the army engineer to be right there.

"In position," Ford reported to Mitchell. The two UUVs were as stationary as their weight allowed, holding just fifty feet above the bottom and three hundred yards out. Tests had shown that they'd have to start "flaring" at twenty-five feet above the seabed, and would slow to two or three knots as they passed over the hydrophones in a gentle glide. Ford looked over at Jerry, who nodded and gave him thumbs up.

"Commence the UUV run," Weiss ordered over the circuit.

Lieutenant Ford ordered, "Half speed to the motor."

"Five knots at level pitch," Lawson reported a moment later.

The glide bombing approach itself started with a dogleg maneuver. First they had to locate the cable, then start running along it until the imaging sonar saw the hydrophones. Then they'd start the dive. The UUVs detected the cable as expected, and Jerry issued the command to secure the propulsion motors and begin the turn. Watching the nav plot on the display carefully, Jerry waited, counting quietly to himself, then said, "Five degrees down bubble, *mark!*"

They felt a slight vibration in the deck as *Carter*'s propulsor pushed her forward.

"José's at four point five knots," Lawson reported. Ford followed with Walter's speed. They were nearing the point where they'd have to pull up into the flare maneuver.

"Conn, Sonar. New contact, Sierra one six, bearing zero one seven, drawing left rapidly!"

What? Jerry pulled up the sonar display, saw a faint, but sharply canted line on the screen, then hit the intercom switch. "Sonar, UCC, what do you hold on Sierra one six?"

"UCC, Sonar. Broadband mostly, very faint narrowband tonals, contact is close aboard!"

Jerry pressed the button for the control room, "Control, UCC, recommend—"

Weiss's voice cut him off. "UCC, Control, abort, abort! Dump ballast, go to creep speed. Turn both UUVs north, straight away from the barrier!"

The UUV operators got very busy as they abandoned the gliding approach and turned the vehicles sharply northward. They used the built-up speed to get them close to the bottom fast and away from the line of passive acoustic sensors. Cavanaugh saw Jerry's expression go from alarm to satisfaction. The deck titled slightly as the sub turned to port.

"UCC, Control, changing course to zero eight zero, three knots. Compute UUV course to rendezvous and follow in trail. Setting ultra quiet throughout the boat."

After that, the intercom was silent, and a hush filled UCC, just a few spoken reports, quietly acknowledged.

After a full minute, everyone seemed to relax, but everyone's attention remained fixed on the displays.

Jerry had a small, grim smile, and Cavanaugh asked, "That new contact, behind us. Another submarine?"

"Yes," Jerry nodded, "and it was frickin' close."

"How could you tell?"

"Because he popped up suddenly, and the bearing rate—how fast it was changing—was high. A high bearing rate means either the contact's going fast, or he's damn close. Since we didn't hear him a long time ago, that means he's going slow, ergo very close. And I have a sneaking suspicion I know which boat it is, too." Jerry then nodded toward the intercom.

"Captain Weiss did exactly the right thing, stopping the approach and heading us away, to the east, since the other sub is probably going west. We'll get some distance, recover the UUVs, figure out who just crashed our party and plan our next move."

Cavanaugh felt let down. He'd managed to prepare himself for the attack, and didn't know what to feel right now. "We aren't aborting the mission, are we?"

"No, not at all," Jerry replied confidently, "but things just got more complicated."

18

TRY, TRY AGAIN

4 August 2021
2000 Local Time
The Admiralty Building
St. Petersburg, Russia

Vasiliy Lavrov was in a foul mood. The president had issued a straight-forward enough order: "Have naval intelligence do a complete check of all Western submarines. Positively confirm the location of any that are capable of reaching the Arctic." Initially, however, the tasking came down as all American submarines, then two hours later was corrected to all nuclear-powered Western submarines—the ones that could reach the Arctic—and then to all Western submarines because some fool bureaucrat insisted that the question be answered in as complete a manner as possible. By early afternoon the extent of the effort had shifted yet again, and now a comprehensive survey of *all* NATO naval assets was needed. And while Lavrov saw the value of the expanded survey, no one had bothered to adjust the completion deadline to accommodate the huge increase in the scope of the work.

Given the size and immediacy of the new tasking, Lavrov had proceeded to draft every naval analyst he could get his hands on, as well as a number of mid-grade officers sitting about in the Admiralty Building. The problem wasn't the order of battle, which was maintained on a daily basis, but positively confirming the locations of all the ships and submarines within each nation's inventory. This was proving to be immensely difficult, as it required good quality electro-optical overhead imagery—and Russia had a small, finite number of imaging satellites. In some instances, all he had was days-old images or infrared shots that weren't as reliable. Worse yet, the results of the preliminary analysis didn't bode well for Mother Russia.

Glancing up at the clock, Lavrov saw that he was already late, and was getting more so with each passing moment. Shaking his head, he went back to editing the final report that was supposed to have been delivered to Admiral Komeyev . . . fifteen minutes ago. Rushing through each page, Lavrov carefully checked the facts—spelling and grammar were of secondary importance. He was almost finished with the final pass when his regular phone started ringing. Ignoring the bothersome electronic warble became impossible, and he jerked the handset from the phone's body.

"Yes!" he shouted indignantly.

"Captain Lavrov?" asked the voice with hesitation.

"Yes, yes, who is this?" grumbled the captain.

"Captain Lavrov, I'm Captain First Rank Anatoly Borovich Bylinkin. Russia's assistant naval attaché to the United States."

Lavrov recognized the name, but he wasn't in the mood, nor did he have the time for a friendly chat. "My apologies for the curt greetings, Captain," he replied. "But I'm terribly busy at the moment, perhaps we could—"

"I'm aware of your urgent report for the president," interrupted Bylinkin. "But I had to make sure you received the e-mail."

"E-mail? What e-mail?"

"The report from our observer in New London, Captain. There was a severe thunderstorm in the area this morning and the canvas covering the graving dock at the Electric Boat shipyard has been partially stripped away. There wasn't anything in the dock, Comrade Captain. He included photos in his account."

Lavrov felt a sudden shiver pass down his spine. *Jimmy Carter* was gone? His fingers raced over the keyboard and brought up the e-mail with the photos. They were only four hours old. Blowing up one of the shots of the graving dock's gate proved conclusively that it was empty.

"Captain, did you hear what I said?" queried Bylinkin.

"Yes, yes, I did. Thank you very much, Captain. Goodbye." Lavrov didn't bother to wait for Bylinkin to acknowledge the send-off.

Pulling up the U.S. submarine order of battle section, he quickly changed the *Carter* entry from "In EB dry dock," to "Location Unknown." He then modified the conclusion, adding a single short but blunt sentence. He saved the file, attached it to an e-mail and sent it directly to Admiral Komeyev, who was already in Moscow. Pausing only long enough to print out a copy of the most alarming photo, Lavrov gathered his notes and ran for the stairs.

4 August 2021
2115 Moscow Time
The Senate Building, Kremlin
Moscow, Russia

The car with Defense Minister Aleksandr Trusov dashed down the street at high speed; he was late for the General Staff meeting with the president. In his briefcase was the report on the locations of all NATO naval assets, along with a photo of the empty graving dock at the Groton shipyard. The minister was troubled. Most of the West's nuclear submarines were at sea. A sudden surge within the last eighteen hours had increased their deployed strength considerably . . . the U.S. alone had fifty-two submarines now at sea, seventy percent of their order of battle. Included in that number was the spy submarine, *Jimmy Carter*, that naval intelligence had repeatedly warned was likely a threat to the Drakon complex. The submarine had been seen entering a shipyard graving dock late in July, but as of five hours ago the boat was no longer there . . . it was missing. No one knew where it was, or when it had left the dock. The report was quite blunt in its conclusion; "*Carter* could be off Bolshevik Island right now, for all we know."

As soon as the vehicle came to a stop, Trusov threw open the door.

He didn't even bother waiting for the young Presidential Regiment guardsman to open the door for him. Formalities were immaterial at this point. The defense minister broke out in an undignified run as he entered the building and started taking the steps two at a time. Even though the elderly minister was in reasonable shape, the several flights of stairs caused him to become short of breath—but it was still faster than taking an elevator.

Waving vigorously for the guard to open the door to the president's main conference room, Trusov strode into the meeting that had already started. Fedorin saw the defense minister enter the room and scowled. He expected his ministers and commanders to be punctual. "I'm pleased to see you could finally make it, Defense Minister Trusov," blurted the president.

"My apologies, Comrade President, but it couldn't be helped. I had to verify some of the findings in the naval intelligence report you requested this morning."

"Findings? What findings trouble you, Minister Trusov?" Fedorin growled. "The chief of the main intelligence directorate submitted his report *several* hours ago. The Americans have a higher than usual deployment of attack submarines, but not appreciably so. He attributes this temporary increase to regular combat patrol rotations."

"I see," replied Trusov with an icy tone. He then saw the grim face on the navy commander, Admiral Komeyev; the man looked ready to strangle someone. The intelligence chief was not an ally, and consistently tried to find ways to embarrass the defense ministry and the services in front of the president. Trusov recognized immediately that General Vanzin was up to his old tricks again.

"Unfortunately, Comrade President, in this instance I believe that Intelligence Chief Vanzin's report was premature. A review of the most recent satellite imagery indicates that the Americans have sortied approximately seventy percent of all their submarines, including cruise missile and ballistic missile submarines."

Fedorin turned, casting a seething gaze at Colonel General Vanzin, while Trusov continued his report. "In addition, two carrier strike groups departed their home ports this afternoon. That means six are now at sea, with indications that another is in final preparations. In short,

Comrade President, the U.S. Navy has surged the majority of its naval assets within the last twenty-four hours. And while I don't have any direct evidence, I believe their air and ground forces are also mobilizing, rapidly. I've instructed the armed forces' intelligence organs to do a complete review by tomorrow morning."

General Vanzin looked shocked. "How is this possible? We haven't seen an appreciable increase in message traffic, or even e-mails sent out to the affected commands . . . how could they possibly surge within a day or two?"

"Probably because they've been secretly preparing for weeks, sending the orders out the old-fashioned way . . . by phone, or by courier," explained Trusov. "Regrettably, Comrade President, there is more unpleasant news."

Fedorin halted the defense minister's report with a sharp hand gesture. A blistering expression showed his disdain as he yelled at Vanzin, "Leave now! Before I have you thrown out!"

Vanzin rose from the chair slowly, his body visibly shaking. He scooped up his leather-bound notebook and papers, bowed slightly and quickly retreated from the room. Many of the other staff members looked quietly pleased.

"Continue!" barked Fedorin as soon as the sharp click from the door reverberated throughout the conference room.

"Yes, sir. It is also apparent that the American spy submarine, *Jimmy Carter*, is not where we thought it was. The shipyard graving dock we saw her moved to late last month was discovered empty this afternoon. We have no knowledge of where she is right now, or when she left the dock. The report from Admiral Komeyev's intelligence section makes the candid conclusion that she could already be loitering off the Prima Polar Station."

Fedorin's face twitched with rage, and he struggled to maintain his composure as he erupted, "How could this have happened!? Why were we unaware of the Americans' activities!?"

"Comrade President, it is clear we have been collectively deceived by a well-executed disinformation campaign . . ." began Trusov.

"WHY WASN'T I INFORMED!?" screeched Fedorin.

Trusov was sorely tempted to march back to the president's desk and throw the reports they'd both gone over in his face, but that would have little effect given Fedorin's current state of mind. The defense minister had to get the discussion back to the main concern at hand. "I can assure you a complete investigation into this failure will be conducted, Comrade President, but we have more important problems to deal with right now."

"Like what!?" Fedorin demanded.

"That the impetus for the disinformation campaign means the Americans probably are aware of Project Drakon, *and* the restoration offensive. We could be facing a fully mobilized NATO alliance if we are not careful."

The room was suddenly filled with low rumblings as the service chiefs and directorate heads spoke to each other. Fedorin initially appeared panic-stricken by Trusov's assertion, but then the president's face became resolute and strangely calm. "No matter, General Trusov, we can still outmaneuver them. We will begin the campaign in two days."

The muted rumors exploded into surprised shouts of alarm as the members of the General Staff protested. Trusov motioned for the crowd to calm down, but the army commander would have nothing to do with that. "You can't be serious, Comrade President, many of our brigades are scattered, conducting training exercises, they are not even close to their stepping-off positions. And they will still need to be reprovisioned before we can send them into a high-intensity conflict. This will take more than two days!"

"General Isayev, we will never get a better opportunity to reclaim that which was lost to us. If we don't go now, then there is every reason to believe that we won't be able to in the future," responded Fedorin evenly. "Yes, our troops will not be at their best, but we have trained more and harder than our adversaries. Need I remind you that the NATO Alliance has been greatly weakened by the Pacific War, the British exit from the EU, and the economic doldrums they are still wallowing in— they are taller, perhaps, on paper. In reality they are shorter than us.

"America is also weakened, and is desperately trying to keep the peace. Hardy is a new president and is still trying to get his feet under him. He has done nothing but react to our movements, we still have the initiative. If we don't take advantage of this opportunity, with our enemies disorganized and war weary, then we are doomed to failure in our great cause. We *must* move forward. Russia *must* move forward."

Pivoting sharply to face the chief of the Main Directorate for Deep Sea Research, Fedorin demanded, "What is the status of the Drakon launch complex?"

Admiral Rogov was uneasy; he was confident the president wouldn't like his answer. Swallowing hard, he told his president, "We have four of the torpedoes loaded as of yesterday. Preparations to load the fifth have begun and are underway as we speak. But, it will take at least another week to finish loading all the weapons."

Fedorin surprisingly didn't launch into another rant, but simply nodded with an air of conviction. "Very well, Admiral. Cease loading any additional weapons and begin system alignment and testing. I need those four torpedoes operational within two days. And as for you, Admiral Komeyev, I want that American submarine found and killed."

4 August 2021
2200 Local Time
USS *Jimmy Carter*
Entrance to Shokal'skogo Strait

The crew remained tense while they recovered the UUVs, constantly looking over their shoulder for the phantom that had brushed by so closely. Jerry headed forward once the second UUV was safely in the ocean interface module. As he walked into control Weiss had already turned *Carter* westward. He needed to head back to the *Toledo* gap, but he also hoped they'd get another glimpse of . . . whatever it was.

Jerry found Weiss and Segerson over at the starboard plotting table talk; the conversation appeared intense, punctuated with rapid hand movements toward the paper plot. Both were trying very hard to look calm. Jerry could feel the tension from all around him. Squeezing by the fire control positions he leaned on the table and asked nonchalantly, "So, just how close did *Kazan* get to our derrière?"

Segerson looked confused, Weiss had more of a poker face, but both were amazed by the abrupt question. Recovering quickly from the surprise, Segerson queried, "How do you know it was *Kazan*, Commodore?"

"Elementary, XO, we know she's at sea, and only a boat as quiet as a Severodvinsk class could get that close to a Seawolf without being detected earlier. So, we're talking, what, four to five thousand yards, give or take?"

Weiss let a taut grin materialize on his face; his commodore was spot on. "We're looking at about five k-yards at CPA, sir, although given the size of the beam widths, she could have been a lot closer."

"Nah, that wasn't all that close!" exclaimed Jerry, waving his hand in dismissal. Then with a little more volume, "That wasn't close, was it COB?"

Gibson, seated in the diving officer's chair, shook his head without turning. "Nope, we had plenty of room, Commodore. I don't know what those two are fretting about."

A collection of quiet snickers broke out from the control room watchstanders. Even *Carter*'s CO chuckled as he rubbed his forehead. "I suppose if one's personal reference for just what defines 'close' is a collision, then anything else is a walk in the park!"

"Sort of like the old adage, 'any landing you can walk away from is a good one.' Come to think of it, I've done that too." This time everyone laughed—the crew was well aware of their commodore's early career as an F-18 pilot. Jerry, noting the stress level had dropped a bit, gestured aft with his head and said, "Captain, let's take the geoplot and retire to the wardroom to nuke this problem out. We'll be less of a disturbance to the control room watchstanders."

"Of course, sir," responded Weiss. The captain then signaled the XO and navigator to join them. While Segerson gathered up the paper plot and the fire control chits, Jerry pointed to the weapons officer. "Kat, please have the sonar techs print out the latest sound velocity profile, as well as range of the day estimates for a *Severodvinsk*-class submarine at slow to moderate speed, say five to ten knots."

"Aye, aye, sir," Owens said as she turned toward the sonar shack.

"Oh, and at a depth of four hundred fifty feet," Jerry called out. Owens waved her acknowledgement.

* * *

For three hours the four men hovered above the geoplot like fortune
tellers over a Ouija Board, trying to piece together what had happened.
Sitting in the quiet of the wardroom, Jerry, Weiss, Segerson, and Malkoff pored over the sparse bearing data trying to refine the intruder's
movements. The contact had been picked up on the TB-33 thin-line
towed array in broadband-search mode. It had passed through the aft
beams quickly, which meant the bearing information was on the fuzzy
side. None of the hull arrays got a whiff, including the wide aperture
array that would have given them range as well as bearing. Classifying
the target was just as difficult, since there was very little narrowband to
go on; and what they did have wasn't consistent. To Jerry, it was bad
case of déjà vu.

By overlapping multiple course and speed scenarios with the calculated sonar ranges of the day, Jerry and the others were able to cut down
the possibilities to a narrow set of solutions. Malkoff drew a line of best
fit through the data and read off the results. "Best course is three one
five, speed six knots, with a closest point of approach of four thousand
six hundred yards."

"That matches pretty much with what I remember when *Seawolf* got
jumped by *Severodvinsk*," Jerry remarked as he stood up and stretched.

"I would have thought we'd have a better detection range than that
with the new fiber-optic towed arrays," commented Malkoff.

"Ah, yes, but this isn't *Severodvinsk* we're dealing with, Nav," reminded Jerry. "*Kazan* is a Project 885M submarine. The *M* means modernized, and one of those mods is supposedly a reduced acoustic signature.
So, it's basically a wash between our better arrays and their quieter
boat."

Segerson pointed to a choppy, faint line on the narrowband display
printout. "The turbine generator line is almost invisible. I can barely
make it out. And it's noticeably weaker than the SSTG lines I've seen
on Akulas. Not that they're all that easy to find, either."

Weiss shook his head; there was a worried expression on his face.
"This guy is going to be a problem."

"Concur, Lou, but now we at least have a better idea of when we can expect to hear him. And it's important to note that nothing suggests *he heard us*," Jerry affirmed, strongly emphasizing the last three words.

Weiss nodded his understanding and took a deep breath. "Okay, XO, let's see if the sonar techs can tweak their search settings to match this target and eke out a few hundred yards or more for us. But use four thousand yards as the initial range for the fire control solution."

As Segerson finished repeating the captain's order back to him, LT Ford knocked, opened the wardroom door, and stepped in.

"Captain, both UUVs have completed their battery charges, and we've reloaded the lead ballast. They're ready to deploy at your convenience."

"Thank you, Ben. We were just getting ready to discuss that—" A sudden growl of the sound-powered phone interrupted Weiss. Reaching over, he grabbed the handset. "Captain."

"Captain, Officer of the Deck, sir. Sonar reports the construction noise from the launch complex has suddenly stopped. And Mario says this isn't according to the schedule."

"Understood, OOD. We'll be right there."

5 August 2021
0145 Local Time
USS *Jimmy Carter*

Jerry and Weiss stared at the displays over the sonar techs' shoulders. Very little could be seen, or heard, from the direction of the launchers. No hammering, no humming, nothing. After thirty minutes of silence, Jerry knew this wasn't just another shift change. He waved to Weiss, and they stepped out of the sonar shack. "I've got a really bad feeling about this, Lou," Jerry whispered.

"Agreed, sir. Do you think it means the Russians are done loading the weapons?"

"Possibly. The intel guys said they didn't have a good handle on the Russians' schedule. But if you're correct, then we are almost out of time." Jerry walked over by the plotting boards, studied the charts for a moment, then strutted back. There was a determined look on his face. "We're going to make another attempt, right now."

Weiss hesitated, then started to speak, "Commodore, I don't think that's a good—"

"I don't like it, either," Jerry cut him off. "I wish we had more time to plot *Kazan*'s movements, but we'll just have to do the best we can, with what we have. I'll get the UUVs deployed. You get us headed to the gap."

0230 Local Time
USS *Jimmy Carter*

"UUVs are back in position," reported Ford. Jerry swiftly glanced at the status display on the command console; Walter and José were holding at fifty feet above the bottom and three hundred yards away from the cable. Ford and Lawson looked over at the commodore, waiting for him to give the order.

"All right, gentlemen, here's to hoping the second time's a charm," Jerry said wistfully.

"Technically, sir, isn't this the *third* time?" joked Lawson.

"Hush up, Thing Two!" snarled Jerry with feigned annoyance. Followed shortly by, "Smart-ass . . . and mind your console." The smile on his face revealed he really wasn't angry.

"Aye, aye, sir!" snorted Lawson. All four UUV operators laughed, even Cavanaugh found the exchange amusing. The junior lieutenant wore a very self-satisfied grin.

Jerry toggled the mike and reported to control that they were ready. A moment later Weiss announced, "Commence UUV run."

Ford exhaled a deep breath, and then uttered optimistically, "Here we go. Half speed to the motors, stand by for the turn."

The UUVs accelerated sluggishly, building up speed. The large-screen display on the bulkhead showed their positions relative to the minefield and the passive sonar net. The UUV icons moved painfully slowly toward their targets.

"Contact!" Frederick and Alvarez reported virtually simultaneously.

"Contact, aye. Stand by to shift to dual-frequency mode," ordered Ford.

So far, so good, Jerry thought. With the shorter-range active mode, they'd have a better feel for range to the first hydrophone, the marker to begin the flare. Once the range to the cable ticked down to fifty yards, Jerry gave the command. "Execute the turn, propulsion motors all stop. Stand by for downward pitch maneuver."

The UUVs arced lazily, with only their forward inertia to pull them through the turn. Once they were lined up with the cable, Jerry had the operators begin the glide, pitching down five degrees. Both vehicles noted a slow increase in velocity as they traded altitude for speed. Comparing the two flight trajectories, Jerry saw that José's speed was creeping up faster than Walter's. "Careful Steven, you're pulling out too far ahead," warned Jerry. "Ease off a bit on the pitch."

"Yes, sir. Backing off to four degrees down bubble."

There was no way to synchronize the movements of the two UUVs perfectly, but Jerry wanted them to be matched as close as possible. The lead shot had to be dropped at about the same time on both hydrophone sections if they were to disguise it as just another ambient noise spike. Staring at both UUV imaging sonar displays, he waited for the telltale bump that marked the first hydrophone. Petty Officer Frederick beat him to it.

"Contact! First hydrophone. Range is seven eight yards."

Alvarez blurted his report out seconds later. Time to bleed off some speed. "Execute flare, ten degrees up bubble!" Jerry commanded. Both pilots responded instantly and the status display noted a decrease in forward velocity.

"Careful now," he grunted softly. The vehicles' depth was dropping quickly; both pilots struggled to keep them on a steady course. All were aware that the UUVs would be very sluggish in their maneuvering. The sonar operators called out the range as they came up to the first drop. Over the intercom Jerry heard, "One thousand yards to minefield."

Once the range dropped to twenty-five yards, Jerry ordered the UUVs level and checked their respective depths. Walter's depth was perfect at three feet above the seafloor. José was a tad higher, but acceptable; speed was just over three knots, which was good enough. Nodding his approval, Jerry instructed, "Pilots, drop lead ballast at your discretion. Remember to allow enough time for the command to travel to the UUV."

Ford and Lawson acknowledged the order and the warning. A few seconds later, they started dumping the lead shot. "Pooping lead!" declared Lawson. Jerry just shook his head in silence.

After another twenty seconds, both pilots announced the glide bombing run had been completed. Jerry ordered the UUVs' propulsion motors started up again, and at a two-knot creep speed, he had the pilots bring the vehicles around to see how they'd done. As each hydrophone location came into view, Jerry noted that each one had been pushed deep into the silt due to the heavy lead pellets resting on top. With a feeling of triumph he reported to Weiss, "Conn, UCC. Sever hydrophone sections are obscured. Recommend we proceed to the target."

"UCC, Conn, concur. Bravo Zulu, UUV operators."

Turning back to the two teams, Jerry added his own congratulations. "Yes indeed, gentlemen, well done. Now let's get to the reason why we are here. Set course one eight five, speed five knots, and get the vehicles down to ten feet off the deck."

Twenty-two minutes later, *Jimmy Carter* slipped through the muffled acoustic fence.

5 August 2021
0030 Local Time
National Cyberdefense Center
Berlin, Federal Republic of Germany

Dieter Hoffmann swilled down another Red Bull, then tossed the empty can across the room. It had been a long day and there was no sign that it was going to end anytime soon. Rubbing his eyes, he suppressed a deep yawn and tried to focus his blurred vision back on to his computer screens. The caffeine and sugar in the energy drink would take a little time to work its magic on his groggy brain. Until then, he'd have to force his way back to work—and there was a lot of work to do.

Russian-based cyber attacks had jumped markedly in the last couple of days; most were annoyances, unsophisticated denial-of-service attacks, ransomeware, and spear phishing attempts, but others weren't quite so easy to figure out. The Moskito virus was proving to be a royal pain in the ass. Reports from several other European countries indicated it was widespread, but the infection appeared to be constrained to business websites only. All twelve of his fake company websites had been infected, but what was even more troubling was that a new version had popped up less than an hour ago. Hoffmann saw the Russian malware's antics as a personal challenge; one he gladly accepted.

Once the malware was safely ensconced in his machine, Hoffmann put it into an isolated test environment, or "sandbox," and attempted to disassemble the code. This wasn't as easy as it sounded, as the malware code itself was encrypted and proving to be quite resilient to cracking. Hoffmann and his colleagues had suspected the Russians were using a polymorphic engine that changed the code's appearance with each infection, but he'd busted more than his fair share of those during his music pirating days. The young German computer geek opened up his special electronic toolkit and got to work.

Recalling that the Moskito virus tapped into a computer's real-time clock, he had a hunch that the revised malware was a last-minute change, and that the change involved time. If the Russians were in a big hurry, then perhaps they hadn't changed the encryption/decryption engine. He pulled down the work from the forensic team and looked at their progress. They'd done a lot of emulation runs and Hoffmann could see they were getting close. Picking up where they left off, Hoffmann pulled out his favorite "nut cracker" as he called it and started more runs.

Thirty minutes later he let out a satisfied chuckle. "Ho-ho-ho, you sneaky little bastards. Got a little sloppy, did we?"

Triggering the now located encryption/decryption engine, the gobbledygook on the screen instantly transformed into readable JavaScript. Scrolling down, he saw over two dozen Internet Protocol addresses, some he recognized immediately; these must be the targets. Breaking down the code further he saw that the virus would be launched by the business websites but the actual attacks would be from a vast network of closed-circuit television cameras located all over Europe. Then he saw the clock function and noted the time and date.

"My God!" he whispered. Grabbing the phone's handset, Hoffmann excitedly punched his boss's home number. Hoffmann fidgeted impatiently as the phone rang. The ringing stopped suddenly, but it was several seconds before a disoriented Klemmer answered, "Hello?"

"Johann . . . Johann, it's Dieter."

"Dieter?" replied Klemmer, still a little wobbly. "What's the matter? Do you know what time it is?"

"Yes, I know it's very late, but Johann, I cracked the Moskito virus."

"You did?!" Klemmer's tone instantly transformed from annoyed to intrigued. "What is its function?"

"Johann it's a huge BOTNET. Designed to execute a massive distributed-denial-of-service attack on the twenty-five largest banks in Europe. This *verdammt* code will disrupt virtually all electronic transactions throughout Europe; commerce will come to a crashing halt. The chaos this thing will cause is on a legendary scale, and Johann, it has a time fuse that is scheduled to go off in a little more than forty-eight hours!"

5 August 2021
0315 Local Time
Prima Polar Station
Bolshevik Island, Russia

The harsh wind tore at Captain-Lieutenant Mirsky's parka, and while it wasn't quite as bad as the day before, it was still blustery. As he approached the small wooden hutch situated at the extreme end of the station, he grumbled that it was as far away from the flight line as it could possibly be and still be considered part of the base. The wind had shifted during the late evening and was now coming from the north. And even though it was the height of summer, the temperature dipped down below freezing. It was with a sense of relief that he closed the outer door, pulled back his hood, and removed the heavy arctic mittens. Walking into the main operations room, Mirsky was immediately struck by how cramped it looked, as well as its haphazard arrangement—he was not impressed.

Two junior ratings sat at what looked like ordinary computer workstations, while another manned a surface search radar repeater. An officer and a fourth enlisted man stood by a table with a chart of the local area spread out on the surface. Mirsky noticed that while there were several portable heaters going, everyone seemed to be wearing multiple layers.

"Lieutenant Zhabin?" he called out loudly. The officer at the plotting table looked up, saw the bundled individual, and shuffled his way around to greet their visitor.

"Captain-Lieutenant Mirsky, I presume," Zhabin remarked while extending his hand.

"Correct," replied Mirsky, and after shaking hands gestured to the work space. "Not the most hospitable of accommodations."

Zhabin shrugged his shoulders. "It's what was available. It took a little time, but we've made it functional."

"Hmmm," Mirsky grunted as he set down his gloves and opened his parka. "Look Lieutenant, I've never done coordinated operations with a fixed acoustic system before. That job is usually done by maritime patrol aircraft, so I've come to see how this system works."

"Of course, sir. Come this way." Stepping up to the plotting table, Zhabin pointed to the workstations and explained. "Those operators monitor the two MGK-608M passive arrays that guard the approaches to the construction basin. We have eleven modules to the north, here, and seven down here to the south, between October Revolution and Bolshevik Islands." He pointed to the two lines of symbols on the chart. "These are relatively short-range sensors, say two to three kilometers against a frontline Western submarine in this environment, but the way the barrier is laid out, any intruder would have to pass very close to one of the hydrophone sections. There is no way to get around either sensor line."

Mirsky nodded. "How do you classify a contact?"

"We have the ability to analyze any narrowband components that we can see, of course, but that takes time. Our current procedure relies on comparing an alerted module's location with the surface radar picture to validate that the contact is probably submerged. That's when I'd call you."

"Very well," said Mirsky with less disdain. The approach Zhabin and his men had adopted was well established in the Russian Navy. At least Mirsky's helicopter crews wouldn't be chasing surface ships. Still, having a better understanding of the system's capability could be useful. Motioning toward the door leading outside, he asked, "How badly affected are you by this wind?"

The junior lieutenant shrugged again. "The wind is actually not as big an annoyance as you might think, however, ice noise, and all that banging from the construction site, can trigger the Sever system's automatic detection feature and cause it to alert. Fortunately, those noise sources are highly transient. They spike quickly and are gone just as fast. A submarine attempting to pass through doesn't sound anything like that and we'd spot the difference instantly."

Satisfied with the explanation, Mirsky grunted again and offered his hand. "Thank you, Lieutenant. I appreciate your time." Pointing over to the flight line, he added, "I have two Ka-27M helicopters on constant combat alert; another four can be airborne within fifteen minutes. The quicker you can relay potential submarine detections, the sooner I can get my helicopters over the alerting module, and we both know how critical that is for a successful prosecution. So, I would lean toward erring on the side of caution, if I were you."

Recognizing an order when he heard one, Zhabin came to attention and barked, "Yes, sir!"

0330 Local Time
USS *Jimmy Carter*

The approach to the launcher had been slow and nerve-wracking. Yes, *Carter* had penetrated the Russians' outer defenses, but now they had to creep up on the launcher while carefully keeping an acoustic eye peeled for any new surprises—the last thing they needed was another row of acoustic sensors, or God forbid, mines. There was little conversation among the UUV operators, only speaking when absolutely necessary, as if their silence would help the boat stay covert.

Jerry watched the starboard large-screen display closely. It always presented the current tactical situation, and right now the situation was complicated. They were just six thousand yards from the launcher, hovering close to the ocean floor, waiting as the UUVs closed in from the northwest at three knots, barely five feet off the muddy bottom. Just to the right of the launcher, nine thousand yards away from *Carter*, were the Russian submarines *Belgorod* and *Losharik*. Jerry could taste the tension in the air.

"Conn, Sonar. Sierra one four appears to be hovering near Sierra one five. There is no apparent bearing rate with either contact."

Weiss's reply was hushed and terse. "Sonar, Conn, aye."

Cavanaugh came up beside Jerry and asked quietly, "What are they doing, Commodore?"

Jerry exhaled loudly before he responded. "I think *Losharik* is getting ready to mate up with *Belgorod*. The modified Oscar is the mother ship. One of its jobs is to transport the smaller, deep-diving boat to where it needs to go. Personally, I really don't care what they do as long as they stay put, or better yet, go away all together."

"Can *Belgorod* hear us? I mean, we're awfully close aren't we?"

Though he spoke carefully, the doctor's tone betrayed his nervousness. "I doubt it, Dr. Dan," Jerry answered. "*Belgorod* would've had to store its towed array because it's been stationary. The SKAT-3 hull array is good, but nowhere near that good. As long as we stay very quiet, she won't have a clue we're here. But one thing is certain. If those two boats are leaving, then the Russians are done loading the launchers."

Jerry took two steps over to the Walter control station and gently put a hand on Ford's shoulder. "Status, Ben."

Ford stiffly shook his head. "Nothing yet, sir. We're still at least three hundred yards out."

"Understood." Stepping away, Jerry looked back up at the tactical display. He'd have to be patient.

A long three minutes later, Frederick quietly cried out, "Contact! Bearing one seven four, range one two zero yards."

Half jumping, Jerry rushed behind Frederick, who showed the commodore the display. "Tallyho," he whispered. Dashing back to the command console, Jerry pointed to Lawson and called, "Steven, alter José's course to close on Walter!"

"Already on it, sir!"

Waving that he'd heard Lawson, Jerry grabbed the intercom mike and called in the detection, "Conn, UCC, Walter has made contact."

Weiss's relieved voice acknowledged the report.

Looking over at Cavanaugh, Jerry saw the man dancing around trying to get a good view over Frederick's shoulder. "Hey Dr. Dan," he shouted. "We can put that up on the big screen! Get your drawings organized, so we can figure out how many beacons we need to deploy and where!"

The digital image on the screen couldn't do justice to the structure's true size, but to Jerry, the launcher complex was huge. From what he could tell, Cavanaugh had pretty much nailed its construction. Six bulky cylindrical vertical supports sprouted up out of massive blocks. The numerous cross members were hefty I-beams that supported six launch tubes, arranged in two rows of three and canted upward at about twenty degrees or so. Jerry almost burst into laughter watching the explosives expert. Cavanaugh was sloppily tossing rejected drawings into the air as he went through his preplanned scenarios.

"Voilà!" he announced, and brought the desired drawing to Jerry. "See here, Commodore, this is almost a perfect match! We'll need four torpedoes to turn this engine of destruction into scrap metal!"

Jerry examined the drawing and agreed that it seemed a good match for what they were seeing. Still, there was something odd about the left pair of tubes. "Dr. Dan, don't the last two tubes on the left look different from the others?" he asked.

Cavanaugh settled down and stared at the screen. "Yes, now that you mention it, those two tubes do look different. Can we get a closer look?"

"You heard the man, Ben," Jerry directed.

"Aye, sir. Stand by."

The image grew and shifted upward as Walter moved in on the left hand side of the structure. Once the UUV was in the same plane and looking right at the tubes, it became clear why they were different.

"They're empty!" declared Cavanaugh. "Those tubes have nothing in them. We can treat this as a four-tube launcher." He jumped down and started rummaging around the deck to find the appropriate drawing. Jerry, on the other hand, was not nearly as pleased as the doctor. *Why would the Russians have stopped before all the tubes were loaded?* he thought to himself. It didn't make a lot of sense. Suddenly, Jerry had a really anxious feeling about the whole thing.

"Dr. Cavanaugh," Jerry exclaimed. "Do we need fewer torpedoes to deal with four launchers?"

"What? Oh, yes, three should do very nicely, Commodore."

"Great, wonderful. Please coordinate with Lieutenant Lawson and get the four beacons on José deployed." Pivoting to face Ford, Jerry shouted, "Ben!"

"Sir?"

"I want you to send Walter to the north, course . . ." he paused while he changed the display screen to a navigation chart, "course zero three five, low and slow."

The UUV pilot looked stunned, perplexed. "You want me to send the UUV away from the structure, sir?"

Jerry understood the junior officer's confusion; the commodore was straying far from the plan they'd been working on for the past several days. "I'll explain later. Course zero three five, low and slow, and I mean now, mister!"

"Aye, aye, sir," jumped Ford.

Reaching over, he grabbed the sound-powered phone handset, selected the control room, and spun the handle.

"Captain," answered Weiss.

"Lou, Commodore Mitchell, we're positioning four beacons now. Cavanaugh says we can get away with three torpedoes; I'm going with four. I've ordered Walter to disengage and head north. I intend to have him scout ahead of us, looking primarily to the north and east. On the way out I'll put José to our left, looking to the west."

Weiss was initially quiet, but then inquired, "Is there a problem, Commodore? I was under the impression we were going to use one or both UUVs for battle-damage assessment."

Jerry took a deep breath, fighting the wild urgency he felt. He needed to sound calm. "Lou, the Russians left two of the tubes empty. The only reason I can think of why they'd do something like that is because they're rushing, because they believe there is an imminent threat. I have a very bad feeling they may be onto us. With four weapons, we'll still have some redundancy, but right now we need the UUVs' passive sensors more than the imaging sonar. I'll inform you as soon as José is finished deploying the transponder beacons. Then we need to get the hell out of here."

0445 Local Time
USS *Jimmy Carter*

If Jerry thought the run in was slow, getting out seemed like an eternity. Both UUVs were now deployed on *Carter*'s flanks. Walter was to the northeast, nearly twenty minutes ahead, José to the northwest. Both UUVs were at six knots, *Carter* at four, crawling ever so slowly to the gap in the minefield and open water. Jerry had insisted that the UUVs cross the passive barrier first, away from the *Toledo* gap; he was betting they would be able to sneak across by coasting over the sensor cable. If they were detected, then they would serve as decoys to enable *Carter* to make good her escape—after she fired the torpedoes.

Glancing over at Cavanaugh, Jerry noticed that the man looked down, despondent actually. "What's the matter, Dr. Dan?"

"I'm not sure, Commodore. It all seems so anticlimactic. I mean we've placed the beacons and now we're essentially on our way home. Not quite as exciting as I thought it would be."

Jerry couldn't help but laugh. "Dr. Dan, we still need to *fire* the torpedoes. That'll generate some excitement, I can assure you. Then there is that vexing little problem of weaseling our way past the minefield with a bunch of very pissed-off Russians all around us. I'd be very happy with a boring transit out, but the odds are—"

"Conn, Sonar," squawked the intercom, interrupting Jerry. "Sharp mechanical transients from Sierra one five. Possible mating collar or docking clamps."

"Well, that will complicate things," Jerry grumbled. "If *Losharik* is docking, then *Belgorod* may start moving."

"Commodore, Walter is nearing the Sever line. Estimated range is three hundred yards," reported Ford.

"Very well. Bring Walter to a depth of fifty feet off the bottom and then secure the propulsion motor. Trade altitude for speed as much as possible to maintain five knots."

Everyone in UCC seemed to hold their breath for the next four minutes as they watched Walter's representative icon move across the digital chart. They saw the cable lying on the ocean floor as Walter passed over it, some thirty feet, with no sign of any hydrophones. A few hundred yards further downrange, Jerry ordered Ford to bring Walter back to power and make four knots. They'd have to do the same thing in about twenty minutes with José. But just before they were to execute the second sneak maneuver, Frederick called out, "Passive contact, bearing zero two zero!"

Jerry nearly launched himself out of his seat as he brought up Walter's passive flank array. There was a weak contact, drawing left rapidly. There could be but one conclusion. Grabbing the handset, he toggled the mike. "Conn, UCC. Walter has gained a passive sonar contact, bearing zero three three from own ship. High left bearing rate. It looks like our friend is back."

Before Weiss could reply, the intercom squawked again. "Conn, Sonar, Sierra one five bears one seven zero. Contact has gotten underway, slight left bearing drift." It wasn't long before the sound-powered phone set growled. Jerry was expecting the call.

"Commodore, we have a serious problem." Weiss's voice was stressed, and rightfully so. "If *Belgorod* keeps coming to the left, we'll be caught between her and *Kazan*. My intention is to get a good firing solution and engage *Belgorod* first, then attack the launch complex."

Jerry almost shouted his reply, but managed to keep it to a firm, "No, Lou, do not concur. Continue to monitor the situation and prepare to fire the four torpedoes at the launcher. That is our first priority."

"Sir, we'll get caught up in a close melee with *two* Russian subs. We need to take one out first, Commodore!"

"Captain." Jerry's voice was even more forceful. "Stay focused on the mission. We haven't been detected yet and I have a plan in mind to—"

"Commodore! I'm responsible for this boat and I don't see the logic in ignoring two highly capable threats!" Weiss's tone was defiant.

That was it. Jerry had had enough. He growled, "I'm coming to control!"

19

KNIFE FIGHT

Fighting his rising temper, Jerry almost forgot to tell LT Ford to take over in UCC and maintain contact on the unidentified approaching submarine. The panicky look on all of the operators' faces helped to remind Jerry that as far as this crew was concerned, he was the next thing to God, and the wraith of a squadron commodore was a terrible thing to behold. As Jerry marched toward the control room, the memories of his own heated debates with his old Squadron 15 commodore, Captain Charles Simonis out in Guam, rushed into his mind. He remembered how he felt when his superior challenged his tactical prowess, and the memory had a calming effect. Jerry decided he wouldn't relieve Weiss the moment he saw him—he'd at least give the man a chance.

He had no sooner entered the operations compartment, than Jerry saw a lone figure standing in the passageway. It was the executive officer, Joshua Segerson. He looked very unhappy.

"I had a sneaking suspicion I'd run into you, Commander," Jerry rumbled as he advanced. "I'm in a bit of a hurry, so state your case while we walk."

Segerson's surprised expression told Jerry the XO had been expecting a knockdown drag-out fight. Recovering quickly, he said, "Sir, we're be-tween two hammers and the anvil. If we don't engage *Belgorod* first, we'll be in a three-way cross fire before we can get all our weapons away!"

"Interesting. I don't see it that way," Jerry replied sharply. "You and your skipper have a bad case of tactical tunnel vision. You've overlooked some clues that should tell you what is actually going on."

The XO grabbed Jerry's shoulder, bringing him to a halt. His ap-pearance was a mix of anger and concern. "Commodore! Lou Weiss is a fine submarine officer, and a good captain. He's proven himself to me, and the crew; I trust his judgment!"

Physically accosting a senior officer like that was unheard of. For a very brief moment, Jerry wanted to slam the man up against the bulk-head, but a fistfight would accomplish nothing. Instead, he took a deep breath, pivoted and faced Segerson. Speaking carefully, he told the XO, "I'm not saying he isn't a good submariner, or a good captain. What I'm saying is that he's about to commit a gross tactical error that will adversely affect the ability of this boat to complete its mission."

Pointing over his right shoulder toward *Toledo*'s wrecked hull, he exclaimed, "My friend and his crew lie over there, dead, and millions more may join them if we don't do this right! I'll give the captain his min-ute in court, but if I'm not satisfied that he understands what he's doing wrong, I *will* relieve him. Do I make myself clear?"

Segerson swallowed hard and nodded. "Yes, sir. Thank you, sir."

Still apprehensive, but now a little more hopeful, the XO followed Jerry into the control room. As soon as the pair emerged by the plotting tables, Weiss saw them and approached. He had a resigned air about him. "I assume I'm to be relieved, sir," he said stoically.

Jerry barked, "Enough with the dramatics, Captain! Get your ass over here!" He then turned and took up a spot by the geoplot. Speech-less, Weiss stepped down from the periscope stand and stood next to his executive officer. "You, too, COB!" Jerry called over toward the diving officer's position.

"Yessir!" responded Gibson.

The master chief quickly squeezed by the fire control consoles and positioned himself to Weiss's right.

"Let me summarize your argument," Jerry spoke quickly. "If we don't engage *Belgorod* first, we may not be able to get all our torpedoes away and escape before being counterattacked by both submarines."

Weiss nodded. "Yes, sir. If we can get a shot off at *Belgorod* first, we can at least force her to evade and withdraw. By firing the weapons at slow speed, we'll be able to delay them from being detected by either *Belgorod* or the fixed array for a little bit—just long enough for us to get some bearing separation."

"And where do you plan on placing this attack, since *Belgorod* is in the towed array's end-fire beam? We'd have to maneuver at least once to get a reasonable firing solution. That will take time; time we really don't have with *Kazan* coming in from the northeast," countered Jerry.

"It doesn't have to be a great solution, Commodore, just good enough to make *Belgorod* run. Her skipper won't know we don't have a good solution."

"But it will still take time, and it all hinges on your assumption that the shot will not be detected quickly. I believe this is an unrealistic assumption, Captain. Either *Belgorod*, or possibly *Kazan*, will likely hear the weapon soon after launch. Those boats have the best ASW sensors in the Russian fleet and even a mod seven ADCAP torpedo isn't that quiet. Either one of the two subs will likely go active and shoot a salvo of weapons down the bearing. Maybe both.

"And once one sub goes active, the other will hear their comrade's pinging and light off herself, and then we *will be* caught in a cross fire. This isn't poker, Lou, it's chess, and you're getting pawn hungry. A good submarine commanding officer is aggressive; a great one knows when not to be."

Weiss's look was one of discouragement. He'd felt so confident. Jerry smiled faintly; he now had the CO's attention. "You've made two big assumptions here, Lou. First, you assumed that *Belgorod* would act like any other attack submarine. This is a bad assumption. *Belgorod* is a Russian navy *strategic* asset. She and *Losharik* are your counterparts in the Russian Navy. They're unique. And don't forget that *Belgorod* is also a strategic nuclear asset.

"I'm convinced that *Belgorod*'s standing orders are to avoid a fight at all costs. She will run as far and as fast as possible from us.

Segerson was shaking his head, trying to follow all of his commodore's finer points, but one thing just kept bothering him. "I don't get it, sir, if you believe any torpedo we launch will be detected quickly, then how does attacking the facility first change anything?"

"Ah, very good, XO," commended Jerry. "That deals with the second assumption, but I doubt you'd realize that you were making one. You were all being good little submariners trying to figure out how you could stay undetected, covert, during the attack. Well, we can't. So we need to be as frickin' loud as we possibly can!"

If human brains had circuit breakers, three of them would have popped then and there.

"What!?" blurted all three men in concert.

"I'm . . . I'm sorry, Commodore, but I don't understand," stammered Weiss.

"All right, then, here's the *new* plan." Jerry motioned for them to close ranks and look at the geoplot. "Walter is almost past the minefield, here, on our right, José is on the other flank about here, and we are in the middle. Once José clears the minefield we have both UUVs come up, say two hundred feet off the bottom, drop their NAEs and run like hell, away from the gap. Yes, that means we're sacrificing them; fortunes of war.

"At the same time, *Carter* will also deploy countermeasures, as well as some mobile decoys. This will cause the majority, if not all of the Sever modules to alarm. But because there will be multiple, very loud, noise sources evenly dispersed along the line, it'll mess with the system's ability to provide good bearings. Even if they do manage to get a glimpse, there will be at least five possible moving targets for them to contend with, the Russians won't know where to send their ASW assets. In the meantime, while they're still crapping their pants, we'll fire four weapons. The first two go out at twenty-eight knots, the second set at forty knots. When the second pair catches up to the first, we put the pedal to the metal on all four torpedoes, cut the wires, close the outer doors and run through the gap.

"By the time *Belgorod* can distinguish the torpedoes through the jamming, we won't be anywhere near that bearing. Her captain will naturally think he's the target of the salvo. He'll probably counter fire and then run to the south as fast as his boat's overweight butt can go."

"What about *Kazan*?" Segerson asked.

Jerry grinned. "That's why I'm having the UUVs dump the NAEs to the north of the minefield. All that noise should trigger the mines' passive sensors and many of them will go active looking for a target to lock on to. I don't think *Kazan*'s captain will want to be anywhere near a pack of activated mines looking for something to kill. He'll evade to the north, just to make sure he's out of range of the mine's torpedo payload."

"And if he goes active first?" pressed Weiss.

"Then he'll see a lot of junk on his screen from all the noise, but even if his sonar system can cut through it, there will be multiple moving targets. He'll have to figure out real fast what's valid and what isn't—if we're lucky, he may even think there are several submarines attacking simultaneously. Regardless, he'll be distracted and that gives us the advantage. Once we get in front of the countermeasures, we'll have a clear line of bearing to *Kazan*. We generate a quick fire control solution, and if necessary, throw a couple of Mark 48s her way while we head north to the pack ice. Any questions?"

Weiss, Segerson, and Gibson initially kept staring at the geoplot, then looked up at each other, and then finally at Jerry. "Um, no, sir," said Weiss.

"Okay, then. We need to do this expeditiously; we'll only have about ten minutes after the first countermeasure is launched. We need to have the torpedoes on the way, and us out of the way before that time is up," Jerry summarized. Then pointing at Segerson, added, "The XO and I will set up the torpedo spread, and you, Captain . . ."

"Yes, sir?"

"Fight your ship."

0540 Local Time
USS *Jimmy Carter*

The enthusiasm in control started ramping up the moment Jerry had given Weiss his instructions. LT Ford, in charge in UCC, successfully navigated José across the fixed acoustic arrays and had just detected one of the PMK-2 mine anchors. Jerry glanced at the navigation plot and saw that *Carter* was only a few hundred yards from the lead-lined passage they'd created. Life was about to get very exciting . . . for the Russians.

"Weps, make tubes one through four ready in all respects," Weiss ordered calmly.

"Make tubes one through four ready in all respects, aye, sir," repeated Owens. Jerry peeked at the torpedo tube status display and confirmed they were being flooded down; they'd be ready to shoot soon. Stepping back from the fire control consoles, Jerry turned and caught Weiss looking his way; his expression was still an odd mixture of relief and bewilderment.

Smiling, Jerry passed by the periscope stand and without looking up remarked, "When this all over, Captain, remind me to tell you a little sea story about a very close friend of mine."

Startled by the unexpected statement, Weiss hesitated momentarily, recovered, and replied, "Yes, sir."

"Captain, we're passing over the acoustic arrays now," reported Malkoff.

"Time to begin the festivities," Jerry muttered under his breath, reaching for the intercom mike. "UCC, Conn. Accelerate UUVs to maximum speed and bring them to a depth of four hundred feet."

As Ford acknowledged the command, Weiss leaned toward the fire control consoles and shouted, "Countermeasures, stand by!"

An intense silence descended on the control room as everyone sat anxiously at the edge of their seat. All eyes were on Jerry, waiting for him to give the order when all hell would break loose. After an insufferable pause, the intercom speaker squawked to life. "Conn, UCC, both UUVs are at eight knots, accelerating to ten. Depth is four hundred fifty feet, coming to four hundred feet."

With an expression of utter resolve, Jerry clicked the mike. "UCC, Conn, deploy countermeasures . . . NOW!"

0550 Local Time
Prima Polar Station

Petty Officer Yolkov yawned and rubbed his eyes. The Sever monitoring station personnel had been at full combat alert for the last twenty-four hours, and everyone was starting to get a bit worn. Glancing at his watch, he was disheartened to see that his shift was only half over. Sighing quietly, the young rating picked up his mug with hot tea. He had to stay awake for another two hours. Yolkov raised the mug, but it never reached his lips. Suddenly, his eyes went wide with disbelief as his display console erupted with alarms.

"Lieutenant! . . . LIEUTENANT!" he screeched.

"What is your problem, Petty Officer Yolkov?" shouted an angry Zhabin. The lieutenant looked up and saw both operators were white as ghosts; Yolkov was trembling, pointing nervously at his screen.

Irritated, Zhabin strutted toward the pair, yelling, "I said, what is the problem, Petty Officer—" He stopped dead in his tracks as soon as he looked over the operator's shoulder and saw the display.

"Mother of God!" he exclaimed. The entire northern line of Sever modules was alerting. The track log kept jumping between three and five possible targets. But there was no track data, and the bearings were all over the place. Stumbling backward, Zhabin almost fell over a chair at a nearby desk. Scrambling to maintain his balance, he grabbed the nearest phone . . . but whom should he call? The helicopter detachment commander? No! He had to alert the entire base. With quivering fingers he punched in the chief of staff's number.

Boris Kalinin had learned to appreciate the early hours of each morning. It was the only time he could rely on to be free of interruptions, allowing him to attack the massive assemblage of paperwork the base generated. Thus, when the phone rang, it was with frustration that he reached for the handset.

"Chief of Sta—" he started to say, but was cut off by an excited, loud, and incoherent voice, shouting something about multiple contacts. Kalinin recognized the voice as the officer in charge of the Sever monitoring detachment. Irritated by the unintelligible report, the captain bellowed, "Lieutenant Zhabin! Get a hold of yourself! Calm down, you imbecile! That's better. Now report properly, Lieutenant."

Zhabin paused and began again. His voice was still very agitated, but he was at least understandable. Kalinin listened, impatient, then with alarm. Jumping to his feet, he exclaimed, "Five submarine contacts!? The entire northern array line is being jammed!? Call the flight line immediately! I want helicopters airborne, right now!"

He slammed the handset down back into the base while shouting for his aide, "Pyotr! Sound a base-wide alert! We're under attack!"

USS Jimmy Carter

"Firing point procedures, Dragon torpedo complex, Mark 48 AD-CAP, tubes one through four," snapped Weiss.

"Solution ready," called Segerson.

"Weapons ready," Owens followed instantly.

"Ship ready," announced Malkoff.

"Shoot on generated bearing!" Weiss roared.

"Set . . . standby . . . shoot!" reported the fire control technician.

Down in *Carter*'s torpedo room, the firing valves on the port and starboard tube nests popped open, releasing high-pressure air to the tube's air turbine pumps. The spinning turbine blades drove an impeller that gulped hundreds of gallons of seawater and thrust it forcefully into the tube. The massive pulse of seawater boosted the two-ton torpedoes into the ocean at nearly thirty knots. Seconds later, the four torpedoes' own engines came to life and the torpedoes accelerated smoothly and quietly.

"Normal launch!" shouted the fire control tech. "Torpedoes are on course one eight three, first set at two eight knots, the second at four zero knots, run-to-enable seven five double oh yards!"

LT Owens then did a quick double take; she didn't like what she saw. "Captain! Loss of wire continuity on weapon number four!"

"Understood," replied Weiss calmly, he wasn't surprised. Statistically, it was a long shot to retain all four wires. Turning to Jerry, he asked, "Do we still accelerate the three torpedoes to sixty-five knots?"

Mitchell paused while he did the mental math. At forty knots, the torpedoes would need an additional two minutes or so to reach the enable point, where the seekers would start pinging. He shook his head; the Russians wouldn't be able to react quickly enough. He decided he'd rather keep all four weapons. "Negative, Captain. Bring all weapons to forty knots."

"Aye, aye, sir," Weiss said then, looking at his stopwatch, counted down the time until his next order. "Weps, accelerate units one and two to forty knots, cut the wires, and shut the outer doors." Weiss gestured for Segerson to follow up on the torpedoes' status. Pivoting, the captain ordered, "Helm, all ahead standard. Dive, keep us close to the bottom!"

Prima Polar Station
Red 48-Helicopter Flight Line

Captain-Lieutenant Mirsky didn't even bother taxiing to the runway. He frantically waved the ground crew away, turned the aircraft to face the wind, and then gunned his machine. The Ka-27M helicopter leapt into the sky. Without waiting to see if the other helo had taken off, Mirsky pushed the throttle to full power and set course for the western end of the hydroacoustic array.

"Petty Officer Mitrov, enter these coordinates into the Lira combat system." Mirsky spoke tersely as he handed the rating a piece of paper. His head was still spinning. How could four American submarines be attacking the complex? Two contacts were detected at each end of the array barrier; Mirsky's flight was to prosecute the ones to the west, as headquarters didn't have a good position on the Project 885M submarine, *Kazan*. She was at last report off to the east of Bolshevik Island, but that had been some time ago. The pilot didn't like the idea of helicopters and friendly submarines operating in the same area. They couldn't communicate easily; coordination was all but impossible. He'd have to be very careful when he dropped his torpedo. Killing one of their own submarines, even in a chaotic battle such as this, would be a career-ending blunder—if he were lucky.

USS *Jimmy Carter*

"Coming up on the minefield," stated Malkoff. "We should be clear in about two minutes."

"Very well, Nav." Weiss leaned over toward the fire control consoles. He needed to prepare for the next phase of their escape. "Weps, make tubes seven and eight ready in all respects."

"Conn, Sonar," blared the speaker. "Regained Sierra one five on the towed array. Contact bears roughly one nine five, drawing left, heading southwest. She's cavitating."

"Run away! Run away!" squealed Segerson with a bad British accent. Mitchell had been right. *Belgorod* was running.

Jerry and Weiss both laughed. "C'mon XO, you'd run too if you saw four torpedoes heading your way!" chided Jerry jokingly. Segerson dismissed the reproach with a haughty wave.

"Conn, Sonar, possible explosion to the east. Acoustic countermeasures are masking bearings between zero seven five and zero eight zero."

Weiss and Jerry looked at each other, perplexed. An explosion? The captain hit the intercom, "Sonar, how confident are you about an explosion?"

"Pretty sure, Skipper. The countermeasures lit off just a moment later."

"*Kazan*? Or Walter?" Weiss wondered.

"Knowing our luck, Lou, I think Walter is toast. Those countermeasures, though, they bother me," replied Jerry as he reached for the intercom with the UUV control center. "UCC, Conn, do you retain contact with either vehicle?"

"Negative, Conn. Countermeasure interference has masked all comms." Ford's report wasn't a surprise. Jerry had expected as much.

Once again, the intercom squawked. "Conn, Sonar, own ship's units are accelerating!"

Prima Polar Station

Zhabin and his operators cheered when a torpedo from a PMK-2 mine hit one of their assailants and detonated. The explosion was clearly heard on Sever modules nine, ten, and eleven. Once the reverberation from the blast died down, there were no longer any signals from the contact—a confirmed kill.

After the initial shock, Zhabin managed to calm down and began adjusting the Sever system's beamformer and signal-processing settings, trying to get the modules to look away from the jammers. He was only partially successful. Modules two through eight were still badly degraded, effectively useless. He still believed that there were at least three confirmed contacts, possibly four, and that they appeared to be attempting to penetrate the defensive barrier at the ends.

Concentrating on the outputs from the four good modules, he saw traces of several fast-moving objects circling near the minefield. That meant a number of mines had actively detected a target and launched their torpedoes. He was amazed that the Americans were so bold as to try a frontal assault. Looking to the south, Zhabin saw a submarine signature with a moderate left bearing rate. It was increasing speed quickly and was fitted with two screws—*Belgorod* was attempting to escape.

"Petty Officer Yolkov, inform central post that *Belgorod* is underway and is steaming to the southwest. Speed is eighteen knots and accelerating; she should be able to . . ." The officer suddenly ceased his report as another contact emerged from the noise clutter and into module nine's field of view. The new contact had an unstable, blurry bearing, but it appeared to be moving incredibly fast.

Zhabin played with the controls in an attempt to tighten up the bearing display, but to no effect. After another twenty seconds, information started coming in from module ten and the fuzzy bearing trace seemed to split out into several close lines. The lieutenant inhaled sharply, it wasn't just one contact; it was many. "Torpedoes!" he shrieked.

USS *Jimmy Carter*

Carter's Mark 48 torpedoes all began pinging nearly simultaneously. They were only four thousand yards away from the launch complex, and the transponders all sent back a strong coded homing signal, each beacon calling to a separate torpedo. After three solid echoes from the beacons, the torpedoes accelerated to attack speed—sixty-five knots—and dove. The weapons ignored the large target moving away to their right. Each torpedo was fixated on its own personal siren song. Two minutes later the first torpedo reached the Dragon launcher and struck one of the large concrete anchors, detonating on contact. Three more explosions followed in a ripple.

The lower row of three launch tubes was heaved upward by the shock wave and the expanding gas bubble. The upper set folded in the middle as the blast and inertia from the lower tubes thrust them upward and back. The pulsating bubbles first pulled the tubes toward each other, then violently pushed them out again, only this time sideways. Five of the launch tubes were crushed, flattened like beer cans over much of their length, while the sixth was badly bent and distorted around its center. The supporting I-beams were twisted like pretzels and wrenched free from the now-crushed cylindrical supports.

"Conn, Sonar, multiple explosions bearing one eight five!" cried out the sonar supervisor. A boisterous cheer broke out in control, but they weren't done yet and Weiss quickly suppressed the celebration. "SILENCE IN CONTROL!" he thundered.

As the noise died down, Weiss turned and pulled on the intercom's switch. "Sonar, report. What do you hear?"

"Skipper, it sounds like someone kicked over an organ—multiple 'gong-like' noises and lots of banging metal. That launcher got thumped real hard."

Jerry rubbed his eyes and took a deep breath. "Rest now, my friend, we have the watch," he whispered. Then glancing up at the periscope stand he saw Weiss looking down. Jerry extended his hand and grasped

Weiss's firmly. "Well done, Captain. Now, let's get the hell away from this beehive!"

Red 48

Mirsky could hear the two Klimov turboshaft engines shrieking above his cockpit. He'd pushed them well beyond the red line on the RPM gauges, and he prayed they'd hold together. Both Helix helicopters were doing better than 150 knots—racing toward the last reported location of a probable American submarine.

Toggling his mike, he passed instructions to his wingman. "Red 45, disregard standard tactics. Drop three RGB-48 buoys to the northeast of the datum, triangular pattern. I'll do the same to the northwest."

The flight commander was desperate to get sensors in the water as soon as possible. If the American was trying to disengage under the cover of the countermeasures, he'd be moving faster than usual, which meant the two helos couldn't afford the time needed to hover and dip. Besides, the dipping sonar would be badly affected by all the noise in the water; the passive RGB-48 sonobuoy with its much lower frequency range would not. The only problem would be in finding enough open water to drop the buoys safely. A crushed sensor wouldn't do them any good.

Mirsky pulled the Helix into a sharp, low hover as Mitrov verified the sea surface below was free of large ice chunks, and then started dropping the buoys. Once in the water, the sonobuoy released its hydrophone assembly, which sank to a depth of fifty meters.

It wasn't even a minute before Mitrov barked, "Contact, bearing one three five. Target appears to be moving to the northwest at moderate speed."

"Got you, you bastard," growled Mirsky, smiling. Pulling up on the controls, he put his machine back into flight mode, streaking low over the water toward the ice-encrusted shores of October Revolution Island. He had to give the American captain credit; running along the rocky coast took courage. The water wasn't even forty meters deep.

Clicking his mike, Mirsky ordered his cohort to follow. "Red 45, submerged contact heading northwest. Fly twenty-five kilometers along course three two zero. Drop another sonobuoy pattern and stand by to release ordnance!"

USS *Jimmy Carter*

"CONN, SONAR, TORPEDO IN THE WATER! BEARING ZERO FOUR EIGHT!" blasted the intercom speaker. Weiss was stunned, his expression asked, "How did they know?"

Jerry spun about and looked at the WLY-1 acoustic intercept receiver; it remained silent. Pointing to the blank display he shouted, "The torpedo hasn't enabled! Turn to the right!"

Weiss caught on quickly. "Helm, right full rudder! Steady on course zero seven zero!"

Carter rolled to starboard as the rudder bit, swinging the bow hard right. The incredibly high bearing rate meant the weapon was close—very close, and yet the torpedo's seeker continued to remain silent as it roared past them. There wasn't time to ask any questions as the intercom blared once again. "Conn, Sonar, new contact bearing zero five five! No, correction. Regained Sierra one six, drawing left rapidly!"

"Range to target?" shouted Jerry instinctively.

"Three eight double oh yards and decreasing!" answered Segerson tensely.

"Bearing rate is left thirteen degrees per minute!" added Owens.

"Jesus! She's right on top of us!" uttered Weiss.

"And may not know it, Lou!" exclaimed Jerry as he snapped his fingers. "Shoot, for God's sake! Shoot!"

"Snapshot! Sierra one six, tube eight! Minimal enable run!" yelled Weiss.

Segerson jumped between consoles, making sure the targeting data was good. Once he was satisfied, the fire control technician grabbed the firing key handle, rotated it to the left and called out, "Set . . . stand by . . . shoot!"

Red 48

The two Helix helicopters barely slowed down as six more sonobuoys were laid out in two triple chevron patterns. Both sensor operators picked up their prey quickly and verified the target was passing amazingly close along October Revolution Island. Mirsky stationed Red 45 ten kilometers to the north, in case his torpedo missed, updated the contact's course and speed, and hit the attack button.

The Ka-27M automatically positioned itself over clear water right along the target's projected path. Once the fire control computer was satisfied the vehicle had met the necessary flight conditions, it released a UMGT-1 torpedo. Mirsky immediately pulled the helicopter away from the ocean's surface and announced, "Weapon dropped!"

The torpedo plunged underwater and drifted lazily for a moment as the seawater-activated battery came up to power. The propulsion motor accelerated the weapon to forty-five knots as it executed a large circle search; the acoustic homing head began pinging. On its second pass, the torpedo detected a faint echo, but with lots of Doppler. Peeling out of its search pattern, the weapon shot toward its target at full speed. Seconds later it impacted and exploded.

Mirsky saw the plume from the explosion break the surface and reach skyward. Petty Officer Mitrov cheered at their apparent success. But the flight commander wasn't ready to congratulate himself just yet; he was more seasoned than that and knew he could have just as easily hit a rock. With an impatient voice he growled, "Shut up and search for the target, you fool! Red 45, monitor your sonobuoys for any sign of the contact; stand by to execute your attack!"

USS *Jimmy Carter*

The Mark 48 ADCAP torpedo catapulted out from the lower port torpedo tube and turned hard left as soon as it was under power. Segerson had set the weapon to run at slow speed initially, to make sure the torpedo's seeker had enough time to acquire and lock on to the target. It was a good call. The acoustic homer enabled a scant seven hundred yards from the Russian attack submarine. Between the strength of the return and the high Doppler shift, the seeker's logic readily locked onto the echoes and accelerated to attack speed.

There was very little the crew of *Kazan* could do. By the time they understood what was happening, the Mark 48 torpedo was at sixty-five knots and had already closed to less than four hundred yards. No decoy or countermeasure could save them now. The weapon hit aft, striking near main engineering and shredding a ten-foot hole in the hull. The submarine heeled over sharply, angling downward, and plowed into the bottom at almost twenty knots—its shattered hull lay within a stone's throw of *Toledo*.

Weiss allowed himself a deep sigh of relief once he heard the explosion. He didn't need a report from sonar; everyone heard the blast through the hull. There were no cheers in the control room this time, just silence as the adrenaline high started to wear off. Even Jerry felt a little ragged, but he'd been there before, and recovered more quickly. "Nice shot, XO," he said quietly.

"Thank you, sir. Can we go home now?" Segerson's little quip got a chuckle out of everyone in control.

Laughing, Jerry replied, "Don't look at me. I don't have the conn."

Weiss looked down at his XO's earnest expression and shook his head in amusement. "Oh, very well. Helm, left standard rudder. Steady on course zero two zero."

The captain then hit the intercom switch. "Sonar, Conn, stay alert and keep your ears sharp to the west. There's an Akula out there and I really don't want to have to do this a second time."

Ten minutes later, *Carter* passed under the ice pack and over the drop-off into the Nansen Basin. Weiss took his boat deep and slowed down. *Jimmy Carter* maintained her northerly course until both Jerry and Weiss were confident that they had given *Vepr* the slip. Only then did the boat turn for home.

0615 Local Time
Prima Polar Station

Vice Admiral Gorokhov had bolted from the command center as soon as the Sever monitoring detachment had reported incoming torpedoes. He ran as fast as he could to the cliff's edge and looked out into the mouth of the Shokal'skogo Strait with his binoculars. With the exception of a slightly darker hue of brown in the water around the mooring buoy, everything looked as before. And yet, he feared that the scene would be drastically different one hundred and eighty meters below the surface.

"Admiral! Admiral!" yelled Kalinin as he approached his senior officer. "Sir, one of the Ka-27M helicopters reports that it has successfully engaged an enemy submarine. That makes two confirmed kills!"

Gorokhov spun about seething, "I don't give a damn about how many American boats we've destroyed, Captain! I want divers down on the launcher complex immediately! I need a full and complete damage report, and I need it NOW!"

"Yes . . . yes, Comrade Admiral. At once," stammered Kalinin as he turned and ran back to the hut.

EPILOGUE

4 August 2021
2105 Eastern Daylight Time
Oval Office, The White House
Washington, D.C.

Afterward, President Hardy would confess that he could not remember who he was meeting with, or why. His visitors were quickly ushered out after Joanna appeared at the Oval Office door, beaming. Without speaking, she handed her husband a single sheet of paper. Hardy read:

FLASH
050200Z AUG 21
FROM: USS JIMMY CARTER (SSN 23)
TO: CNO WASHINGTON DC
INFO: COMSUBFOR, SUBRON TWELVE
TOP SECRET//SCI
SUBJ: MISSION QUICKLOOK REPORT
1) OVERCHARGE EXECUTED. FOUR TORPEDOES FIRED, FOUR EXPLO-
SIONS HEARD CONSISTENT WITH TARGET'S LOCATION 0558G. NU-
MEROUS METALLIC TRANSIENTS DETECTED POST DETONATION.

2) SUBMARINE KAZAN ENGAGED AND SUNK DURING EGRESS FROM OP AREA.

BT

"It's done," Hardy said, almost without thinking, then pulled himself up short. "This doesn't say much about the launch facility's status—'metallic transients detected post detonation.'"

Patterson sighed and admitted, "They probably don't know, Lowell. If *Kazan* was in the area, they were likely too busy to watch the results."

Instead of sitting on one of the couches, Joanna came around and perched on the edge of Hardy's desk. He reached up to her and she took his hand, giving it a squeeze.

She observed, "We know *Carter* managed to launch the attack, sink a submarine nearby, and felt safe enough to send us a message."

"And, even if they'd said the facility had been destroyed, we'd need independent confirmation," Hardy agreed.

"I've had all the intelligence agencies listening hard to the Russian Navy communications network. Message traffic in the Northern Fleet and the Arctic has almost doubled, and the time frame for this activity is consistent with the time in *Carter*'s message. Better yet, some of it's been in the clear, and they all describe an underwater attack and some sort of calamity."

"Then that's it." Hardy called out for his chief of staff, who appeared instantly. In response to Sellers's expectant look, he answered, "It's good news, Dwight. Set up the press conference for an hour from now."

Sellers nodded and disappeared. The first couple sat for a few moments, smiling like proud parents.

Joanna finally stood and announced, "If you're going to have a press conference, I've got work to do." She stroked his cheek. "And you'd better shave."

5 August 2021
0430 Moscow Time
The Senate Building, Kremlin
Moscow, Russia

First word of the attack reached Defense Minister Trusov early that morning; the phone call from Admiral Komeyev seemed too incredible to believe. Unwilling to take the commander-in-chief of the Russian Navy at his word, or hopeful that he had somehow been misled, Trusov took the time to speak directly to the Prima base commander. The minister spent precious minutes absorbing the news, questioning Admiral Gorokhov for specifics, and struggling to overcome the surprise and shock he felt. He couldn't delay reporting to the president for long, though, and finally yielded to duty. He called the president's aide to arrange the earlier than usual meeting, got dressed, and headed for the Senate Building

As soon as Fedorin saw General Trusov's expression, he knew it was bad news.

"Comrade President," the minister started out slowly. "I regret to inform you that the Drakon launch installation has been destroyed." Before the president could ask the obvious question, Trusov continued, "It appears to have been a direct frontal assault by multiple American submarines. The Sever sensor net reported torpedo noises and explosions near the launcher, as well as numerous submarine engagements between our forces and the enemy. The Navy CINC reports that two American submarines were hit and sunk during the battle." Trusov sighed heavily, and added, "We have also lost contact with *Kazan*, and it is likely she was sunk."

The Russian president listened to Trusov; he seemed distant at first, then furrowed his brow, concentrating, as if trying to understand the minister's words. "That can't be right," he finally responded. "The launch site is heavily defended. There must be an error."

"I confirmed the Navy's report with the base commander himself," Trusov answered patiently. "The recordings from the Sever net will be sent to St. Petersburg for analysis and confirmation, but at the same time as the explosions, the control station on the island showed alarm lights on all six launch tubes, as well as the four loaded torpedoes them-selves. Gorokhov reports that it's impossible to launch any of the weap-ons. He was sending divers to survey the damage."

"Yes, absolutely," Fedorin suddenly responded. "It's vital that the launchers be repaired immediately. The weapons as well, if they have been damaged. When did you speak to the base commander?"

Trusov checked the wall clock. "Perhaps an hour ago."

"Then call him now. We will hear what the divers have discovered."

Trusov had expected this, and it only took a few moments to arrange the call. He handed the receiver to Fedorin. "The base commander is Vice Admiral Gorokhov," he reminded the president.

Fedorin almost snatched the receiver from the minister's hand, while Trusov listened in on a second handset. "Admiral Gorokhov, how quickly will you be operational again?" demanded Fedorin. Trusov even heard an optimistic tone in the president's question.

"Operational?" Gorokhov sounded astonished, even incredulous. "Comrade President, the divers have only completed a preliminary ex-amination, but the damage is severe. They say the supporting launcher frame is completely wrecked. The Drakon torpedo transport launch canisters are either crushed or badly deformed. Radiation in the area is above norms, as well."

"But can it be repaired?" Fedorin repeated sharply. "How long to restore the complex so that any undamaged weapons can be launched?"

Trusov could almost hear Gorokhov shrug. "Comrade President, I would need a detailed survey, which will take several days, before I could give you even a rough estimate of the time to repair—if it is possible at all."

"Possible?" Fedorin had trouble with the word.

Gorokhov's voice softened, as if he was bracing someone for bad news about a family member. "All the divers agree that the damage is quite extensive. Comrade President, please remember, they have all been involved in building the structure since the beginning, and they know it well. They report it may be faster to just start over. As for the weapons themselves, I fear they are damaged beyond recovery and will—"

Fedorin suddenly hung up, backing away from the phone. Trusov had to thank the admiral for his report before breaking the connection. The president laid his head down and covered it with his hands.

"It's gone, Aleksandr Aleksandrovich," Fedorin groaned, his voice filled with grief. "The entire operation depended on that single installation. It was the foundation for everything else that we planned. It was supposed to hold the Americans in check, and free us to act. And without the operation, what of Russia?"

Fedorin's sadness washed over Trusov like a wave. The president had always identified with his country, and often spoke of his fears for its future. The invasion they had planned was designed to forestall that fate. But there were worse fates, like starting a war they could not win.

"Comrade President." Trusov had to repeat himself before Fedorin lifted his head to face the defense minister. "We should begin issuing recall orders." Fedorin didn't respond immediately. The minister reminded him, "Some special warfare elements have actually infiltrated their targets, waiting for the code word to begin the operation. We have to extract them before they are discovered."

"But why . . ."

"Every minute our troops are deployed is costing us millions. If we are not going to go forward, then we should stand down. We will need to conserve . . ."

"No! Just that quickly, we're giving up?" Fedorin straightened up in his chair. "Let's launch the operation now, this minute. NATO isn't ready. They have admitted their military forces can't stop us." Fedorin's sudden enthusiasm almost convinced Trusov, but that option had been studied and gamed out long ago. The West always won.

"With American reinforcements they can push us back, and even if they eventually lose, it would be a long war, which would ruin us."

"We can increase the attacks by special forces and cyber warfare. Paralyze Europe, and then move." Fedorin was animated, excited by the idea.

"It would take too long to have any effect, Comrade President. And they would only encourage NATO to fully mobilize. Remember the American reinforcements that are already coming. Time is against us."

"Then let's just concentrate on one part of the original objective. Focus on the Baltic States . . ."

"No, Comrade President." Trusov felt like a schoolmaster, correcting a student's recital. "They would be able to concentrate their forces in that region. And even if we won, the reward would be far less."

Out of ideas, Fedorin sat back, shrunken. "I could see the future so clearly, Aleksandr Aleksandrovich."

"And you shared your vision with us, Comrade President. We wanted it as well, but it's over now."

Fedorin's secretary opened the door with only a perfunctory knock. "Comrade President, Comrade Minister, the American President Hardy is on the television . . ."

Trusov cut her off. "Yes. I know. He's announcing that America is sending reinforcements to NATO."

She shook her head, with a worried look. "No, sir. He's past that. Now he is talking about a Russian base in the Arctic."

Fedorin reached the remote first, and turned on the wall screen. It only took a moment to find a channel carrying the American president's speech. A Russian-language translation scrolled across the bottom.

". . . weapon announced just a short time ago. This secret Arctic base, armed with a new nuclear weapon system capable of a covert first strike, was an immediate and direct threat to American lives and territory. On my authority, I ordered a U.S. Navy submarine to destroy the launch facility, which they did a little over three hours ago."

Fedorin muted the sound and carefully set the remote down on the corner of his desk. He remained silent, but his expression spoke of failure and ruin.

Trusov, who had been standing since he'd entered Fedorin's office, sat down heavily. "They knew," he whispered. "Somehow they learned of the base . . . the weapon . . . and our plan. My God, Comrade President, they knew it all!" The silent TV showed Hardy was continuing to speak. Trusov thought the American president looked grim, almost angry.

They both sat quietly for some time. Fedorin finally said softly, "Give the orders."

12 August 2021
0900 Eastern Daylight Time
New London Submarine Base

Jimmy Carter's transit back home had been much quicker because she could steer a direct route and transit at a higher speed. Although they had accomplished their mission, Weiss gave the crew little rest. Too many routine tasks had been deferred during the transit north, and the captain insisted on a thorough field day of the entire boat, with an inspection the day before they reached port.

They could have arrived as early as the evening of the eleventh, but had been ordered to arrive off the sub base at 0830 the next morning, and be docked half an hour later. *Carter* had been ordered to dock at Pier Six, because its landward end adjoined a large parking lot, which had been taken over for the occasion.

Ensign Truitt brought the submarine in. Jerry wasn't sure if Captain Weiss was training, testing, or punishing the young officer. There was a slack tide, and only a gentle breeze from shore, so the navigational hazards were minimal. If the ensign could ignore the distractions, like the spectators, the band, the media, and the distinguished guests, it should be a simple landing.

With some bargaining, Dr. Cavanaugh had been authorized to act as a lookout during the maneuvering watch, happily wearing a parachute harness and snapping photos every few moments as *Carter* smoothly approached the pier. The lookout's perch was the only way he could be topside, since the cockpit was more than crowded with the bridge crew, Captain Weiss, and Commodore Mitchell.

Public works had set up bleachers, with reserved places in front for the family members who had flown out from Bangor. A separate box with more comfortable seating held the president's party and the navy brass. The media had chosen the pierside corners for their cameras. Cavanaugh thought his position, precarious as it was, gave him the best view.

He heard the Navy Band serenading the crowd during their approach and the sub's turn toward the pier. Even *Tug Paul* looked a little neater than usual as it gave *Jimmy Carter* the nudges it needed to maneuver against the river current. The bandmaster timed it so that there was only a brief pause between the last popular song and "Anchors Aweigh," which began as the first line was wrapped around the bollard. With only the gentlest of bumps, the sub's hull kissed the fenders and she was secured to the pier.

As arranged, the moment the gangplank was in place, the entire crew, except for the duty section, in their best whites, hurried out of the access hatches onto the pier and formed ranks in front of the distinguished visitors' box. The band continued to play, following "Anchors Aweigh" with Sousa marches.

Jerry was the second to the last to disembark, with Captain Weiss the last to step ashore. The two senior officers walked quickly down the pier and, after Weiss received the XO's report that the crew was "present or accounted for," took their places in front.

President Hardy stood and approached a microphone. "Welcome back, *Jimmy Carter* and her valiant crew. I won't even try to describe the service you have performed for your country, because it would take too long to do it justice. I will say that it was difficult, a little dangerous, and performed brilliantly, in the best tradition of the U.S. naval submarine service. Attention to orders!"

Carter's crew came to attention, and the chief of naval operations assisted President Hardy with the decorations. Captain Weiss was awarded the Navy Cross, and Jerry received one as well—his fourth. After teasing Jerry about "his collection," President Hardy ended the ceremony with "I am pleased to award USS *Jimmy Carter* with the Presidential Unit Citation, and also to announce, with the exception of the duty section, liberty for the crew!"

The cheer that followed almost drowned out the first notes of "Victory at Sea." Jerry and Captain Weiss quickly disengaged from the many well-wishers, and hurried back aboard. They had a reception to host.

Everything was in readiness when the two arrived in the wardroom. This left Jerry and Weiss at loose ends, especially when word came down that the president and first lady were taking time to shake hands and pose with the crew and their families.

"Never too early to think about the next election," Weiss commented philosophically.

"I think he'd get their votes anyway," Jerry replied. "By the way, a word of warning. The first lady is a hugger."

Weiss's eyes widened a little. "Really."

Jerry nodded sagely. "Just go with it. She was probably sweating our safe return more than the president."

"I can do that," Weiss answered. His hand kept going up to touch the medal Hardy had pinned to his uniform. Jerry wasn't sure if he was worried about it being on straight, or was just checking to see if it was real.

A mess specialist suddenly popped out of the pantry; two cups of fresh, steaming coffee in his hands. "Here you go, Skipper," he said.

"Thank you, Olson. I've been waiting for this."

Jerry graciously accepted his cup and raised it . . . the smell was incredible, and the taste was even better. "Whoa! Lou, where did you get this coffee? This isn't standard Navy issue, that's for sure!"

Weiss was slow to answer; there was an awkward look on his face. No, a better word would be sheepish.

"What?" asked Jerry with concern.

"I, uh, got this from the EB engineer that runs *Shippingport*, Commodore . . . before we left."

"You mean to tell me you had this coffee with you for the *entire* run north!?" Jerry's expression was one of utter disbelief.

"Ahh, yeah . . . I, uh, kind of forgot I even had it, sir."

"Forgot about it!? Coffee this good!? Mister, we need to have a serious talk about your priorities!" Both men laughed heartily.

The wardroom fell silent as they enjoyed their relaxing time together. Weiss looked down at his award again and slowly shook his head.

"Something wrong?" Jerry inquired.

"No, sir. I've just been looking for the right opportunity to say 'thank you' for not relieving me during that fight."

Jerry shrugged. "Sometimes not shooting something is the best course. What matters is that you grasped the situation and handled the boat brilliantly. You'll be a much better captain now because of what you've learned. And truth be told, Lou, that's really the best part of my job—to help train my COs."

Weiss nodded, appreciating his boss's compliments. Then his expression suddenly changed and he motioned toward Jerry. "You said something during the fight about a friend of yours?"

"Oh yeah, I did, and it's completely ironic too. You see, my friend, Alex, was the commanding officer of *Severodvinsk*, *Kazan*'s sister."

Weiss abruptly leaned forward in the chair, his eyes wide with curiosity. "Seriously?"

"Mm-hmm," Jerry muttered while taking another sip. "Alex was over the top aggressive. I was on *Seawolf*, we were doing a northern run and he snapped us up, had us dead to rights. But he couldn't just embarrass us and let it go. He kept getting closer and closer, scared the crap out of us. Then something went wrong and he plowed into us. *Seawolf* got smashed up pretty bad, tore open the sonar dome and sliced up a couple of the main ballast tanks. *Severodvinsk* slammed into the bottom . . . really, really, hard.

"We managed to help save Alex, and most of his crew, but he lost eighteen men. We lost one young sailor as well, one of my guys. Alex has been haunted by that tragedy ever since. He learned a hard lesson that day, letting your aggressive tendencies get the better of you can be costly . . . in more than one way."

Carter's commanding officer listened with rapt attention to Jerry's story. He wanted to ask a host of questions, but a 1MC announcement cut him off before he could even start.

"UNITED STATES, ARRIVING."

"Well, that's our cue," observed Jerry as he put the cup on the table, stood, and adjusted his uniform.

Hardy and a gaggle of guests in trail arrived a minute later. Photographers snapped the handshakes and greetings, and Joanna's hugs of both COMDEVRON Five and Commanding Officer, USS *Jimmy Carter*.

As guests continued to enter the already-crowded wardroom, Hardy pulled Jerry into what had to serve as a quiet corner. He asked, "Jerry, you know, I've got some connections now. What can I do for you, besides giving you another Navy Cross?"

As Hardy asked the question, Jerry spotted Emily, with Charlotte resting on her hip, entering the wardroom. He'd spotted her in the VIP seats, but hadn't had a chance to talk. She didn't look happy to see him. In fact, she looked a little mad.

She hadn't spotted her husband yet, and Jerry slid over a little so that he was hidden from her view. "If you could run interference with Emily, Skipper, I'd be eternally grateful."

Hardy glanced over his shoulder, and saw Mrs. Mitchell acquire her target and commence an approach. He laughed, and answered, "Not a chance, sailor. She'll chew my ass off, even if I am the president. I'll delegate that responsibility to my national security advisor," gesturing to Joanna, a few feet away.

Seizing on the advice, Jerry maneuvered to place Patterson between Emily and himself, and more importantly, placing the approaching threat in the first lady's field of view . . .

"Emily! And Charlotte! I'm so glad you could fly out. Carly, how big you've gotten!"

Patterson reached out, and the child allowed "Auntie Joanna" to pick her up for a hug and compliments about her fancy dress. Emily, delayed but now unencumbered, circled Joanna to port and caught Jerry. To his surprise, there were no harsh words, just a hug almost fierce in its intensity, while she buried her face in his shoulder.

Jerry knew he had to say something, and finally confessed, "I'm sorry that I worried you."

She pounded his shoulder with her fist, just once. "It's no better finding out after the fact what you were doing. I don't know how Navy wives do it."

"But you're a Navy wife," he countered.

"And it's hard work." She punched his shoulder again, but more lightly. "Next time you go on a mission like that—*if* there is a next time—you have to tell me ahead of time, so I can brace myself."

Jerry protested, "Emily, I didn't know myself until I got to New London, and we left port the same day. Besides, it was classified."

"That's no excuse."

Jerry felt a tap on his shoulder and it was Hardy. "Can I break in?" the president asked, smiling. He gave Emily a peck on the cheek, and said, "Carly looks more like you every time I see her."

He turned to include Jerry as well. "After lunch, during the memorial service for *Toledo*, you're sitting with us."

Hardy glanced at Carly, who was interested in a brooch that Joanna was wearing.

Emily read his mind and explained, "Jerry's sister Clarice came out from Minnesota. She'll watch Charlotte while we're in the chapel. She's really being an angel," Emily remarked, "but this afternoon is nap time," she said firmly.

"What about the meeting tomorrow with the *Toledo* families?" Jerry asked.

Hardy nodded. "It's on for 0900. I put my foot down and declassified the whole bloody thing. We'll show them the photos, and tell them what happened—everything. We owe them that much, at least. Devil take the complications."

The president checked his watch. "Do you think Captain Weiss would let me look around if I asked nicely?"

"It could be arranged, Skipper. I know the duty section would get a charge out of it."

"Then let's get going."

GLOSSARY

ADCAP: Advanced Capability (a variant of the Mark 48 torpedo)

ADM: Admiral

ARDM: Auxiliary Repair Medium Dry Dock

ASAP: As Soon As Possible

ASW: Antisubmarine Warfare

BND: Bundesnachrichtendienst, Germany's Federal Intelligence Service

BZ: Bravo Zulu, U.S. Navy shorthand for "Well Done"

CAPT: Captain

CDR: Commander

CIA: Central Intelligence Agency

CINC: Commander-in-Chief

CO: Commanding Officer

COB: Chief of the Boat

COMINT: Communications Intelligence

CPA: Closest Point of Approach

CSO: Chief Staff Officer (of a submarine squadron staff)

CTML: Conventional Twelve-Mile Limit (the edge of a nation's territorial waters)

Datum: Last known location of a submarine

DCI: Director of Central Intelligence (Agency)

DEVRON: Submarine Development Squadron

DNI: Director of National Intelligence

EAB: Emergency Air Breathing system

EB: Electric Boat

EDT: Eastern Daylight Savings Time

ENS: Ensign

EPM: Emergency Propulsion Motor

ESM: Electronic Support Measures (detecting radar transmissions)

ETA: Estimated Time of Arrival

EU: European Union

Fortify: Code name for the plan to reinforce Europe

GRU: Russian Military Intelligence

HUD: Heads Up Display

HUMINT: Human Intelligence (spies)

JCS: Joint Chiefs of Staff

Ka-27M: Helix antisubmarine warfare helicopter

LCDR: Lieutenant Commander

LT: Lieutenant

LTJG: Lieutenant, junior grade

MAD: Magnetic Anomaly Detector

MGK-608M: Modernized Sever fixed acoustic array

NAE: Naval Acoustic Electromechanical (a type of acoustic countermeasure)

NATO: North Atlantic Treaty Organization

NSA: National Security Advisor (position)

or

NSA: National Security Administration (organization)

NSC: National Security Council

OOD: Officer of the Deck

Overcharge: Code name for the plan to destroy the Russian launch facility

PBXN-103: A powerful high explosive

PMK-2: Russian propelled-warhead mine (MPT-1UM torpedo)

RADM: Rear Admiral

RGB: *Radiogidrakustichesky* buoy, Russian designation for a sonobuoy

SCI: Sensitive Compartmented Information (a special type of classified information/data)

SCIF: Sensitive Compartmented Information Facility

SIGINT: Signals Intelligence

SSAN: Nuclear-powered auxiliary submarine

SSBN: Nuclear-powered ballistic missile submarine

SSN: Nuclear-powered attack submarine

SSTG: Ship's Service Turbine Generator

SUBFOR: Submarine Forces Commander

SUBRON: Submarine Squadron

SVR: Sluzhba Vneshney Razvedki, Russian intelligence agency, successor to the Cold War KGB

Tensor: Code name for information related to the Russian Drakon weapon

UCC: UUV Control Center

UKSK: *Universal'nyy Korabel'nyy Strel'bovoy Kompleks*, Universal Shipboard Firing Complex UMGT-1: Russian 40cm electric torpedo

UUV: Unmanned Underwater Vehicle

VADM: Vice Admiral

XO: Executive Officer